4 to 16 Characters

Kelly Hourihan

Lemon Sherbet Press
Boston, MA

The characters and events in this book are the products of the author's imagination. Any similarity to persons, living or dead, is coincidental and not intended by the author.

©2013 Kelly Hourihan

All rights reserved. With the exception of brief quotations for critical articles or reviews, no part of this book may be reproduced in any manner without prior written permission from the publisher. You can contact Lemon Sherbet Press at publishing@lemonsherbetpress.com.

Published 2013 by Lemon Sherbet Press
Cover design by Jacqueline Gallagher
Interior design by Kerianne Hourihan
The text of this book is set in Minion Pro
Printed in United States

Publisher's Cataloging-In-Publication Data
(Prepared by The Donohue Group, Inc.)

Hourihan, Kelly.
    4 to 16 characters : [a novel] / Kelly Hourihan. -- 1st ed.

    p. ; cm.

    Summary: Fifteen-year-old Jane Shilling devises a number of online personas, each with a distinct personality, in order to escape a difficult home life. But things become trickier when she finds herself drawing close to some of her online friends, and winds up struggling with the question of how to maintain a real friendship while masquerading as a fake person.
    Interest age level: 011-014.
    Issued also in Kindle and ePub formats.
    ISBN: 978-0-9897411-0-1 (pbk.)

    1. Online social networks--Juvenile fiction. 2. Teenage girls--Conduct of life--Juvenile fiction. 3. Friendship--Juvenile fiction. 4. Identity (Psychology)--Juvenile fiction. 5. Online social networks--Fiction. 6. Teenage girls--Conduct of life--Fiction. 7. Friendship--Fiction. 8. Identity--Fiction. I. Title. II. Title: Four to sixteen characters

PZ7.H687 Fo 2013
[Fic]
2013946698
First Edition

For Carol, whose unflagging faith in this book kept me going through more than one time when I was ready to give up;

and for Eve, who was there when all this started.

Date: 2/8/2013

What's your name?: Rachel

How old are you?: 20

Boy or girl?: Excuse me, young meme-maker, but I am a *woman*. ::tosses hair::

Single?: There's a boy. I call him The Boy.

Want to be?: Not at the moment; The Boy is very nice.

Your living arrangement?: College, baby! One roommate, who plays the tuba very badly, as anyone who lives within half a mile can attest, and is constantly sneaking her senile cat in to stay the weekend when her parents jaunt off to Bermuda or some such. The cat has quite the fetish for my bedspread. Other than the tuba and the cat, though, Liz is great.

Your family: Two parents, a sister two years younger, and a dog. We're pretty classic-boring-American all the way. :)

Obsessions?: Look to Tomorrow, Brad Memphis, writing, Brad Memphis, Scrabble, Look to Tomorrow, Brad Memphis, and OMG BRAD MEMPHIS.

Do you have a webpage?: Yep, there's the Look to Tomorrow page with episode guide, quotes page and Subtextometer, the Diary-Now, fanfiction. com and ourownfanhome.com profiles, and, of course, the ReCirclr. Oh, and have a direct link to the FriendsLink you are looking at right now, just for the hell of it.

FIRSTS

First date: Peter White, a nice boy from my high school who, halfway through the date, revealed that he was not interested in dating me so much as in converting me to the Jehovah's Witnesses. He kept assuring me that it was an honor that he was talking to me about this -- that no one else at school had the "spiritual depth" for him to be able to get through. I told him thank you, but I was really much shallower than he thought, and stuck him with the check. The way I figure it, I was making it that much easier for him

1

and his camel to get through that needle's eye.

First real kiss: Well, needless to say, it wasn't Peter. My first kiss was six months later, with Neil Harding, who, from the way he kissed, apparently had some sort of localized muscular dystrophy that only affected his tongue. He'd slobbered all over my chin in ten seconds. Poor boy.

First break-up: About thirty seconds after that. :P

First love: He's sitting on my bed drawing semi-pornographic anime cartoons on the inside cover of my English notebook. Basically, he's ensuring that he'll be impossible to forget even after he leaves the room. I'm pretty sure he does it on purpose.

First car: Current and only car, my ghetto little used Kia Spectra. I have painted it silver and anointed it Xronia. Despite its LtT-sanctified namesake, it doesn't exactly zip me through the centuries instantaneously -- if you put it up above fifty, in fact, it starts vibrating and clunking in manner that is very alarming, so I tend to keep it at a nice slow pace better suited to meandering cattle. On the plus side, I might just get it to go *backward* in time one of these days. Still, the passenger seat never has held my Brad, so the minuses reign where my car is concerned. :(

First musician: First musician what? First musician that I listened to, liked, slept with, bought at auction to keep chained in my basement for entertainment on demand? This question does not make sense.

LASTS

Last car ride: Why you care is beyond me, but to the 7-11 about a half hour ago. Yes, my college campus is so spread out that I have to drive to the 7-11. I suppose I could have just grabbed a couple of chickens and maybe a cow from the field next door, instead of going all that way, but they're so messy to cook.

Last movie seen: I FINALLY managed to trade for a crappy, staticky, beautiful taped-off-TV copy of *Jesus' Sandals* -- okay, not great cinema, but Brad was very young and very hot and these are the things that matter in life.

Last annoyance: A few weeks ago, when CKN announced they're canceling next week's LtT for the eighteen millionth People's Choice Awards-knockoff in the last six months. NO ONE CARES, CKN.

Last disappointment: See above.

Last time wanting to die: See above. ;) No, seriously, do most people think a lot about wanting to die?

Last book read: Mark Haddon's *The Curious Incident of the Dog in the Night-time.* Good book, go read it.

<u>74 hearts</u>   <u>53 comments</u>   <u>42 Shares</u>

Date: 2/8/2013
Security level: Private

Top Ten Things Anyone Who Knows Me Would Notice About That Survey:

1.) None of it's true.

2.) ...

Okay, so we'll stick to one for now.

I've done a lot of thinking about this lately, actually. What is "truth"? Before you go rolling your eyes figuring I'm some irritating college philosophy major with an ego the size of Canada, let's get this straight. Of course, I know what it means in common usage. Truth is what you did after you got up this morning, right? It can also be what you did after you got up yesterday, or the day before. And maybe it's what someone you know did, or what someone they know did. You can even stretch it into what you thought, as long as what you mean is that yes, it's true that you had that thought. Truth is about what happened, right? If it didn't happen, it's not true.

Well, here's something that's "true", something that happened: Today in English class Ms. Frolich told us she wants us to keep a diary for class. "I'll check to make sure you've written enough pages, but I'll never read what you write," she told us, in that high, reedy little voice she has. Lots of people rolled their eyes at that; no one believes she won't read the diaries. "I know it will be important to you, in later life, to have a record of your teenage years --" more eyerolls -- "to remember things not as your memory would want to paint them, but how they really were." Then she gave us fifteen minutes to free-write while she laid her head on her desk and closed her eyes.

So I wrote the truth in my diary. I wrote all about how I got up that morning and I put on blue jeans and a green shirt and white socks, and I picked up my backpack and I went to school. I wrote about how yesterday I got back a geography test that I got a D on. I wrote about how my math textbook is heavy and I gave myself a paper cut in Spanish class. All of these things absolutely happened. Not a single one of them matters, and every single one tells you less about me than that quiz about Rachel does, even though not a single line of the Rachel quiz refers to anything that ever actually happened.

Which is where things get interesting. I mean, think about this for a minute. You double-click on Firefox, and suddenly two finger twitches have put you in this place where no one knows anything about what "really" happened to you that day at all. There's six squillion people on the Internet and all you have to do to ensure that no one knows you is pick a forum or an IRC chat, make a new screen name, and head in. You can tell them anything -- tell them you just got out of prison on bail for the murder of both your parents plus your mom's lesbian lover, but you only did it because they were all ganging up to kill *you* because you knew their dirty secret about the drug/prostitution ring in the basement. Sounds ridiculous, right? Until you realize that this stuff does happen to *someone*, *somewhere* out there in the world -- and in a chat room, can anyone really be sure that it wasn't you?

And it's even simpler when you're not going for the melodrama. You go onto a message board and say you're Jessica, sixteen years old and a die-hard Taylor Swift fan. Someone posts a message in reply to say they love Taylor Swift too. You start talking about Taylor, and even if you know nothing about her there are plenty of websites that will tell you way more than you ever wanted to know. You keep talking with her, and maybe she chats you at some point once you get Jessica her own FriendsLink, and pretty soon Jessica is her best friend. And if she found out you're "lying" she'd be devastated, sure, but how's she ever going to find out? And if she doesn't find out, does it even matter that you're making it all up?

The philosophical aspect of the Internet is vastly underrecognized.

Unfortunately, most of the world doesn't much go in for that kind of philosophy. And the ordinary, non-philosophical truth is that my name is Jane -- yep, boring old plain Jane; any parent who names their kid that is just begging for this kind of trouble, IMO -- and I'm a sophomore in high school. Every morning I get up and go to school, and every afternoon I come home and, after saying hello to my father, who is fifty-eight years old and is invariably sitting in the living room drinking a beer and staring blearily at some Drew Barrymore movie on TV, I go upstairs and go online. We don't talk again all night -- sometimes I'll hear footsteps outside my door, like he's poised to knock, but he always chickens out, probably because he's always drunk by then -- and there's no one else to interrupt me. And I do my homework on the ride into school, so from 3 pm to 10 pm I'm free to surf the Internet, except for dinnertime when I heat up a TV dinner and eat it in my room. That's it. I have no friends in "real" life, no extracurricular activities, no hobbies, no nothing.

Online, though, there's plenty going on. I tend to have between four and eight Internet personalities running at any given time. I started out small, with Rachel. In fact, at first it wasn't even meant to be an elaborate scheme to get out of my skin -- I was just joining a *Look to Tomorrow* mailing list for the very first time, and I was nervous about all the rumors I'd heard about people stalking you through the Internet, so I changed my name and some key details about myself. This was two years ago. Rachel was a few years older than me, in her senior year of high school, and she lived in a small unnamed suburb "west of Boston". At first I was wary of saying anything about her at all, afraid someone would magically catch me out. But it became pretty clear pretty soon that no one was the slightest bit suspicious. I mean, why should they be? I can't be the only one out there doing this, but unless you're being an awful troll, the amazing thing is that online no one seems to *care*. No one's being all paranoid and hacking into some central database that checks IP addresses against your home address and name. Why should they? At first they don't care, and by the time they know you well enough to care they'd never believe something like that about you.

Anyway, once I figured that out, Rachel grew and grew, until by now I feel like I know her life better than my own. Rachel isn't a short dork with medium-brown stick-straight hair. Rachel's tall with gorgeous dark brown curls, and she won't admit to being a knockout but she is. Rachel doesn't scurry around between classes with a giant dorky backpack monogrammed with her initials, trying to get to class before the bell without bumping into anyone. She saunters between classes with a group of friends, laughing and chatting the whole way, and if she's a few minutes late it doesn't matter because classes never start on time in college anyway. And Rachel doesn't have a dead mother and a father who'd be creepy if he weren't so sad.

Rachel's got two lively, bustling parents who heckle her lovingly about her grades and a younger sister who's such a pain in the butt but they're so close anyway. She's also got a dog. Named Shamrock, because the first week she got him he ate an entire patch of shamrocks in their backyard and had to be taken to the vet. Before she got to college her sister used to steal her clothes all the time and her mom, embarrassingly, chaperoned all her school field trips.

True story, now. The last time I had to have my dad sign a permission slip, for a trip to see *The Glass Menagerie* at the local theatre for English class, he was deep into his sixth beer and the DVD of *The Wedding Singer* that he stole from Redbox and watches seven times a day. He asked me, without moving his eyes from the screen, what this was for, and I told him "The class is doing a volunteer project ministering to the poor in Zambia. I'll be back in a few months." He said "All right, be careful." I think next time I'm going to bring him a check for a few thousand dollars made out to myself.

Anyway, so Rachel came about first, but once I got the hang of it I started coming up with other personalities. It sort of became a game I played, you know. I figure it might help my fanfic writing -- it's basically just creating characters, right? So it ought to help with characterization. And it turned out to be a lot of fun. At first I just created whoever I felt like being in the moment, playing it by ear. There were a lot of abandoned characters early on, people who had just one or two conversations and never showed up again. But after awhile I started getting more attached to a couple of particular characters, and pretty soon I had a roster of personality alters. Eventually I made a folder for each of them, where I keep a dossier on who they are, all the elements of their life history, and any other details I need to remember so they don't trip me up in later conversations. I also copy-paste all of their conversations and posts into a Word file, so that if someone asks me about something we talked about that I don't remember, I can do a quick ctrl-F to find the specific conversation we had and keep the details consistent.

I know, I know, it sounds a little obsessive. But it's all in good fun, and besides, although there are dozens of personas I've invented for kicks over the years, there are really aren't that many of them that I use with any regularity. You know, there's the bog-standard angry-feminist troll that I use when I feel like yelling at random people on the Internet to let off steam, or the English-lit grad student writing her dissertation on Edna St. Vincent Millay (who was one of Mom's favorite poets, and now is one of mine.) The yelling's therapeutic and the Millay research is totally academically productive, right? I may hate doing assigned schoolwork, but I love doing my own research and learning at my own pace, and I think playing Elana (that's the grad student) will really give me a jump-start in college English. And then there are the characters who have a ton of crazy backstory, like Ethan -- he's this goth who went straight-edge after his drug addiction led to an OD, but he keeps backsliding and getting high even though he's trying to stay clean. He's been in and out of psych wards, he has a couple of suicide attempts in his past, his older brother was killed in a motorcycle accident a few years ago, he got expelled from his private school because he wrote a story about a school shooting and now he's at a special boarding school for troubled youth, and to top it all off he's starting to wonder if he's gay. I post to his journal pretty regularly, sometimes with suitably bleak LtT fanfics if I'm feeling inspired to write one, but more often with the newest installments in the Ethan soap opera. Which has about 70 readers now and averages about twelve sympathetic comments per entry. If that's not a good education in learning how to tell a gripping story and pull in readers, I don't know what is.

So all the alters have a point, really. And even so, I don't use any of them nearly as often as Rachel. In all honesty, a lot of the time I feel like I'm really more like Rachel than I am like Jane. I'm not *really* this small socially inept little geek living a shit home life with a depressed alcoholic father and nothing but an Internet addiction to fill the hours, right? I can't be. What it comes down to, really, is that I refuse to be.

From: margaretbaker@spectrum.org
To: janeshilling@spectrum.org
Subject: Missing homework assignments
Date: 2/12/2013
Attachments:

> Feb2.PDF
> Feb5.PDF
> Feb9.PDF
> Feb10.PDF

Dear Jane,

In the last two weeks, you've failed to turn in four homework assignments. These were due on 2/2, 2/5, 2/9, and 2/10. The two assignments that you have turned in have also been incompletely and carelessly done, with many unanswered questions. For the record, I did note that you turned in a paper for the homework assignment of 2/8, but I cannot accept it as complete because you failed to answer any of the questions. Recopying the problems and putting a question mark next to each of them is not acceptable in my class.

I am attaching the four homework assignments you have missed in PDF format, in case you've lost the papers. If you are unable to complete your homework because you don't understand the concepts, please come to me for extra help, and I'll be happy to work the material through with you on a one-on-one basis. I'm available each morning before school from six-thirty on, and every day after school until four o'clock.

Sincerely,
Mrs. Baker

http://www.diarynow.com/users/thejanethe/5301.html
Date: 2/12/2013
Security level: Private
Mood: annoyed

Ugh, what is WRONG with Mrs. Baker? God, she's been teaching our class for less than a month -- Ms. Fallon went on maternity leave two weeks after Christmas break -- and she's already driving me nuts. You know, I've been at Spectrum for two years. And I have seen plenty of nonsense in my time there, but I have never before met a teacher who could not understand the concept that Spectrum is *not a mainstream school*. If anything, the teachers and staff go the other way: for some reason, the only teachers the administration will hire (or maybe the only teachers stupid enough to work here) are these skinny chicks in their twenties with tentative smiles and an addiction to the honorific "Ms.", and half of them seem to have a whole lot of trouble with the concept that "behavioral problems and/or learning disabilities" is not the same thing as "psychotic disorders and/or developmental disabilities." They usually treat us like we're all either potential school shooters or afflicted with Down's Syndrome until they've been here at least six months. Still, they tend to look at all our personalized IEPs and "reasonable accommodations" and psych profiles and goals-and-standards sheets with an almost religious awe, and you can bet that they never forget for an instant that we're not "normal". And, you know, okay, there are plenty of times when that makes me crazy. I don't really see why having this stupid "nonverbal learning disability" (which I do not care to write about, except to say that it is stupid) necessitates my dealing every day with doe-eyed teachers and counselors who talk to me in a slow, soothing voice like they're trying to calm down a bucking bronco. And after Mom died they nearly drove me batshit with all their grief stages and processing and counseling -- seriously, people, I am much more capable of handling things when you just LEAVE ME ALONE. But they let me write fanfic in class for three months (I'm not all that sure how they came to the conclusion that that was part of my Process of Grieving -- I think they thought I was journaling all kinds of morbid thoughts about death and mourning and whether there is an afterlife -- but hell, why complain?), and then I got excused from my finals so I could write an end-of-semester thesis on a topic of my own choice. So while I emphatically Do Not Like the doe-eyed Ms.-es, I know how to manage them. I can't wait to graduate, but at least I know how to deal with Spectrum in the meantime, as long as things go the way they're supposed to go.

Unfortunately, in Mrs. Baker's class, things do not go the way they are supposed to go. Mrs. Baker is this middle-aged matronly woman with really thick ankles sheathed in wrinkled-up pantyhose, together with the kind of clunky lumpy shoes the Wicked Witch of the West wore that drove her to such lengths to try to steal Dorothy's slippers. She has awful hair the color of tumbleweeds that she pulls back tight enough to make the veins stand out in her temples and that she cements in place with what must be enough aerosol hairspray to kill a rainforest a week, and she's always wearing dark maroon lipstick that she's never managed to apply quite right, so she winds up with an outline of lipstick around her mouth that makes her look like Mrs. Potato Head. And she only ever wears camouflage colors -- dark green, olive green, brown, beige -- and her clothes are always totally baggy, like she's trying to smuggle grenades and extra magazine rounds under her blouse. I keep expecting to see her show up one of these days wearing a canteen slung over her shoulder. Amid the sea of recent college grads in shiny purple blouses and imitation-Hermes scarves that is the Spectrum faculty, she looks like a drill sergeant who stumbled into a beauty salon.

Her personality is nearly as charming as her appearance. In a school that's all about positive reinforcement and affirming that our learning difficulties are serious but manageable challenges, Mrs. Baker somehow got it into her hairspray-hardened head that it was a good idea to lecture kids on "not making excuses." This, predictably, has prompted a *lot* of angry calls from parents, arguing that a doctor's diagnosis of autism/ anger-management problems/severe OCD/dyslexia/whatever does not constitute an "excuse". And then she goes into backtrack mode, spinning all this crap about how she's not minimizing our problems, she's encouraging us to push through them and come out stronger; and then the parents' email list that Mom used to subscribe to floods with furious debate that quickly degenerates into pointless capslock; and finally the administration intercedes or something, or occasionally a parent pulls their kid from Spectrum entirely, and it all blows over. Another lesson in crack teaching skills from Mrs. Baker! Keep up the good work, Marge!

And now she's on my back. Fantastic. (Seriously, she's bugging me about *four homework assignments*? One of which I actually *turned in*? Who even cares about homework assignments?!) The crowning glory on what was already shaping up to be an awesome year! Seriously, I thought it was annoying last year when people were all crowding around me trying to get me to Process My Grief for my mom, but this year they're *not*, and in some ways that's actually worse. There may be a lot of assholes at my school -- well, maybe a quarter of them actually have legit behavioral problems that make them act like assholes, but then a bunch more have decided that having diagnoses of behavioral problems gives them an excuse to act that way -- but even the ones who pick on other kids the most seemed to have qualms about harassing a kid whose mom had just died. It probably wasn't chivalry so much as fear that I would suddenly puke grief all over them and then sob convulsively on their shoulders for the rest of the day, but it kept me under the radar. But now people seem to have decided that my mom died so long ago I must have forgotten about it by now, because I've already been taking shit from some of the other kids. (Apparently I am ugly, clumsy, and geeky. Who knew?) Bizarrely, I get a particularly rough time from a lot of the kids who aren't exactly stone hotties themselves; it's like they think picking on other geeks will make them less geeky themselves. For God's sake, Jason friggin' Malone won't leave me alone, and he hasn't improved much in cool quotient since preschool, when he peed his pants while he was at a playdate at my house and had to wear a pair of my Tinkerbell underpants for the rest of the day.

But it just sucks. Kids are teasing me, teachers are expecting me to "come out of my shell" more, and now Mrs. Baker is shaping up to be a giant pain in the ass. And I just... I don't know, I feel way more lost at Spectrum than I ever have before. Even though I've always liked being alone, somehow the fact that some of the kids are making fun of me makes me wish I had some friends too -- for a buffer, I guess. But there aren't exactly a lot of candidates... I mean, even if I sometimes get to feeling lonely or whatever, in practice I really am so socially awkward that I never know what to say to anybody, so I'm sure the whole friend thing would be way more trouble than it would be worth.

But when you come right down to it -- who does need it, anyway? See, everyone thinks it's weird or obsessive or something to spend as much time as I do on the Internet, but that's just because people don't understand Internet culture. People are always saying things like "you're just hiding from your real life!" What they don't get is that who I am on the Internet IS real, even when I'm using a fake name. The friendships I have online are real friendships; the interests I share with people online are real interests. There's absolutely no reason I need to waste my time freaking out about how to maintain three-dimensional friendships when I'm so awkward in 3D and so much more comfortable online. Rachel has 350 friends on ReCirclr, both because her posts are funny and well-written and because the *Look to Tomorrow* fanfiction she writes is really popular. In the "real" world people laugh at me for liking LtT, and if anyone ever found out I write stories about the characters, they'd think I was a total loon; online, those same things have made me hundreds of friends -- incidentally, probably a couple hundred more friends than even the most popular kids at school have. If that's not real life, maybe someone should explain to me why I should *want* a real life.

So, all in all, I think it makes perfect sense to keep my head down through as much of my "real life" as I can manage. Which only makes it more annoying, of course, when people like Mrs. Baker try to drag my "real life" online and mix the two worlds up. I hate to break it to you, Mrs. Baker, but I am not any more likely to do my homework assignments just because you sent them to me via email. Sorry your grand hep-to-the-Internet scheme failed. Maybe next time you can try sending me my homework via text message. But right now I'm heading to the LtT chat.

13

http://racheltessers.recirclr.com/post/52327064990/omg-omg-omg
2.16.2013

OMG OMG OMG

OMG OMG OMG OMG OMG OMG OMG

OMG OMG OMG!!!!!!!!!!!!!!!!!!!!!!!!!1111

OMG, people, DID YOU SEE THIS DID YOU SEE IT

Am I the first one to post about this? I think I'm totally the first one to
post about this, I think THAT FACT ALONE should win me the Lookies
and the SDGISFIODSGEWOWQDQODUY FLAILMAKING AMAZING, I
think I should post this entry before someone else beats me to it and I am
no longer the first and OMG OMG OMG OMG OMG!!!!!!!!!!!!!!

#themostamazingthingthateveramazinged #icannoteven #howdocope
#looktotomorrow #ltt
#omgomgomgomgomgomgomgomgomgomg

178 comments   374 reblogs

Comment   Reblog   Favorite

14

http://www.lttweb.com/lookies/2013

This year, for the first time ever, the Lookie fanfiction awards will be **officially sponsored** by Alan Shaughnessy and the production staff of *Look to Tomorrow*. Their sponsorship is an extraordinary gift to the show's fans, affirming that fandom and fanfiction, so far from threatening the producers and writers of the show, can only help it to become stronger and more vibrant. Their support of the Lookies fanfiction contest is an unprecedented acknowledgment of the creative power of fandom and its importance to network television. And now, with their support, the Lookies are able to give back to the fan community with a contest that's bigger and better than ever before, with a new twist and AMAZING new prizes!

This year, the Lookies are teaming up with the staff and crew of Look to Tomorrow in the fight against breast cancer. The powers that be at *Look to Tomorrow* know what an amazing, dedicated, passionate fandom we are, and they know that together, we can make great strides in defeating this terrible disease. But to do it, we need your help. Here's how it works:

On the signup page for the 2013 Lookies, you'll see a DONATE HERE button, which provides a link to a special donation page for the Hannah J. Christiansen Breast Cancer Foundation. **NOTE: A donation is not a prerequisite to enter the 2013 Lookie awards.** You may enter without making a donation. We understand that not everybody has money to spend on this, and we are sensitive to that. However, if you can afford it, you are strongly encouraged to give whatever you can give. We have some fantastic incentives; read on.

Beside the donation button, you will also see a graphic that tracks how much money is given. The graph tops out at $15,000. For every dollar donated to breast cancer research through the link on the Lookies signup page, the producers of *Look to Tomorrow* will make a matching donation. And now for the REALLY exciting part:

If the 2013 Lookie fanfiction awards raise $30,000 in the fight against breast cancer -- in other words, if the Lookies are able to raise $15,000 from fan donations, which will be matched by the producers -- the prizes for the winners will change. The GRAND PRIZE in this case will be:

-An all-events-included pass to the 2013 *Look to Tomorrow* convention in Los Angeles, AND

-A special, once-in-a-lifetime chance to be present at the preliminary round-table script reading of an actual episode of *Look to Tomorrow.*

Two days after the ending of the convention, on Monday morning, there will be a script reading for an episode of *Look to Tomorrow*; this means that all the writers and actors will be gathered to run through the script of the episode for the first time. The winner of the grand prize will be there with them. You'll get to sit in a room with Brad, Joscelyn, Danielle, and all the rest of the cast, PLUS the writing crew and some members of the production staff, and hear their very first run-through of a real episode of the show.* This is a not-to-be-missed opportunity for one very lucky and very talented fanfiction author -- and it's not the only one! The incredibly generous sponsorship provided by the show means that we can offer more authorized, official show merchandise than ever before, plus some very special prizes that are completely unavailable commercially. Below is a chart of what the prizes will be if we raise less than $15,000, and then what they will be if we DO raise the $15,000:

	ORIGINAL PRIZE	**$15,000+ PRIZE**
Grand Prize	All-inclusive pass to 2013 *Look to Tomorrow* convention	All-inclusive pass to 2013 *Look to Tomorrow* convention AND an exclusive sit-in on a preliminary round-table reading of a new, 2013-season episode of *Look to Tomorrow!*

First Place -- Drama and First Place -- Humor	Season 3 *Look to Tomorrow* DVD	Season 3 *Look to Tomorrow* DVD AND an AUTOGRAPHED POSTER of the full cast of *Look to Tomorrow*. Autographs WILL BE personalized.
Second Place -- Drama and Second Place -- Humor	Official *Look to Tomorrow* T-shirt	Official *Look to Tomorrow* T-shirt AND novelty *Look to Tomorrow* alarm clock, featuring the *Look to Tomorrow* theme. Wake up every morning to LtT!
Third Place -- Drama and Third Place -- Humor	Official *Look to Tomorrow* baseball cap	Official *Look to Tomorrow* baseball cap AND your choice of official Thorin Lancet action figure OR official Jaela Sher action figure
Honorable Mentions -- Drama and Humor	Official *Look to Tomorrow* cast poster (not autographed)	Official *Look to Tomorrow* cast poster (not autographed) AND official *Look to Tomorrow* playing card deck
Special Prizes for Drabble, Vignette, and Songfic	Copy of *The Official* Look to Tomorrow *Guide: Interviews, Behind-the-Scenes Moments, Episode Guide and More*	Copy of *The Official* Look to Tomorrow *Guide: Interviews, Behind-the-Scenes Moments, Episode Guide and More* AND your choice of *Look to Tomorrow* wall poster (not autographed)
Special Prize -- Voters' Choice Award	Official *Look to Tomorrow* board game	Official *Look to Tomorrow* board game AND an AUTHORIZED, AUTOGRAPHED SCRIPT of episode 2.16, *A Night to Forget*

*Winner will be required to sign a nondisclosure agreement prohibiting him or her from discussing any aspect of this episode of the show with any third party prior to the episode's airing. Violation of this agreement will incur substantial monetary fines. The producers reserve the right to change these rules or to rescind the prize altogether at any time. In the event that this prize is given, further rules and restrictions shall be presented to the winner at that time. Void where prohibited by law.

http://www.diarynow.com/users/thejanethe/13796.html
Date: 2/16/2013
Security level: Private
Mood: !!!!!!!

OKAY OKAY OKAY

...OMG

OKAY

OMG OMG OMG

OKAY.

I have GOT to calm down. Right now I'm running around kind of screaming and flailing incoherently and jumping on chairs and things, and, dude, I HAVE NOT WON THE CONTEST YET. There's not even a "yet" yet. I am not within ten million thousand lightyears of having won the contest yet, and I will never BE within ten million thousand lightyears of winning unless I calm the hell down and start planning for this. And even if I DID win, I can't GET there unless I do even MORE planning. Holy crap. This is huge. And it's pure fantasy at this point. And... huge.

Oh my God.

This is just... oh my God!

I have to win this. I HAVE to. Oh my God, the competition is going to be CRAZY. I don't even know -- is Audra entering? Oh, Jesus, I'm so screwed if Audra's entering, and of COURSE she's entering, EVERYONE will be entering, and how do I beat Audra? And Audra's the best in the fandom but Maxxi's good too and she's a friend of Rashida's, who's one of the judges, and they say the judging is anonymous but OBVIOUSLY it's not when you are FRIENDS with one of the judges and WHY AM I NOT FRIENDS WITH ONE OF THE JUDGES?!?! Shit. Shit, shit, shit! I'll have to figure something out. Pandering -- but even if I get into blatant pandering to the judges I don't know if that will be enough, and then Jolene is one of the judges too and she has that totally obsessive bizarre Jaela/Tamar quirk, and how am I supposed to pander to her and still write the kind of big Thorin/Jaela epic that I'll need to win with the rest of them? I'll have to just forget about Jolene, but maybe I can throw something in there, like Jaela and Tamar had a fling a long time ago -- or maybe I can

19

write a different fic, like a Jaela/Tamar vignette, that I won't submit to the contest but that might make her like me -- but come on, everyone will be pandering to the judges, they'll be able to see right through that -- but then what do I DO? I have to write a GOOD fic, is what I have to do. A great one. Better than anyone's ever seen before, and oh crap, oh crap, oh crap, I'm not good enough to win this, there's no way I'm good enough to win this, and I HAVE TO BE. I just have to be, and oh my God oh my God

I have to calm down first. I just... this is not helpful. LOL

...Okay, trying to calm down.

...still trying.

...still trying...

OMG OMG OMG AAAAAAAAAAAAAAAAH!!!

Okay. I have to get off the computer and stop thinking about this and calm down. Normally I would watch LtT to calm down but I don't think that will help. Maybe I'll take a bike ride. Or watch something else on TV, a stupid sitcom or something. Or... something.

Right. Okay.

(help)

Date: 2/16/2013
Subject: Kin to Sorrow (1917)
    So I've been reading some of Edna St. Vincent Millay's older poems for background on my thesis, and I just came across this one:

Am I kin to Sorrow,
    That so oft
Falls the knocker of my door--
    Neither loud nor soft,
But as long accustomed,   5
    Under Sorrow's hand?
Marigolds around the step
    And rosemary stand,
And then comes Sorrow--
    And what does Sorrow care   10
For the rosemary
    Or the marigolds there?
Am I kin to Sorrow?
    Are we kin?
That so oft upon my door--   15
    Oh, come in!

You know, I love Millay, but I am pretty sure she succumbed to a minor fit of lunacy while she was writing this poem. Yes, okay, Sorrow ignored your flowers, how terribly sad, and I'm sure the knocking is annoying. But Edna, honey, you have Sorrow *locked outside* --

-- so why on *earth* would you open the door?

I'm pretty sure anyone who has a lock on the door but lets Sorrow in anyway *deserves* to be depressed. Sheesh.

http://www.diarynow.com/users/thejanethe/15426.html
Date: 2/16/2013
Security level: Private
Mood: slightly calmer

    ::deep breath:: I am now several hours calmer. I started watching *Frasier* at first, which was the only thing that we had in the house on DVD that didn't have either Drew Barrymore or Brad Memphis in it. But I wasn't in the mood -- we only had the DVD because Mom and I used to watch it together, it's not a show I'm all that into myself. So I switched to Elana's Millay thesis for awhile to keep myself distracted. And now here I am. Calmer.
    So. Yeah.
    ::smallflail::
    ::cough::
    Yikes.
    You know, it's kind of ridiculous how, now that I've calmed down a bit, I'm practically tiptoeing around this Lookies thing in my head. It's crazy. The prize is SO AMAZING and I'm already so crazy-nervous about it, you know? I can already feel myself getting all revved up and melodramatic about it, as if I'm going to die or something if I don't win. But that's just how I feel. I mean, I tend to get obsessive about the Lookies anyway, no matter what the prizes are. But losing a prize this big would be just -- I don't even know how to describe it. I'm honestly not sure how I would cope. It sounds crazy, but I just don't know if I could keep on going on in fandom after that. And... I can't lose that.
    It's like... well, a lot of it is about Rachel. You know, she is who I wish I could be, she has the life that I wish I could have. If I were writing a story about Rachel, Rachel would totally win this contest, because that's what Rachel *does*. She always gets the things she *really* wants out of life, because she's awesome and hardworking and likable and all that sort of thing. And then there's me. And I never get the things I want out of life. Ever. I hate my life and I suck. And... if I could win this contest, then it would be like I finally *did* something. I wouldn't just be playing Rachel anymore. I'd *be* Rachel. And I don't mean that I'd go to the con

22

pretending to be someone named Rachel Williams or something, either -- I'm sure they'll do background checks and things for the script reading; if I win the prize the fandom will have to know my real name and age and so on. But if I win the prize, *none of that will matter.* There would be no *reason* to hide Jane Shilling anymore, because if I can win the grand prize and get to the con and the script reading, I could tell people I'd just been guarding my identity because the Internet can be creepy -- *and they'd believe me*. Because if I win this contest and this prize, I won't be a loser anymore. Why would someone who could win a writing contest this awesome and get a chance to do something so amazing need to hide who she is?

I have to win.

I need this so badly that I almost feel like I have to try to take some space from it. It scares me. I'm afraid to even check the comments on my entry or to read the rest of my friends list. Everyone else wants this just as much as I do and I'm terrified I'll lose, but I also just can't stand the excitement. I literally feel like I'm about to have a heart attack.

Not that I'll be able to forget about it and go to sleep tonight, either.

Well, I suppose now's as good a time as any for an LtT marathon. I can start trying to think of fic ideas (I have to do something AMAZING, obvs.) and watch until I fall asleep. Theoretically, I suppose I should be doing math homework -- Mrs. Baker's been glaring at me owlishly for the last few weeks, like she bit into her Tootsie Roll Pop and there was no Tootsie inside. On the other hand, I'm not all that interested in being Mrs. Baker's Tootsie, and besides, I'd probably just wind up doodling bad sketches of Brad Memphis all over the margins of my homework. I think the marathon's a better idea. I wouldn't be good for anything else right now anyway.

Spectrum High School Email
"Where achieving potential is just the beginning"
Compose Mail

Mark Unread As: Bold
Check to Delete

☑	**Lorilynn Meisner, LICSW**	**Happy New Year! :)** -- Hi Kids -- It's great to have you back!!! I hope you all had a wonderful break, whether you celebrate the holiday of your choice or just relax! We...
☑	**Margaret Baker**	**Start of New Term** -- Dear Class: Welcome back. As you may have heard, I will be teaching your Algebra I...
☐	Laine Elsing	Working in library this semester -- Hi Jane! I'm putting together the list of volunteers for this...
☑	**Spectrum High School Administration**	**Rules and Regulations** -- PLEASE READ CAREFULLY. The following rules will apply to all students in the new...
☑	**Spectrum High School**	**Start-of-Term Bulletin** -- Welcome to the start of the new semester! We hope you have all had...

So, on the subject of real-life friends… maybe you should be careful what you wish for?

Or maybe not. I'm not sure. It's all… weird.

Well, starting at the beginning. There's this guy who's in a couple of my classes -- Gary Huang. He sits diagonally from me in math class, and I guess, come to think of it, he's been kind of friendly all year. Most of the kids at school who don't tease me just ignore me, but I've caught him staring at me a couple of times, and sometimes he smiles at me or rolls his eyes at me when Mrs. Baker is being stupid. I've never really said much of anything to him, though. I mean, to begin with, he's a little bit weird. He's kind of a funny-looking kid, kind of skinny and gangly, with tufty, slightly electrified-looking hair. He has this nervous giggle that he seems to append to the end of everything he says, since I hear it floating across the aisle like every five minutes. He also has an occasional minor facial tic -- I think it pops out when he's nervous -- and even though he has a nice enough smile, when the tic is acting up he looks kind of creepy. I mean, I don't mean to sound shallow, and I certainly don't have a problem with the guy. He seems nice enough when he's on his own, and I'm not going to shun him for having a facial tic or whatever. But last I knew he was tending to tag along at the edges of Louie Vitelli's crowd, which was last made famous when Louie got suspended after he was caught doing crack in the teachers' bathroom. (Apparently he was smart enough to realize the staff bathroom was the only one with a lock, but not smart enough to realize that the fact that it is a staff bathroom meant that the odds were good that a coffee-addicted teacher would be standing out there waiting when he stumbled out of the bathroom and dropped his pipe on the floor.) I don't think Louie Vitelli and his crowd have much more use for me than I do for them, in general. So smiles or no smiles, I was not really thinking of Gary Huang as a potential BFF. Frankly, sometimes I wished he'd find someone else to trade Baker-provoked eyerolls with. I'm just not 100% sure what his deal is.

25

But then he sat with me at lunch today. Okay, so, explanation, let's put this right out there on the table: people do not sit with me at lunch. They don't want to and I don't want them to. (Just another reason why I know, when I think about it logically, that "friends" are one of those things that sound a lot better in my head than they would be in practice.) I read during lunch; I may spend most of my free time on the Internet, but I like having forty-five minutes to spend alone with a book. It's me-time, and so I wasn't so happy when Gary sat down in front of me. He was being ridiculous, actually; he was so uncertain that he actually sat down, completely, but didn't put his tray down on the table, as though that would somehow finalize the whole deal and he'd have no chance to change his mind if it looked like I was going to throw up on him. So there he was, perched on the seat as though he might get up and flee, with the tray poised like a foot above the table. Which also put it only like three inches under his chin. He sat there like that for a couple seconds, neither one of us sure what the hell he was doing, until some freshman bumped into him from behind. His chin hit his tray, his tray hit the table, chocolate milk went everywhere, and I started laughing. I couldn't help it. His glasses were all speckled with milk and he was sitting there rubbing his chin and looking totally befuddled and... I'm sorry, it was funny.

Anyway, he wiped down his glasses and we mopped up the milk together, and that broke the ice a little. But only a very little. As soon as the milk was cleaned up we lapsed back into silence, and he'd gained just enough confidence to try and break it with periodic little stabs at conversation. At one point he asked me, in all seriousness:

GARY: ::nervous up-glance, prefatory giggle:: "So... um... do you think Mrs. Baker drinks more coffee or more tea?"

I have to give him credit, it's not an icebreaking line I'd ever heard before.

Eventually he got to more mundane topics, like "What do you like to do for fun?" for example. I hate that question, though. I mean, I'm not going to tell Gary about writing fanfic, or LtT, or anything like that. I don't know why that seems so personal, but it does -- I guess it's because most people would think I'm crazy. But that really just doesn't leave a whole lot. I finally wound up saying "I'm pretty into Scrabble," and figured he'd let it

26

die there. No one ever has any answer to that.

I should have thought again. "Really? That's cool, I heard about that," he said, leaning forward and nearly upsetting his bowl of pudding as well. "Do you do, like, those tournaments and stuff? Those are hardcore."

He seems to have some sort of fetish for that word. "No, they're too -- uh -- hardcore for me," I said, which is true. I play a lot on gameaddiction. com, but I'm fairly certain I'll never graduate from Expert rank to Pro. (I slaughter everyone in Wordsmith with Friends on FriendsLink, but that doesn't really count.) "Why'd you think I was in tournaments?"

"I dunno, you seem... uh..." He went red in the face, and I could tell he was trying to find some way *not* to say that I seem obsessive. I had to laugh. He may be weird, but he's sort of endearing.

"Well, Scrabble pros are way beyond my level," I said, trying to spare him the embarrassment. For some reason that made him blush even darker. I think in general, conversations with Gary are likely to flow much more easily once you give up trying to figure him out.

"No, it's cool," he said, as though I had contradicted him. "I mean, my friends think what I'm into is geeky too -- I mean, um, not that your friends think you're geeky, or that I think you're geeky, or --"

I was trying so hard to keep the laughter to some kind of minimum that I nearly choked. When I could talk again, I tried to tell him it was okay, really, but the more he talked the more embarrassed he got. God, I wonder what his deal is; most of the time he's okay, and then every so often he loses the social thread, so to speak, and it looks like he'll never be able to pick it up again. In an effort to deflect him from embarrassing himself into hyperventilation, I asked him what he's into that his friends think is so geeky. He glanced automatically back over his shoulder when I mentioned them, and suddenly it became crystal-clear why he was sitting with me; over at Vitelli's table, bags were spread strategically across chairs in a way they never are unless a clique is trying to prevent infiltration. Or to send a tough message to an ex-clique member. Poor Gary.

"You have to promise not to laugh," he said. This was not an easy promise to make at that point in time, as he still had chocolate milk droplets on the edges of his glasses and his face had only faded to strawberry so far. But I nodded anyway.

"Louie and them think it's lame that I'm so into Skee-Ball," he said, and for a minute I stared blankly, wondering if I'd heard him correctly. But then he went on, dead serious, and I felt the giggles start to rise like bubbles in an Efferdent commercial. I bit my lip and tried really, really hard to keep them in. "That's why I asked if you did tournaments, right. My team just won the state championships," he said, with no little amount of pride.

"The -- the state Skee-Ball championships?" I queried.

"Yeah," he said, his face brightening. "The league isn't real big yet, not too many people know about it, but we do recruiting at arcades and stuff."

"What arcades?" I said, trying to think. We don't really have any arcades in town -- we used to have one, but it got converted to a roller rink/ bowling alley awhile back.

"Well, since Aerial turned into a goddamn *bowling* alley," he said, the bitterness heavy in his voice, "mostly at, uh..." He mumbled something, staring at his tray.

"Mac and cheese?" I said, bewildered.

He giggled and grimaced simultaneously. "No. Chuck E. Cheese."

The bell rang then, and I just managed to make it to the girls' room before bursting into laughter.

I know, I know, I'm sorry, I am so not the one to be pointing fingers at other geeks, but I couldn't get the image out of my head of Gary, totally focused, one hand curled around a Skee-Ball, attempting to sink a 100-point shot, whipping his hand back... and knocking the head off a gigantic puppet mouse.

Gary... that boy is an odd duck. And I still have not figured out why he is latching onto me. Was today a one-time thing, or is he, like, really set on this friendship thing?

...the state SKEE-BALL championships?!?!?!

Date: 2/19/2013
Security level: Private
Mood: enraged

OH MY GOD I AM GOING TO KILL MRS. BAKER I AM GOING TO KILL HER I AM GOING TO KILL HER.

(Yeah, that ought to be enough to get me expelled from school in the era of school shootings, huh? Great. Show me the door, folks, and I'll be out of your hair.)

Mrs. Baker... she got the administration to call my dad. She TOLD THE ADMINISTRATION I AM NOT PARTICIPATING IN CLASS and then the administration GOT MS. MEISNER TO CALL MY DAD, and I HATE MS. MEISNER, I've been stuck in counseling with her all year and SHE DRIVES ME CRAZY AND SHE CALLED DAD AND NOW HE'S ALL FREAKED OUT AND

I think I had better calm down and try to get rid of some of these capital letters.

Look. I'm not going to pretend I participate in math class, okay? It's true. I don't. But this is REALLY NOT A PROBLEM, and Mrs. Baker hadn't gotten half her brain left behind when they beamed her down from Planet Helmet-Hair, she'd know it. At Spectrum, there are kids who have tantrums in the middle of class, who do drugs in the bathrooms between classes, who get in fights, all sorts of disruptive stuff. Two days ago Joe Collins all but kicked his desk over *in Mrs. Baker's class* before he stormed out of the room in the middle of a lecture on linear equations. Me, I go to my classes, and I sit at my desk. I pay attention in the classes that matter to me and engage in "independent study" (i.e., reading and writing) in the classes that don't. Then I do my end-of-term theses, eventually, and that's where my grades come from. No one has EVER had a problem with this before. God, I'm like a model student by Spectrum standards. Sure, I wouldn't be one in a mainstream school, but that's why I'm not IN a mainstream school.

And then Mrs. Baker goes and -- and what is she doing? She's reporting to the administration that I don't do my homework, for starters. And, I mean -- *homework?* Who cares about homework? She should be glad I'm not kicking over desks in the middle of class. And then, even better! Mrs. Baker told the administration I'm being "withdrawn" and "uncooperative" in class! My God! Withdrawn and uncooperative! The horror, the horror!

I mean, I just... I do not understand why Mrs. Baker felt the need to involve my father in this. Honestly. I cannot even begin to imagine where that idea came from. My father is just -- look, he has enough stress in his life. Just a couple of days ago *Ever After* and *Never Been Kissed* were airing at the very same time on different cable channels, and two weeks before that *Everyone Says I Love You*, which he's *never even seen omg*, was airing on a pay channel that we don't get. He has not yet come out of mourning. He does not need to be getting ridiculous calls from school saying I am not handling things well. I am handling things fine. I am handling things much better than he handles things.

I just can't get over the fact that somebody decided to call him about this. My dad... I don't know what he needs right now, but it's not this. And I sure don't need this either. We just don't... oh, I don't know! Here, why don't I simplify this and transcribe the conversation we had after he got the call.

Dad: ::knocks, very timorously::
Me: Hello?
Dad, sounding frightened: Jane?
Me: ::under breath:: Who else would it be? ::gets up, opens door to find **Dad,** cowering back as though I were about to hit him:: Uh... what's up?
Dad: Oh. Can I come in?
Me: Ummm... [Note: Dad never comes in my room. No one ever comes in my room. I'm not so comfortable with having people in my room.] Uh, sure, I guess.
Dad: Okay. ::sits on bed, having gained some confidence from the fact that no one has blown up or spontaneously caught fire thus far in the conversation::
Me: Uh... is something up, Dad?
Dad: Yes. No. I mean, okay, yes, Jane. I mean, I just got a call from your school.
Me: ...what?

30

Dad: Yeah. I got a call from a, um, a Miss Meyer or something?

Me: Uh... ::realizing:: Oh God. Dad, she's a moron. Why the... *why* was she calling?

Dad:: She said, um, well, this math teacher, she talked to her, you know, she said she's your counselor? And she said, well, that you haven't been paying attention in class... [Here insert, with many "ums" and "ahs" and prompts from me, his eventual account of the withdrawn/uncooperative/ non-homework-doing business. Dialogue is one thing, but if I tried to transcribe all my dad's confused, out-of-it ramblings, I would run out of space. On the Internet. Anyway, cut to...]

Me: ::floundering:: Are you SERIOUS? I... look, I have no idea what's going through Mrs. Baker's head, but I promise you, this doesn't matter. The whole point of my *being* at Spectrum is that I don't NEED to do all this stuff.

Dad: What do you mean, you don't need to? Math is important, Jane. School is important.

Me: Really, Dad, in this case it's not. She's a ridiculous teacher, and she's got a grudge against me, I don't know why. I'm not going to learn anything from her.

Dad: She's your math teacher, honey. I mean, Jane, you have to work in your classes, you know? Your education -- it's the most important thing, what your mother and I -- [I groaned. He got discombobulated and lost his train of thought.] And, I mean, you're so smart. So smart... If you... The lady who called, she said your teacher said that... I think... well she said, I mean, the teacher said, but she, the Meyer lady, she told me, you've been "abusing the system" --

Me: What is that supposed to mean? It's THEIR system! [I was yelling by now. This was a bad move. Dad looked like he thought I was going to clock him over the head with a bedside lamp at any minute. Oh boy.]

Dad: I don't know, I don't know what it means, I mean, I don't know what's been going on, this is just what they said, you know? But I figure, I mean, they never called before, and I worry, you know, because it -- you -- they...

Me: ::before he could finish declining the personal pronoun:: Dad, please don't worry. *Please.* Nothing is wrong. I swear to God.

Dad: But she, the lady who called, says she's concerned for you...

Me: That's total bull. The only problem is Mrs. Baker hates me.

Dad: I don't think -- I mean, it didn't sound like that, Janie. [I hate being called Janie.] I think... I think they're just concerned, you know? About -- I mean, it's what schools are for, right? For --

Me: Dad, I have this under control. I'm not "abusing" any system. If they let me do things my own way it's because my own way works.

Dad: What does that mean? [By this point he was starting to look really pained and sad. I *hate* when that happens.] I hardly know anything about what you're up to these days... I shouldn't...

Me: ::quickly:: Dad, it's okay. Really. I just do my own thing at school, I do my own projects -- good ones, really. I wind up learning at my own pace. The librarian -- you should talk to her after talking to Mrs. Baker, she knows me a lot better -- she says she's amazed at my drive to learn.

Dad: You work in the library, right?

Me: Yeah, I have for a long time. I'm good friends with the librarian, she lets me help her pick what books the library should order and stuff.

Dad: See, your mother would have known all this. Your mother --

Me: You did know that.

Dad: No, I thought that, I wasn't sure. I didn't know anything about it, I don't talk to you the way she did, I... It's bad enough you don't have a mother without me --

Me: Dad, this has nothing to do with anything. Really, it's okay.

Dad: -- without me not paying you any attention. You were never in trouble at school when she was around --

Me: Dad! This isn't about that! And I'm not in trouble! Mrs. Baker just hates me!

Dad: You spend all your time in your room, on your computer. And I, I just watch TV all the time, I drink too much, I know it, no one has to tell me that --

Me: Oh my God, this SO DOESN'T HAVE ANYTHING TO DO WITH ANYTHING!

And he started to cry. Jesus. I mean, obviously he was on the sentimental side of a few beers, but Jesus Christ. Ms. Meisner makes one phone call to the house and all of a sudden Dad's sobbing about how he's a horrible parent and how he hasn't seemed to be able to hold anything together since Mom died. I had absolutely no idea what to do. I mean, how are you supposed to comfort your own father when he's -- being like that? (Especially when he's sort of right; he doesn't understand that I don't mind that much that he's sort of in his own shell. I mean, whatever, let him deal with things however he has to deal with them. I'm doing fine.)

I wound up patting him awkwardly on the shoulder a bunch of times, just saying "it's okay, really, there isn't a problem, Dad, it's fine" like a broken record. And he kept insisting it wasn't. And he kept crying and I kept patting and glancing at the computer and thinking *It would all be okay, Dad, really, if you'd just go back to your movie and I could go back to my computer. I can't do this.*

Finally he pulled himself together enough to say he thought Ms. Meisner was right, he should be more involved in my life at school, we should maybe even try family counseling at some point. I was too relieved that he'd stopped crying to notice what he was saying, really. But this is so, so, so very not good. Ms. Meisner drives me crazy; she's one of those superficially cheerful bouncy types -- her favorite word is "super!" and she never goes anywhere without a colorful scarf with some ridiculous abstract pattern or other on it. And there is a picture on her wall of an eggshell breaking open and blueberries falling out of it, with the caption "Expect the Unexpected." What in GOD'S name is that supposed to mean? It's bad enough seeing her every week myself; now I'm supposed to drag *Dad* in there? I mean, look at the three of us: I don't do my homework, Dad watches too much TV, and Ms. Meisner thinks blueberries hatch from eggs. Which one of those people seems to need the most help, here?

My point is, I hate her and she's useless and stupid and totally unhelpful to me, solo, singular. So how she's supposed to help my dad and me, plural, is just beyond me.

Ugh -- how is it still two hours until LtT is on?

http://www.diarynow.com/users/thejanethe/25437.html
Date: 2/19/2013
Security level: Private

Managed to get into the LtT chat, FINALLY! It's been acting up ever since they made the Lookies announcement, and forget about getting onto any of the forums. But anyway, everyone in the world was in there, and at times it was practically illegible what with all the capslock and exclamation points, but I did learn some things. Here are a few of the most salient points:

1. Everybody who is anybody in the entire fandom is entering. Audra, Jenna, Fanfictionista, Skye, TealDeer, Allie S. Even that friggin' "Tooxian Taleteller" with all the dippy grammar-impaired fangirls is entering, and she hasn't written a fic in two years.

2. The judging is theoretically anonymous, which I knew, but practically not anonymous at all, which I should have known. People always gossip about what other people are submitting, even though they're not supposed to, and the big-name writers' prose styles are always recognizable anyway. (Skye didn't take it too kindly when Jenna noted that you can always identify one of Skye's fics because they contain no complete sentences, just a lot of fragments and em-dashes. Jenna's such a bitch. And so right.)

3. The roster of judges, which did a little bit of shifting early on, is now set in stone and is comprised of Jolene, SiqanGoddess, Mara, Rashida, Floam23, and Tim. I don't know any of them except SiqanGoddess, who likes my quizzes. Must post more quizzes.

4. The judges' friends always win.

All in all, it wasn't the most encouraging conversation I've ever been in.

Ack, I can't let them get to me! People were TOTALLY doing the psych-out thing -- it was ridiculous. Srsly. Jenna was OUT OF CONTROL. She ripped everyone to shreds and then gave them little smiley faces for Band-Aids. I don't know what's more annoying, that she actually stands a shot at winning, or that she took pot shots at all the big-name writers in the room -- Skye, Audra, Teal, and even JTGenie, who to my mind is totally irrelevant -- and ignored me completely. Ignored Rachel completely.

34

Whoever. Either way I think I've been way overrating Rachel's popularity in the fandom, which is totally depressing. The whole point of Rachel is that she's supposed to be charming and witty and brilliant and, like, everyone's favorite person! If Jenna considers her less of a threat than JTGenie, how popular can she possibly be?

So I have to do some name-boosting. Rachel's latest fic, "Stars May Fall," is pretty popular, but obviously it isn't popular enough. I'm going to have to step that up -- cross-post it to more communities, do more networking on ReCi

...omg, I just got an email. Is that what I think it --

OMG!!!!! Audra just friended me on DN!!!!!!!! HAHAHA, JENNA, EAT THAT!!!!!!!!!1 Dude, AUDRA IS THE MOST AMAZING PERSON IN THE FANDOM AND THE MOST AMAZING WRITER IN THE FANDOM AND SHE HAS LIKE 600 FOLLOWERS ON DIARYNOW AND SHE'S FRIENDED LIKE 75 OF THEM BACK. Hahahahaha, she DOESN'T EVEN HAVE JENNA FRIENDED! I *KNEW* she thought Jenna's dumbass pretentious-dreamy-AU stuff sucked, I KNEW IT! We were joking together in the chatroom just now -- she'd told me that she likes Rachel's "Stars" fic, but I didn't know whether she meant it, but she was being really nice to me, and we were sort of joking around a little about some of the crazier drama that's already been going down, especially late in the chat when like a whole contingent of non-fanficcers got so annoyed with all the Lookies discussion that they huffed off and formed a splinter chat and we were joking about how the whole fandom was going to split off into warring factions and eventually start the Internet equivalent of a nuclear holocaust, which in reality would probably translate to a whole bunch of ostentatiously deleted ReCirclrs and poorly-spelled and -punctuated anonymous comments and a switch to moderated posting on the lttfans forum. And... and somewhere in the last ten lines I forgot about the concept of sentence-ending. LOL

And... but dude! Audra is AMAZING. She just is. I mean, she's an amazing writer, but she's also incredibly sweet and funny and nice. And she's a legitimate fandom celebrity -- everyone loves her and her fics. I've been following her on every site ever since about a week after I joined the fandom. I love reading her public posts and I adore every single one of her fics, and for the longest time I honestly *yearned* for her to friend me back. I sort of idol-worship her -- for someone who *is* so popular, there's nothing snotty or pretentious about her at all, and I love her sense of humor and her way of looking at things. But over time I sort of resigned myself to the idea that I could be popular in fandom and I could even have a fair number of admirers of my own, but I was never going to be *that* popular. Why would someone like Audra want to waste time on someone like me? Even Rachel-me?

I love how two seconds before she friended me I was writing about how I wasn't popular enough in the LtT community. I am pretty sure there is no way to *be* any more popular in the LtT fandom than to have Audra Scanlon friend you. ^.^

This is really, really great. In fact, it could turn the whole Lookies around, no lie. I found out today in the chat that when they said the fandom had to raise $15,000 in donations in order for the script reading to be part of the prize, that number was chosen specifically because there was a similar contest last year in the *Alien Fantasies* fandom, which is just slightly larger than the LtT one, and it raised $12,000. So the producers picked a limit they figured was just out of our reach, so they could get a publicity stunt going without having to deal with the hassle of actually letting an outsider into a script reading. Thanks, producers.

Anyway, while people were chatting about it I hit on the idea of having a fandom auction. I've seen it done before. You can't auction off actual show merchandise, I don't think, but you can auction off custom-ordered fanfiction, beta reading services, fanart, webpage design, stuff like that. From what I've seen, you can raise a lot of money by doing that, particularly if you get talented enough people to donate. If Audra donated a fic or two, I bet they would raise *hundreds*. And if she were participating, a whole lot of people would follow suit. Maybe we could even co-manage the auction. I should talk to her about it soon. I'll tell her I'll do most of the work (which I totally will) -- she could just post about it on her FL/RC/DN/etc., donate some stuff, contact some other big-name writers and artists about donations. There is a very good chance that this could tip things over the $15,000 marker.

And, what's maybe the best part... I think I'll finally have the guts to submit a drabble to the fanfiction page she mods. It's the only one in the entire fandom with quality standards -- she has to personally approve you as a talented writer before you can get posting access -- and *everyone* reads it. I was always too scared to even try; your initial submission has to be a drabble, so she can review it quickly, and I suck at drabbles. But if she's friended me on DN, I think I'll just go for broke and send one. Apparently she already thinks I'm a good writer (!!!).

Okay, this entry sounds kind of nuts, like I maybe have a secret stash of love letters to Audra hidden in my drafts folder or something. From the tone of this you'd think I just got friended by Brad Memphis himself. But... it really is a big deal to me. It'll be good for my fandom standing and good for the auction.

...and plus, I really just think she's kind of awesome.

Haha, I'm looking back at the entry before this and I can't believe now that I was so upset about school. I mean, yeah, Mrs. Baker is being a bitch, but she's just one teacher. So she reported me to the administration -- so Ms. Meisner called the house. So what? Dad, I'm sure, will remember none of this in the morning, so whatever. It's fine. The worst that's going to come of it will be that Ms. Meisner will probably crease her brows a notch more when she does her frowny-concerned look. I should start, like, keeping a chart of estimated millimeters that her brow creases when I say or do specific things, and then see if I can figure out how to give her specific patterns of wrinkles over time or something. And school might feel anxiety-provoking, but it is Spectrum, after all. I think I can handle Spectrum, no problem.

...

OMG AUDRA FRIENDED ME YAAAAAAAAAAAAAY!!!

livelongandfangirl:

Way to go with yet another bullshit sexist plot, Look to Tomorrow. Isn't it special that Jaela the hysterical little woman is disrupting the whole history of her planet and endangering everyone on Qaetas to try to get her dead parents back? Obviously it's the woman who has to be too stupid to get that she's risking destroying her whole planet for the sake of rescuing two people from a Zyerlean guerrilla raid that happened 20 years ago. Why can't she use logic to figure out that if she gets caught by the Zyerleans they'll know that in the future people will figure out that Saureshan was backing the raid, and at that point they'll probably cover it up by blowing up the whole goddamn planet? Oh, right: BECAUSE SHE'S A WOMAN. Women aren't logical! They're emotional, hysterical idiots! Thanks for creating yet more popular media totally grounded in sexist garbage, LtT writers.

#sexism #bullshit #feminism #looktotomorrow

racheltessers:

I should say at the outset that I understand your point here, and I'm certainly not going to argue that the Look to Tomorrow writers are 100% free of sexism (cf Jordana's response to the assault in Cicruccia). However, I don't think what Jaela is doing here is an enactment of that sexism. I think it's actually a moving example of how grief for (a) loved one(s) can take over someone's world, how subsumed in that grief people can become and how much they'd risk or sacrifice to get their loved ones back. I don't think Jaela's being "hysterical". This has been building up for her for a long time, and Saureshan's election was just the tipping point. She's just been destroyed by it, and the way they've done it feels pretty real to me. Between Paula Grayson's writing (it's nice that they put one of the three female writers on staff on it, anyway :P) and Joscelyn's amazing acting, I've actually found it pretty heartrending. I really think it's been handled fairly sensitively, and I'm looking forward to seeing where they take it.

#looktotomorrow #ltt #sexism #feminism #rachelexplainstheworld #rachelislongwinded #rachelcaresaboutthings #rachelusestoomanytags

To: janeshilling@spectrum.org
From: adowning@clearwater.org
Date: 2/24/2013
Subject: Re: Hi

Hey sweetie,

I just wanted to check in and make sure everything's going well for you. I've been feeling badly lately that I fell so out of touch with you and your father while I was living in Oregon. When I call your phone usually goes straight to voice mail, but I did get your dad on the phone the other day. He didn't sound good, although of course it's hard to tell over a telephone line. I thought of dropping by but he told me it was too late on a school night and to come another time. So I thought I'd drop you a line and ask you when a good time would be. What's your schedule like?

Oh, I almost forgot. I found some pictures, when I was unpacking, that I thought you'd want to see. I barely remembered packing them all, but back then the divorce was so stressful, and Jess dying right in the middle of it all... oh, Jane, honey, I'm just so sorry I handled all of it so badly. I barely know any of what's been going on with you and your father, and... I know this is all awkward, but sweetie, if he's drinking again, you'd tell me, wouldn't you? I know about his drinking before he and Jess got married -- I was her confidante through that, I guess you'd say. So you can talk to me too, I promise, I'll understand. I can imagine how rough things must be... When he showed up like that at the funeral... I was such a mess with everything going on, I didn't even know what to do. I did talk to him and he said he was going right back into AA, and then I called once or twice to see how he was and he always seemed fine, and he told me he was in AA. So I thought it was working, I guess. I didn't know... well, if anything's been wrong, I didn't know, and I'm so sorry.

I'm sure this email isn't making any sense -- I'm sorry. I was talking about the pictures I'm sending, wasn't I? I scanned them all for you before I put them in an album, and I'm attaching them as a zip file. (As a side note, it took me just about two hours to figure out how to make them into a zip file, so you'd better be grateful for them, kiddo.) There are all sorts of them, lots from when you were a kid, and some even from when your mom and I

39

were kids. The last bunch are the last roll of pictures I ever had taken with your mother. They're from when we went to Arizona the summer before the accident. They're so strange to look at... I know they might be hard to see, but I wanted you to have them. You know I'm just a phone call away, right? I'm always there to talk to.

All right, sweetheart. I'll be in touch, OK? Let me know about the movies. I'd love to see you.

Love,

Your Auntie Amy and Fairy Godmother

***

To: adowning@clearwater.org
From: janeshilling@spectrum.org
Date: 2/24/2013
Subject: Re: Hi

Dear Aunt Amy:

Everything here is fine. I know you're worried, but seriously, we're fine. Dad's not drinking. There isn't a problem. You might have caught him when he had taken some Benadryl or something, he had a cold last week. Everything's totally okay, and you don't have to feel guilty -- that doesn't help anything; it just makes me feel bad that you're feeling bad, and anyway, really, it doesn't do anyone any good for you to

To: adowning@clearwater.org
From: janeshilling@spectrum.org
Date: 2/24/2013
Subject: Re: Hi

Dear Aunt Amy:

Everything here is fine. I know you're feeling all guilty because you were all the way across the country when Mom died and then you couldn't visit for more than like three days but that's fine, I mean, you've got your own life and your own priorities, so that's the way it goes, I get it. And anyway, I'm fine and Dad's fine and really the only problem is when horrible stuff that it sucked slogging through the first time gets dragged up again, so if you could please not send all these photos of Mom and stuff like that because it's not like anyone ever tried to say a single thing to make you feel guilty about running away three days after the funeral but then you can't exactly expect when you move back nine months later that suddenly you can just be a part of things and be some kind of shoulder to cry on or

http://www.twistedart.net/users/blackwingedsoul/22342.html
Date: 2/24/2013
Security level: Public

it's all pointless

there is no use

evan's out for the weekend. no one to talk to. he is the only one i can talk to, his eyes so brown and understanding. his face settles into perfect lines of stillness and i know he cares. there is no one else who cares.

i miss jeff

that's what i would tell evan if he were here. i need to tell him, he isn't here. he left an ounce of pot under his bed. i've never stolen drugs from evan, never. i wonder if he would mind. i don't know what to do

i hurt, oh, god, i hurt

the motorcycle accident. mom was at home, she got the news, i was at jordan's house and she called and said jeff had been hurt, come home, and jeff was already dead when she told me that. he was dead. he was dead. why didn't she tell me he was dead? why did she give me hope that he was alive? i got home and i found out he was dead and the whole universe crumpled in and all i could think was she lied, she gave me ten minutes when i thought he was alive and he wasn't, ten minutes when i didn't know my world had changed forever, ten minutes when my insides had been scooped out with a melon baller and i didn't even know it yet. i wanted to yell at her, why didn't you tell me right away? i wanted to yell at her, why did you *ever* tell me? if you could lie to me for ten minutes you could lie to me for the rest of my life, tell me he was fine but he moved to costa rica, i wouldn't question, i would know how important it was that the lies not be disturbed, know how important it was that the house of cards that was my life stay standing, no matter the lies, the worst lie is better than this truth

the loss of him is a deep black hole and i tiptoe around it every day, i turn my back to it and feel the adrenaline rush as my heel catches on the edge of the drop and i almost go over, almost go in. every day i expect the hole in the universe to get smaller, to shrink back to normal, every day i expect that time will heal me as everyone told me it would, but it doesn't, it doesn't heal, it doesn't help, the abyss grows larger every day, every day more earth crumbles in, and i know someday it will swallow me whole. it swallowed him and it will swallow me. i know. *i know.*

and then there are days like today. something trips me up and i go in. i feel like i am clinging to a cliff face. i can't let myself drop. i don't have the strength to pull myself up. just hanging onto the cliff is the most i can manage. maybe more than i can manage.

i need something

i need him

i can't find any more words

<u>Leave a Comment</u>   <u>9 Comments</u>

To: <u>adowning@clearwater.org</u>
From: <u>janeshilling@spectrum.org</u>
Date: 2/24/2013
Subject: Re: Hi

Dear Aunt Amy:

Thanks for emailing -- it was really nice to hear from you. You're right, it is a shame that we live so close now and hardly ever see each other. But no worries, everything's fine here, and I'm sorry you were so worried by Dad on the phone -- he had a cold last week, so he'd probably taken some Benadryl or something, I don't know. He's not as young as he used to be, as you know :) -- he probably just fell asleep early and was groggy when you called. Anyway, I'd love to see a movie with you. I really wanted to see *In Flanders Fields,* that war movie that's out now (I know I'm not usually into violent movies, but, well, it's got Brad Memphis in it and he's my pet celebrity, so how could I say no? :)) Do you want to go see it next week, maybe Wednesday? I could meet you at the theater -- I've been biking a lot lately, which I'm really loving. The weather's been crazy nice for this time of year, huh?

Love,

Jane

From: racheltessers@yippee.com
To: stormgoddess72@yippee.com
Date: 2/26/2013
Subject: Drabble submission for "Tales of Tomorrow"

Hi Audra,

    I'd like to apply for posting access to your *Tales of Tomorrow* fanfiction page. My drabble submission is attached; please let me know if there's any problem with the attachment or with my application. I adore the site and would love to be a part of it, but I'll understand if my writing isn't ready for your site yet. Just let me know -- thank you so much for maintaining such a great page and for looking at my submission! :)

    All best,

    Rachel

* * *

Drabble: *Reminders*
Author: Rachel (racheltessers)
Word count: 112 (sorry! Just a bit over)

    Thorin would be fine if they'd leave him alone.

    Jaela's pod had been lost for weeks -- he knew she wouldn't be back. But he could handle it, her being gone. Work eighteen hours, sleep six. Chase the adrenaline rush of ever-more-dangerous jaunts. He could've done it. He knew how.

    But they wouldn't let him. Jordana asking if he needed time off to cope; Tamar's awkward condolences. And then stumbling over the reminders no one had thought to expunge. Her sprawl-scribbled paperwork left on his desk. Her Ciccrucian jade still on the wall.

    And sometimes, he didn't know what was worse: that she'd left him alone without her… or that no one else would.

http://www.diarynow.com/users/thejanethe/27254.html
Date: 2/25/2013
Security level: Private
Mood: determined

It's really late, but I can't sleep. I've been lying awake twitching, staring at the ceiling, trying to figure things out, trying to let all of this go long enough to sleep. None of it's working, of course. But my resolve has been growing all night. The only thing that's hard is putting it down in words.

Still, I'm going to, here at three in the morning, in a private post where nobody can see but me. I'm putting it down in words so that tomorrow morning, when I'm still thinking about this, I won't keep pushing it to the back of my mind and trying to pretend it isn't there. This *is* what I'm going to do, and I *am* going to plan on it, and I don't care if anyone else would call it crazy, because I'm not going to waste any more time worrying about what other people would think.

Here it is:

1. I am going to submit a screenplay-format alternate-season episode in the drama category of the Lookies, and I am going to win the grand prize.
2. I am going to go to the con and to the script reading. (Duh.)
3. I am going to submit my alternate-season episode to the show's producers as a spec script, and I am going to speak with them at the script reading about said spec script.
4. I am going to join the writing staff of *Look to Tomorrow*.

OKAY, OKAY. Look, I KNOW how ridiculous that sounds. Totally. I do. I get it. I feel like I should be writing about it in invisible ink. White font, white background. And yet I've thought this through a million times -- this isn't starting today. It didn't even start with the announcement of the special Lookies prizes. It's been floating around in my mind for I don't even know how long... but the second I start trying to put it into words I feel like a four-year-old planning to meet Mickey Mouse at Disney World, thinking the guy in the giant plastic costume is the real thing. But now here are the Lookies with this amazing new grand prize, and it's like the opportunity is dropping into my lap. Crazy as it sounds, I *know* it's true.

46

I'm going to make it happen. I swear to God.

Because I CAN. I know I can. It *sounds* insane, sure. It sounds insane until you realize that this *is* how people get hired to write for TV shows. I've looked into it; I know. You write a spec script and you submit it. They don't usually produce your spec script or actually make it an episode of the show. They just want to know how well you write the characters, how good you are at plot and suspense and that kind of thing. Well, look. There are a whole host of things in this world I am really bad at: math and social skills and playing the violin and even telling my left from my right, for God's sake. I am not the world's most well-rounded individual, but there is one thing I can do, and that is that I can write. I know it. My mom was an amazing writer; she was working on a novel when she died. I've read what she had written -- it was fantastic. (I still want to know what happens next... but anyway.) She would have been a published novelist, I know it. And I know *I* can write. It's genetic. And Lord knows I've written enough fanfic in the last year and a half to get all the practice I need. Everyone always says that my characterization is perfect -- better than Sean Davies', Teresa likes to kid. (He's one of the not-very-good writers on staff. We all groan when we see on CKN.com's LtT page that there's a new Sean Davies episode coming out.) I know how to write, and God knows I know this show. Writing the spec script will be just like writing a screenplay-format fanfic. It's even been done in fandom before: some Xena-fic girl got a writing gig on the show based on her fanfics. I've read her fics, and honestly, if she could do it, I certainly can.

Of course, all I've got to do is stop typing for a second, and the doubts start flooding in once more. It's a self-image thing, obviously. I know how I look to the rest of the world -- even to myself, a lot of the time. I'm not exactly blazing a red-hot trail of success through life, here. Anyone looking at me'd peg me for a plain old lazy slob, sleeping her way through high school. Heading into a fascinating career in convenience-store clerking and gasoline pumping. And I know everyone else thinks that, although the people at school would never phrase it so unkindly as "lazy slob". They're full of kind, forgiving talk and sympathetic looks from those soft cow's eyes that make me want to cram wads of chewing gum up their nostrils. And every so often, one of them lets the bovine look slip for just a second; there's a faint narrowing of the eyes, a little vertical crease down the brow, and I know that behind all the kind looks and stupid jargon, they're thinking what everyone else is thinking. "Lazy slob." Right.

It's all bull, though. The central problem is the assumption that because I don't apply myself in high school, the rest of my life is going to be similarly unsuccessful. The fact of the matter is that it doesn't matter what they think of me at Spectrum, and it doesn't matter what I do at Spectrum. I *do* have plans for my life, believe it or not. And they emphatically do not involve writing high school papers on the Industrial Revolution or acing tests on Fibonacci sequences.

And you know what, I don't even care that I'm fifteen. I don't even care that I haven't finished high school yet and I have no means of supporting myself and I can't even go to college for another three years. There's such a thing as emancipated minor status, right? If I can prove that I can make a living writing -- and that's just what I'm planning to do, make it as a writer -- then they can't keep me here. No one in their right mind would tell me I can't go to California to write for *Look to Tomorrow* because I have to stay in this dirty smelly house in the custody of a depressed drunk. It would be better for everyone. I hate seeing Dad this way, but if I went to California, I could make the money to actually get him into a decent rehab. We wouldn't have to be scrabbling to make it through each day, living in this crummy town, hoping his Social Security kicks in before Mom's life insurance runs out. I could get him somewhere where they'd take care of him and I could take care of me. I've been doing it for a year now, with Dad and my stupid school holding me down. Anyone who thinks that I couldn't take care of myself in California has no idea what it takes just to take care of myself here.

I know I can be mature enough and talented enough to do this. If I can just get this one break, I know I can make it work. And then, you know, there'd be the chance to write for *Look to Tomorrow* into the bargain. And, uh, spend some time around Brad Memphis every once in awhile. Or more than every once in awhile. Maybe when I'm a writer for the show I can write an episode where Thorin has a hot makeout scene with a pale, mysterious young girl with straight brown hair and a wry smile...

AHEM. Back to reality.

And to what I'm going to MAKE into reality.
I'm going to do this.   California, here I come.
(Oh God, did I just say that?   Time for bed.)

From: ra016eltessers@yippee.com
To: looktotomorrowfans@yippeegroups.com
Date: 2/28/2013
Subject: Auction!

Hi all!

It's been just two short weeks since I sent that first email proposing an auction to earn money for the Hannah J. Christiansen Foundation through the Lookies -- and what a time it's been! The auction has gone live now at http://racheltessers.recirclr.com/post/6729895669/auction, with items and bids accepted on a rotating basis. And the short version of this is -- you guys ROCK! XD The auction has only been live for five days, and already the sum total of the top bids is up at **$986**, with **at least** five more days remaining on each item! Most of the items will be up much longer than that, and there will be a constant influx of new items as well. So keep checking back!

Here's some numbers to break it all down for you:

-We have **17 items** that are already live for bidding, including **one piece of fanart with pairing of your choice by Emmaline L.**, one **custom-ordered fanfiction (<5,000 words) by Jenna Fann**, one *Chicago* **playbill autographed by Joscelyn Winters**, and **one full-length fanfiction beta by Audra Scanlon!**

- **36** more items have already been lined up for donation and are awaiting confirmation, including some very exciting stuff!
- The average high bid on each of the donated items as of this morning is **$58**
- The average amount bid on each item daily is **$18**
- The average number of days left on each item currently up for bidding is **7 days**
- According to my tracking of several items on eBay, bidding rates are usually **300% higher** (!) in the final eight hours before an auction ends
- By this math, the items that are **already posted** ought to earn us **$3,336** within the next 7 days -- and if we extrapolate this data out to make a rough estimate of how much the unconfirmed donations

will bring in over the course of the auction, and then add on an extra 25% of that as a conservative estimate of the proceeds from items that will be donated later, we come out with a whopping **$12,675!**

A few more thousand after that and we've got the $15,000, no sweat!

This is all possible, guys. Look at the numbers, and then look at the fandom. If anybody's got the enthusiasm and the coordination to pull a thing like this off, it's us! But we've got to live up to our potential and make it happen. Email me to donate items, go to the auction to bid on the stuff you like, and go just that one small step further than you otherwise might have -- it's for charity, after all! You'll be doing the world some good, and you'll be doing some awesome things right here within the *Look to Tomorrow* fandom. Let's show the world what fandom can do!

Again, the auction is NOW LIVE and is posted at http://racheltessers.recirclr.com/post/6729895669/auction.

See you there!

Love,

Rachel

* * *

http://www.diarynow.com/users/thejanethe/28092.html
Date: 2/28/2013
Security level: Private
Mood: satisfied

Well, that only took five hours and eighteen different wrong versions. I think I should be allowed to turn that post in as my math homework for the night.

To: <u>kanyefan2010@whalemail.com</u>, <u>laalaalaand@yippee.</u>
<u>com</u>, <u>hyphopboi@spotmail.com</u>, <u>janeshilling@spectrum.org</u>,
<u>bitchinsk8rgrrl@whalemail.com</u>
From: <u>rawkdaskeeball@yippee.com</u>
Date: <u>3/2/2013</u>

Subject: sign my petition!!!!!

Hi evry1

Plz sign the petiton my skeeball league made its here ----> http://www.
petitiononline.com/skbl564/petition.html Were trying to make skeeball an
olympis sport & we need evry1 2 sign it!!! & fwd it to all ur freinds!!! it will
b hard 2 convince them but if u all sign WE WILL PREVIAL!!!!

gary :)

_____

Bring Skee-Ball To The Olympics!!!!!

<u>View Current Signatures</u> - <u>Sign the Petition</u>

To: The Olympics

We the undersigned want SKEE-BALL to be an Official Olympic Sport.
Skee-Ball does not get the recognition it deserves as a REAL SPORT and it
is time that the Olympics changed this!!! Skee-Ball is much more of a sport
then things like curling, which is people pushing big rocks along ice, or
javiline throwing, which is stupid since all you have to do is throw a stick.
Skee-Ball requires much more skill and talent then these "sports" as well as
alot of others. For these reasons, and because the American Championship
Skee-Ball Leagues are full of talented individuals who want to recieve some
reasonable recompensation for all there hard work, we ask that SKEE-
BALL be recognized as an OFFICIAL OLYMPIC SPORT.

Sincerely,
The Undersigned

<u>View Current Signatures</u>

52

http://www.diarynow.com/users/thejanethe/32203.html
Date: 3/2/2013
Security level: Private
Mood: amused

Haha, this guy is cracking me up. An online petition about OLYMPIC SKEEBALL? Oh, man, Gary.

Honestly, I don't know what to think of him at all. He keeps sitting with me at lunch now. At first I was kind of weirded out by it and I thought maybe if I just kept reading he'd take the hint, but whenever I did that he always looked so awkward and sad that I'd give up and put my book away. But I never know what to say to him at all. He's so anxious and stuttery a lot of the time -- which, to be fair, is probably in no small part because I'm anxious and stuttery too. (NB: This is one not-insignificant reason that I prefer books to people. Books never make me stutter.) We keep making stabs at talking about things like Mrs. Baker or the lunch menu or whatever, but we're both so terrible at it that the conversations always seem to career around manically for two seconds and then run out of air completely, like a balloon with a hole in it. Lunch is a half an hour long; I can dawdle in the lunch line for maybe seven or eight minutes, pretending to pick out just the right bag of chips, but then we've got twenty minutes to kill. I would estimate that we usually spend about five minutes trying to have a real conversation, and then I give up and ask him about his Skeeball team. At that point, he starts going back and forth between getting really revved up and talkative, and then all of a sudden getting apologetic and even more awkward than before because he's afraid he's been monopolizing the conversation. I have to keep telling him, no, it's really interesting, even though I can't hear three-quarters of what he's saying anyway because the cafeteria is so loud. Part of my particular brand of learning disability is that I have trouble with auditory processing when things are really loud or chaotic, but I haven't wanted to try to explain that to Gary because I don't want to sound like a weirdo. But I think he can tell I'm not really with him, because he just keeps on jabbering and getting embarrassed and jabbering and getting embarrassed. And… augh. I mean, he's a nice guy, but lunch with him is exhausting.

53

On the whole I wouldn't say I'm 100% thrilled that he's apparently decided to take our friendship-or-whatever online. I've always kept my online life separate from my three-dimensional life for a reason. (And although the fact that none of my online friends would ask me to support Olympic Skee-ball through the medium of an e-petition was never part of that reason, maybe it should have been.)

Well, give credit where credit's due, he's right about the curling thing. And -- oh, I don't know. He's a really nice guy, whatever else he has going on. And social rejection sucks. I kind of wish he hadn't latched on to me, but... oh, whatever. What'll it take to keep from hurting his feelings? Like a paragraph? I think I just need to convince myself that my computer is not actually going to explode if I start getting emails from real-life people.

* * *

To: rawkdaskeeball@yippee.com
From: janeshilling@spectrum.org
Date: 3/2/2013
   Subject: Re: sign my petition!!!!!

Hi Gary,

I signed your petition and I hope it helps, but I'm not sure the Olympics are going to listen, sadly. :(There are a whole bunch of steps you need to go through to get a new sport added to the Olympics (which is not to say it can't be done; check out this article here -- they're trying to get ballroom dancing included in the next Olympics.) The biggest thing, though, is that you need a certain number of participants in a certain number of countries on three different continents before you can even start lobbying. There are more details in the article I linked. So I don't know if Skee-Ball is ready for that yet, but you can always try to start it by trying to increase awareness and popularity of the American national team. That way, even if the Olympics are a long ways away, you could maybe get some more Skee-Ball competitions going, which means more prizes, which means more money for you. :) Getting it recognized as a sport on a widespread basis in America would be a huge coup... maybe by the time we graduate, there'll be Skee-Ball scholarships! I can see it now: you'll be heading to Harvard on a full ride to play Skee-Ball, and I'll be stuck at the community college slinging burgers twenty hours a week and playing Scrabble online in my spare time. ;)

Anyway, hope that helped. See you tomorrow!

-Jane

Date: 3/9/2013
Security: Private

I hate Spectrum. SHIT, but I hate Spectrum. I try to talk a good game about how it isn't that bad, how at least most of the staff leave me alone and I can write fanfic in class and stuff, but… I don't know, I hate it! I hate the looks that everyone gives me when they find out where I go to school, and I hate the short bus so much that I refuse to ride it. I hate that they censor the library because they think Holden Caulfield will give us ideas. I just… I hate it.

If I weren't at Spectrum, today wouldn't have happened. I… I don't even know how to deal with what happened today.

It was never going to be a good day. It was pouring rain outside, and Dad "overslept" (i.e., was too hungover to get out of bed) so I had to walk to school. I'd idiotically put on a new red shirt that I'd gotten on sale at Wal-Mart or somewhere -- that and a pair of khaki pants. My umbrella blew inside out within five minutes of my leaving the house, and I outgrew my three-year-old windbreaker last year, so there you go. By the time I got there I was drenched, and the dye from my shirt had leaked all over my pants. I was stained completely red from the waist to the thighs, with random pink drops all over the rest of my pants. And I just looked awful. I had three huge zits on my face, my hair was plastered to my skull, my shirt was clinging to me so that every wrinkle in my bra was showing… it was awful. Really.

I got there late and made a nice showy entrance to first-period English. We were having "twenty minutes of quiet reflection and journal writing", which meant Ms. Frolich didn't feel like teaching. Actually, in this particular case, it meant she was asleep, probably sharing whatever drunken dreams Dad was having at home. So there was plenty of smirking and whispering when I walked in, but Ms. Frolich didn't so much as twitch. Emboldened, Bruno Vega leaned across the aisle and whispered to Andrew Schmidt, just softly enough that they might not have heard him in Argentina. "Hey. Check it." He gestured at me.

"What -- awwww," Andrew groaned, feigning disgust.

Don't react. It's what they want.

"I know, right? *Dis*-gusting." I flung my bag down next to me, hard, and heard something snap.

"Dude, that shit is nasty. She couldn'ta cleaned up before she got to class?" Forcing myself to ignore them, I dug around in my bag for a pen and notebook, but my fingers came out dyed blue and dripping: a pen had snapped in half when I'd thrown my bag and was leaking all over the place. If I ever carried any of my textbooks around, that would have been a disaster, but sometimes being a slacker pays off, I guess. I slipped the notebook with my LtT fic in it onto my desk. Safe and sound.

"Forget cleaning up -- she never heard of Tampax?"

I thought for one suicidal moment of explaining that period blood is not the same shade as cherry Kool-Aid, but managed to stop myself in time. Instead, I turned and I flicked some ink at Bruno, leaving a very satisfactory spatter pattern on his face, and went looking for another pen.

"Bitch!" Bruno cried, stung, trying to get a stray drop of ink out of his eyes.

"Yeah," chimed in Jason Malone. I glanced up at him, rolled my eyes. Jason and I go way back -- we went to daycare together back when we were in diapers, for Christ's sake. He would have done much better if he'd stayed four years old forever. Nowadays, he's the sort of guy who gives puberty a bad name: all gawky arms and bony elbows, with volcanoes of acne all over his face. He's the sort of guy that you can't look at without thinking about farts and sweaty jockstraps. As you might imagine, this does not make for great popularity, and he's one of those kids who spends all his time hanging on the edges of the in-crowd, trying to worm his way in. He'd been goggling at sideline of Bruno's and Andrew's conversation for the last few minutes, trying to find an opening. Apparently he'd decided this was his chance. "Anyway," Jason said, with that trademark hawking snort that's probably half the reason he's not in the in-crowd, "that ain't her period."

"Nnn," Bruno mumbled, mopping at his face with what looked like a used Kleenex.

"Yeah. You know what I bet?" No one answered, but he plunged in anyway. "Looks like someone puked up a fuckin' Bloody Mary on her."

I froze. What he'd said made hardly any sense at all, as witness the eyerolls from several of the kids sitting nearby, but -- had he just picked that out of air?

"Huh?" Bruno said, momentarily ceasing to smear dried germs all over his face.

"Yeah," Jason said, more animated now -- it was probably the first time Bruno had ever shown even mild interest in anything he had to say. "What, you didn't know? Dude, her dad is like a *total drunk.*"

Bruno poked me in the back again. "That true?" he said, and from his tone I knew this was not going to go well -- as if it ever could have, once those words were out. *A total drunk.* I was just frozen to my chair. How could this be happening? How could Jason know -- anything? And why on earth would anyone *care*? I keep to myself at school. I leave everyone else alone, and they usually leave me alone. And now -- this? Of all things, it had to be *this*? I felt like asking him, *Can't we get back to talking about my period?*

"*Yeah*," said Jason, practically hiccuping with laughter now. "I saw her dad coming out of the liquor store, right? I was in waiting outside with my brother, he was getting me beer, and, like, seriously, dude, he's always totally down for getting booze for me, he's 18 and his ID looks *totally* real and if you ever want to come over, like, I can totally hook you up with booze and even weed sometimes when this guy my brother knows is in town? But yeah, so I'm sitting there in the parking lot, acting like it ain't no thang -- " YES HE DOES IN FACT TALK THAT WAY AND YET SOMEHOW I AM THE ONE THEY LAUGH AT -- "and Jane's dad comes out and he's, like, *sixty* or something, this total old geezer, my mom used to know him from PTA and stuff but like -- "

"You ever stop talking and get to the point, man?" Bruno said.

"Yeah, right -- and Jane's old fart of a dad comes out and he's got like *four* twelve-packs of beer and he slings them all in his car and I'm like, all right, so he's having a party, right? But then I'm in the bodega over on the corner of Pike and Elm last week and there he is buying two bottles of vodka, and, shit, man, dude is *weaving* all over the aisle. He knocked over a fucking rack of porno mags. Dude behind the counter looked like he wanted to throw the old geezer out. Meanwhile I'm acting all cool and shit and walking out the store with two six-packs a Mike's Hard behind my back." He let out a loud braying noise that almost woke Ms. Frolich up.

"Fuckin' Mike's," Bruno muttered, then spoke louder. "That true, Jane? Your dad's a drunk?" I wondered if he would shut up if I shoved a pencil in his throat. "He ever cut you in on any of the booze? You too fucked up this morning to notice you look like you fell in a vat of fuckin' raspberry Jell-O?"

I sat in my chair like my shoulders had been stapled to it, my face crimson, wondering what in *God's* name I could possibly do to *make them stop.*

"Awwwwwwwwwww, lookit, da widdle Janey is *bwushing!*" Jason shrieked, not even pretending to keep his voice down now. Everyone was staring. "Hey, everyone!" Jason yelled, seeing everyone's eyes on him. "This is what Jane's dad looks like when he's *plastered!*" He jumped out of his chair and began doing some sort of lurching, Frankenstein-style walk that looked like his left leg was paralyzed. "Huuu-uuhh," he said, even drooling a little bit. Probably wasn't part of the act. "Huuuh, like, I'm a *total boozebag* and I'm like *eighty* and I sit at home all day and pour booze down my throat and jack off to pornos and -- " He started to mime that last bit.

I needed to cry -- *needed* to -- but I wouldn't let him see me. With my last ounce of composure I snatched the notebook with my LtT fic in it, then grabbed my bag and jammed it down over his head. A flood of ink cascaded down over his shoulders, pens and notebooks and random crap fell all over the floor, and the last thing I heard from him was a very muffled "WhaFUH?" I leapt out of my chair and ran for the door. I'd almost made it to the bathroom before I collapsed in tears.

I went home early. Right after that. I couldn't stand to go back to class and listen to the whispers and know that they *knew*, everybody *knew* now. I went to the nurse and made up a story about having a headache, but I was so flipped out -- trying not to cry and choking on sobs anyway, my face all red from crying and ink smears all over my cheeks from where I'd tried to wipe the tears away -- that she just decided I was a head case and sent me to Ms. Meisner, my ludicrous dip of a guidance counselor with the strange blueberry-egg delusions. I didn't go, obviously; I thanked the nurse very nicely for the hall pass and then walked the three miles home in the rain, again. As soon as I got home I realized I was trailing drops of red dye everywhere I went; we'd need to shampoo the carpet to get rid of them, and since Dad will never bother and I don't know how, they're there for good. I stripped out of all the wet crap I was wearing and threw it all away. I tossed on an old oversize T-shirt. Then I curled up in bed and cried until my head hurt.

I spent the rest of the day huddled under the covers, watching LtT torrents. Dad never noticed I was home and I sure wasn't going to tell him. LtT helped, a lot. While I was watching it I could almost forget. But it was like there was this tight, hard ball lodged in my stomach, and no matter what I did, no matter how hard I tried to focus on Thorin and Jaela, I couldn't get it to dissolve.

Jason. Of all people. Jason.

I kept seeing his face when he was four years old. He had a bowl cut and a lazy eye, and even in kindergarten the kids knew enough about what cool was -- and wasn't -- to cut him out. Meanwhile, I didn't have any friends either, though that was more of a mutual decision between me and the other kids; I preferred books, they preferred chasing each other around and screaming about cooties. I spent a lot of time holed up in a corner of the kindergarten classroom reading a book, and Jason used to spend a lot of time with me, pretending to read even though he hadn't learned how yet. It wasn't exactly an idyllic childhood friendship; I'd always tell him, with the kind of scorn only a kindergartener can muster, when the book he was "reading" was upside-down. But he stuck to me and we got along OK most of the time. Sometimes after class we'd go out to the playground and look for snails. Jason had a snail collection.

That was kindergarten.

I knew he'd turned into an asshole. I mean, water under the bridge -- for God's sake, it was *kindergarten*. I never even liked him that much! But he got picked on and I got picked on and back then we used to hide together. In the corner, with our books. His upside down.

The whole school knows about my dad now, and Jason Malone's the one who told them.

I don't know what to do.

I can't write about it for ten seconds without crying.

He's going down. I don't know what I'm going to do yet. But I want to put him in so much pain... I want to...

oh, fuck

http://www.diarynow.com/users/thejanethe/40002.html
Date: 3/9/2013
Security level: Private
Tagged: grip of a moment, spec script first draft

SCENE #SOMETHINGOROTHER
NOT TOO EARLY
(Yeah, it's probably time to pull together an actual outline of this thing. But anyway.)
[Jaela and Thorin are standing motionless, staring at one another. Jaela is holding a piece of paper in her hand. The scene is frozen for a long moment.]
JAELA: Tell me you didn't write this, Thorin.
[Thorin opens his mouth, but is unable to speak. Jaela reads from the sheet of paper.]
JAELA: "Given that Jessamyn's recent actions constitute a very serious threat -- perhaps the primary threat -- to the Institute and its long-term goals, any internal division as we seek to negate this threat could have extremely damaging consequences. In this light, Agent Apaerna's recent attempts to exclude the Zyerlean contingent from our alliance against Toös should be discounted as personally motivated attacks that are counterproductive to the Institute's current needs."
THORIN: You're taking that out of context. In the next line I told them --
JAELA: In the next line you told them you didn't think I was so far gone that they needed to fire me! This is support?
THORIN: Frankly, yes!
JAELA: [mimicking him] "Oh, guys, she's off her rocker about this Zyerlean thing, but don't worry. I'm sure we can find a desk job for her." You're supposed to be my partner!
THORIN: I am your partner! But that doesn't mean -- [Catching himself, with effort.] It was a private memo. Only top-echelon members of TIME --
JAELA: You *cc'ed Saureshan.*
THORIN: He's top-echelon.
JAELA: He's the Zyerlean PM!

62

THORIN: Like I said.

[Jaela exhales sharply. When she speaks, it's in a whisper.]

JAELA: Everyone at TIME has thought I'm nuts for years, Thorin.

THORIN: Jaela, no one --

JAELA: Believe me, I hear the whispers. I'm the token Siqan, right? TIME needs to fill its quotas, show how much they care about the oppressed minorities. I know half the people I work with think that's why I'm there. I know they look at me and instead of seeing my face, they see two murdered parents and a burned hometown.

THORIN: [helplessly] Jaela, none of this has anything to do --

JAELA: And I've handled that! I've stuck with it for years because I love the work, and because no one else can do what I do. But I'll tell you what I'm not going to handle, Thorin. I'm not going to handle my own partner misjudging my motives and casting me as the emotional, irrational little woman when I try to protect more innocent civilians from being killed by the regime that killed my parents.

THORIN: The regime that killed them! Jaela, no one ever found a shred of proof that those guerrillas were acting on the orders of --

JAELA: Oh, *don't* give me that! I've put up with all kinds of crap here at this institute, but you can be damn sure that I have my limits, Thorin, and you're dangerously close to breaking them!

THORIN: [losing his temper] Like it or not, there's something to be said for the idea that if every single other employee of TIME thinks of Saureshan as an ally, you might just be the one who's off base. The rest of us do have priorities here, and a random guerrilla raid in your hometown twenty years ago is just not at the top of the list -- and whether you believe it or not, neither are your murdered parents!

[Jaela's face collapses in on itself, then goes blank. An endless moment passes. When Jaela speaks, her voice is level but deadened.]

JAELA: I'm not staying.

THORIN: What are you *talking* about, you're not staying? You have nowhere else to go!

JAELA: Nowhere's better than this, Thorin. If I spend the rest of my life scrubbing toilets it'll have more dignity and worth than what you're doing right now. Whatever integrity you ever had just blew away like a scrap in the wind.

THORIN: Jaela, this is nuts. You're talking about defecting from TIME, losing your job, your --

JAELA: It doesn't matter! You really think I can't pick up from here? You think I'm stuck working for a place that would sanction genocide for political gain?

THORIN: Sanction genocide! Jaela, you --

JAELA: I'm not stuck working here --

THORIN: What are you going to do, go renegade?!

JAELA: If I do it's no concern of yours. I'm not stuck working this job, and I'm not stuck living this life. [With acid dripping from her tone] And I am definitely not stuck having this conversation with you. [half a beat] We're through.

THORIN: Jaela!

[Jaela spins on her heel and walks out the door.]

http://www.diarynow.com/thejanethe/40694.html
Date: 3/10/2013
Security: Private
Mood: enraged

Oh God, I am so done with Spectrum right now. SO. DONE. One more day like today and I am going to lose it, I swear. I am about one-tenth of a millimeter from my breaking point and if I have to live through one more *second* like what I went through today I am going to run off with the circus and spend the rest of my life shoveling elephant shit and loving it as long as I can ship a nice warm package of it back to the lovely students and staff back at Spectrum Alternative High because, seriously, SO DONE

This morning I got a message in homeroom to go see Ms. Meisner. Now, Ms. Meisner, as I believe I have mentioned before, is completely insane -- a fine trait in an adolescent counselor, I'm sure we can all agree! Blueberry-hatching eggs on her wall, a "Hang in There, Kitty" page-a-day calendar on her desk, and waaaaaay too many cutesy little cartoon patterns on her clothing and accessories. This is a woman I can barely tolerate under the best of circumstances. And today's were not the best of circumstances. I'd been hoping no one would notice that I cut yesterday afternoon instead of going to Ms. Meisner's office, but obviously someone had. I got my little blue slip in homeroom, asking me to report to Dipsy Doodle's office first thing. Because, you know, the absolute best way to help kick off a great day for a kid who's been having a tough time at school is to drag her into a guidance office for a Serious Conversation about it with a woman wearing ladybug clips in her hair.

I didn't go, of course. It would have made about as much sense as going to her office yesterday would have. Let me put it this way: they're always talking about "knowing your boundaries" and "respecting your emotions" (yes, really) at Spectrum, right? Ms. Meisner talks that crap all day long. Kids with anger management problems are supposed to learn to excuse themselves from class and go to the guidance office or the quiet room instead of throwing chairs. Kids with learning disabilities are supposed to ask for special services instead of getting frustrated and giving up. So on and so forth, blah, blah, blah. So here I am, and when I do *exactly*

65

that -- evaluating exactly what I need to do to stay sane, and then doing it, period! -- instead of *them* respecting *my* boundaries, somehow it becomes a disciplinary case? Um, WTF? Believe me, lady, I know exactly where my boundaries are and how to "respect my emotions". It involves NOT DEALING WITH YOU WHEN I'M ALREADY ON THE BRINK OF A COMPLETE BREAKDOWN. I understand we are only supposed to deal with our problems via the pre-approved means outlined in whatever $12.95 70-page pamphlet you got at the last guidance counselors' convention, but I am not a case study and I am NOT letting some wide-eyed 24-year-old LICSW drag me into a nervous breakdown in the middle of school.

So I skipped -- went to the girls' room instead of to Meisner's office, and then carried on with my day. I figured I'd made my point. I figured that was the end of it.

And then she showed up to get me.

In my English class.

This is... she's unbelievable. I cannot believe she would do that. She KNEW I'd left during English yesterday, and she HAD to know it was because something bad had gone down. I wanted so badly to cut English today, and the only reason I went was to show them all that nothing was wrong at all, that I was completely fine, that nothing they could say or do could get to me. I mean, that's about the only reason I went to *school* today. I pulled together everything I had because I knew how much worse the gossip would be if I didn't go in and pretend everything was normal. If I started skipping, dodging away from everyone, they'd all know just how much Jason got to me. Dumping my bookbag over his head was bad enough, but I could pass that off as a fit of temper. If I started acting like something was really wrong over the long-term, I was sunk.

And then my fucking guidance counselor shows up in the room and asks me to come with her for a special conference.

And when Ms. Frolich, hungover as usual and slow on the uptake, asked her to repeat herself, instead of just *repeating herself for Christ's sake*, Ms. Meisner furrows her brow and says in this quizzical tone, "I'd heard Jane had some difficulty yesterday --?" and Ms. Frolich is still looking befuddled because she was goddamn passed out for the whole scene, so Ms. Meisner KEEPS GOING -- " -- something that I might... well... Jane? Why don't you come to my office so we can talk?"

That was it. The class went from snickers and whispers to open laughter, neither Ms. Frolich nor Ms. Meisner herself had a clue what was going on, and I was ready to kick her teeth in, I swear to God. Everyone at Spectrum has a nose for this sort of thing anyway; if you're humiliating other people you're drawing attention away from how fucked-up your own life is, so everyone's always gossiping, trying to deflect. Jason Malone is enough of a jackass that yesterday *might* have gotten written off as more of the same, but Ms. Meisner literally went into class and *told everybody that what happened yesterday was a big enough deal that my guidance counselor had to get involved.*

The slurps, glug-glug-glug noises, and invisible upturned bottles at the lips of everyone who wasn't smirking and whispering made it pretty clear what everyone made of that.

So we went to her office, where she helpfully informed me of the following things:

1. She has been A Little Concerned about me for awhile, based on teachers' reports that I am "withdrawn" in class and "isolated" in general;
2. She became More Concerned when Mrs. Baker spoke to her about my "refusal to participate" in math class, as it seems that my "lack of engagement" (why does *everything* this woman says beg for quotation marks?!) may cause a "serious disruption to my long-term performance and well-being at Spectrum" (OMG WHERE DID SHE GET THE IDEA THAT THERE IS SUCH A THING AS "WELL-BEING" AT SPECTRUM);
3. She became Very Concerned when she heard that I had become "distraught" in English class yesterday, and that
4. She would like to address these Concerns by holding a joint meeting with me, my dad, Mr.-Sheehan-the-head-of-the-guidance-department, and herself, so we can discuss how to amend my IEP to address my needs more fully and -- here's the part she tried to slip in casually, so I wouldn't notice it -- to determine whether there are any "issues in the home that we might be able to help address to make things easier for me" thenabunchofstuffaboutahappyproductivesunshine'n'lollipopsyear that she tacked on all in a runon-sentence hurry so I might not

notice that she just basically said she wanted to drag my fucked-up dad and my fucked-up life into her office and put it all on display for Mr. Sheehan and whichever other members of the guidance office are peeking through the two-way mirror that I'm sure she has stashed behind the blueberry eggs.

So those were the four things she explained to me, very kindly and of course (of course!) with great Concern, about the particular charge and chemical composition of the dynamite she was planning to apply to my personal boundaries and right to privacy. In turn, I explained the following things to her, with rather less Concern but considerably more Venom:

1. My dad is never, ever going anywhere near her office
2. I am never, ever again going anywhere near her office
3. She is the worst therapist I have ever encountered and her office feels less like a "safe space" than a carnival horror house and she is completely crazy and I hate her and she has been prying and poking and subjecting me to emotional harassment for months now and I am so not dealing with her anymore and also did I mention she's crazy, because blueberries don't come from eggs, okay, so I don't know what in the hell her problem is but I don't care what it is anyway because I am never seeing her again, ever
4. She had lipstick on her teeth
5. She is still completely insane
6. I still hate her
7. I AM NEVER GOING ANYWHERE NEAR HER OFFICE AGAIN.

But all this time I was yelling and she was not yelling, which was basically the most infuriating thing in the world. She always has the most goddamn smug face, as though nothing you ever say to her could possibly matter because she knows that you're just *misdirecting healthy anger* or *experiencing an externalizing disorder* or *maladaptively processing your grief.* I yelled so much that the guidance counselor next door stuck her head in to check on us, and Meisner still did not raise her voice once.

And then the bell rang and I left her office and immediately Andrew Schmidt was there in the hallway, and he smirked and did the glug-glug thing, and it hit me again like a punch to the gut. She *came to my English class.*

And the family therapy thing... I'm not... she's not budging on that either. And I don't know what to do. I can't have Dad in that office. I just... I can't!

I just need to figure out what I'm going to do now. I can't let her do this. I can't let her keep acting this way. And she set up *another* special session for tomorrow, and even if she doesn't talk about Dad anymore she's just prying and poking and hammering and tearing at me all the time, she's making me a total wreck, and if there were just some way to

oh, *wait*

Be back in a few, dear diary. I think I just found the answer.

Zooooooooom

Web   Images   Groups   News

Results 1-5 of 5 for "lorilynn meisner"

Directory of Psychologists
...**Lorilynn Meisner**, LICSW, Partners Health Care Center, 115 Brookstone Rd., Lexington, ME...
www.psychresources.com/states/me.html - 12k

Harrisburg Daily Record | People Notes
...and Mrs. Leonard P. **Meisner** announce the engagement of their daughter, **Lorilynn Meisner**, to physician Rupert Avery. Avery graduated summa cum laude from the University of... wedding is scheduled for June 2012. The **Meisners** look forward to...
www.harrisburgdaily.com/events/engagements.htm -- 67

Spectrum High School, 2010-2011 Staff Listing
... jellerbee@spectrum.org. Health Room 467-555-7685. **Lorilynn Meisner**, LICSW, Student Counselor. E-mail **lmeisner**@spectrum.org. Guidance Office 467-555-7689. Hanne...
www.spectrum.org/staff.html - 87k

[PDF] Unity Chapel Retreat Scrapbook
...pictured above, Shari Coleman, Lisa Johnson, Karen Edelman. "It's just such a refreshing experience," said **Lorilynn Meisner**, who has attended the retreat for three years running. "It's interdenominational but what you really feel is a sense of transcending...
www.uc-lexington.org/retreats/scrapbook01.pdf

[PDF] Spectrum Notes, Sept-Oct 2010
...welcoming **Lorilynn Meisner** to Spectrum's staff. Ms. **Meisner** is a licensed social worker who earned her B.S. in child psychology. Having interned at CareFirst's psychiatric center for troubled children ...
www.spectrum.org/notes/SeptOct10.pdf

http://www.diarynow.com/thejanethe/38790.html
Security level: Private
Mood: Triumphant :-D
Date: 3/11/2013

Aha! Ahahahahahahaha!!! :-D ::does the dance of kickassery:: OMG I SO RULE. WOOOOO!!!!

I mean, OK, I rule, but my luck was also fantastic this time around. Maybe God wanted me to get shot of this woman, I don't know. But the story -- oh, screw the story; I'd lose so much in summarizing it. I'm putting down the direct transcript, this is one for the permanent record, baby.

THE ANNIHILATION OF LORILYNN MEISNER
Or, How I Gave the Prying Counselor a Taste of Her Own Medicine

CAST OF CHARACTERS
Ms. Meisner, a youngish, friendlyish, not-so-very-competent-ish social worker/therapist.
Jane Shilling, an ordinary-looking high school girl. She is not much to look at but is clearly possessed of a remarkable intelligence.

SETTING: A lame guidance office, decorated with multicolored throw pillows on a Big Comfy Couch. Therapist sits in cut-rate executive-style chair across from the door. A strange picture of an egg hatching blueberries features prominently on the wall, prompting the audience to question the sanity of the woman sitting center stage.

JANE enters the room, sullen but with an air of suppressed vindication. This apparently goes unnoticed by MS. MEISNER, which, as we shall soon see, is not an unusual state of affairs.

LM: (overly cheerful) Hi Jane! Why don't you sit down?
J: I had been counting on standing through the session, but sure.
LM: (looks uncertain for a moment, then laughs) Right. So how have you been?

J: Fine.

LM: Sure?

J: Absolutely.

LM: It seemed as though you were experiencing some difficult emotions yesterday.

J: Oh, not in the least.

LM: Well, this is a safe space where you can process those emotions, Jane --

J, silently: *If you say "safe space" one more time I am going to shove a pen through your jugular.*

LM: -- a safe place --

J: Where do you keep your pens?

LM: *(on a roll, does not hear J)* -- to work those things through.

J: Well, that's just super nice of you, Lorilynn -- *[Ms. Meisner gives a startled glance, but does not reply]* -- but I really feel just A-OK about everything right now. No problems here.

LM, *condescending:* Now, Jane, there's no need to pretend here. There's nothing wrong with having emotions.

J: Oh, I'm having emotions.

LM, *practically clapping:* That's good, Jane. Can you say more about that?

J: Absolutely, Lorilynn. Right now I am feeling pissed off.

LM: Well, you can let it out here, and then we can talk about it, okay?

J: Great. I am feeling pissed off because this entire setup is bullshit.

LM: How so? Let's work this through together, Jane.

J: Oh, yes! Let's. [sits forward, suddenly energized] Here is the basic issue with the way you run this place, Lori: you keep hammering at me, pushing and pushing, thinking you're entitled to know everything about me, thinking you have some kind of right to dig out every horrible thing in my life that I am not willing to talk about, calling all the shots. What gives you the right?

LM: Well, I'm your therapist, Jane. And I understand how you feel, and I want to honor that feeling. But you've been in a great deal of denial about everything that's happened to you in the last year, and it's important that --

72

J: Oh, no way. You don't understand how I feel at all. You have never sat in a room and had someone take digs at your personal life --

LM: No one's been taking digs --

J: Oh really. Then what do you call it when I tell you that I'm not comfortable talking about something and you completely blow past me? First session here you had a long spiel about how therapy was founded on mutual trust and respect -- so tell me, Lori, how are you *respecting* me when you don't listen to a thing I tell you about what I can deal with and what I can't? And what makes you think you could ever earn my trust?

LM: (Clearly taken aback.) I -- hm. I'm sorry if you felt I haven't respected your boundaries. I --

J: (laughs) Oh, no you don't. Don't start talking about boundaries and all the rest of your psychobabble crap, okay? It's too easy, like if you can make me fit into one of your textbooks it matters less, right? It's got nothing to do with boundaries. It's not *fair*.

LM: ...fair?

J: Right. You're the one holding all the cards, and I figured, well, that's not cool.

LM: What do you mean?

J: (Pulls out printed-off ZoomSearch information.) Has anyone ever made you sit in a room and be bombarded with really personal questions about stuff you can't stand to talk about?

LM: I... all therapists are required to go through at least a year of therapy themselves to become certified.

J: I see. Was this the preferred method when you were in therapy?

LM: I'm sorry... what do you mean?

J: Well, did your therapist keep harassing you about stuff you didn't want to talk about, trying to get you to have a nervous breakdown?

LM: (laughs a little) No one's trying to get you to have a nervous breakdown, Jane.

J: Really. Because it sure has seemed like it. So anyway, what happened with Rupert?

LM: (pause) I'm sorry?

J: Rupert Avery, your fiance? You were scheduled to be married in June 2012, but it's March 2013 and you're still Ms. Meisner, not Mrs. Avery, so

-- what's the deal? Problem with the caterers?

LM: I -- where did you get that?

J: We Internet addicts have our sources. So what happened?

LM, (tight smile): I'm guessing the engagement announcement was online somewhere?

J: Of course. Funny thing, though, how quickly he moved on. Do you follow him on FriendsLink, Lori?

LM: I don't really think this is germane to --

J: Because there, it says he's been married since 2012, to someone named Marie Jansen. Well, Marie Jansen Avery, now. That's a pretty quick switch, being engaged to you in 2012 and then married to someone else in 2013. So, was he cheating on you?

LM, eyes widening: I don't -- it's -- (Takes breath to steady herself) Jane, I understand why you're playing this little game, but --

J: I mean, I'm sure it's not a reflection on *you*, Lori. There are all kinds of reasons why he could have dumped you. Maybe this Marie person is just better in bed than you, you know? It's not like you could help that, really --

LM: *Jane!*

J: -- maybe you were just too vanilla for him, you know? Or maybe kind of a prude?

LM, *raising voice, eyes wild*: Jane, this is extremely inappropriate --

J: Because Marie there sure isn't any prude. She really loves to post selfies at the beach in string bikinis, huh? And --

LM: (frantically grasping at LICSW straws) Jane, let's explore why you're doing this. Let's not --

J: -- obviously it's not *your* fault that her tits are bigger than yours --

LM: Jane, you need to *stop this right now* --

J: -- so between that and all the weird kinky stuff on Rupert's page, like his favorite movies being *Secretary* and *Nine and a Half Weeks*, which, you know, if you're not into that stuff --

LM: -- because I *seriously* cannot take this from you right now, so --

J: Oh! I'm so sorry! Did I pry into something you didn't want to talk about? Well, I'm sure you're just in denial about it. We have to work through these feelings! So let me ask again: was he into, like, whips and chains and stuff, or --

LM: -- just -- [shrieking] just GET OUT OF MY OFFICE RIGHT NOW!

J: Excellent! I think we'll have to leave it at that for today, Lori. Good work today. (casually dropping ZoomSearch page on desk) You know I'm not coming back, right?

LM: I certainly hope not.

J: Good! I'm glad we understand each other. Have a lovely day.

[JANE exits. As she closes the door, one can hear the faint sound of something hitting the desk, then a creative variety of swears.]

FIN

ETA: UPDATE -- Mr. Sheehan emailed me and I have officially been kicked out of therapy with Ms. Meisner. Can we just take a moment to note that I AM THE AWESOMEST PERSON IN THE WORLD. *\o/* *\o/* *\o/*

Anyway, the rest of the email was kind of good-news/bad-news: the good news is he didn't say anything about a family session with Dad, so I think the school is letting that drop. The bad news is I have to see another therapist, and I'm pretty sure if I skip out on sessions with that one, they really are going to get Dad involved. So here we go with Eleanor D. Acton, M.S., APBB, Psy.D. Obviously as soon as I got the email I ZoomSearched her, hoping for a Meisner reprise, but unfortunately, there was nothing good on her, just a bunch of LinkedIn-style sites which, boiled down, say "There is a therapist named Eleanor Acton who practices in Denton". The bare-bones info told me plenty, though. All those alphabet-soup degrees she's got make it clear that she is an Older Therapist; one of the sites said she'd been licensed since *1984*. If I'm very charitable and assume she got licensed when she was 25, what does that make her now? Mid-fifties? Oh, I'm sure she's wonderful at relating to teenagers. *eyeroll* And anyway, I know Older Therapists. Hell, I know all the therapists -- I've been to enough of them. The Older Therapist is usually large of frame and dresses in dark clothes. Her office decor is very different from that of the sprightly little LICSWs with their demented posters (thank God): instead, her office is full of super-drab furniture -- brown couch with beige or moss pillows,

75

dark rug with gold trim, cherry desk. The bookshelves along the walls are filled with actual books, not inspirational trinkets, but the books are all about alcoholism and trauma and incest -- you know, fun, cheery stuff like that. And she takes assiduous notes on a yellow lined-paper pad, occasionally glancing up to peer at you intently over her glasses. (They always have glasses.)

Better than Meisner, of course. Anyone's better than Meisner, but... ugh! I'm trying to be blase about it, but... this has me really anxious now, and I don't know what to do at all. Ms. Meisner scared the hell out of me, talking about bringing Dad in for a family session. I keep trying to forget about it, but it's hard -- he just came in a little while ago, and now that I'm all worked up about this I'm super-aware of him wandering around the house. I didn't even know he'd gone out, but I guess he ran out of booze, since that's the only reason he ever leaves the house anymore now that I do all the grocery shopping and stuff online. And I just feel so jumpy. I wish he'd just settle down in front of the TV, but he's on one of those stupid nostalgic kicks he gets on, wandering around the house and fingering everything Mom ever touched and getting all weepy. I hate it so much. Any minute he's going to stumble up to my door and wait out there for like twenty minutes trying to decide whether or not to knock, and I'm going to pretend I don't know he's there, and eventually he'll go away, and if he wasn't already crying he will be by then, and... this is what Ms. Meisner wanted me to deal with *in her office? *Seriously?*

I can't deal with her. I just... I'm not dealing with any of this. This is stupid. I got rid of her, I don't have to do a family session, GET OVER IT.

I'm supposed to be doing math homework now but I so don't care. I'm putting on an LtT DVD. At least then if Dad comes to my door it'll be easier to pretend not to hear him.

http://www.diarynow.com/thejanethe/50481.html
Date: 3/11/2013
Security level: Private
Mood: ecstatic

But OMG OMG OMG!!!!!   All of that is TOTALLY IRRELEVANT because today is THE MOST AMAZING DAY IN THE HISTORY OF THE WORLD and HERE, MY NONEXISTENT FRIENDS, IS WHY:

- Audra accepted my drabble to her fanfiction page and made me an approved poster (!!!)
- Audra said she "loved" my drabble and it was "haunting" and "everything a drabble should be" (!!!!)
- Audra FRIENDSLINK-MESSAGED ME TO TELL ME ABOUT THIS AND WE CHATTED FOR HOURS (!!!!!!!!!!!!!!!!!!!)

Okay, I might be overdoing the exclamation points, but seriously!!!!!!!!!!! Audra friending me on DN was one thing, but this is something else again. Audra doesn't really do DN comments, and even though I'm on her flist, a lot of her posts seem to be private or filtered. Which is fine, of course it's her life and her business, but I have to admit that I was a little irrationally disappointed that we didn't immediately get, like, super-close after she friended me. And now suddenly we're chatting online and she's acting like we're good friends and omg omg omg!!! SOMETHING IS WRONG INSIDE MY HEAD, I AM MUCH TOO EXCITED ABOUT THIS

Of course, in the moment it did not feel like the most thrilling thing in the history of ever. In the moment, in fact, it pretty much felt like the most agonizing and horrific thing that had ever happened. And why, do you ask? Why, merely for this reason: I had no idea she was going to message me. And at the precise moment that she messaged me, I was in an IRC chat as Zelda, the ass-kicking lesbian feminist environmentalist vegan pro-choice anti-fur man-hating bitch who runs around burning down animal testing labs in her spare time. This meant that I was engaged in industriously bitching out some girl with the sn "WetnHot4U" for being just one among a vast contingent of modern women contributing to female objectification. And you know how sometimes when you're typing in another screen and then a new message pops up before you notice, you finish your original message in the new screen and send it without even realizing? Yeah, so my conversation with Audra definitely started out:

Audra S (7:06:52 PM): Hi there!

Rachel W (7:06:53 PM): th your heads stuck too far up your ASSES to realize how badly you're damaging the movement!

Uh. Yeah. When I looked up and realized what I'd done I pretty much died. But Audra, as we know, is awesome, and she was just as cool about it as you'd expect:

Audra S (7:07:02 PM): Wow, one line into the conversation and I've already managed to grow multiple heads *and* asses. Go me! :)

After nearly biting my lower lip off, I tried to explain, but it was kind of difficult. I mean, I've never told anyone about all the personalities and stuff, and I certainly wasn't going to tell Audra -- she'd think I was a total fruitcake. At the same time, there's no context in which that comment wouldn't be bitchy, and I didn't want her to think I was a bitch either. I wound up going with:

Rachel W (7:07:14 PM): Oh, erm, sorry. I was messing with some of my friends in a chat room; one of them bought her boyfriend a "wife-beater" today, so I was acting all feministy and whatnot about it. ::sheepish smile::

It sounded kind of ridiculous to me, but I guess she bought it. I mean, there's no reason for her not to have bought it.

Audra S (7:07:21 PM): np. That is an awful name for them. LOL

Rachel W (7:07:30 PM): Tell me about it! I joke about being all feministy about it, but the last time The Boy bought one I made him return it. Actually, though, I was only claiming that was for feminist reasons -- it just didn't look so good on him and I didn't have the heart to tell him. ::g::

78

Excellent. We were chatting casually, just as if my head hadn't almost exploded when she messaged me, and I even managed to sneak The Boy in; I love The Boy.

Audra S (7:07:38 PM): Ah, you've got a Boy, then! Now, does he have a Christian name, or did his parents decide that the generic was sufficient? :)

This is a tough one -- people are always asking me what The Boy's real name is, and I never have an answer. The problem is, and this is embarrassing to admit, that I haven't named him because I'm waiting for him to name himself... see, The Boy is my dream boy, and I don't want to name him because, well, what are the odds that when I actually meet my dream boy he'll have the same name I picked? I'm kind of waiting for him to show up in real life and then I'll know what his name is. Which is all ridiculous because I've figured out like everything about him *except* his name. But, hey, a girl can dream, can't she?

Rachel W (7:07:49 PM): Oh, the name thing. He actually asked me if I'd give him a new name online; he's a little self-conscious about me posting about him, and he doesn't want too many Vital Details Known. But I couldn't think of him by any other name, so I just call him The Boy now. I like it, actually, there's a certain mystique. ;)

Audra S (7:08:02 PM): Gotcha. Anyway, hi! First time talking in real time, huh? Sometimes that's a little awkward, but your comment about me having my heads up my asses definitely broke the ice. ;)

Rachel W (7:08:05 PM): LOL! I told you that wasn't for you!

Audra S (7:07:09 PM): Yes, but you don't expect me to let you forget it, do you? ;)

And so on. She's SO easy to talk to -- we talked for literally three hours on end. Mostly we talked about LtT, which was pretty awesome in itself,

79

discussing the show with someone so intelligent *and* who knows as much about it as I do. We talked for awhile about the Lookies, too, which was definitely cool. She said she's working on a collection of drabbles and vignettes, which is super gutsy of her because giant Jaela/Thorin epics almost always win, but if anyone can pull off a different style, it's her. I would estimate we spent an hour and a half just squealing over the prize though. XD I was kind of hoping to be able to bring the conversation around to the auction -- time *is* running down on that -- but somehow we didn't really get into it. I'm sure I can get her on board with it, though. There's no one in the fandom who'd be better at helping me organize it. And that'll take care of the money thing, and being on her site will do wonders for my name recognition, and between that and the reception "Stars May Fall" has been getting, my popularity ought to be shooting through the roof right about the time the judges are deliberating. With any luck all the judges will recognize my writing style by then, which will put me on equal footing with the other big-name authors. And if I can fight my way through all of *that* stuff, I know getting to the con and finding somewhere to stay and stuff will fall into place. I'll take a super-cheap Greyhound, one of those ones that takes three weeks to get there and stops in every podunk town along the way; I'll get a gross roach-infested hostel and eat nothing but granola bars for the whole trip. AND IT WILL BE AWESOME.

I am so loving the direction my life is heading in right now.

Spectrum High School Email
"Where achieving potential is just the beginning"
Compose Mail

1 - **10** of **10** Older › Oldest »
Mark Unread As: Bold
Check to Delete

	Lorilynn Meisner, LICSW	**This week's progress report** -- Hi Jane! Since we missed our last meeting, I thought I would scan this week's report from your teachers and email it. Actually, I...
☑	**Amy Downing**	**Hi sweetie** -- Hi, hon, how are you? I thought I'd drop you a line because we seem to be playing phone tag at...
☐	Gary Huang	Fwd: funny lolcats -- ok i kno u hate fwds but these r rly funny & 1 of the lolcats iz BRAD MEMPIS so u beter check it out! haha ok so its not...
☑	**Lorilynn Meisner, LICSW**	**Checking in** -- Hi Jane! How is your week going? Well, I hope! I thought I would email you because now that we are not seeing one another in...
☑	**Margaret Baker**	**Missing assignments** -- Jane -- You have not yet responded to my last email, nor turned in any of your late assignments. In addition, you have...
☑	**Paul Sheehan**	**Missed classes** -- Hello Jane, I hope all is well. I'm writing to notify you that according to your teachers' records, you have missed 12 classes since...

81

☑	Juanita Montoya	**Missing assignments** -- Hola Jane, Como estas? I wanted to speak with you about your missing homework papers and Actualidades report, which…
☑	**Spectrum High School**	**March Bulletin** -- Welcome back! We hope you all had a fun and relaxing break and are ready to hit the books once more! Some…
☑	**Margaret Baker**	**Syllabus** -- Dear students: Attached please find your class syllabus for the coming weeks. We will be covering chapters 6 and 7 this…
☑	**Paul Sheehan**	**Signature Required on IEP** -- Hello Jane, According to our records, you have not yet returned your signed individualized education plan (IEP). Both you and your parent or…

Date: 3/13/2013
Security level: Private
Mood: Annoyed :-(

Well, on the up side, things are still going well in fandom: the auction is rolling along pretty steadily, the donations are piling up, I'm making some progress on Grip (though frankly I'm doing a lot better with "Stars May Fall", which is ironic, since I can't submit it), and best of all, Audra and I are still chatting almost every night (!!!) On the down side, I had the not-so-pleasurable pleasure of meeting Eleanor D. Acton today. She did in fact meet most of my Older Therapist checkboxes -- sedate clothes, yellow lined pad, books with depressing titles. In fact, I think I've figured out their rationale in sending me to this Acton woman: I didn't like Ms. Meisner, so if they found me someone who they figured was Ms. Meisner's polar opposite in every way, I'd be sure to love her! So if Ms. Meisner wears shiny faux-satin blouses and pencil skirts, my new therapist should wear polyester pant suits. If Ms. Meisner's face goes up and down like a marionette manipulated by a cokehead, my new therapist should limit herself to twinkly eyes and understated smiles. If Ms. Meisner displays blueberry-hatching-eggs, my new therapist should have hideous gold-trimmed decorative plates on the wall. If Ms. Meisner is 22, my new therapist should be 78. You get the idea.

But when you come right down to it, a therapist is a therapist is a therapist, and thus a pain in the ass.

In keeping with this truism, today's session started the way most of them do. The therapist introduces herself. I mumble something. She offers a few pleasantries. I stare at her and raise an eyebrow. She stares back. Some of them say something at this point; some of them wait for me to take the lead. Usually if they wait long enough I explain that I am being forced to be here, and then I pull out a notebook and start working on a fanfic. 'Nuff said.

The problem is that this Acton woman wouldn't leave well enough alone at that point. I mean, I'll give her credit, she didn't jump right into prying into my life, but she kept going on about how she works in therapy, how she handles this that and the other thing, working together on goal-setting and blah blah blah -- I only caught half of it, but I was annoyed that I was hearing even that much; I really needed to be working on Grip. So when she told me she's pretty informal and I'm welcome to call her by her nickname, "Nora", I decided to see if I could get a rise out of her. "Oh, you go by Nora? That must be why I couldn't find too much information about you on ZoomSearch," I said. I was watching her reaction. If there was stuff I could find about her on Zoom under the name Nora, I'd be a lot happier about the whole situation. I can't afford to get myself kicked out of therapy with this woman like I did with Meisner, but I'd like to have some leverage, anyway.

Unfortunately, she seemed pretty unfazed. "Actually I think you'll find more about me under Eleanor," she said. "That's what I go by professionally, so you'll find any info about my career searching on that name. You might try Eleanor D. Acton -- sometimes that's how my name turns up."

I laughed. "Nora, I'm not looking for professional information. I already found all that, and it's boring. All it told me was that you're like every other therapist I've ever seen -- there have been twenty-three of them, did you know?"

She consulted her file. "I have twelve listed here, plus five consultations. But you're right, that is a lot." She smiled nicely.

I got pissed. I don't need your smiles, lady. "Look. The number doesn't matter. You're all alike. And you think we're all alike -- all of your patients. You parcel us all out into neat little DSM-IV diagnoses and call it done, right? And maybe most of your patients fit in those, I don't know. But let me tell you something: I don't. I'm not a check box, and you have no idea about who I am, and I am definitely not interested in telling you, and no matter what you think, you don't have any kind of *right* to harass me about every single private thing in my life just because you got a degree in poking around in people's heads thirty years ago." She was supposed to be getting annoyed, or defensive, or *something* by now -- instead, she was nodding, like she was actually taking me seriously. It was making me madder than ever, honestly. What a hypocrite. "That's why the Zoom search. If you get to know personal things about me, I get to know personal things about you." Not a blink from her; instead she gave me this nice, unruffled smile, like everything was perfectly copacetic in Dr. Decrepit!Land. By this point

I was hoping like hell that she'd turn out to be some sort of ex-cult leader who'd bilked a bunch of yellow-robed followers out of millions of dollars, just so I could wave the Zoom results in her face next week.

"Well, if that's how you feel about it, I'm sorry it didn't work out very well for you," she said, sounding way too blase to support my cult-leader theory. Damn. "I think I must be too old to have much of an Internet presence. We dinosaurs don't hold much truck with the Internet, and I guess it ignores us in return. But, you know, if there's anything you want to know about me, you can always ask. I can't promise that I'll answer. But you can ask."

That was flat-out ridiculous. "You know perfectly well you're not going to answer any personal questions," I said. "But somehow I'm supposed to. I get forced to come in here and I know you're going to ask me questions about how I have a dead mom and an alcoholic dad and how does that make me feel, like you're going to be able to help me, and you know what? Those aren't things anyone can help, and I do not care to discuss how I feel about them with some stranger who thinks I am a case of depression and social anxiety and learning disabilities rolled into one big giant ball of crazy!" I had to stop for a breath at that point. I was madder than I thought I'd been.

She leaned forward intently and steepled her fingers under her chin, for all the world like I hadn't just blown my top at her. What is up with this lady? I don't get her at all, I swear. "Well, tell you what," she said. "I can tell you've been through the therapy mill a good few times, so I'm going to dispense with all the preliminaries -- I'm sure you know them all. And I'll also tell you, I'm not going to be able to help you today."

I raised an eyebrow. "You're not?" Like, seriously, if she's not at least pretending that's what she's there for, why was I sitting in her office?

"No," she continued. "Not today. Probably not for awhile yet. I have to know you before I can help you. I mean, there's no magic wand I can wave and make it so your mother's not dead and your dad doesn't drink, right?"

"Exactly," I said heatedly. "Remind me why I'm here?"

She smiled faintly. "Because your school is making you be here, if I understand correctly. Do I?"

"Yes," I said, completely lost.

"So I'm not going to be able to fix everything for you right away, and I also can't do any therapy work until I get to know you and you learn to trust me. So I guess that's where we start."

I snorted. "I don't trust therapists."

I swear to God, she actually laughed. She covered it up, or tried to, but she laughed. My therapist laughed at me, is that even allowed?

"I had an idea," she said.

"So you can't work with me until I trust you. And I don't trust therapists. So I'll never trust you. So maybe you can write a note to my school and tell them therapy won't do me any good?" I asked hopefully.

She shook her head. "Uh-uh. I have higher hopes than that for the future." That damn smile again; the woman's a regular ball of sunshine. "Call me an eternal optimist."

I rolled my eyes. "You'd better be." Then something else occurred to me, something I never said out loud to a therapist before, but then I'd never been quite so committed to just laying it all out on the line before. "What makes you think you could help me even if I trusted you? I'm probably smarter than you."

"Oh?" she said.

"Yeah. I'm smarter than almost everyone." I had a major conscience twinge at that one; it's not something I like to go around saying, or even thinking, it seems so snotty. And it's not like "intelligence" counts for much, or even makes that much sense as a concept, when you have learning disabilities and stuff balancing it off. But all my IQ tests say my intelligence is genius-level, so why not put it on the table? She's already got my IQ scores anyway.

"Yes," she said, confirming that, "I can see that from your neuropsych report. You certainly are smarter than most people."

"So?" I said.

She smiled. "So am I."

This woman. "Yes, I'm sure your IQ is hiiiiiiiiighly satisfactory," I said, drawing it out, really being a bitch now. "But that doesn't matter. If I'm smarter than you are, then this isn't going to work. I'm going to throw up roadblocks, and you're going to get distracted by them, and we'll wind up talking around the issues all the time. Things would be so much simpler if

86

you'd write my dad that note. Really."

"I see your point," she said. "But let me ask you a question."

She seemed to be waiting for some kind of a response, so I said "Yeah?"

"Have I gotten sidelined by any of your roadblocks so far?"

So she'd been doing better than most. So what.

"I haven't even gotten started yet," I told her.

"Well, I look forward to it," she said. Then she checked her watch. "I think that's a good place to end for today, don't you? You and your father both have some paperwork to fill out. All right?"

"Whatever," I mumbled.

I don't know what her deal is. I think she thinks therapy is supposed to be like an Abbott and Costello routine or something. Fine. Bring on the repartee. But I'm not going to like her. If she thinks being casual and off-the-cuff and refusing to be intimidated is some way to get me to spill my guts, she is sorely mistaken. I don't like therapists, and I don't like her, and she can labor under the misapprehension that she might win me over for as long as she wants, but it doesn't matter. I am definitely writing fanfic in my next session.

Gary Huang has sent **Jane S** a guest-chat request.

Jane S (4:13:54 PM) Oh, hi, Gary.

Gary H (4:13:55) hay :)

Jane S (4:13:57 PM) What's up?

Gary H (4:14:02 PM): i prolly shouldnt have msged u?

Jane S (4:14:06 PM): No, no, it's fine. I was just surprised.

Jane S (4:14:08 PM): I'm not on FriendsLink much.

Gary H (4:14:11 PM) yah i nevr see u on

Gary H (4:14:14 PM) I sent u a freinds request awile ago

Jane S (4:14:18 PM) Oh, right. Sorry, I just signed in, I haven't dealt with messages and stuff. Hold on a sec, I'll go approve it.

Gary H (4:14:21 PM): its ok if u dont want 2

Jane S (4:14:24 PM): No, it's cool. I have about five friends here, so you can be number 6. :)

Gary H (4:14:26 PM): awsum :)

Jane S (4:14:52 PM): Okay, all set.

Jane S (4:14:55 PM): So what's new?

Gary H (4:14:55 PM): wats up

Jane S (4:14:57 PM): nmh

Gary H (4:14:58 PM): nmh

Jane S (4:15:00 PM): LOL

Gary H (4:15:03 PM): what?

Jane S (4:15:06 PM): Nothing. We're just both bored. In the same words.

Gary H (4:15:09 PM): :)

Gary H (4:15:16 PM): did u do the geograffy homework yet

Jane S (4:15:20 PM): Some of it. But my scanner's broken, so you can't have it. ;)

Gary H (4:15:23 PM): na I wasnt gong 2 ask 2 copy

Gary H (4:15:26 PM): just cureous

Jane S (4:15:29 PM): No, no, I know. I was just kidding.

Gary H (4:15:52 PM): what r u doin now

Jane S (4:15:57 PM): Nothing much. I was going to be watching TV, but those stupid Hot Teen Hollywood Awards got in the way.

Gary H (4:16:00 PM): o

Gary H (4:16:04 PM): u into look 2 tommorow?

Jane S (4:16:06 PM): How'd you know that?

Gary H (4:16:09 PM): i stock u lol

Gary H (4:16:14 PM): no but 4 real the hot teen w/e awardes are on CKN

Jane S (4:16:17 PM): Oh, right.

Gary H (4:16:20 PM): look 2 tom is suposed to be on CKN now

Jane S (4:16:24 PM): Tell me about it. ;)

Gary H (4:16:29 PM): do u write fanfictons and stuff tho?

Jane S (4:16:31 PM): Where are you getting all this?! Dude, HAVE you been stalking me?!

Gary H (4:16:35 PM): how would i stalk ur fanficytons

Gary H (4:16:39 PM): i watch u writting in class tho

Gary H (4:16:42 PM): those arent class notes :)

Gary H (4:16:46 PM): n 1 time u had ur notebook out during lunch n it said sumthing abt jaila n thorin

Jane S (4:16:48 PM): ...oh my God.

Gary H (4:16:50 PM): no dont freak out

Gary H (4:16:51 PM): i think its cool

Jane S (4:16:51 PM): Have you read any of them?

Gary H (4:16:53 PM): no

Gary H (4:16:56 PM): where r they

Jane S (4:17:11 PM): It's just… sort of personal.

Gary H (4:17:14 PM): personal?

Jane S (4:17:18 PM): Like… I don't know. It's hard to explain.

Jane S (4:17:21 PM): People sort of tend to think you're crazy when you tell them you write fanfic.

Gary H (4:17:23 PM): dude

Gary H (4:17:28 PM): ur talking 2 the state skeeball champeon

Jane S (4:17:29 PM): LOL!!!

Gary H (4:17:32 PM): i dont think ur crazy

Jane S (4:17:34 PM): Well, thanks.

Gary H (4:17:37 PM): so can i c them?

Jane S (4:17:37 PM): NO

Gary H (4:17:38 PM): LOL

Gary H (4:17:40 PM): annother day

Jane S (4:17:42 PM): Try never, hon.

Gary H (4:17:47 PM): i coud serch 4 them online

Jane S (4:17:50 PM): No you couldn't, but I hope you wouldn't anyway.

Gary H (4:17:53 PM): no i woudnt if u didnt want me 2

Gary H (4:17:56 PM): but how come i coudnt?

Jane S (4:17:58 PM): They're not up under my name. I use a pen name.

Gary H (4:18:01 PM): rilly? what name?

Jane S (4:18:02 PM): Nice try!

Gary H (4:18:05 PM): no :) just cureous

Jane S (4:18:07 PM): Well, you'll have to live with your curiosity.

Gary H (4:18:24 PM): so how come u dont like FriendsLink?

Jane S (4:18:29 PM): I dunno, it's just not my scene.

Jane S (4:18:34 PM): I spend enough time being ignored by people at school without spending time being ignored by them online. :P

Gary H (4:18:36 PM): lol

Gary H (4:18:39 PM): well if u use fl I wont ignore u

Jane S (4:18:43 PM): Yes, I see that. :)

Gary H (4:18:49 PM): so witch othr sites do u use?

Jane S (4:18:56 PM): Um, I don't know. I'm not really online that much.

Gary H (4:19:00 PM): exsept ur always cuttin class 2 go to the cpu lab ;)

Jane S (4:19:03 PM): OMG, dude, you do not give up, I'll give you that. LOL

Gary H (4:19:06 PM): :)

Jane S (4:19:12 PM): Look, if you really want to chat, my ZIM handle is thejanethe. I'm on there sometimes.

Gary H (4:19:16 PM): zim?

Jane S (4:19:19 PM): Zetta Instant Message.

Gary H (4:19:23 PM): o I dont no any1 who uses that

Jane S (4:19:25 PM): Well, now you do.

Gary H (4:19:28 PM): hbow come u use that

Jane S (4:19:35 PM): It's just easier to deal with. On FL anyone can chat you if they know your name. On ZIM you have to give them your screen name first before they can chat you.

Jane S (4:19:40 PM): I'm not all that excited about the prospect of Jason Malone being able to track me down online, for instance. :P

Gary H (4:19:44 PM): lol I wdnt b either

Jane S (4:19:46 PM): So, yeah.

Gary H (4:21:22 PM): ok I downloded zim

Jane S (4:21:25 PM): Wow, that was fast.

Gary H (4:21:29 PM): my sns rawkdaskeeball

Jane S (4:21:32 PM): Of course it is. LOL

Gary H (4:21:36 PM): & ur thejanethe

Jane S (4:21:38 PM): Right.

Gary H (4:21:40 PM): ok

Gary H (4:21:44 PM): how come u picked that 1?

Jane S (4:21:49 PM): Dude, you ask more questions than anyone I have ever met in my life. LOL

Gary H (4:21:52 PM): thats me, the queston man :)

Jane S (4:21:56 PM): Anyway, it's a Simpsons reference. Do you ever watch that?

Gary H (4:21:59 PM): a litle

Gary H (4:22:04 PM): more into south park and family guy

Jane S (4:22:11 PM): Oh. Anyway, it's from one of the old episodes. This murderer Sideshow Bob has "Die Bart Die" written on his chest, and at his parole hearing he tells the judge that it's German for "The Bart the". :)

Gary H (4:22:15 PM): lol

Gary H (4:22:17 PM): does he get off?

Jane S (4:22:21 PM): For half an hour. Anyway, that's what it's from.

Gary H (4:22:25 PM): it makes u sound boring tho

Gary H (4:22:28 PM): like ur just a… the

Gary H (4:22:29 PM): lol

Jane S (4:22:32 PM): Oh. Well, I kind of am.

Gary H (4:22:34 PM): no ur not

Jane S (4:22:36 PM): No, really, I am.

Gary H (4:22:37 PM): y?

Jane S (4:22:39 PM): Why? I don't know.

Jane S (4:22:43 PM): Because I have stick-straight mousy hair and a C average in school and my name is Jane, as in Plain Jane?

Gary H (4:22:45 PM): no, ur too smart 2 b boring

Jane S (4:22:47 PM): I don't do anything with it though.

Gary H (4:22:50 PM): whats that mean

Jane S (4:22:52 PM): Oh, I just feel like I waste a lot of my life.

Jane S (4:22:55 PM): I guess I'm just not very good at the stuff that matters.

Gary H (4:22:57 PM): like what

Jane S (4:23:01 PM): …I don't know, life? LOL

Gary H (4:23:05 PM): haha im noyt so good at that either

Gary H (4:23:06 PM): exceped for skeeball

Jane S (4:23:09 PM): Which, by the way, you are going to have to show me how to play one of these days.

Gary H (4:23:11 PM): yea?

Gary H (4:23:13 PM): what r u doing tonite?

Jane S (4:23:21 PM): …nmh?

Gary H (4:23:23 PM): o yea

Jane S (4:23:25 PM): LOL

Gary H (4:23:27 PM): wanna go out?

Jane S (4:23:42 PM): Umm… I should check with my dad.

Gary H (4:23:44 PM): ok

Jane S (4:23:46 PM): brb

Gary H (4:23:47 PM): ok

Jane S (4:24:36 PM): Well, my dad said okay. He can't drive me though.

Gary H (4:24:38 PM): :)

Gary H (4:24:39 PM): my mom can drive us

Jane S (4:24:41 PM): You already asked?

Gary H (4:24:42 PM): :)

Gary H (4:24:45 PM): be there in a half hr?

Jane S (4:24:47 PM): Sure.

Gary H (4:24:48 PM): k!

Jane S (4:24:50 PM): See you then!

http://www.diarynow.com/thejanethe/63765.html
Date: 3/15/2013
Security level: Private
Mood: Thoughtful :-/

Well. Well, that was… interesting.

(Why does it seem that every entry I make about Gary starts off that way?)

It was kind of fun, actually. Before I went, I was expecting it to be like the most awkward experience of my life. I don't even remember the last time I went out with a friend my own age -- God, what was it, like fifth grade? It's just never been my scene. I'm really bad in social situations like that. I always feel like I've missed the conversational beam, somehow, like I'm a step behind and a beat off. I don't really know how to explain it. I'm sure the people I used to try to hang out with (when you're in fifth grade, if you invite a kid out to ice cream or the movies, no matter how dorky you are, they will come; at that age, the parents always pay) could explain it better. I get twitchy. I laugh too hard, at the wrong things. My brain starts working overtime, and I'm either blurting strange things out or not saying anything at all. Seriously, it's really, really painful.

Gary's easier, and I probably could have predicted that if I'd been looking at it from the right angle. There are probably a lot of people at Spectrum who would be easier to hang out with than my old friends in grammar school. I mean, the whole social anxiety thing is one of the reasons I'm at Spectrum in the first place, and I'm not the only one. I may not be able to catch the rhythm of social interaction very easily, but if the other person can't either, at least I feel less left out.

Which is not to say that the first part of the evening with Gary wasn't ridiculously awkward. The boy was terrified. I don't know whether he had second thoughts after he invited me -- maybe he functions better on the Internet too? -- but he sure was nervous when we met up. His mom drove us to Chuck E. Cheese; we sat in the car in complete silence for about two minutes, and then he turned some punk-rock CD on as loud as it would go to try and cover the silence up. If I wake up tomorrow morning with blood leaking out of my ears I won't be at all surprised. The music ended when we

95

got out of the car, though, and there we were. For a minute I was placing mental odds on which one of us was going to turn and run pell-mell back home first.

But we got our tokens, and he made a beeline for the Skee-Ball machine. And... oh my Lord. It really reminded me of the way I used to be back in elementary school, how whenever school got to be too much for me I'd have to sneak a book under my desk and read a few pages (or as many as I could get away with). I've never forgotten the amazing relief that would wash over me then. Gary had the same expression on his face when he hit the Skee-Ball machine.

He's so cute.

You never think much about what it takes to be good at Skee-Ball, do you? I mean, obviously some people are better at it than others, but it's not like other sports (*other sports?* oh *man*, Gary is getting to me!) where you can really see what they're doing right or wrong. I mean, you pull your arm back, you swing it forward, you throw the ball, and it goes wherever it's going to go. Right?

Oh, wrong, wrong, wrong. So wrong.

Gary... he starts about four feet back from the machine. No farther than that -- apparently he needs room for three long steps, no more and no fewer. It's not like bowling, he told me with a superior sort of an eye-roll -- he has a real grudge against bowling. It's not about how *hard* you throw the ball. It's about how *well* you throw the ball.

He starts four feet back, he takes his three steps, he brings his arm up and then back down in a long arc, and he throws it with this fancy twist of the wrist that is impossible to describe. He tried to slow it down enough for me to see what he was doing, but I couldn't do it to save my life. You don't have to twist it that way unless you're aiming for the 100-point holes, he explained; they're the only ones on the sides of the board, so putting a spin on the ball is the best way to aim for them. Some of his friends shoot from the corner of the ramp and try to get the ball to run a long diagonal, but he thinks that's too risky -- the wrist-twist is much more consistent once you get used to it. He's been working on a ricochet shot too, but that's really just for effect -- it gives you a lot of power but it's not practical because you can't aim as well, so it's really only good for the free-form part of the

96

competition.

Yes. They have a free-form part of the competition.

For this, Gary has specialty shots. There's the double-hander, in which you shoot two balls simultaneously and each one hits one of the 100-point holes. There's the cross-wise double-hander, which is the same as the standard double-hander except the balls roll on a diagonal and cross paths on the ramp. There's the "short-step", where you trade in those long three strides for this weird, jerky little hop that sort of makes you look like a hiccuping frog. There are ricochet shots and skip-shots and reverse-spin shots and oh, dear Lord, so many. So, so many. Gary showed me every single one of them. It was surreally fascinating.

After awhile he stopped messing around and started playing to win. 100-point shot after 100-point shot, all nailed cold. The Chuck E. Cheese employees were eyeing him disdainfully -- apparently everyone in his Skee-Ball league (WHO ELSE IS IN THIS THING?!? WHO?!?) is well-known to the employees of the local CEC. (Gary tends to call it that, I think because it's just too embarrassing to him to keep talking about the passion of his life in the context of a Chuck E. Cheese.) They've actually made a rule that no one in the league is allowed to play Skee-Ball except on three designated lanes out of the ten; the machines are wired so that if you get a score of 700 or over you get 200 tickets, but the league people were winning way too many tickets, so they disabled that on three machines. However, when there were no employees in sight, Gary snuck over to the other machines and got 200 tickets out of each one of them. He brought all his tickets to an employee who he said was new, and he "bought" me a highly ticket-expensive and unbelievably gaudy bedside lamp. It is a round black ball with multicolored light-up facets, the base of it is lined with neon trim, and it is indescribably ugly. It is sitting next to my bed right now, revolving slowly. Gary looked so gleeful upon winning it for me that I burst into giggles and couldn't stop for a very long time.

I played a few games of Skee-Ball myself, and won a total of fourteen tickets. In the spirit of reciprocity, I bought and gave to Gary a curious oblong piece of lime-green plastic with Chuck E. Cheese's face imprinted on it. It is of indeterminate purpose, but Gary didn't seem to mind. He pocketed it and said -- I don't know if he was serious or not -- that it would be his good-luck charm from now on. I think it's ironic that he's using a trinket that was won via several of the worst Skee-Ball games ever seen by mankind as a good-luck charm for intense Skee-Ball competitions. But I didn't say so. If he suddenly loses his touch he can always throw it away.

On the ride home, in stark contrast to the ride there, Gary was a regular chatterbox. Apparently not too many people are willing to listen to him talk about Skee-Ball very much, and I think he's sussed that I never hear a damn thing he says during lunch, so he felt at liberty to repeat all of it. Skee-ball wasn't all we talked about, though; I think at one point we may have actually gossiped about some of the students and teachers at school. You know, the way teenagers are supposed to do. My mind is officially boggled.

When his mom dropped me off, he reached out for a second as if to hug me, then froze, then clammed up again, then got a hold of himself and took my hand and shook it firmly. Up-down-up... down-up... down-up. I was still trying to figure out why he looked so flustered, he was trying to figure out how long the handshake was supposed to last, and after a minute we both burst out laughing and I hit him on the shoulder. Then I got out of the car and went inside.

I have a bunch of questions rattling around in my head, none of which I really want to formulate, but maybe I should:

1. Was tonight a date? (No, the answer to that one is definitely "no". Okay, so moving on...)
2. Are Gary and I officially friends now? (I'm thinking yes on this one.)
3. Do I actually need to follow through on that bullshit story I told him and start using Zetta Instant Messenger more than like once every six months? (Uh, I think I'll play this one by ear.)
4. What the *hell* am I going to do with that revolting lamp next to my bed? (God only knows.)

Rachel W (4:09:11 PM): Hey Audra!

Audra S (4:09:16 PM): Hey girl. :) What's up?

Rachel W (4:09:18 PM): nmh. Looking over the latest chapter of "Stars", trying to get Thorin to be a good boy and do what I want him to do.

Rachel W (4:09:22): He's supposed to be keeping his head down and spying on Distra's illicit jaunt activity, but somehow he keeps trying to rip off his shirt and drop-kick her into the next century instead.

Audra S (4:09:24): And... that ISN'T what you want him to do? :)

Rachel W (4:09:25): Well, I suppose you have a point. XD

Audra S (4:09:25): ;)

Rachel W (4:09:27): I think it's probably about time for me to set that aside for now, though. But, hey, I wanted to bounce some thoughts off you about the auction -- wanna brainstorm?

Audra S (4:09:30): Oh, the auction. Would it be all right if I took a rain check on that for tonight? We can talk about it soon, tomorrow or whenever. It's just been a rough day -- I've been looking forward to relaxing and NOT thinking for awhile. :)

Rachel W (4:09:31 PM): Oh. Totally, no problem.

Audra S (4:09:32): Wanna play a game instead?

Rachel W (4:09:34): ...that would depend on what game, hon. Because I'll tell you, I won't be recovering anytime soon from the thrashing I took in chess last week. :)

Audra S (4:09:36 PM): Oh, like you didn't kick my ass twice as hard in Wordsmith with Friends. :P QAT? QI? 64 points? Whatever, dude!

Rachel W (4:09:37): QAT AND QI ARE SO TOTALLY IN THE SCRABBLE DICTIONARY GO LOOK OKAY

Audra S (4:09:39): LOL Man, let's not get into this again, agreed?

Rachel W (4:09:40): Agreed. (But THEY ARE. :P)

Audra S (4:09:42 PM): Anyway, no board games. I'm sick of board games.

Rachel W (4:09:44 PM): ...what are you trying to suggest, charades?

Rachel W (4:09:45 PM): ::pantomimes... something::

Rachel W (4:09:46 PM): ::that I can't tell you what it is::

Rachel W (4:09:47 PM): ::but it involves waving of arms. or something::

Rachel W (4:09:47 PM): Okay, now guess! :P

Audra S (4:09:48 PM): LOL Stop being a wiseass. Charades isn't the only non-board game in the world.

Rachel W (4:09:50 PM): Yeah, but this whole online thing is limiting. Are you talking another round of name-the-LtT-quote?

Audra S (4:09:52 PM): Nah, that's no challenge for either of us. Between us we've probably got every ep memorized.

Rachel W (4:09:52 PM): *grin*

Audra S (4:09:55 PM): ::flicks open old book of slumber party games::

Rachel W (4:09:57 PM): Do you REALLY have one of those to hand?

Audra S (4:10:01 PM): No, but it makes a suggestion of Truth or Dare seem less out of the blue. ;)

Rachel W (4:10:03 PM): OMG TRUTH OR DARE! I haven't played that since, like, second grade! LOL

Audra S (4:10:06 PM): Nobody has. I like reverting back to childhood though.

Rachel W (4:10:14 PM): Then you must have had a good childhood. All I can remember is my sister daring me to moon the window in my Rainbow Brite panties for a full minute. She timed me too. Brat. LOL

Rachel W (4:10:38 PM): ...you there?

Audra S (4:10:43 PM): Sorry, got distracted for a sec.

Rachel W (4:10:45 PM): np, I thought you were going to have to restart.

Audra S (4:10:49 PM): Nope -- for the moment, at least, my computer is not actively pitching a fit. Anyway, what do you say?

Rachel W (4:10:54 PM): I dunno... I mean, how do you play T or D online?

Rachel W (4:11:57 PM): How would you ever know if I did the dares?

Audra S (4:12:01 PM): Well, two options. One is you only take truths.

Rachel W (4:12:04 PM): But that takes all the fun out of it! *pouts*

Audra S (4:12:07 PM): Let me finish. The other option, obviously, is that we only give dares that can be done online.

Rachel W (4:12:12 PM): waitaminutewaitaminute.

Audra S (4:12:16 PM): ::waits, hoping some spaces are forthcoming::

Rachel W (4:12:20 PM): What kind of dares could you do online?

Rachel W (4:12:22 PM): oh piss off. LOL

Audra S (4:12:27 PM): I can't tell you beforehand, then you wouldn't take them! ;)

Rachel W (4:12:32 PM): OMG YOU WERE GOING TO MAKE ME FL-SEX-MESSAGE THAT CREEPY GUY WHO WRITES ALL THE JAELA/DISTRA PORN, WEREN'T YOU?!?!?!

Audra S (4:12:35 PM): ROFLMAO

Audra S (4:12:37 PM): I hadn't had the idea, but I wish I had!

Rachel W (4:12:41 PM): Omg I SO don't trust you now!

Audra S (4:12:46 PM): I don't know why, it's your own dirty mind!

Audra S (4:12:51 PM): Anyway, does that mean you won't play?

Rachel W (4:12:58 PM): No, but it means I'm not taking any dares. LOL

Audra S (4:13:03 PM): Fine. :P You start.

Rachel W (4:13:09 PM): Uh, okay.

Audra S (4:13:44 PM): ::checks watch::

Rachel W (4:13:49 PM): Aagh, I can't think of anything!!

Audra S (4:13:57 PM): ::Miss Helpful:: You should probably start by saying truth or dare.

Rachel W (4:14:06 PM): LOL You're just not cutting me any breaks today, are you?

Audra S (4:14:11 PM): ::throws up hands helplessly:: I just want to play a game! :P

Rachel W (4:14:17 PM): Fine, fine. Truth or dare?

Audra S (4:14:20 PM): Truth.

Rachel W (4:14:32 PM): …::wasn't expecting that::

Audra S (4:14:39 PM): I'm a little frightened of your dares since you came up with the idea of sexting Mr. Creepazoid!

Rachel W (4:14:43 PM): But I thought *you* were going to do that! I -- okay, truth.

Audra S (4:14:46 PM): Yes. Truth.

Rachel W (4:14:54 PM): Hmm. It strikes me that I don't really know much about you, you know?

Audra S (4:14:58 PM): Yeah. Kind of the point of the exercise.

Rachel W (4:15:11 PM): Huh, right. Uh… okay, what's the most embarrassing thing that ever happened to you?

Audra S (4:15:17 PM): You're the only person I know who doesn't start Truth or Dare by asking if the other person's a virgin.

Rachel W (4:15:25 PM): Hey, my question could be related to that. ;) Are you stalling?

Audra S (4:15:31 PM): No. My answer's not a funny story, though.

Audra S (4:15:36 PM): You are hereby forewarned and may change your question if you like.

Rachel W (4:15:42 PM): No, I don't mind, unless it's too personal.

Audra S (4:15:49 PM): No. Like you said, we don't know that much about each other, so what better way to find out?

Audra S (4:16:01 PM): When I was in middle school I passed out and fell down an entire flight of stairs. Between classes, in the middle of school.

Rachel W (4:16:06 PM): OW!! Were you okay?

Audra S (4:16:13 PM): The worst of that was a few bumps and bruises, but then the nurses' office decided I was anorexic.

Rachel W (4:16:22 PM): …you don't have to answer this if you don't want to, but were you?

Audra S (4:16:30 PM): No. My dad had gotten laid off his job recently and we didn't have much money. I mean, we weren't, like, trash--picking poor or anything, but I was too young to really get what was going on and I overheard my mom talking about how she was having to cut back on the groceries.

Audra S (4:16:41 PM): I'd just been reading all these books like The Little Princess -- you know the scene where she's had no food for a day and then she runs into the orphan who's had no food in three days and she gives all her rolls to her, or whatever? -- and I had this melodramatic eleven-year-old idea that as the oldest sibling I had to give my little brothers my food.

Rachel W (4:16:43 PM): Wow.

Audra S (4:16:49 PM): I wasn't *starving* myself or anything, don't get the idea I'm some huge martyr. Though I certainly liked to think of myself as one. :P I think it was just that I'd had some kind of super-sugary cereal for breakfast, which always makes me wonky after awhile, and then no lunch.

Audra S (4:17:02 PM): But the nurses' office had been noticing me losing a bunch of weight anyway, so they weighed me and spewed out a bunch of crap about body-mass index and then called my mom and kind of accused me of starving myself and accused her of incompetent parenting in the same sentence.

Audra S (4:17:06 PM): She was not happy.

Rachel W (4:17:09 PM): Jesus, jumping to conclusions much?

Rachel W (4:17:11 PM): What did your mom do?

Audra S (4:17:18 PM): Yeah, I think the nurse had just read an article about early-onset anorexia in Time Magazine and was dying to diagnose someone with it, or something. :P

Audra S (4:17:26 PM): She probably had a quota of cases of all the hip new preteen disorders that she had to diagnose each year or the guidance office would write her up.

Rachel W (4:17:28 PM): LOL

Audra S (4:17:32 PM): Oh, my mom gave the nurse a piece of her mind.

Audra S (4:17:36 PM): Mom's loudmouth Bronx through and through. The nurse was holding the phone six inches from her ear by the time she was done. ::eyeroll::

Rachel W (4:17:38 PM): Fair enough, as long as she wasn't yelling at you. LOL

Rachel W (4:17:51 PM): Is your computer being stupid again?

Audra S (4:17:56 PM): Sorry, another message came through. No, mostly she just spent a lot of time yelling at the nurse.

Audra S (4:18:02 PM): She mostly got defensive of me. Although she wasn't happy that I was skipping food unnecessarily.

Audra S (4:18:08 PM): None of it made the school nurses like me any better though. :P

Audra S (4:18:31 PM): They kept on making all these insinuations about my home life and they made me go to the school psychologist for months.

Rachel W (4:18:32 PM): Ugh! That sucks!

Audra S (4:18:39 PM): And the story got out in school and I got teased for months for being a welfare kid. Not that we actually were on welfare, but you know how kids are.

Rachel W (4:18:42 PM): :(Yeah.

Audra S (4:18:46 PM): Oh, well, water under the bridge. Truth or dare?

Rachel W (4:18:49 PM): Oh, uh, truth.

Audra S (4:18:51 PM): Sure? You sound kind of tentative.

Rachel W (4:18:54 PM): Yeah. Sorry, I was distracted for a minute. Roommate drama. :)

Audra S (4:18:57 PM): np. Hm...

Audra S (4:19:04 PM): Well, this one is general, but just for the sake of getting to know one another better -- what's your family like?

Rachel W (4:19:10 PM): My family?

Audra S (4:19:13 PM): Sure. However you define it. :)

Rachel W (4:19:20 PM): Oh, no, I wasn't hesitating because there's any question about how to define it, they're just not very interesting. Heh.

Rachel W (4:19:25 PM): Mom, dad, sister, dog. The .4 kid hasn't shown up yet, but my parents say give them time. :)

Audra S (4:19:26 PM): The .4 kid?

Rachel W (4:19:28 PM): You know, how all the studies say the average family has like 2.4 kids?

Audra S (4:19:29 PM): Oh, right. Gotcha.

Rachel W (4:19:38 PM): That's us. Dad's an accountant, Mom's stay-at-home, they've got the white picket fence around the nice middle-class home in the suburbs... we're like the definition of average. It's kind of obnoxious actually. LOL

Rachel W (4:19:46 PM): And you know what, that was such a terrible answer to that truth that I think I should take a dare instead!

Audra S (4:19:48 PM): Wait, so you want to redo it? Like, [truth redacted] or something?

Rachel W (4:19:50 PM): ::laughs:: Why not?

Audra S (4:19:52 PM): And you don't want to take another truth?

Rachel W (4:19:55 PM): I could, but I doubt it'd be any more interesting than the first one. Heh.

Audra S (4:19:59 PM): And, wait, you're not afraid of my making you sext Tim the Creep anymore?

Rachel W (4:20:03 PM): What can I say? I guess I trust you more than I thought. ;)

Audra S (4:20:05 PM): Well, OK.

Audra S (4:20:12 PM): Hmm.

Rachel W (4:20:13 PM): What?

Audra S (4:20:17 PM): No, no, just thinking. OOOH!

Rachel W (4:20:20 PM): ::is wary::

Audra S (4:20:22 PM): Got it!

Rachel W (4:20:23 PM): Uh-oh…

Audra S (4:20:30 PM): In the next twenty minutes, you're going to write an angsty Twilight/LtT crossover. Edward/Thorin.

Audra S (4:20:32 PM): With at least one sex scene.

Rachel W (4:20:33 PM): OMG OMG NO I'M NOT!!!!

Audra S (4:20:36 PM): And post it under your own name. On fanfiction. com.

Rachel W (4:20:38 PM): You are so. not. serious.

Audra S (4:20:46 PM): Since twenty minutes is a short period of time in which to write a fic, you have the following guidelines to kick-start the piece: the theme song, from which you are to draw the title and part of the inspiration, may be -- hmm, let's see --

Rachel W (4:20:49 PM): I AM SO NOT DOING THIS!!! I don't know how to write guyslash and I don't know how to write a guyslash SEX SCENE and I ESPECIALLY DON'T KNOW HOW TO WRITE TWILIGHT/THORIN SLASH AAAAAAAAAAAAIEEEEEEE

Audra S (4:20:51 PM): Taylor Swift's "You Belong with Me" --

Rachel W (4:20:52 PM): AAAAAAAAAH!!!

Audra S (4:20:56): Oh, don't worry, I'll give you a few options. Let's see...

Audra S (4:21:03 PM): Beyonce's "Irreplaceable" --

Rachel W (4:21:06 PM): Wait, what? What's that?

Audra S (4:21:32): http://www.elyrics.net/read/b/beyonce-lyrics/irreplaceable-lyrics.html

Rachel W (4:21:45): Oh -- waitasecond, THAT song?! That's about a girl kicking her asshat boyfriend to the curb!

Audra S (4:21:48): Indeed.

Rachel W (4:21:53): HOW AM I SUPPOSED TO WRITE GUYSLASH ABOUT BEYONCE BREAKING UP WITH HER BOYFRIEND

Audra S (4:22:02): Hey, I don't have to write the fic. ;) Adele's "Rolling in the Deep" --

Rachel W (4:22:10 PM): OMG dude in the context of guyslash Rolling in the Deep is the SKEEVIEST TITLE EVER and also have you not HEARD any music since 2009 because these songs are all A MILLION YEARS OLD and WHY AM I EVEN DISCUSSING THIS I AM NOT WRITING A TWILIGHT CROSSOVER!!!!

Audra S (4:22:15 PM): Or Rihanna's "Take a Bow". Go.

Rachel W (4:22:19 PM): Dude, I am NOT putting this up under my name! I'd never be able to show my font face in the fandom again!

107

Audra S (4:22:23): Oh, if you're going to be like that... :P Fine, you can put it up on a Twilight site. That's as much mercy as I'm showing you.

Rachel W (4:22:25): WHAT IF SOMEONE READS BOTH BOARDS

Audra S (4:22:28): This, my dear, is the risk you run when you take a dare. ;)

Rachel W (4:22:30 PM): yes but but but

Audra S (4:22:32 PM): You want to take it back and go for a truth?

Rachel W (4:22:35 PM): ...

Rachel W (4:22:36 PM): FEGUIEFIGFDKB

Rachel W (4:22:40 PM): ::goes to write::

Rachel W (4:22:42 PM): ::mumblegrumblegrumpbitchmumblegrump::

Audra S (4:22:45 PM): Excellent.

From: "Elana Landry" <elandry@yippee.com>
To: millay_discussion@yippeegroups.com
Date: 3/19/2013
Subject: Sonnet V, Renascence and Other Poems -- Some Thoughts :)

If I should learn, in some quite casual way,
　That you were gone, not to return again --
Read from the back-page of a paper, say,
　Held by a neighbor in a subway train,
How at the corner of this avenue
　And such a street (so are the papers filled)
A hurrying man -- who happened to be you --
　At noon to-day had happened to be killed,
I should not cry aloud -- I could not cry
　Aloud, or wring my hands in such a place --
I should but watch the station lights rush by
　With a more careful interest on my face,
Or raise my eyes and read with greater care
Where to store furs and how to treat the hair.

-Edna St. Vincent Millay, Sonnet V, from Renascence and Other Poems

* * *

　(Hey, y'all -- just bouncing some thoughts off you that I was percolating in preparation for my thesis! I'm narrowing my thoughts down now -- any thoughts on the subject would be very welcome.)

　The representation of grief in the above poem by Edna St. Vincent Millay is one of the most unique and authentic that I've yet read. For starters, in sharp contrast to the effusions of emotion that characterize most writers' poems on grief, the tone of Millay's poem is deliberately careful, restrained, and measured. The strict meter and rhyme scheme of the sonnet form add a further sense of constraint. Furthermore, the description of the central loss is as sparse as possible, using a hypothetical situation and deliberately casual phrasing. Paradoxically, though this is a poem about grief, we are given no access to the author's emotions whatsoever.

And as the poem goes on, it becomes clear that this is because <u>she</u> has no access to her emotions. She cannot allow herself to react: "I could not cry/Aloud, or wring my hands..." Yet, straitjacketed by the tight structure of the sonnet and by Millay's refusal to use any but the most mundane and casual terms to describe an event as titanic as the loss of a loved one, we sense what we are not allowed to see in the poem: the wave of the speaker's grief, struggling against the constraints the speaker has imposed. We sense, too, that she has imposed these constraints because they represent the only safety she can find. Her grief is so great and so painful that she <u>cannot</u> let it go. The idea that Millay ultimately expresses is that such grief, given free rein, will destroy the griever. It will tear the griever apart. Grief like that -- grief stemming from the loss of a loved one, someone who is needed desperately, someone without whom one cannot imagine one's life -- it is limitless. It has no boundaries. It *consumes.* The idea that one can "cope with" such grief is a myth. Millay's speaker recognizes this, and recognizes the need to lock it down as tightly as possible.

That's how the process of grieving works: how it must work, if one is to preserve one's sanity at all. You (generically speaking) can't process your grief by writing 131 poems like Tennyson did in the wake of his friend Hallam's death. Nor by writing existential poetry on the tragedy of life's inevitable ending in death. You don't do it by crying at graveside four days a week. You don't do it by letting your grief tear through you and tear you apart.

You do it by getting a new haircut. You do it by reading the advertisements in the paper and on the train very, very carefully. You do it by finding something else to focus on, and focusing in on that with tunnel vision until the pain recedes. You do it by getting on with your life and structuring things as precisely as possible. You do all of that so that you don't fall into the hole the person's death has left in you.

Millay conveys all of this in her poem. She allows the grief to remain below the surface, where it should stay. Where it needs to stay. This underrated little poem is the clearest evidence of Millay's genius that I've yet seen, and I plan to make it central to my upcoming thesis on her life and work.

From: eleanor.acton@firstgroupnet.com
To: janeshilling@spectrum.org
Date: 3/22/2013
Subject: Appointment Confirmation

Hello Jane,

I'm just emailing to confirm our next appointment on 3/26 at 4:30 pm. Thanks again for your flexibility in changing the time.

Also, as a side note, I did in fact remember what you said at our last session about my knowing nothing about the Internet or the world you live in. I've elected to take that as a challenge. Learning about the Internet is pretty circuitous, isn't it? I tried one of those books they sell at Target but I don't think anyone who writes those books is any younger or cooler than I am. So I went to this online encyclopedia that I saw an article about in the paper, and "Internet trends" had links to a bunch of things that seem to be popular, and now here's what I know:

- People like to take pictures of their cats and put funny, badly spelled captions on them. They have a certain charm, don't they? My favorite one so far is the one with the kitten in the tissue box that says "When out of tissues, a cat is fine too". It seems like something I should have in my office, to offset that stack of Kleenex boxes you love to make fun of.
- "Memes" are things that are popular on the Internet. (Is that right?)
- That boy who plays the vampire in the "Twilight" series seems to have a lot of stalkers. He's popular on the Internet, but I don't think he's a meme, because he's a person, not a thing. Is that right?
- There is a site called Urban Dictionary that will tell me lots more about current slang and Internet expressions, but it does seem to focus rather narrowly on the filthier side of things.
- There is also a site called Snopes that I can use to get people to stop sending me forwarded emails. Thank the Lord!
- On that note, the deposed king of Nigeria doesn't really need my bank account information. This is good news. I was worried about the poor soul.

I'm not sure that I know that much more about the Internet as a whole than I did when I started, but it definitely seems like a much more entertaining place than it did before. What would you add to all of this to round out the list of things I should know? Think about it, and maybe we can talk about it next session.

--Nora

Notice: This email contains PRIVILEGED AND CONFIDENTIAL INFORMATION for the intended recipient(s). If you are not the intended recipient of this email or the agent responsible for delivering it to the intended recipient, you are hereby notified that any dissemination or copying of this email and its attachments is strictly prohibited. If you received this in error, please immediately notify me at the address above, and permanently delete the email and all files from your computer. This statement is in accordance and compliance with the Health Insurance Portability and Accountability Act (HIPAA).

* * *

http://www.diarynow.com/users/thejanethe/69860.html
Date: 3/22/2013
Security level: Private

OMG U R SOOOOOOOOOOOOOOOO KEWL DOCTOR NORA LADY ::facepalm:: ::facepalm:: ::FACEPALM::
On the plus side, if she is trying to be funny, she is in fact succeeding. In fact, she is being far funnier than she could ever have dreamed of being. Not in a good way, precisely. But still, very funny. Much more entertaining than Meisner. If the worst she is planning on slinging at me is questions as to whether Robert Pattinson is a meme (HAHAHAHAHAHAHAHA), I can handle her, no sweat.

(I do not even want to picture her reading UrbanDictionary, omg, it should be illegal for anyone over the age of 20 to read that site)

thejanethe (3:36:02 PM): WHAT THE HELL

thejanethe (3:36:02 PM): Did you do it?!

RawKdaSkEEbaLL (3:36:04 PM): woah whaht

thejanethe (3:36:05 PM): Tell Jason Malone that I write LtT fanfic!!!

thejanethe (3:36:05 PM): It has to have been you, NO ONE ELSE KNOWS

thejanethe (3:36:06 PM): How could you do that to me?!

RawKdaSkEEbaLL (3:36:07 PM): wait wait wiat

RawKdaSkEEbaLL (3:36:09 PM): I dident tell anyone

RawKdaSkEEbaLL (3:36:11 PM): not Jason or noone

thejanethe (3:36:12 PM): Then how did he find out?!

thejanethe (3:36:12 PM): omg, I so can't deal with this

RawKdaSkEEbaLL (3:36:15 PM): hold on slow donw

RawKdaSkEEbaLL (3:36:17 PM): waht hapened exactley

thejanethe (3:36:18 PM): JASON MALONE FOUND OUT I WRITE LOOK TO TOMORROW FANFIC IS WHAT HAPPENED

thejanethe (3:36:19 PM): Jesus

> **Audra S** (3:36:19 PM): Hey Rach, you there?
>
> **Rachel W** (3:36:27 PM): oh
>
> **Rachel W** (3:36:27 PM): yeah
>
> **Rachel W** (3:36:28 PM): Hi, Audra!

RawKdaSkEEbaLL (3:36:28 PM): ok see thats not slowing down :P

RawKdaSkEEbaLL (3:36:32 PM): srsly tell me wat hapened

RawKdaSkEEbaLL (3:36:37 PM):

I herd sumthin at scool from amy
goodman but she dident know much
abt it

thejanethe (3:36:38 PM): Amy
Goodman?

thejanethe (3:36:39 PM): She's not
even in that class!

> **Audra S** (3:36:41 PM): Sorry, am I
> catching you at a bad time?

> **Rachel W** (3:36:43 PM): No, no, sorry,
> I just didn't know I was logged in here.

RawKdaSkEEbaLL (3:36:43 PM):
what class

> **Audra S** (3:36:44 PM): Yeah, that
> happens with FL chat sometimes.
> Whenever you're checking your page it
> assumes you're ready to chat. :)

thejanethe (3:36:44 PM): Oh, God, is
it already making the gossip rounds at
school?!

RawKdaSkEEbaLL (3:36:45 PM):
probly

RawKdaSkEEbaLL (3:36:47 PM):
what hapened??!

> **Audra S** (3:36:51 PM): I'll leave you
> alone if you're busy or something, I'm
> sorry.

> **Rachel W** (3:36:53 PM): No, don't
> worry about it.

> **Rachel W** (3:36:55 PM): What's up?

Audra S (3:36:59 PM): Oh, not that much.

thejanethe (3:37:00 PM): Okay.

thejanethe (3:37:02 PM): You really didn't tell Jason about the fanfic thing?

RawKdaSkEEbaLL (3:37:04 PM): no i nevr talk to him

RawKdaSkEEbaLL (3:37:05 PM): WHAT HAPENED

thejanethe (3:37:07 PM): Okay. ::deep breaths::

Rachel W (3:37:16 PM): :) "Not much" sounds nice.

RawKdaSkEEbaLL (3:37:17 PM): yea breatheing is good

Rachel W (3:37:28 PM): I'm in the middle of a crazy project for school.

RawKdaSkEEbaLL (3:37:29 PM): :)

Audra S (3:37:36 PM): Your school must be really rough, you have so many crazy projects. :)

Rachel W (3:37:38 PM): Eh, it's not that bad.

thejanethe (3:37:58 PM): Jason and I have English class together.

thejanethe (3:38:01 PM): We haven't exactly been getting along well this year.

RawKdaSkEEbaLL (3:38:04 PM): yea u sorta mencioned that b4?

thejanethe (3:38:07 PM): We used to be friends, like, back when we were five years old.

RawKdaSkEEbaLL (3:38:09 PM): rilly? i dident know that

thejanethe (3:38:11 PM): Yeah, it was a long time ago. We went to Starling Elementary together.

thejanethe (3:38:23 PM): So a few weeks ago he was trying to be cool and he told Bruno Vega and everyone else in English class that my dad's a drunk.

RawKdaSkEEbaLL (3:38:26 PM): u dident tell me that, that sux hardcore

RawKdaSkEEbaLL (3:38:27 PM): wut an asshole

thejanethe (3:38:29 PM): Yeah.

thejanethe (3:38:31 PM): So I told some people that Jason's first kiss was with a guy.

RawKdaSkEEbaLL (3:38:33 PM): omg u started tat rumor??? lol

thejanethe (3:38:35 PM): Dude, it is so TOTALLY not a rumor! I just sort of left out the part where he was seven years old.

Audra S (3:38:36 PM): Everything going all right for you?

RawKdaSkEEbaLL (3:38:38 PM):
huh>

> **Rachel W** (3:38:38 PM): Sure, why
> wouldn't it be?

thejanethe (3:38:40 PM): He used to
get along better with girls than with
boys when he was a kid. As opposed
to now when he doesn't get along with
anybody.

thejanethe (3:38:42 PM): He wanted
to have more friends who were boys,
though -- he was starting to figure out
it wasn't cool for all your friends to be
girls.

> **Audra S** (3:38:44 PM): Oh, I don't
> know. School stress sucks.

> **Rachel W** (3:38:45 PM): Eh, it's not so
> bad.

> **Audra S** (3:38:48 PM): Well, everyone
> has crises from time to time, don't
> they? :)

thejanethe (3:38:48 PM): Anyway, he
found out a couple of the girls he was
friends with had had a sleepover where
they decided to find out what kissing
was like by kissing each other. You
know, how seven-year-old girls do. So
he tried to kiss some boy in our grade.
He thought that would make them
friends.

RawKdaSkEEbaLL (3:38:50 PM):

> **Rachel W** (3:38:57 PM): Sure. Right now my great crisis is having to get through 400 pages of Middlemarch by tomorrow at one. :)

> **Audra S** (3:39:02 PM): Oh, I'm sorry. I should let you get to that.

thejanethe (3:39:02 PM): Yeah, that's Jason. As socially clueless at seven as he is at fifteen.

RawKdaSkEEbaLL (3:39:03 PM): hay do girls still do that

thejanethe (3:39:05 PM): ...dude, do you want to hear this story or not?!

RawKdaSkEEbaLL (3:39:06 PM): yea sorrey

thejanethe (3:39:09 PM): ANYWAY. Jason had to know I was the one who told people that, because no one else knew. But there wasn't much he could do about it, so I figured that was that.

thejanethe (3:39:16 PM): Then today Ms. Frolich had to leave the room to go spike her coffee with kahlua or whatever. You know how she still thinks appointing a student proctor will keep everyone in line while she's gone.

> **Rachel W** (3:39:25 PM): No, no, I'm mid-procrastination. :)

RawKdaSkEEbaLL (3:39:25 PM): yea she needs to hook up with aa or sumthing

RawKdaSkEEbaLL (3:39:27 PM): neway go on

> **Audra S** (3:39:28 PM): You just seem so rushed sometimes.

thejanethe (3:39:28 PM): So I was writing fic in my notebook and Jason started giving me shit.

> **Audra S** (3:39:35 PM): You know, if the stress is ever getting to you or whatever, I'm here to talk.

RawKdaSkEEbaLL (3:39:36 PM): coud he c what you were writting

thejanethe (3:39:37 PM): NO. I'll get to that in a minute, hold on.

RawKdaSkEEbaLL (3:39:38 PM): ok

thejanethe (3:39:40 PM): He was hamming it up for Bruno or whoever, and then all of a sudden he's like, "She's writing stories about Brad Memphis."

thejanethe (3:39:41 PM): IN FRONT OF THE WHOLE CLASS

thejanethe (3:39:43 PM): Everyone was staring. Everyone. You know how Jason gets when he gets going, all loud and stupid and, like with the gestures and shit, and -- oh, fuck

thejanethe (3:39:44 PM): Then HE

GRABBED MY NOTEBOOK AND
TRIED TO READ IT OUT LOUD

RawKdaSkEEbaLL (3:39:46 PM):
tryed 2?

thejanethe (3:39:47 PM): Yeah, that
was kind of awesome, even if the rest of
it sucked hardcore.

thejanethe (3:39:48 PM): You
remember when you saw some of my
fanfic in my notebook?

RawKdaSkEEbaLL (3:39:51 PM): yea
thats y i wonderd if he saw it 2?

thejanethe (3:39:52 PM): No, no. After
that I got nervous about writing fanfic
in school, especially because I'm doing
so much more of it now.

RawKdaSkEEbaLL (3:39:53 PM): yea
y is that

thejanethe (3:39:54 PM): Hold ON.
After you saw my fic I learned how to
write in mirror writing.

RawKdaSkEEbaLL (3:39:56 PM):
mirror writting?

thejanethe (3:39:57 PM): Yeah, you
know, in reverse, so you can only read
it in a mirror?

RawKdaSkEEbaLL (3:39:59 PM):
rilly?

thejanethe (3:40:01 PM): Yeah. In
cursive.

thejanethe (3:40:03 PM): If you don't know what it is, it's really hard to tell. I can read it and write it now, but no one can read what I've written.

RawKdaSkEEbaLL (3:40:04 PM): wow thats cool

RawKdaSkEEbaLL (3:40:06 PM): ull have 2 show me sumtime

thejanethe (3:40:06 PM): Well, it sure surprised the hell out of Jason.

RawKdaSkEEbaLL (3:40:07 PM): haha

> **Audra S** (3:40:09 PM): Rach?

> **Rachel W** (3:40:11 PM): Sorry, I was away for a second.

> **Rachel W** (3:40:11 PM): Really, everything's fine.

> **Rachel W** (3:40:12 PM): I'm lucky, I guess. My life seems to be totally resistant to major crises. LOL

RawKdaSkEEbaLL (3:40:14 PM): wut hapend?

> **Audra S** (3:40:15 PM): I wish mine were so resistant.

thejanethe (3:40:15 PM): He grabbed the notebook from me, and, you know, I was already freaking out.

thejanethe (3:40:19 PM): Like, I just -- I'm sorry I ragged on you, but I totally thought you told him, and I still

121

don't know how he knew, and when he grabbed the book like even though logically I should have known he couldn't read it it just felt like -- I don't know -- the whole book is personal.

thejanethe (3:40:20 PM): I don't know. I was flipping out.

thejanethe (3:40:21 PM): But of course he got hold of it and he couldn't read a word of it.

thejanethe (3:40:24 PM): And he's standing there with the whole class watching him, and this expression is slowly dawning on his face, and the whole thing started to switch gears.

thejanethe (3:40:25 PM): Because the expression on his face totally said "I can't read."

RawKdaSkEEbaLL (3:40:26 PM): haha o shit

RawKdaSkEEbaLL (3:40:29 PM): i sorta feel bad 4 him tho i think he mite be dislexic like me

thejanethe (3:40:29 PM): DON'T

        Rachel W (3:40:30 PM): Aww.

        Rachel W (3:40:31 PM): Still haven't heard back from that guy?

RawKdaSkEEbaLL (3:40:31 PM): that woud be embarasing if he isnt a good reader alredy

thejanethe (3:40:32 PM): He is SO not worth your pity, dude

RawKdaSkEEbaLL (3:40:33 PM): ok ok

> **Audra S** (3:40:34 PM): Well, no.
>
> **Rachel W** (3:40:35 PM): Don't worry about it. I'm sure he'll call.
>
> **Rachel W** (3:40:36 PM): You're too awesome for him to pass up. ;)

thejanethe (3:40:37 PM): So he's just standing there, shifting from foot to foot, his face almost as red as his acne. And then he starts MAKING STUFF UP.

thejanethe (3:40:38 PM): It just -- I can't even write down the stuff he was saying. oh my god

RawKdaSkEEbaLL (3:40:39 PM): did ppl think u wrote what he said

thejanethe (3:40:41 PM): No, it was pretty obvious he was making it up. He is not very good at improvising.

RawKdaSkEEbaLL (3:40:42 PM): yea i bet

> **Audra S** (3:40:43 PM): Well, thanks.

thejanethe (3:40:46 PM): Mostly he just looked like a moron some more, and people started laughing at him instead of me, and then Mrs. Frolich came back and whatever.

thejanethe (3:40:48 PM): But it was still incredibly embarrassing! Everything he was saying was really sexual and gross and oh, jesus

        Audra S (3:40:51 PM): I'm sorry if I'm bugging you, you seem distracted.

thejanethe (3:40:51 PM): And I still don't know HOW HE KNEW

thejanethe (3:40:53 PM): omg I SO CAN'T DEAL WITH THIS everyone will know now!!!!

        Audra S (3:40:54 PM): I guess I'm just feeling a little blue today.

RawKdaSkEEbaLL (3:40:55 PM): no hold on tho

RawKdaSkEEbaLL (3:40:58 PM): whaht dd he say abt what u were writting exactly

RawKdaSkEEbaLL (3:41:00 PM): did he say u were writting fanfictons?

thejanethe (3:41:02 PM): No, he said "stories about Brad Memphis", but what the hell ELSE is that going to mean??/

RawKdaSkEEbaLL (3:41:04 PM): but mayb he dident know u write fanficts

RawKdaSkEEbaLL (3:41:06 PM): maybe he just made that up abt brad mempis

RawKdaSkEEbaLL (3:41:10 PM): i

124

mean like evry1 knows u like him rite?
& u were writting in ur notebook so
mayb he just made it up abt the storys
sence he knows u like brad

thejanethe (3:41:12 PM): What do
you mean, everyone knows I like him?
How would everyone know? Are you
going around saying THAT instead?
Because that is SO not any better, Gary,
I swear to God!

RawKdaSkEEbaLL (3:41:14 PM): i
dont go around talking abt u ok

RawKdaSkEEbaLL (3:41:16 PM):
dude u have like 10 picturs of him in ur
locker

thejanethe (3:41:16 PM): Not
ten! Four, maybe!

RawKdaSkEEbaLL (3:41:17 PM): ok
4 then

RawKdaSkEEbaLL (3:41:18 PM): its
still alot

RawKdaSkEEbaLL (3:41:20 PM): &
ppl can still see wen they go bye

RawKdaSkEEbaLL (3:41:22 PM):
mayb jason just saw the pictures &
decided 2 mess w/ u abt it

thejanethe (3:41:23 PM): ...I don't
know

thejanethe (3:41:24 PM): That's not
exactly less embarrassing

RawKdaSkEEbaLL (3:41:26 PM): y is it so embarassing neway

> **Rachel W** (3:41:28 PM): Aww, hon. ::hugs::
>
> **Rachel W** (3:41:30 PM): You're not bugging me. Sorry I'm distracted, I'm just running around like a madwoman

RawKdaSkEEbaLL (3:41:30 PM): so u like a tv show & u write storys abt it

RawKdaSkEEbaLL (3:41:31 PM): so wut?

> **Rachel W** (3:41:37 PM): Hey, nothing to fix a case of the blues like a pint of Ben & Jerry's and an extended marathon of undiluted Brad, huh? :)

thejanethe (3:41:38 PM): oh, I don't know

> **Audra S** (3:41:39 PM): Nothing like it!

thejanethe (3:41:40 PM): it's really hard to explain

> **Audra S** (3:41:42 PM): That sounds good, I think I'll do that.
>
> **Rachel W** (3:41:43 PM): :) I hope it helps!
>
> **Audra S** (3:41:43 PM): Later!
>
> **Rachel W** (3:41:44 PM): Later, Aud!

thejanethe (3:41:51 PM): It just makes me feel... vulnerable, or something?

thejanethe (3:41:58 PM): Like... people aren't supposed to like TV shows this much. It... I don't know.

RawKdaSkEEbaLL (3:42:00 PM): lots of ppl are rilly into difrent tv shows

RawKdaSkEEbaLL (3:42:02 PM): ltt has lots of fans even

thejanethe (3:42:11 PM): No, but... it's not that.

thejanethe (3:42:13 PM): The whole fanfic thing... I don't know, it's really personal.

RawKdaSkEEbaLL (3:42:16 PM): yea u said that b4

RawKdaSkEEbaLL (3:42:18 PM): i dont rilly get it?

RawKdaSkEEbaLL (3:42:21 PM): cuz ppl online read ur fanfics rite

thejanethe (3:42:23 PM): That's totally different. Those are people who are in the fandom too. They... I don't know, they get where I'm coming from.

thejanethe (3:42:24 PM): It's TOTALLY different to have people at school know about it.

RawKdaSkEEbaLL (3:42:26 PM): but how come

thejanethe (3:42:27 PM): I DON'T KNOW, dude, it just is

RawKdaSkEEbaLL (3:42:29 PM): ok ok ok

thejanethe (3:42:39 PM): It's just really important to me. And it's how I ESCAPE from all of the bullshit at school.

thejanethe (3:42:43 PM): It was really awful to have Jason make it part of all that. Like it makes it less of an escape.

thejanethe (3:42:46 PM): It's been my private world, you know? It was... really awful to have Jason take that away.

RawKdaSkEEbaLL (3:42:48 PM): that sux :(

thejanethe (3:42:53 PM): And I can't deal with the thought of Bruno and Andrew and all them making fun of me for liking Brad. Doing all the disgusting stuff they do to the girls they choose to pick on, you know. I've been really lucky I've slipped under their radar.

thejanethe (3:42:56 PM): You know how they treat Claudia and Jessica and them. Sticking their tongues in their cheeks or their fingers in their mouths whenever they walk by. The thing with Claudia's locker.

RawKdaSkEEbaLL (3:43:01 PM): ok 1st thing the claudia thing is b/c her & bruno broke up

RawKdaSkEEbaLL (3:43:04 PM): theyre not gunna treat u like her, thats totalley difrent

RawKdaSkEEbaLL (3:43:07 PM): & 2nd thing if they try anything w/ u i will kick their ass

thejanethe (3:43:08 PM): Gary!

RawKdaSkEEbaLL (3:43:10 PM): i'm so serius

RawKdaSkEEbaLL (3:43:11 PM): i totalley will

thejanethe (3:43:13 PM): Gary, that's really sweet, but PLEASE don't fight Bruno Vega. LOL

RawKdaSkEEbaLL (3:43:14 PM): what u think i cant take him??

thejanethe (3:43:16 PM): ...do you want me to be honest here? LOL

RawKdaSkEEbaLL (3:43:18 PM): HEY

RawKdaSkEEbaLL (3:43:20 PM): i know some karrate & stuff

thejanethe (3:43:21 PM): ...you do?

RawKdaSkEEbaLL (3:43:22 PM): ok no

RawKdaSkEEbaLL (3:43:25 PM): but i can lern

RawKdaSkEEbaLL (3:43:28 PM): & he mite be scared cuz us asians all know karrate rite

thejanethe (3:43:29 PM): ROFLMAO

thejanethe (3:43:31 PM): I think they might know your interests run more to Skee-ball.

RawKdaSkEEbaLL (3:43:33 PM): ok so ill throw a skeeball @ his head

thejanethe (3:43:34 PM): LOL Now, see, one of your spin shots might actually do some damage.

RawKdaSkEEbaLL (3:43:38 PM): neway maybe im not gunna fight bruno

thejanethe (3:43:39 PM): GOOD.

RawKdaSkEEbaLL (3:43:42 PM): but i coud ttly take jason malone

thejanethe (3:43:44 PM): Heh. You probably could.

thejanethe (3:43:46 PM): But seriously, don't pick any fights, with Jason or anybody. I don't want your death on my conscience. ;)

RawKdaSkEEbaLL (3:43:49 PM): u have so litle faith in me

thejanethe (3:43:50 PM): I'll be fine.

thejanethe (3:44:03 PM): Today could have been worse... nothing *actually* got spilled, I guess

thejanethe (3:44:05 PM): I like your idea that he could have just been talking about the pictures in my locker...

RawKdaSkEEbaLL (3:44:08 PM): yea he probly was

thejanethe (3:44:10 PM): I think Jason came off worse in the whole thing than I did.

RawKdaSkEEbaLL (3:44:13 PM): yea it sounds like it

thejanethe (3:44:14 PM): What did Amy say about it though?

RawKdaSkEEbaLL (3:44:16 PM): not much

thejanethe (3:44:18 PM): Is that code for "I don't want to tell you"?

RawKdaSkEEbaLL (3:44:21 PM): no she dident rilly know much

RawKdaSkEEbaLL (3:44:24 PM): she said u got upset w/ jason or sumthin thats all

thejanethe (3:44:36 PM): Yeah. I... yeah. I was pretty upset.

thejanethe (3:44:41 PM): That was the worst part of it. Like, if he really doesn't know anything, then whatever, it shouldn't have been a big deal, right?

thejanethe (3:44:44 PM): But I was... well, kind of crying. In the middle of class. I don't know if anyone noticed, it's not like I burst out into sobs or anything, but... yeah.

thejanethe (3:44:48 PM): I'm worried that even if no one believed what he was going on about beforehand, my reaction gave me away.

RawKdaSkEEbaLL (3:44:51 PM): im sorrey

thejanethe (3:44:53 PM): It's okay.

thejanethe (3:45:06 PM): All I know is that he's not getting away with this.

RawKdaSkEEbaLL (3:45:07 PM): huh?

RawKdaSkEEbaLL (3:45:10 PM): what r u gunna do, fight him urself :)

thejanethe (3:45:13 PM): No. My getting beaten up by Jason Malone does not equal him not getting away with it. :P

thejanethe (3:45:16 PM): No, I don't know what I'm going to do yet.

thejanethe (3:45:18 PM): Something, though.

RawKdaSkEEbaLL (3:45:20 PM): yea i cant wait 2 c

thejanethe (3:45:24 PM): Look, DON'T TELL ANYONE I'm planning to get him back. I want him to think I forgot about it.

RawKdaSkEEbaLL (3:45:26 PM): mayb u will forget abt it :)

thejanethe (3:45:28 PM): ...no.

RawKdaSkEEbaLL (3:45:31 PM): & dude i dont go around talking abt u

RawKdaSkEEbaLL (3:45:33 PM): i dont know how come ur so possitive i do

thejanethe (3:45:35 PM): I don't know. Sorry. I know you didn't tell anyone about the fanfic thing.

RawKdaSkEEbaLL (3:45:36 PM): no

thejanethe (3:45:52 PM): Okay. I'm going to try to figure this out. Or something.

RawKdaSkEEbaLL (3:45:54 PM): just relax ok?

thejanethe (3:45:56 PM): I'll try.

thejanethe (3:45:57 PM): Thanks, Gary.

RawKdaSkEEbaLL (3:45:48 PM): ok

RawKdaSkEEbaLL (3:45:51 PM): call me if u want 2 talk latr?

thejanethe (3:45:52 PM): Okay.

thejanethe (3:45:52 PM): Bye for now.

RawKdaSkEEbaLL (3:45:53 PM): l8r :)

http://www.talesoftomorrow.com/pt/6841.html
Title: *Event Horizon*
Author: Rachel (racheltessers@yippee.com)
Pairing: Gen
Type: Drabble
Author's Notes: Set in the time frame of "Hell Jar". Jaela's perspective.

I would have expected it to be cold. All speculation, of course; no one gets sucked into a black hole and comes out to tell about it. God knows where they wind up -- where I'm going to wind up. There's no empirical evidence for me to go by here.

What I didn't expect, what I should have, is how completely time stops. I'm just here, hovering between two universes. I'm being dragged towards an entirely new reality, but I can't feel the pull; I'll never see the people I love again, but I can't feel the distance. All I feel is suspension. And the only plus to the stopping of time is that it leaves no time to feel the terror.

And if I wind up dead, it might be all for the best.

From: "System Administrator" sysadmin@spectrum.org
To: janeshilling@spectrum.org
Subject: Automatic Notification: Mailbox size exceeds limit
Date: 3/30/2013

Your mailbox has exceeded one or more size limits set by your administrator.

Your mailbox size is 22148 KB.

Mailbox size limits: 20000 KB.

You cannot send or receive mail when your mailbox reaches 21000 KB. You may not be able to send or receive new mail until you reduce your mailbox size.

To make more space available, delete any items that you are no longer using. You may find it helpful to begin with old items, or items with large attachments.

Items in all of your mailbox folders, including the Deleted Items and Sent Items folders, count against your size limit.

You must empty the Deleted Items folder after deleting items or the space will not be freed.

To: janeshilling@spectrum.org
From: jessieshill@owletpublishers.com
Subject: Banned Books Week
Date: 5/14/2012

Hi sweetie,

I forgot to mention this morning -- could you ask Mrs. Elsing if she needs any parental help with Banned Books Week next September, and if so, could you get a list of any books there's been a fuss over this year? I'd email her directly but she never seems to check her Spectrum email. Tell her I'd like to help, but I'll need to work around the Arizona trip, so I'd prefer to get the info sooner than later. Of course, there's no way you could possibly see this email or respond to it unless you're checking your e-mail on the sly during your computer class, so I'm sure I'll just have to mention it to you again tomorrow, huh?   Because my Janiekins would _never_ do a thing like that.

Speaking of Arizona, you could use some new clothes for the summer, couldn't you? If so, we should go shopping before I go. Pick a weekend, and I'll put it in my calendar.

Love,
Mom

* * *

To: jessieshill@owletpublishers.com
From: janeshilling@spectrum.org
Date: 5/13/2012
Subject: Re: Banned Books Week

Mom -- What am I, four? Can we quit with the "Janiekins" stuff?

I hate clothes shopping. Can't I just wait until the weather gets warm and go with Dad if I need more stuff?

Also, for your information, I'm in study hall, not computer class. Checking email from the computer lab during study is totally legit.

J

To: janeshilling@spectrum.org
From: jessieshill@owletpublishers.com
Date: 5/13/2012
Subject: Re: Re: Banned Books Week

"J --"

I was at your christening. You've been my Janiekins ever since. Itchy kitchy kootchy coo.

As for the clothes shopping, I'd rather go with you myself, if you can stand it. I need to make a mall trip to get clothes for myself for the trip anyway, so we may as well do it all together. And we could have a nice day together before I go. We'll hit the bookstore, eat at Mollie's, the whole deal. What say?

M

* * *

To: jessieshill@owletpublishers.com
From: janeshilling@spectrum.org
Date: 5/13/2012
Subject: Re: Re: Re: Banned Books Week

I was at my christening too and JANIEKINS IS NOT MY NAME. That nickname practically constitutes child abuse -- cut it out before I report you to DSS. Also, kootchy coo yourself.

I still think we could go out to Mollie's and the bookstore and skip the clothes. Why do you need new clothes for Arizona anyway? Do you have to dress in desert tones before they let you across state lines?

JANE

* * *

To: janeshilling@spectrum.org
From: jessieshill@owletpublishers.com
Date: 5/13/2012
Subject: Re: Re: Re: Re: Banned Books Week

Oh _fine_. Stop growing up, would you?

You know, for all that everyone thinks of you as my little clone, at times you're your father's daughter through and through. How is it that I have to _convince_ my daughter to go clothes shopping? Anyway, pick a date.

Mom

* * *

To: janeshilling@spectrum.org
From: jessieshill@owletpublishers.com
Date: 5/13/2012
Subject: I CHANGE THE SUBJECT LINE IN VICTORY

Saturday the 24th, how about. *Maybe* we'll do clothes.
Jane

* * *

To: janeshilling@spectrum.org
Cc: dennshill@yippee.com
From: jessieshill@owletpublishers.com
Date: 5/13/2012
Subject: Re: I CHANGE THE SUBJECT LINE IN VICTORY

Jane,

In your triumphant capslock I'm guessing you've forgotten to ask Mrs. Elsing about Banned Books Week? Let me know -- I may be able to get her discount copies on the ones that Owlet prints, assuming there are any, but only if she gives me enough notice. Also, your father will have to pick you up today -- see below.

Dennis,

I'm going to be running a little late at work. Would you mind picking Jane up from school and throwing together some supper? I'll be home by six at the latest.

Love,
Mom

136

To: janeshilling@spectrum.org, jessieshill@owletpublishers.com
From: dennshill@yippee.com
Date: 5/13/2012
Subject: Re: Re: I CHANGE THE SUBJECT LINE IN VICTORY

double-jays--
I will handle dinner. Does pepperoni sound good
d

***

To: jessieshill@owletpublishers.com, dennshill@yippee.com
From: janeshilling@spectrum.org
Date: 5/13/2012
Subject: Re: Re: Re: I CHANGE THE SUBJECT LINE IN VICTORY

It's so nice to have a hardworking gourmet chef in the family. Pepperoni
and extra cheese, please. -Jane

To: janeshilling@spectrum.org, dennshill@yippee.com
From: jessieshill@owletpublishers.com
Date: 5/13/2012
Subject: Re: Re: Re: Re: I CHANGE THE SUBJECT LINE IN VICTORY

Caesar salad for me, thanks, dressing on the side. From MJ's?
And Jane, how are you replying to your email hours after your study
hall ended? I don't want to get another email from your guidance counselor
telling me you're cutting class to hang out in the computer lab, do you
understand? Neither of us will be happy if I wind up going back to calling
the school every week to make sure you're going to classes, but I will if I
have to, so get to class.
Mom

To: jessieshill@owletpublishers.com, dennshill@yippee.com
From: janeshilling@spectrum.org
Subject: Re: Re: Re: Re: Re: I CHANGE THE SUBJECT LINE IN VICTORY
Date: 5/13/2012

Mom -- chill. We're between classes. Checking email on my cell. --J

* * *

To: jessieshill@owletpublishers.com, dennshill@yippee.com
From: janeshilling@spectrum.org
Subject: Re: Re: Re: Re: Re: Re: I CHANGE THE SUBJECT LINE IN
VICTORY
Date: 5/13/2012

Mjs it will be. 1 ceasar salad 1 large pizza extra cheese extra pepp. Jane,
your chariot will be waiting at 2:45. Also listen to your mother & go to
your classes young lady. I got tix for us to go to the pawsox game this
weekend but if your behind on your schoolwork you will be at home doing
homework while your mother & I go. - d

* * *

To: dennshill@yippee.com, janeshilling@spectrum.org
From: jessieshill@owletpublishers.com,
Subject: Re: Re: Re: Re: Re: Re: Re: I CHANGE THE SUBJECT LINE IN
VICTORY
Date: 5/13/2012

Dennis, are you asking me on a date? Because I can call Jane's teachers
and ask them to assign her extra schoolwork. -Jessie

To: <u>dennshill@yippee.com</u>, <u>janeshilling@spectrum.org</u>
From: <u>jessieshill@owletpublishers.com</u>,
Subject: Re: Re: Re: Re: Re: Re: I CHANGE THE SUBJECT LINE IN VICTORY
Date: 5/13/2012

    Ew, you guys, can you not cc me on your marital flirtation? Dad, it's 2:53, where are you? -J

From: margaretbaker@spectrum.org
To: janeshilling@spectrum.org
Subject: Missing homework assignments
Date: 3/30/2013
Attachments:

> Feb12.PDF
> Feb17.PDF
> Feb18.PDF
> Feb23.PDF
> Feb24.PDF
> Feb26.PDF
> Feb27.PDF
> Mar2.PDF
> Mar3.PDF
> Mar4.PDF
> Mar10.PDF
> Mar12.PDF
> Mar16.PDF
> Mar17.PDF
> Mar18.PDF
> Mar23.PDF
> Mar24.PDF
> Mar25.PDF
> Mar26.PDF

Dear Jane:

Attached to this email are the 19 homework assignments you have missed since the last time I emailed you. This makes a total of 23 assignments you have not turned in.

I have attempted repeatedly to schedule meetings with you and with your father. You've ignored every request I've made to speak with you after class, every note I've sent to your homeroom, and every attempt I've made to work with the administration to help you get on the ball. The few times I have spoken to you one-on-one, you stare right through me. You remain entirely withdrawn in class, and you've missed two tests and performed poorly on two others.

There isn't going to be a magic bullet that will fix all of these problems from you. As I told you in one of the one-sided conversations I had with you, you may turn in a written thesis as an extra-credit project to boost your grade, but I will not accept it as a substitute for a term's work.

I need to tell you that your behavior is entirely unacceptable, and although the rest of the school seems to be willing to let you continue to refuse to put in any effort, I am not. If you believe that you can continue to skate by on your innate intelligence, you are mistaken. I am not interested in enabling you to waste your abilities by allowing you a free pass to ignore all your responsibilities without consequence. If you don't pull yourself together soon, you will be attending summer school. Consider this an unofficial but very serious warning. Your performance in the next month will determine whether or not you will pass my class for the year.

Please speak with me after class regarding the schedule on which you will make up your 23 missing homework assignments.

Sincerely,

Mrs. Baker

http://www.diarynow.com/users/thejanethe/48452.html
Date: 3/30/2013
Security level: Private
Mood: numb

No. She can't do that.

She floods my inbox, she makes me go through all my old emails and -- and -- never mind, I just had to go sorting through all this shit to make room (NINETEEN GIANT PDF FILES IS SHE OUT OF HER MIND) and now she's threatening me with *summer school*?

She *can't* make me go to summer school. No. Just... no!

This is not happening. This is SO not happening. No, no, forget it! This is ridiculous -- she should be sued for talking to people like this. This is Spectrum! The whole point is that they're supposed to help kids, not just -- I don't know -- hammer at them and insult them and then send them to summer school! What the hell is wrong with an end-of-term thesis? So I learn at my own pace! That's why I'm at an ALTERNATIVE school! And if she has a problem with the way I act in her class, she ought to consider how SHE'S treating ME. What, I'm supposed to be all sweetness and light when she's treating me like a total piece of shit? All she ever does is make a huge big show of writing down a zero next to my name whenever she collects homework -- and then she calls on me in class, like, every two seconds, as though I'm going to start getting embarrassed and do all the work just so I can give the right answer or something. And just... all the shit she's saying... where the *fuck* did this woman get the idea that *humiliation* was an appropriate motivational tactic at *Spectrum Alternative High?*

She's just exactly like every teacher I ever had back in mainstream school, and I can't deal with it. Every time I see her, every time I sit down in her class, I feel as horrible as I did every day of my life back at in elementary and middle school, when I was anxious all the time and the teachers were always snapping at me for not paying attention and insisting that if I was so good at English I must be faking all this other stuff, like how I still can't really tell time on a non-digital clock or how I couldn't learn my times tables until I thought to study them written out in words in like sixth grade. And people kept basically insisting that learning disabilities and anxiety and stuff were, like, imaginary concepts and that if I just applied myself... you know, whatever! It doesn't matter. The point is that Mrs. Baker is exactly like the mainstream teachers, she doesn't CARE what issues we have, everyone just has to act like they're normal and it's all their fault if they can't do it and I seriously CAN'T and WTF am I supposed to do? Does she think it somehow makes everything better for her to make me feel COMPLETELY HORRIBLE? Like, why does she think I don't pay attention in class in the first place? Why does she think I focus on the stuff I can do and shut out the stuff I can't do? Because the stuff I can't do makes me feel like a piece of shit!

And the way she's treating me is bad enough, but now she's threatening everything that really does matter. How am I supposed to win the Lookies if I can't write during class? The deadline's coming up in three weeks and the fic is not working out at *all*. It's so stupid -- I'm working on three fics right now plus a bunch of one-shots, and Rachel's popularity is soaring just like I thought it would, but the one fic that I'm writing for the contest is coming out horrible. I'm not getting the hang of screenplay format at all. Honestly, I'm starting to feel like spec scripts and fanfics are just too different from one another... but I'm not going down that road. I've already decided what I'm going to do.

But I'm completely freaking out. Ever since the day they announced the new Lookies prize I've been staking my whole future on winning, you know? I need to win. I need to have this opportunity to make it, I need to... I just need to get out of here! The Lookies are my only chance. And now the fanfic's going really badly. And the auction's going really badly. Everyone wants to *have* an auction, but no one wants to do any work to actually make it happen, and I can't do it all myself -- people need to donate stuff, for Christ's sake. So I'm scared I won't win, and I'm scared if I win there won't be any script reading prize because the fandom won't hit the $15,000 and now Mrs. Baker is threatening me with summer school, and I just can't. The convention is on July 15. Dad would never let me go if I'm supposed to be in summer school. And, like, not that I couldn't sneak out in the middle of the night -- but... I'm afraid to do that. I'm seriously afraid it would kill Dad if he woke up one morning and found out I'd taken off on a trip to California.

Come to that, I'm pretty sure me winding up in summer school would kill him, too.

Why did she have to send those huge PDFs? Why did she have to make me go through all those old emails? None of this would be happening if Mom were here. She'd never let Mrs. Baker do this to me. I mean, she used to help me with my homework, and it's not like she let me get *away* with stuff or whatever -- she'd probably even get on my ass about the same stuff Mrs. Baker is complaining about, even, but she'd NEVER let someone talk to me that way. She always knew what it was like -- if anyone ever tried to lay shit on me because of my NLD or start demanding stuff I couldn't do, she fought them like a lynx -- she'd never let...

Fuck Mrs. Baker. She's giving me a fucking panic attack, and I haven't had one of those since Mom died. I am NOT letting her get to me like this, and I'm certainly not doing her 23 fucking homework assignments. I'll work something out -- talk to Mr. Sheehan or even the principal or something, I don't care. But I'm not letting her psych me into freaking out over *algebra homework* when the Lookies are at stake. When *my future* is at stake. My future away from all of this.

No way. No. Just, no.

http://www.diarynow.com/users/thejanethe/55502.html
Date: 4/1/2013
Security level: Private
Mood: jubilant

I. AM. AWESOME.

Hahahaha, I am SO PROUD of myself right now. You know what? Never let it be said that Jane Shilling will lie down and take shit from other people passively. I've been starting to feel helpless in the face of a lot of the crap that's been piling up lately -- Mrs. Baker being ridiculous, the parade of stupid therapists trying to get into my head, and Jason Malone on top of it all. Well, I don't have to take it anymore. I dealt with Jason Malone tonight, and rather awesomely, if I do say so myself. It's good to feel like I have some *power* over some of this shit for a change. I dealt with Ms. Meisner, I dealt with Jason Malone. I can figure out a way to deal with Mrs. Baker & Co. too. I am woman, hear me roar. ::pumps fist, Rosie-the-Riveter-style::

The Jason thing was ridiculously simple, too. I can't believe I never thought of it before. I kept tossing around these ideas for what to do, but somehow they were all school-based. I don't know why it never occurred to me that if I really wanted to get back at Jason, I'd probably do best sticking to my own home turf. I.e., the Internet.

But it all clicked when I was looking through my folder of alters earlier today. I was just trying to find some minor LtT alters, looking for someone who might be friendly with Jenna -- she's been really hush-hush about her Lookies fic and strategy, but I thought I had an old alter who'd kissed her ass a bit back in the day, and it was worth trying to get her to open up that way. It was weird looking through all my minor alters, though -- these imaginary people, most of whom I'd created on a whim one day when I was bored, posted or guest-chatted with once on FL, saved the chat, and never used them again. There was everything from a wiseass standup comic to a psych-ward inmate with a crayon-eating compulsion to Bristol Palin's best friend, all of them made back when I started making up alters and was just playing around, concocting crazy personas just because I could.

And then I came across Heather, the slutty cheerleader. And just like

145

that, the plan fell into place.

I did a FriendsLink search on Jason. He's in the Springfield network, I'm in the Springfield network; his entire pathetic profile was viewable. He'd been online since 3:20, precisely twenty minutes after school ended. Why wouldn't he be? At our school -- probably at everyone's school -- there's two kinds of kids: the kids who have someplace to hang out after school, and the kids who come home and go online. Jason is not and has never been in Group A. Which is kind of what I was counting on. I steadied myself for what was sure to be one of the least enjoyable online experiences of my life. Then I sent him a guest-chat request.

SexyHeather C (4:54:01 PM): hay sweet thang wuts goin on :-* :-*

It was all down to whether he would accept a guest-chat request from a girl named SexyHeather Cheergrl with a picture of a blonde girl in a skanky cheerleader outfit. You can imagine the suspense.

Jason M (4:54:04 PM): whose this

Yeah.

SexyHeather C (4:54:06 PM): o........ :-[

Jason M (4:54:08 PM): ?

SexyHeather C (4:54:09 PM): u dont know me but ive been tryin 2 get up the nerve 2 im u 5 awile

Jason M (4:54:11 PM): ur proffile says ur from denton?

SexyHeather C (4:54:13 PM): yea

Jason M (4:54:16 PM): so rite around here then

SexyHeather C (4:54:22 PM): yea i sortaaaa........ admiered u from affar? like?

Who the HELL would buy this? Jason, that's who. And if I hadn't figured he would I wouldn't have tried it in the first place.

Jason M (4:54:24 PM): oic

Jason M (4:54:25 PM): B-)

The sunglasses face. I shit you not.

Jason M (4:54:28 PM): so u didnt say where do i know u from?

SexyHeather C (4:54:30 PM): welllllll my cuzin iz anna cole

Jason M (4:54:33 PM): anna cole r u srs??

Very tactful, Jason. Anna Cole is the hottest, most popular girl at our school. She wouldn't spare Jason a glance if he was a piece of gum on her shoe. She wouldn't need to. There'd be plenty of boys crowding around begging to lick her shoe clean for her.

SexyHeather C (4:54:36 PM): yea, & she said u were rilly kewl

"Rilly kewl." Sometimes the stuff I type as Heather almost causes me physical pain.

Jason M (4:54:38 PM): rly?

Jason M (4:54:41 PM): yea ana & me r kinda tight

At that point I laughed so long and hard I almost forgot where I was.

SexyHeather C (4:54:48 PM): yea so.......... she pointed u out 2 me @ the mall when we were in hot topix...... u were bying sumthin w/ a silver skull on it

Mostly I just floated that one for my own amusement, even though it

147

was a completely unnecessary risk. I felt like an idiot for getting so cocky the second that I'd typed it. But I should have trusted my instincts more:

Jason M (4:54:52 PM): o yea i remember........ not liek i go their alot just that 1 time i liked that 1 chain

Uh-huh, like he's not in there every weekend.

SexyHeather C (4:54:54 PM): i know.......it wuz superkewl

Jason M (4:54:58 PM): u licked it?

I knew that was deliberate. Heather wouldn't know.

SexyHeather C (4:55:00 PM): yea alot

Jason M (4:55:02 PM): awsum

Jason M (4:55:07 PM): soooooooooooooo......... wutz up?

I chatted him up awhile. It got very, very boring. I pretended to be Very Interested in his status as a Super Awesome Sk8r D00d and blown away by how awesome Nine Inch Nails and Blink 182 are and completely weak in the knees over how amazingly hawt he is. 'Round about there I started gagging, but you can hide those things on the Internet! And I sent him some pictures of Heather, and he was very interested indeed, as he goddamn well should be given that her pictures are those of some chick on an amateur photo site who I'm pretty sure is an aspiring porn model. I don't know what goes on in Jason Malone's head, but he never did seem to ask himself, when faced with a super-hot girl slobbering all over him, what was wrong with this picture. Was he just that desperate to believe he could be popular? Or does he really have that inflated of an ego? The world will never know.

So here was how the crux of the conversation went down:

SexyHeather C (5:06:38 PM): sooooooooo........ maybe this iz lyke 2 forwerd or sumthin

SexyHeather C (5:06:40 PM): but...................

Jason M (5:06:41 PM): ?

SexyHeather C (5:06:43 PM): do u think we couldd meet?

Despite how well things had been going, I was nervous he wouldn't go for it. There's no one who's *really* dumb enough these days to arrange an in-person meeting with someone they met five minutes ago online, is there?

Jason M (5:06:48 PM): wen?

Apparently there is.

SexyHeather C (5:06:52 PM): tonite, if u can...... im just so exited were gettin along so well & i rilly wanna meet!!!!!!!!!!

Jason M (5:06:56 PM): tonite? wut time? & were?

SexyHeather C (5:06:58 PM): 630? @ the mall>

Jason M (5:07:03 PM): sure...... didnt have any big plans 4 tonite

Big shock there.

Jason M (5:07:07 PM): u wanna just grab a burger or sumthing

SexyHeather C (5:07:09 PM): y dont we see were the nite takes us

Long pause, then:

Jason M (5:07:33 PM): ok

Uh-huh.

SexyHeather C (5:07:36 PM): but jason im a litle afriad i wont reckonize u

Jason M (5:07:39 PM): y? u said ud seen me b4?

SexyHeather C (5:07:41 PM): yea and ur fl pics but its sometimes diffrent in person

SexyHeather C (5:07:44 PM) so i was wondrin

SexyHeather C (5:07:49 PM): mayb u coud ware somethin that i coud reckonize u by?

Jason M (5:07:52 PM): like wut?

SexyHeather C (5:07:56 PM) welllll... did u evr see those glowin the dark susspendars @ hot topix? they hav black skulls on tem?

The fact that Hot Topic actually sells glow-in-the-dark suspenders with black skulls on them made it clear to me that the universe was on my side here.

Jason M (5:07:59 PM) yea i saw them last time i was in their

Jason M (5:08:02 PM): y u licked them 2?

FFS Jason it was a TERRIBLE JOKE THE FIRST TIME

SexyHeather C (5:08:06 PM): yea!

SexyHeather C (5:08:08 PM): their so sexy

Jason M (5:08:10 PM): rly?

You know something's dorky when even Jason Malone knows it. Luckily I'd prepared for that eventuality.

SexyHeather C (5:08:13 PM): well i was thinkkin

SexyHeather C (5:08:16 PM): annas havin a rave 2nite

Because that's a thing tenth-graders do in the middle of the week.

Jason M (5:08:19 PM): o rite

Jason M (5:08:22 PM): i herd about that

BRB FACEPALMING FOREVER

SexyHeather C (5:08:24 PM): yea!

SexyHeather C (5:08:28 PM): I thot we cd go 2 that

Jason M (5:08:30 PM): word up

Word up?

SexyHeather C (5:08:34 PM): yea & if u wear glowin the dark it lookz soooo kewl under teh blacklites

Jason M (5:08:36 PM): rly?

Nope.

SexyHeather C (5:08:39 PM): yea deffinately :-*

Jason M (5:08:41 PM): ok

Jason M (5:08:44 PM): i cn get those from hot topix on my way

SexyHeather C (5:08:46 PM): awsum :-*

So, glow-in-the-dark suspenders were a go. Time for the punch line:

SexyHeather C (5:08:49 PM): but theres 1 more thing

SexyHeather C (5:08:52 PM): that woud be SOOOOOO amazing

SexyHeather C (5:08:55 PM): u know, bc i'm such a gurl, i like a romantic toutch :)

Jason M (5:08:59 PM): yea? liek wut

SexyHeather C (5:09:07PM): welllllll

SexyHeather C (5:09:09 PM): i know its rly silly

SexyHeather C (5:09:12 PM): but i alwayz lyked old movies

SexyHeather C (5:09:14 PM): lyke w/ carry grant & humpry bougart?

Jason M (5:09:17 PM): i dunno much about them

SexyHeather C (5:09:18 PM): their so sexy

SexyHeather C (5:09:21 PM): & so i have this thing about....... fedoras?

Jason M (5:09:24 PM): wut r those?

Oh, for Christ's sake.

SexyHeather C (5:09:25 PM): u know, the hats!

SexyHeather C (5:09:27 PM): they have a brim & their super sexxxy

SexyHeather C (5:09:30 PM): ur dad prolly has 1

I knew his dad had one, actually. There's a picture of a bunch of parents from our elementary school at a fundraiser the school had a long time ago -- one of those murder-mystery things where everyone shows up in historical costumes. The absolute, utter dorkiness of Jason's dad and his fedora in that picture was what gave me this whole idea.

Jason M (5:09:32 PM): i dunno

Jason M (5:09:35 PM): i never wear hatz cept for baseball caps

SexyHeather C (5:09:38 PM): i know most guys dont

SexyHeather C (5:09:40 PM): but ur not lyke most guys

SexyHeather C (5:09:43 PM): & their reeeeeeeeeally sexy

SexyHeather C (5:09:46 PM): maybe u could look in ur dads closet & c if he has 1?

Jason M (5:09:50 PM): no srsly i rilly dont like hats

SexyHeather C (5:09:56 PM): cmon, will u wear 1 just 4 me? look im takeing a pic w/ my camra phone -- heres me makeing a poutey face just 4 u

A pouty face, and a tank top cut about three millimeters above her nipples.

SexyHeather C (5:10:40 PM): so will u look in ur dads closet? :-*

Jason M (5:10:42 PM): hold on 1 sec

Jason looked. After a pause that seemed rather lengthier than it needed to be, a fedora was obtained. Photos were taken. Heather confirmed that it was, in fact, a fedora.

SexyHeather C (5:16:26 PM): purrrrrrrrrrrfect :)

Jason M (5:16:29 PM): i just tryed it on

Jason M (5:16:31 PM): i gess it looks ok

Jason M (5:16:35 PM): well anything lookz good on me B-)

AAARGH THE SUNGLASSES

SexyHeather C (5:16:36 PM): o & 1 more thing woud make it sooooo hott

SexyHeather C (5:16:39 PM): do u have a flower 2 put on it???

SexyHeather C (5:16:42 PM): like carry grant in the maltiese falcon

I don't know anything about Cary Grant. I don't know if he was in that movie. I don't know if he ever wore a fedora with a flower on it. I do know how to make a guy look stupid.

Jason M (5:16:44 PM): wat do u think i am a fag!!!!!!!!!!!!!!!

Don't be silly. If you were you'd have entirely too much fashion sense to let yourself be caught dead in public wearing your dad's dust-covered fedora. Especially not because some cheerleader girl sent you sexy pictures.

SexyHeather C (5:16:46 PM): plz i know it sounds wierd but u cd TOTALLEY carry it off

SexyHeather C (5:16:48 PM): & its just, lyke, my fave movie

SexyHeather C (5:16:51 PM): its alwayz been a fantasey of mine 2 date a guy waring a fedora w/ a flower

SexyHeather C (5:16:53 PM): here look, isnt it hott?????

Here I inserted a black-and-white picture I had photo-edited of Cary Grant wearing a fedora with a flower on the brim. It looked pretty good on him, actually, edited or not. That's because he's Cary Grant. Jason is not Cary Grant, although he seems somehow to have skated through fifteen years of life without becoming wholly aware of the fact.

SexyHeather C (5:17:06 PM): cmon i know none of te guyz @ ur school would wear sumthing lyke that....... but thats y i lyke U not THEM. ur so origginal

Jason M (5:17:08 PM): u think

SexyHeather C (5:17:11 PM): lyke theres ppl who follow trendz & ppl who set them

SexyHeather C (5:17:13 PM): i bet alot of guyz @ ur school wouldent shop @ hot topic

SexyHeather C (5:17:14 PM): & thats were i 1st knew i liked u :)

Jason M (5:17:16 PM): ....

Jason M (5:17:20 PM): well my mom has a gerraneum bush

OH MY GOD HE WAS GOING TO SHOW UP WEARING A GERANIUM ON A FEDORA. THIS WAS SO MUCH MORE AWESOME THAN I COULD EVER HAVE ANTICIPATED.

SexyHeather C (5:17:22 PM): omg!!!! that is SO PERFECT

Jason M (5:17:26 PM): ok ok

Jason M (5:17:30 PM): illl put it on like rite b4 we meet

Jason M (5:17:33 PM): witch reminds me were will we meet?

SexyHeather C (5:17:37 PM): how abt bartlys burgers

SexyHeather C (5:17:39 PM): at the mall?

Jason M (5:17:40 PM): awsum!!!!!

I knew there'd be tons of kids from school around the mall then. And Victoria's Secret is just across from Bartley's, the restaurant/ice cream shop where all the cool kids hang out for hours and occasionally leave without paying their bill. I figured he'd get noticed, but just in case, I knotted a scarf around my head and threw on one of Mom's old trench coats -- not strictly necessary for the proceedings, but it added nicely to the sense of intrigue -- and then grabbed my cell phone, complete with camera, and bused it out to the mall. I waited outside Victoria's Secret on a bench, noting with satisfaction that there was in fact a large group of cool kids, including none other than Anna Cole herself, sitting inside Bartley's. Jason showed up soon enough, wearing the suspenders and his fedora -- it had a *plaid lining* on the underside of the brim -- with the geranium perched uncertainly atop it. And, I kid you not, he was wearing those *fake nylon tattoo sleeves*. But his arms are too skinny. So they wrinkled around the elbows. And he was wearing the hideous Hot Topic skull chain that Heather said she loved. And I bet he felt like one sexy stud. But he clearly had enough sense to know that the hat, at least, was ridiculous, so instead of going into Bartley's to wait for Heather in the middle of the school crowd, he hung around outside. And the store across from Bartley's was Victoria's Secret. And there was a sales rack of lingerie outside. And he was nervous. So he started riffling through the lingerie.

I don't even know why I set up the whole thing with the hat. Clearly all I had to do was tell him to show up in public somewhere, and he'd take care of the rest.

So there he was, in full view of everyone at Bartley's, wearing two-inch-wide glow-in-the-dark suspenders with skulls on them and a fedora with a geranium on it, feeling up a rack of women's lingerie. He was fidgeting with the fedora the whole time and it was pretty clear the thing was going to come off in about two seconds if I didn't act immediately, so I snapped four pictures with my camera phone, then, adopting a cracked, hoarse voice as though I'd spent a lifetime smoking, I turned so my face was hidden from both Jason and the crowd in Bartley's and yelled "Oh my *God*, look at *that!*" I didn't turn to watch the heads swiveling -- the last thing I need is for Jason to track this back to me. But as I walked away, a few snickers and comments began to turn into a roar of laughter, and I figured I'd done enough. And when Jason, red-faced and panting, shoved by me at an all-out sprint as I strolled towards the exit a few minutes later (maybe Anna Cole had told him she didn't have a cousin Heather?), that pretty well confirmed it.

Just to be safe, I posted the pictures of him I took to a dummy FriendsLink that night and friended all the kids at school I could find.

I hope he's *writhing* right now. I hope he's gotten a million emails about it already. I hope the kids at school spend so much time laughing at him that they'll forget all about me. I almost hope he *does* figure out it was me who did this. The logical part of me knows he'll probably beat me up if he figures it out, but what the hell. He ought to know who did this and

156

why. He's a wimp and he deserves every bit of this -- deserves MORE than this, actually. This was fun but it doesn't begin to even the score. The score won't be even until I get hold of a secret every bit as personal and awful as what he spilled about me, and tell the whole school about *it*.

But for now, this is pretty awesome.

Dude. I SO RULE.

thejanethe (11:43:09 AM): HAHAHAHAHAHAHA

thejanethe (11:43:09 AM): OWNED, JASON MALONE, OWNED!!!!11

RawKdaSkEEbaLL (11:43:11 AM): woah, hi :)

RawKdaSkEEbaLL (11:43:13 AM): were r u?

thejanethe (11:43:14 AM): At home, where else would I be?

thejanethe (11:43:15 AM): And why the hell did YOU not email ME last night? I HAVE HAD TO WAIT LIKE NINETEEN HOURS TO GLOAT WITH SOMEONE

RawKdaSkEEbaLL (11:43:18 AM): uh at scool lol

thejanethe (11:43:18 AM): Well, you know that I'm not there. :P

thejanethe (11:43:19 AM): Nah, school wasn't happening today.

thejanethe (11:43:20 AM): I had some stuff to finish up at home, and besides, as much as I would like to be watching the fallout today, I thought I'd maybe better steer clear.

RawKdaSkEEbaLL (11:43:23 AM): i was @ skeeball practice & got home late sry

RawKdaSkEEbaLL (11:43:25 AM): fallout?

thejanethe (11:43:25 AM): Yes!

thejanethe (11:43:26 AM): From the Jason thing!

thejanethe (11:43:27 AM): Didn't I tell you I was going to get him back, didn't I tell you? ::does the dance of awesome::

thejanethe (11:43:27 AM): Where are you, anyway?

RawKdaSkEEbaLL (11:43:29 AM): holy crap ur typeing fast

thejanethe (11:43:29 AM): I'm accused of this frequently.

RawKdaSkEEbaLL (11:43:31 AM): im in the cpu lab, its studdy hall

RawKdaSkEEbaLL (11:43:34 AM): i thot u mite b online :)

158

thejanethe (11:43:36 AM): How well you know me. :P

thejanethe (11:43:37 AM): But yes, I am online, and so are you, and what's going on there?

RawKdaSkEEbaLL (11:43:40 AM): whaht do u mean

RawKdaSkEEbaLL (11:43:42 AM): & y r u skiping scool?!?!!/

RawKdaSkEEbaLL (11:43:45 AM): u ttly cant aford 2 miss more, mrs bakers on ur ass

thejanethe (11:43:46 AM): Look, I have bigger problems than Mrs. Baker.

RawKdaSkEEbaLL (11:43:48 AM): u do??

thejanethe (11:43:50 AM): Yes. I need to have this fanfic finished, edited, and submitted to the Lookies in three weeks, and I'm not even done with the first draft yet.

RawKdaSkEEbaLL (11:43:53 AM): uh how is that a bigger problm then mrs baker

thejanethe (11:43:54 AM): Because if I win the Lookies then I get a ticket to the con and to a SCRIPT READING FOR THE NEW SEASON. To which you agreed to drive me, might I add.

RawKdaSkEEbaLL (11:43:56 AM): well yea if u win :)

thejanethe (11:43:57 AM): HEY

thejanethe (11:44:00 AM): Some faith in me you have!

RawKdaSkEEbaLL (11:44:02 AM): ok sry

RawKdaSkEEbaLL (11:44:04 AM): but the thing w/ jason

RawKdaSkEEbaLL (11:44:06 AM): i got ur email abt it & saw the pix

RawKdaSkEEbaLL (11:44:09 AM): i still dont get how u did it???

thejanethe (11:44:11 AM): Let's just say that a sexy girl can be very persuasive.

RawKdaSkEEbaLL (11:44:13 AM): well yea :)

RawKdaSkEEbaLL (11:44:16 AM): whatd u do act all sexy 2 jason?

thejanethe (11:44:18 AM): NO! At least, not how you're thinking. I pretended to be some random sexy girl online and said I'd meet him at the mall.

RawKdaSkEEbaLL (11:44:22 AM): haha jason i cant believe he fell 4 that

thejanethe (11:44:23 AM): I know, right?

RawKdaSkEEbaLL (11:44:26 AM): but wtf hat?!?!?!

thejanethe (11:44:28 AM): All part of my genius. :) I told him they were supersexy.

RawKdaSkEEbaLL (11:44:32 AM): HAHAHAHAHAHHAHAH

RawKdaSkEEbaLL (11:44:34 AM): man poor jason

thejanethe (11:44:35 AM): How come you keep saying that? He is so not "poor Jason."

thejanethe (11:44:37 AM): He is asshole Jason, Jason who wrecked my life at school. He is loathsome Jason. He is "I am so not done fucking with him yet" Jason.

RawKdaSkEEbaLL (11:44:41 AM): wait wut?

thejanethe (11:44:43 AM): What I said. I'm not done.

thejanethe (11:44:47 AM): He told the whole school my dad's a drunk AND that I write "stories about Brad Memphis." A few pictures on FriendsLink are NOTHING in comparison. Last night was, like, a warmup.

RawKdaSkEEbaLL (11:44:50 AM): um i think mayb the pix are enuf?

thejanethe (11:45:03 AM): ...no.

thejanethe (11:45:06 AM): I just explained. Seriously, do you not get how badly he's fucked things up for me at school?

160

RawKdaSkEEbaLL (11:45:10 AM): i know ppl make fun of u sumtimes & that sux

RawKdaSkEEbaLL (11:45:13 AM): but i think what u did is enuf payback

thejanethe (11:45:14 AM): How the hell would you know!

thejanethe (11:45:17 AM): Did anyone ever blab all over YOUR school that YOUR dad was a drunk?!

RawKdaSkEEbaLL (11:45:19 AM): yea actully

thejanethe (11:45:40 AM): Really?   .

RawKdaSkEEbaLL (11:45:42 AM): yea

RawKdaSkEEbaLL (11:45:45 AM): ill let u feel silly quietly now :)

thejanethe (11:45:58 AM): I'm sorry. I didn't know he drank.

RawKdaSkEEbaLL (11:46:03 AM): yea i know i nevr brot it up

thejanethe (11:46:05 AM): Did he quit or something?

RawKdaSkEEbaLL (11:46:09 AM): no he left

thejanethe (11:46:23 AM): Oh. I'm really sorry.

RawKdaSkEEbaLL (11:46:26 AM): its ok it was a long time ago

thejanethe (11:46:37 AM): So, wait -- when people were gossiping about your dad at school, what did you do, then?

RawKdaSkEEbaLL (11:46:39 AM): nothing

thejanethe (11:46:40 AM): Are you serious? How could you stand to do nothing?

RawKdaSkEEbaLL (11:46:42 AM): i dunno

RawKdaSkEEbaLL (11:46:46 AM): i punched walls alot

thejanethe (11:46:59 AM): Punched walls...?

RawKdaSkEEbaLL (11:47:02 AM): yea

RawKdaSkEEbaLL (11:47:05 AM): @ home, not @ scool

thejanethe (11:47:06 AM): Didn't that hurt?!

RawKdaSkEEbaLL (11:47:08 AM): sort of

RawKdaSkEEbaLL (11:47:11 AM): idk, it made me feel beter

thejanethe (11:47:20 AM): Oh.

thejanethe (11:47:23 AM): Well, I don't think it would help me much to punch walls.

RawKdaSkEEbaLL (11:47:26 AM): no it probley wasent the best thing 2 do

thejanethe (11:47:28 AM): But, I mean, you see why I have to get back at him, don't you?

thejanethe (11:47:30 AM): All the snickering, and just... EVERY personal thing that I EVER wanted to hide from the people at school, he told about! What am I supposed to do, just forget about that?!

RawKdaSkEEbaLL (11:47:33 AM): but u alredy did get back @ him

thejanethe (11:47:33 AM): Not enough!

thejanethe (11:47:34 AM): I don't know how you can think this is all fair and square now, dude, I seriously don't

RawKdaSkEEbaLL (11:47:38 AM): u asked whaht its like @ scool 2day, its rly bad four jason

thejanethe (11:47:42 AM): Come on! As bad as having the whole school gossiping about your father's alcoholism and your own fantasy sex with Brad Memphis? Whatever!

RawKdaSkEEbaLL (11:47:44 AM): yea, im serius

RawKdaSkEEbaLL (11:47:46 AM): their calling him queer & fag & stuff

thejanethe (11:47:49 AM): Right. Because THAT'S totally as bad as everyone knowing my dad's a drunk.

162

RawKdaSkEEbaLL (11:47:51 AM): no it rly is bad

RawKdaSkEEbaLL (11:47:54 AM): after the storey abt kissing guys & now him w/the victorreas secrt stuff

RawKdaSkEEbaLL (11:47:57 AM): u know how they do 2 clodea & them, we were talking abt it

RawKdaSkEEbaLL (11:48:00 AM): they do the same stuff 2 jason

thejanethe (11:48:08 AM): ...ew.

RawKdaSkEEbaLL (11:48:10 AM): yea

thejanethe (11:48:12 AM): Okay, that's pretty gross.

RawKdaSkEEbaLL (11:48:15 AM): yea & its prolly just gunna get wurse 4 awhile

thejanethe (11:48:16 AM): I didn't even set that part up. He was just supposed to show up at Bartley's in the stupid hat and suspenders. He started feeling up the lingerie on his own. :P

RawKdaSkEEbaLL (11:48:19 AM): whaht?! lol

thejanethe (11:48:16 AM): I think he was nervous or something. Whatever. I just wanted people to make fun of him for looking like an idiot.

RawKdaSkEEbaLL (11:48:19 AM): yea & sum ppl r but sum of the guys are being way rouf on him

thejanethe (11:48:22 AM): Dude, if you're a guy sexually harassing another guy, doesn't that make you gay yourself?

RawKdaSkEEbaLL (11:48:23 AM): lol

RawKdaSkEEbaLL (11:48:25 AM): dare u to say taht 2 bruno

thejanethe (11:48:27 AM): LOL No thanks!

thejanethe (11:48:43 AM): Oh great, now I'm feeling sorry for JASON MALONE.

thejanethe (11:48:46 AM): This totally sucks, you know it? He screws me over at school, and then when I get back at him I wind up feeling all guilty about it. WTF?

RawKdaSkEEbaLL (11:48:50 AM): i dident mean 2 make u feel bad, i just think u dont need to do anething else

RawKdaSkEEbaLL (11:48:52 AM): it was a good trick

thejanethe (11:48:53 AM): Heh. It was, wasn't it?

RawKdaSkEEbaLL (11:48:55 AM): yea deffinately :)

RawKdaSkEEbaLL (11:48:58 AM): u dident know the guys wd start up w/ this shit

RawKdaSkEEbaLL (11:49:01 AM): but it can all b sorta ended now

RawKdaSkEEbaLL (11:49:03 AM): he did stuff 2 u, u got him back, its over

thejanethe (11:49:15 AM): Yeah. ::sigh::

RawKdaSkEEbaLL (11:49:19 AM): cuz i dont know if he knows it was u who did it but hes not gunna mess w/ u no more :)

thejanethe (11:49:20 AM): You don't think so?

RawKdaSkEEbaLL (11:49:23 AM): no wai, after this hed be scarred shitless of wut u'd do 2 him next :)

thejanethe (11:49:25 AM): Heh. Okay.

thejanethe (11:49:27 AM): So I get to not do anything else, and hope they forget about me and lay off him eventually.

thejanethe (11:49:29 AM): Less of a cymbal-crashing triumph than I'd been hoping for, but whatever.

RawKdaSkEEbaLL (11:49:31 AM): yea probley

RawKdaSkEEbaLL (11:49:34 AM): lol sry i dont have any simbols so i cant help

thejanethe (11:49:36 AM): Maybe you can get people gossiping less about the lingerie and more about the hat. :P

RawKdaSkEEbaLL (11:49:39 AM): lol how wd i do taht

thejanethe (11:49:42 AM): By gossiping about it yourself, of course. :P He's still a jerk, and he deserves to have people making fun of him for SOMETHING.

RawKdaSkEEbaLL (11:49:46 AM): haha i dont think ppl will suddenly swich wyut their gosiping abt cuz of me

thejanethe (11:49:47 AM): Why not? :)

thejanethe (11:49:50 AM): Hey, I know what, tell people he joined your Skee-Ball team! ;) ;)

RawKdaSkEEbaLL (11:49:52 AM): NO WAY

thejanethe (11:49:55 AM): What, you don't want to taint the image of Skee-Ball by association with Jason Malone? ;)

RawKdaSkEEbaLL (11:49:59 AM): jason is so not cool enuf 2 play skeeball

thejanethe (11:50:02 AM): Ha! You may be right at that.

RawKdaSkEEbaLL (11:50:03 AM): oh hey the bell just rang g2g

thejanethe (11:50:04 AM): Okay.

thejanethe (11:50:05 AM): Talk to you later.

RawKdaSkEEbaLL (11:50:07 AM): ttyl

http://www.diarynow.com/users/thejanethe/40002.html
Date: 4/2/2013
Security level: Private
Tagged: grip of a moment, spec script first draft

SCENE #SOMETHINGOROTHER
RIGHT AFTER JAELA TEARS UP ANOTHER ZYERLEAN
ENCAMPMENT
[Jaela is standing looking out over the rubble on the ground in front of her. All of the Zyerleans who are not dead have fled. Her expression is turned inward. Behind her, Distra steps out from behind a tree and emerges from the shadows. Jaela doesn't hear her.]
DISTRA: Did it help?
JAELA: [jumps, badly startled] I -- *Distra?* What are you -- how -- what are you *doing* here?!
DISTRA: Oh, I was just watching the show. [settles cross-legged on the ground]
JAELA: What show?
DISTRA: Oh, please. Seriously, Jaela, how many destroyed Zyerlean encampments does that make for you this week? Three? Four?
JAELA: It -- [Catches herself. Coldly --] It's none of your affair.
DISTRA: Oh, of course not. Nothing to worry about here. Still, while we're on the subject, why don't you answer my question? Purely to satisfy my curiosity.
JAELA: What question?
DISTRA: Did it help?
JAELA: I don't understand. Help what?
DISTRA: You.
JAELA: What do you mean, did it help me? It's not about helping me.
DISTRA: Oh, the hell it's not, Jaela!
JAELA: It *isn't!* I have been taking out Zyerlean encampments, yes. I have been taking out encampments of *armed militants* supporting a regime that starves its citizens, enslaves minorities, tortures dissidents into silence --
DISTRA: Oh, right! Sorry, I get it now. You smashing up a few camps of

166

six or seven Zyerlean soldiers who probably got drafted two weeks ago -- that's going to crush the regime. Why is everyone at TIME after your head? They should be hanging a medal around your neck.

JAELA: They should be *fighting on my side!*

DISTRA: Well, they're not.

JAELA: That -- and you think that's all, do you? You think I can sit back and go "Oh, well, torture and slavery and starvation and all that are pretty rotten, but what the heck, as long as no one at TIME cares, why should I?"

DISTRA: [sits forward, suddenly energized] What I think is you should be honest about why you're doing this. What I think is you should stop acting like you're on some holier-than-thou crusade here when everyone from Hou'phan on up knows why you're really --

JAELA: Do NOT bring my parents into --

DISTRA: Oh, please, Jaela, they're already in it!

JAELA: The Zyerlean encampments go around abducting kids and making them into child soldiers, they --

DISTRA: And I'm asking you: does it help?

JAELA: Does *what* help? Those Zyerleans aren't going to be kidnapping any more kids! They --

DISTRA: And five hundred more encampments of them across the planet will keep kidnapping kids, and another few thousand will just go around sitting around their fires bitching about the cold like those guys were doing before you shot them all to hell and gone, so I am asking you, *did it help?*

JAELA: I don't know what you're --

DISTRA: No more lies! [suddenly shouting] *Did it?*

JAELA: [finally snapping] *I don't know!*

DISTRA: [dripping with disdain] You know, all right. [more her usual snide tone] Jaela, hon, you think I care how many camps you tear up? You think I'm with TIME here, trying to cart you off to prison? I mean, because I always play by the rulebook, right? [Jaela shakes her head briefly, eyes still snapping.] I don't really care what you do, Jaela. I don't think it's going to help anything, but nobody else is doing any better, so you might as well keep going. But if there's one thing I can't stand, it's a hypocrite. So let's be straight here, okay?

[The silence spins out between them. The dying Zyerlean fire is still crackling in the background; firelight plays over their faces.]

DISTRA, *cont:* The time for fantasy games is over, sweetpea. You go ahead and do whatever you're going to do, but you better know why you're doing it and what you really want.

JAELA: I want Saureshan taken down.

DISTRA: So you want Jessamyn to take over everything between Alpha Centauri and Echo Seven's second moon, then.

JAELA: That's not going to --

DISTRA: [impatient] Whatever. Not the point. The point's simple and it goes something like this. Say you go around demolishing all these camps, say for the sake of argument that it would even be *possible* to take out enough of them to somehow destabilize the regime and get things rolling. Great, now you've got the country in chaos. What happens next?

[Jaela is silent.]

DISTRA: Well, it's obvious what comes next, right? You go ahead and assassinate Saureshan, is what comes next. [Jaela opens her mouth to protest, but hesitates for a second.] Oh, come on, we know it's what you're planning. It's why you've been hacking the SendScope records around his trip to Ciccrucia, isn't it? And let's even say for a minute that you manage it. So here we are, you're the only assassin of a major intergalactic emperor ever to walk free and gloat about it. And where does that get you?

JAELA: [slightly strained] When an emperor gets taken out, everything gets shaken down to the ground. You overturn a dictatorship, there's a power void, and there's a chance someone good will step in.

DISTRA: But there *isn't*. TIME backs Saureshan's regime. The minute anything goes haywire, they're sending troops in to lock everything down and ensure the situation stays at full status quo, and his next-in-line moves right into position to keep the citizens pinned under the government's thumb. I mean, that puts Luko in power, right? Don't even pretend you don't know he's at least as bad as Saureshan. Zyerlea is screwed no matter what you do, Jaela. So -- [She stands now, walks over to look Jaela straight in the eyes.] Say you killed Saureshan. Say you looked straight into his eyes and sent him to hell. What happens then?

{and... what does happen then?}

{shit, I don't even know what Jaela wants anymore -- I mean, she was
going to assassinate Saureshan, but Distra is totally right in this scene,
as long as Zyerlea is a member of TIME, assassinating Saureshan is not
going to do anything at all}

{so what am I going to do, devote the second half of the fic to diplomatic
wrangling to get TIME to expel Zyerlea? who CARES? yeah, that'd
be a rip-roaring end to the fic, a bunch of suits talking politics in an
intergalactic conference call}

{and Distra keeps going on about how this is all about Jaela's parents, but
is it really? Saureshan is totally evil and Jaela's 100% right that he needs
to be taken down, so why does this thing with Jaela's parents keep coming
up when it's not the point at all? I mean, okay, I know why it keeps
coming up, because Thorin and Distra *think* it's the point, but by now
it's taking over the fic, so I basically need to edit it all and cut about 60%
of that out and AAAAAAAAGH}

{Okay. Right. So -- ugh, I wish Dad would go away. Why is he ALWAYS
hovering around outside my door? God, can't I like booby-trap the hall or
--

Oh Christ, he's knocking. He's actually knocking! He never knocks. I
have to get rid of him, I'm right in the middle of trying to figure this out
and I can't afford the

RawKdaSkEEbaLL (1:53:21 AM): hey jane

RawKdaSkEEbaLL (1:53:25 AM): what r u doing online so l7

thejanethe (1:53:27 AM): …what am I doing online so l7?

RawKdaSkEEbaLL (1:53:28 AM): lol

RawKdaSkEEbaLL (1:53:30 AM): so l8 i mean

thejanethe (1:53:31 AM): Ah.

thejanethe (1:53:32 AM): I am really frigging pissed right now.

RawKdaSkEEbaLL (1:53:34 AM): at me?

thejanethe (1:53:36 AM): No, why would I be mad at you?

RawKdaSkEEbaLL (1:53:37 AM): idk

thejanethe (1:53:38 AM): No. It's my dad.

RawKdaSkEEbaLL (1:53:48 AM): what did he do

thejanethe (1:53:49 AM): He took away my computer, is what he did.

thejanethe (1:53:49 AM): He TOOK AWAY my fucking COMPUTER.

RawKdaSkEEbaLL (1:53:51 AM): huh?

RawKdaSkEEbaLL (1:53:52 AM): y?

thejanethe (1:53:54 AM): Because he says I spend too much time on it.

thejanethe (1:53:58 AM): So, what, the solution is to take it away entirely?! WTF! I have a paper to write tonight, for God's sake!

RawKdaSkEEbaLL (1:54:02 AM): u never do ur papers & stuff at home anyway

RawKdaSkEEbaLL (1:54:05 AM): u always do them in study hall @ thw cpu lab

thejanethe (1:54:06 AM): …yes, well, he doesn't know that.

RawKdaSkEEbaLL (1:54:08 AM): lol

RawKdaSkEEbaLL (1:54:11 AM): so wait

RawKdaSkEEbaLL (1:54:13 AM): how r u online now

thejanethe (1:54:14 AM): What?

RawKdaSkEEbaLL (1:54:17 AM): if ur dad took ur cpu away

RawKdaSkEEbaLL (1:54:19 AM): how r u online now?
thejanethe (1:54:21 AM): Oh. I took it back.

RawKdaSkEEbaLL (1:54:24 AM): how?

thejanethe (1:54:38 AM): It's a laptop. It wasn't hard.

RawKdaSkEEbaLL (1:54:41 AM): he left it out?

thejanethe (1:54:43 AM): No, I just took it out of his room.

RawKdaSkEEbaLL (1:54:45 AM): wile he was asleep

thejanethe (1:54:46 AM): Yeah.

RawKdaSkEEbaLL (1:54:55 AM): lier :)

thejanethe (1:54:55 AM): What?

RawKdaSkEEbaLL (1:54:57 AM): ur lieing

thejanethe (1:54:59 AM): What are you talking about, dude?!

RawKdaSkEEbaLL (1:55:02 AM): ur font is diffrent

RawKdaSkEEbaLL (1:55:04 AM): ur usully dark blue & bold

RawKdaSkEEbaLL (1:55:07 AM): & now ur just black

RawKdaSkEEbaLL (1:55:11 AM): ur font woudnt be diffrent if u were on ur own cpu

RawKdaSkEEbaLL (1:55:14 AM): did u go 2 an allnite internet cafe or sumthing>

thejanethe (1:55:26 AM): Shit.

RawKdaSkEEbaLL (1:55:28 AM): wat?

thejanethe (1:55:32 AM): Okay, okay. But you had seriously better not make fun of me because I am already NOT in a good mood.

RawKdaSkEEbaLL (1:55:36 AM): i woudnt make fun of u

thejanethe (1:55:38 AM): I'm at my neighbors' house.

RawKdaSkEEbaLL (1:55:40 AM): y woud i make fun of u 4 that

thejanethe (1:55:54 AM): Because... um. They're not... technically home right now.

RawKdaSkEEbaLL (1:55:55 AM): lol!!!!!!!!!!

thejanethe (1:55:56 AM): They're on vacation for the week.

thejanethe (1:55:58 AM): I told you not to make fun of me, damn it!
RawKdaSkEEbaLL (1:56:00 AM): im not

RawKdaSkEEbaLL (1:56:01 AM): rilly

RawKdaSkEEbaLL (1:56:04 AM): im not making fun of u

RawKdaSkEEbaLL (1:56:08 AM): its just...... kind of funny

RawKdaSkEEbaLL (1:56:19 AM): dont u think

thejanethe (1:56:22 AM): I don't know. I just wanted to finish some stuff.

thejanethe (1:56:25 AM): I wanted to do at least part of this paper tonight.

RawKdaSkEEbaLL (1:56:28 AM): bullshit

RawKdaSkEEbaLL (1:56:30 AM): internet addict much? ;)

thejanethe (1:56:31 AM): You know what, FUCK YOU!

RawKdaSkEEbaLL (1:56:32 AM): woah

RawKdaSkEEbaLL (1:56:32 AM): sorry

RawKdaSkEEbaLL (1:56:33 AM): i didnt mean it like that

thejanethe (1:56:34 AM): I'm so sick of people saying that!

RawKdaSkEEbaLL (1:56:36 AM): y

thejanethe (1:56:38 AM): Because that's why my dad took the fucking computer away in the first place.

RawKdaSkEEbaLL (1:56:39 AM): bc ur an addict?

thejanethe (1:56:40 AM): STOP FUCKING SAYING THAT, I am NOT FUCKING KIDDING

RawKdaSkEEbaLL (1:56:42 AM): woah sry

RawKdaSkEEbaLL (1:56:44 AM): i just ment, thats what he said

RawKdaSkEEbaLL (1:56:45 AM): calm down a minute

thejanethe (1:56:48 AM): Why the hell should I calm down? My dad is going around taking my goddamn computer away and the only IRL friend ihave is accusing me of being an Internet addict and I'm fucking SICK of all of this!

RawKdaSkEEbaLL (1:56:50 AM): ok

RawKdaSkEEbaLL (1:56:51 AM): im sorry i said that
thejanethe (1:56:54 AM): ::sigh::

RawKdaSkEEbaLL (1:56:58 AM): ur dads been on ur back about spending time on the net?

thejanethe (1:57:02 AM): Only every minute of the goddamn day?

RawKdaSkEEbaLL (1:57:04 AM): ok

RawKdaSkEEbaLL (1:57:07 AM): did he take iot away 4 like a week or sumthing

thejanethe (1:57:09 AM): No. Until I've "conquered my addiction" or someshit.

thejanethe (1:57:12 AM): Keep in mind this is the former alcoholic talking. Former my ass. He's been off it for like a week so far.

RawKdaSkEEbaLL (1:57:15 AM): oh I dident know he was quiting

thejanethe (1:57:17 AM): He's not. I mean, whatever. There's no sense in talking about it yet.

thejanethe (1:57:17 AM): I refuse to be stupid enough to figure he's quit forever after nine days.

RawKdaSkEEbaLL (1:57:20 AM): well 9 days is beter than my dad evr did, maybe urs will stay sober

thejanethe (1:57:22 AM): Whatever. I'm not getting my hopes up.

thejanethe (1:57:39 AM): Anyway, ever since he "quit" he's been off on this need-to-be-a-better-parent kick.

RawKdaSkEEbaLL (1:57:42 AM): & thats y he took away ur cpu?

thejanethe (1:57:44 AM): Apparently.

RawKdaSkEEbaLL (1:57:46 AM): that sux

thejanethe (1:57:47 AM): Yeah, no shit.

RawKdaSkEEbaLL (1:57:49 AM): so wait

RawKdaSkEEbaLL (1:57:50 AM): sorry 2 keep bugging u abt it

RawKdaSkEEbaLL (1:57:52 AM): but u broke into ur neibors house 2 use there computer?

thejanethe (1:57:54 AM): I didn't break in! We have a spare key.

thejanethe (1:57:57 AM): I'm good friends with them, it's not like I'm not allowed to come in when they're not here.
RawKdaSkEEbaLL (1:57:59 AM): i c

thejanethe (1:58:00 AM): WHAT?

RawKdaSkEEbaLL (1:58:01 AM): ok

RawKdaSkEEbaLL (1:58:03 AM): nothing

RawKdaSkEEbaLL (1:58:05 AM): rilly

thejanethe (1:58:17 AM): Sorry. I'm just a little touchy. ::sigh::

RawKdaSkEEbaLL (1:58:20 AM): no wai :)

thejanethe (1:58:41 AM): It's just... I dunno.

RawKdaSkEEbaLL (1:58:44 AM): hey it makes sence

thejanethe (1:58:47 AM): What does?

RawKdaSkEEbaLL (1:58:52 AM): for u 2 be upset

thejanethe (1:58:54 AM): Well, yeah.

RawKdaSkEEbaLL (1:58:58 AM): r we freidns tho?

thejanethe (1:59:03 AM): ...yes?

thejanethe (1:59:04 AM): Why?

RawKdaSkEEbaLL (1:59:07 AM): cuz i have 2 b ur freind 2 ask u this

RawKdaSkEEbaLL (1:59:10 AM): n i know ur gonna yell at me neway

thejanethe (1:59:13 AM): Whatever. I don't think I can exactly get *more* upset than I already have been.

RawKdaSkEEbaLL (1:59:15 AM): r u mad cuz ur dad hit a nerve?

thejanethe (1:59:28 AM): ...obviously?

RawKdaSkEEbaLL (1:59:30 AM): no i mean

RawKdaSkEEbaLL (1:59:32 AM): b/c he hit close to home?

thejanethe (1:59:43 AM): Oh.

thejanethe (1:59:46 AM): Here we go again. Okay, so why don't you tell me?

RawKdaSkEEbaLL (1:59:49 AM): what?

thejanethe (1:59:51 AM): Tell me what an Internet addict I am, Gary.

thejanethe (1:59:53 AM): Tell me what a crazy fucking freak I am and how you've never seen someone waste as much time online as I do and I'm just totally beyond belief.

RawKdaSkEEbaLL (1:59:56 AM): NO

RawKdaSkEEbaLL (1:59:57 AM): wouldu cut it out for 1 sec?

thejanethe (1:59:59 AM): This is NOT helping. Jesus CHRIST I don't know why I put ZIM on in the first place.

RawKdaSkEEbaLL (2:00:02 AM): ok ok ok ok ok

RawKdaSkEEbaLL (2:00:04 AM): look

RawKdaSkEEbaLL (2:00:07 AM): i wont talk abt it

RawKdaSkEEbaLL (2:00:09 AM): ok?

RawKdaSkEEbaLL (2:00:13 AM): what do u want to talk abt

thejanethe (2:00:14 AM): Nothing. Fucking forget it.

thejanethe has signed off.

thejanethe has signed on.

thejanethe (2:12:46 AM): Gary?

RawKdaSkEEbaLL (2:12:52 AM): yeah

thejanethe (2:12:56 AM): Sorry. I'm just a total mess tonight.

RawKdaSkEEbaLL (2:13:01 AM): its cool

thejanethe (2:13:05 AM): I was just taking stuff out on you that had nothing to do with you.

RawKdaSkEEbaLL (2:13:08 AM): better then busting up walls

thejanethe (2:13:10 AM): Huh?

RawKdaSkEEbaLL (2:13:12 AM): or beating up old ladys or sumthing

thejanethe (2:13:14 AM): LOL I guess so.

RawKdaSkEEbaLL (2:13:17 AM): ooo i made u laugh :)

thejanethe (2:13:19 AM): Yeah, I guess you did.

RawKdaSkEEbaLL (2:13:22 AM): do u want me 2 call u

thejanethe (2:13:33 AM): It's the middle of the night.

RawKdaSkEEbaLL (2:13:35 AM): yah but ur at ur neibors house

RawKdaSkEEbaLL (2:13:37 AM): noones there 2 wake up :)

thejanethe (2:13:40 AM): :) Point taken, but I don't have my cell phone and I probably shouldn't use their phone.

RawKdaSkEEbaLL (2:13:44 AM): u probly shoudnt use there internet either then

thejanethe (2:13:57 AM): LOL

RawKdaSkEEbaLL (2:13:59 AM): hey made u laugh agian!

RawKdaSkEEbaLL (2:14:03 AM): n i thot u were gonna bitchslap me 4 that 1

thejanethe (2:14:06 AM): :) Lucky for you you're not in the room.

RawKdaSkEEbaLL (2:14:09 AM): want me 2 come ovr?

thejanethe (2:14:11 AM): So I can bitchslap you?

RawKdaSkEEbaLL (2:14:13 AM): whatever

thejanethe (2:14:15 AM): No, it's cool.

thejanethe (2:14:17 AM): I'm better at talking on the Internet anyway.

RawKdaSkEEbaLL (2:14:18 AM): makes sence

thejanethe (2:14:19 AM): What does?

RawKdaSkEEbaLL (2:14:21 AM): that ud like the net better

thejanethe (2:14:24 AM): How come?

RawKdaSkEEbaLL (2:14:26 AM): b/c u read so much, ur a writer & everything

RawKdaSkEEbaLL (2:14:30 AM): u always use the rite grammer & spelling & stuff in ur chats

RawKdaSkEEbaLL (2:14:32 AM): i dont :)

RawKdaSkEEbaLL (2:14:35 AM): but im not usully so good in person either

thejanethe (2:14:38 AM): Yeah, life sucks.

RawKdaSkEEbaLL (2:14:41 AM): how come

thejanethe (2:14:43 AM): Just, I don't know. Don't you get tired of trying to blend in with the world?

RawKdaSkEEbaLL (2:14:45 AM): i dont try nemore

RawKdaSkEEbaLL (2:14:48 AM): i just play skeeball n try 2 have fun
thejanethe (2:14:50 AM): :) It's a good attitude to have.

thejanethe (2:14:52 AM): I'm not very good at doing that. Except online.

thejanethe (2:14:55 AM): Do *you* think I'm an Internet addict?

RawKdaSkEEbaLL (2:14:59 AM): sure & y dont u askme if ur fat while ur at it!!!!

thejanethe (2:15:01 AM): LOL!!

thejanethe (2:15:02 AM): I'm serious though.

RawKdaSkEEbaLL (2:15:05 AM): i dunno

RawKdaSkEEbaLL (2:15:07 AM): i see u online alot but, most ppl r online alot

RawKdaSkEEbaLL (2:15:10 AM): y wat do u think?

thejanethe (2:15:13 AM): ...have you been taking lessons from my therapist?

RawKdaSkEEbaLL (2:15:15 AM): oh, r u seeing a therapist

RawKdaSkEEbaLL (2:15:18 AM): i thot miss miesner kicked u out?

thejanethe (2:15:20 AM): She did. There's a new one now.

RawKdaSkEEbaLL (2:15:33 AM): oic

RawKdaSkEEbaLL (2:15:33 AM): but..... i rilly dont know if ur like an adict

RawKdaSkEEbaLL (2:15:36 AM): i dont think u r just cuz u write fanfictons & stuff

RawKdaSkEEbaLL (2:15:38 AM): but um

RawKdaSkEEbaLL (2:15:41 AM): dont go into ur neibores house nemore 2 go online

RawKdaSkEEbaLL (2:15:42 AM): ok?

thejanethe (2:15:45 AM): It's really not a big deal. Seriously, they're good friends of mine.

RawKdaSkEEbaLL (2:15:47 AM): ok

RawKdaSkEEbaLL (2:15:50 AM): just woried u coud get arested or sumthing

thejanethe (2:15:52 AM): No one's going to arrest me.

RawKdaSkEEbaLL (2:15:56 AM): no but rilly

RawKdaSkEEbaLL (2:15:59 AM): dont do it again tommorrow ok?

RawKdaSkEEbaLL (2:16:04 AM): u cn come ovr my house if u rillyu want 2 go online

thejanethe (2:16:06 AM): ::rolls eyes:: And how would I get there?

RawKdaSkEEbaLL (2:16:10 AM): im like 15 blocks away

RawKdaSkEEbaLL (2:16:12 AM): take ur bike

thejanethe (2:16:14 AM): Hopefully this won't still be a problem tomorrow. I'm going to try to talk my dad out of it.

RawKdaSkEEbaLL (2:16:17 AM): maybe its just a 1 nite thing

thejanethe (2:16:34 AM): I don't know *why* I flipped out so badly.

thejanethe (2:16:36 AM): I don't like this, I really don't. I'm kind of flipping out now.

RawKdaSkEEbaLL (2:16:38 AM): rilly? u seem better

thejanethe (2:16:43 AM): No, I am, I'm just... upset. I don't know why I was reacting the way I was, it was like I was having a panic attack or something, and I came over here to try to calm down, and it actually worked for a little while, but it's not working now because now I'm having a panic attack about having a panic attack.

thejanethe (2:16:45 AM): How dumb is that?

RawKdaSkEEbaLL (2:16:46 AM): dont have a panick attack

RawKdaSkEEbaLL (2:16:48 AM): its ok

thejanethe (2:16:51 AM): I think it's just the idea that my dad has this *control* over me, you know?

thejanethe (2:16:55 AM): Like as long as I'm living with him, he can do whatever he wants. He can take away my computer, he could take away my TV if he wanted, books, whatever. I'm fifteen and he can still punish me like I'm four.

thejanethe (2:16:57 AM): I'm stuck with him until I leave for college, and God knows if I'll ever get *into* any college, my grades are way below my PSAT scores and colleges hate kids who don't live up to their potential and OMG I am going to be stuck in my house with my dad FOREVER.

RawKdaSkEEbaLL (2:16:59 AM): woah
RawKdaSkEEbaLL (2:17:00 AM): slow down

RawKdaSkEEbaLL (2:17:03 AM): ull b in colledge in 3 years just like me, k

RawKdaSkEEbaLL (2:17:06 AM): & ur dad isnt going 2 take away ur books & tv

RawKdaSkEEbaLL (2:17:08 AM): u need sum sleep 2nite, thats all

RawKdaSkEEbaLL (2:17:10 AM): ill totally call u if it will help

thejanethe (2:17:12 AM): I don't have my cell with me. And I don't know the number here.

RawKdaSkEEbaLL (2:17:15 AM): their ur close freinds & u dont have there number

thejanethe (2:17:17 AM): I have it at home, but if I'm going home I should probably just go to bed.

RawKdaSkEEbaLL (2:17:18 AM): ok

RawKdaSkEEbaLL (2:17:21 AM): if u cant sleep or w/e u cn still call me

thejanethe (2:17:27 AM): Thanks, but I think I'll watch some LtT episodes before I go to bed. Maybe that will put me to sleep.

RawKdaSkEEbaLL (2:17:35AM): yah that brad mempis sure is boring looking

RawKdaSkEEbaLL (2:17:37 AM): KIDDING

thejanethe (2:17:39 AM): ::reaches out for the strangle::

RawKdaSkEEbaLL (2:17:41 AM): haha

thejanethe (2:17:43 AM): Okay. Thanks, Gary.

RawKdaSkEEbaLL (2:17:44 AM): np

RawKdaSkEEbaLL (2:17:46 AM): c u in scool tomorrow

thejanethe (2:17:47 AM): Okay. Night.

RawKdaSkEEbaLL (2:17:48 AM): bye

http://www.twistedart.net/blackwingedsoul/182693.html
Date: 4/3/2013
Mood: somber
Security level: Public

don't do drugs, ethan. stay in school, ethan. don't be so emo, ethan. try acting normal, ethan. listen to us, ethan. we know what's best for you, ethan. we know your life is ruined, and we know we helped to ruin it, but we are adults, and we know what you should do. and we have papers and contracts to say so, ethan.

we own you, ethan.

for your own good.

these are the nights when i want it more than anything.

a line of powder, glittering in the moonlight. smoke coiling up from a pipe, thick and luxurious. a small foil package and a needle. a tab. a pill

i have a bottle, stored away. it won't be enough.

it won't be enough as i listen to andy's breathing deep and slow across the room and know that i don't even know what it is that i want, but that i want, i want, i want. more than that: i need. i need an escape or a break or a second chance, i need someone, and there is no one, and the needing and the terror and the loneliness bang around inside my skull until i think i will go crazy if i can't blunt them. with the powder. with the smoke. with the needle.

they've taken away all my lifelines and left me floundering. they told me i was sick and they told me they would make me well and they took it all away, everything i had that let me cope, but the everything is still banging and clanging in my head and the world is one long drawn-out shriek of pain and there is no one who will stop the banging, quiet the shrieking, take my hand and guide me to a safer place, to a place where things make sense the way they used to. they took it all away and told me it was the wrong way to cope, the <u>wrong way</u>, but they will not show me a right way and that is because there is none, there is no right way for someone like me when the whole world is wrong.

i will drink the bottle, and i will drink it straight, and i will fall asleep listening to andy's breathing. and it will not be enough. nothing will ever be enough. not since jeff died and the first cloud of pot fumes filled my lungs. the world changed then and nothing will ever be normal again.

i do not want to move into the future. i do not want to learn new coping techniques. the future is blank and opaque and it scares me. i want to move into the past, when things were safe. when the blankets i drew around me for warmth were not ragged and torn and the comfort i could find was more solid than ephemeral smoke, more sustaining than a bottle of booze.

i want things back the way they used to be.

<u>Leave a Comment</u>   <u>8 Comments</u>

http://www.diarynow.com/thejanethe/40010.html
Date: 4/9/2013
Security level: Private
Mood:

Oh, my God, lady, STOP STARING.

At therapy now. Do not intend to make an actual DN post. Intend to write fanfic. This is why I brought my laptop.

She WON'T QUIT STARING AT ME. This is why I have had to open a DN post, because I don't want to stop typing because she might take it as an invitation to conversation but I cannot concentrate because SHE IS STARING AT ME. She said it was fine for me to work on my story but she HASN'T STOPPED STARING for the last five minutes. How am I supposed to concentrate on my fic if she won't stop staring?

Now she's on about how Dad called her this morning and asked her what to do about my "Internet addiction", whether he should keep my computer, and blah blah blah. Apparently she told him to give it back to me -- something about coping mechanisms, not taking one away if you don't have anything better to offer in its stead (STOP CALLING IT A "COPING MECHANISM," HELLO, YOU ARE NOT WINNING ANY POINTS HERE NO MATTER WHAT YOU THINK) and oh, God, some sort of crap about openness and transparency and honesty and *trust*. Because that all makes total sense. Yes, Dr. Acton, please tell me all about how you were gossiping on the phone about me with my dad. That totally makes me trust you. I mean she probably thinks I should be grateful that she told him to give it back, I don't know, but one half-sensible moment does not a trustworthy adult make.

Okay, she shut up. Good. Now focus. Jordana just hauled Distra in for questioning about Jaela. Does Distra want Jaela caught, or not? I don't really think she does, plus it screws up the plot if she turns Jaela in -- but Distra is totally self-centered, so why would she risk her own neck lying to TIME for Jaela's sake? But she's got to. So work it out, Jane. Go to.

...OMG LADY STOP STARING.

...Great. Now she's talking again. "I don't mind if you bring your laptop into session, Jane," sez she, "but I'm wondering why you felt the need to bring it today, when you've come in without it before." I brought it in today because I'm in the middle of a big scene in my story, okay? Like I can't tell that you don't believe me. Why don't you therapists ever say what you mean?

...omg, you're not serious.

OMG. My therapist wants to *chat online with me*?

I am so not kidding. She just said. "You know, for all the reading I did on that online encyclopedia, I still don't feel like I know very much about Internet culture." Snort. *Internet culture*. Although I guess she's right; it kind of is a different culture. Still. Who calls it that? Old people, that's who. "It strikes me that that's probably something of a barrier to communication between us, you know?" Yeah, the barrier is that you're like A HUNDRED AND TEN. "So why don't you teach me? My laptop's right here, it's got wireless. Show me how to use that instant chat thing you see in all those news exposes about the dangers of the Internet." I think she was kidding about that last bit -- she loves doing the twinkly-eye repressed-smile thing. Well, better than if she'd been serious about "the dangers of the Internet," I guess.

Lord, she does not quit, and it's driving me crazy. "Let's just give it a try. At worst you get nothing out of it, but you can have a good laugh at the old fogey." Lady, you don't need to sign onto the Internet for me to do that. Meanwhile, I can't concentrate on my fic at all. STOP TALKING.

This is so *weird*. She seems completely not-disconcerted by the fact that I haven't given her an answer yet.

Distra is still standing in front of Jordana, ready for questioning. So what happens next?

...

Still staring. Still can't concentrate.

...

AGH! Oh, okay, FINE. What the hell. I have to give her credit for originality. She's fairly willing to roll with the punches -- I suppose I have been a bit of a bitch. Considering I haven't, you know, said anything to her all session. And she's right, if she knows nothing about the Internet she'll never know anything about me. Not that I want her to know anything about me, but I'll consider it a service to her next teen patient. I'm so not talking with her on FriendsLink or anything else that has any actual information about me on it, but there's always ZIM, I guess. Let me go see if I can get her set up with an account.

NoraActon48267382 (3:27:07 PM): Hello?

thejanethe (3:27:10 PM): LOL That's one heck of a username.

NoraActon48267382 (3:27:14 PM): When I told it my real name it suggested this online name for me.

NoraActon48267382 (3:27:16 PM): Am I doing this right?

thejanethe (3:27:18 PM): Oh, brother. Yeah, it's working fine.

thejanethe (3:27:21 PM): No, you can't talk out loud. You set this system up, you play by your own rules. :P

NoraActon48267382 (3:27:26 PM): You're right.

NoraActon48267382 (3:27:29 PM): I apologize.

NoraActon48267382 (3:27:34 PM): Oh, goodness, I feel so out of my element.

NoraActon48267382 (3:27:38 PM): It's hard to break the habit of verbal speech.

thejanethe (3:27:40 PM): If you say so. And dude, you don't have to hit send at the end of *every sentence*. Just wait for a natural stopping place.

NoraActon48267382 (3:27:43 PM): Oh. All right.

NoraActon48267382 (3:27:47 PM): What's LOL? And :P?

thejanethe (3:27:49 PM): Oh, sorry. LOL is "laughing out loud". :P is the same as :-P, which, as you can see, ZIM makes into a nice cartoony smiley face for you. It's the tongue-sticking-out one.

NoraActon48267382 (3:27:54 PM): Goodness, you type so much faster than I do.

NoraActon48267382 (3:27:58 PM): I see. There's a picture of one of those next to the button that says "Send," too.

thejanethe (3:28:01 PM): Yes. Good work.

NoraActon48267382 (3:28:05 PM): What's that for?

thejanethe (3:28:07 PM): Click on it and see.

NoraActon48267382 (3:28:11 PM): Oh, wow, look at all these little faces!

NoraActon48267382 (3:28:16 PM): :) :-(;-) :-P :-o B-)

thejanethe (3:28:18 PM): Whoa there. LOL

NoraActon48267382 (3:28:22 PM): I take it LOL isn't literal? I haven't yet heard you laugh.

thejanethe (3:28:26 PM): Oh. I guess it isn't. Ha, I've never IMed with someone in the same room before.

NoraActon48267382 (3:28:30 PM): First time for everything... even more so in my case.

thejanethe (3:28:33 PM): I guess LOL mostly means "I'm amused, I'm smiling", or something along those lines.

NoraActon48267382 (3:28:39 PM): Then what are the little faces for?

thejanethe (3:28:46 PM): Ummmm... I'm... less amused?

NoraActon48267382 (3:28:51 PM): Ah. LOL

NoraActon48267382 (3:28:54 PM): Did I do that right?

thejanethe (3:28:57 PM): ::snerk:: Yeah, you're catching on.

NoraActon48267382 (3:29:05 PM): Does "snerk" mean "snicker"? And what are the colons for?

thejanethe (3:29:09 PM): Um, that's sort of what it means, I guess. And the colons denote action.

NoraActon48267382 (3:29:15 PM): So, if I said ::pick up a pen:: that would mean I was picking up a pen?

thejanethe (3:29:18 PM): You'd probably say it ::picks up a pen::,

187

actually. We tend to refer to ourselves in third person when we write things in colons like that.

thejanethe (3:29:22 PM): You can also use asterisks. *picks up a pen*

thejanethe (3:29:26 PM): I prefer to use colons, though, because I use asterisks for emphasis.

NoraActon48267382 (3:29:35 PM): Oh, my. I see I was right in suspecting that you have an entire dialect on the Internet.

thejanethe (3:29:38 PM): It's really not that complicated.

NoraActon48267382 (3:29:42 PM): So how come you didn't say ::snerks::?

thejanethe (3:29:51 PM): ...I think I was using it as a noun. You can do that with laughs and smiles and things. And did you get a screen name so you could harass me about points of Internet grammar? Because I would rather be writing my story if that's all I'm here for.

NoraActon48267382 (3:30:00 PM): You're here for whatever you want to be here for, Jane. Our sessions are yours to shape.

thejanethe (3:30:06 PM): Great. I get to do all the work. Couldn't I just stay home and shape my own sessions then? Seriously.

NoraActon48267382 (3:30:15 PM): Oh, come on, Jane, if you're going to try to trip me up you can do better than that! You know that the point of therapy is that you bounce your thoughts and ideas off the therapist in order to try to acknowledge and better understand your thoughts and feelings.

NoraActon48267382 (3:30:16 PM): :)

NoraActon48267382 (3:30:19 PM): (Can I send a little face in its own message like that?)

thejanethe (3:30:22 PM): Man, you are all about this Internet-grammar thing. Sure.

NoraActon48267382 (3:30:56 PM): So why did you decide to bring your laptop to today's session?

thejanethe (3:31:04 PM): I thought I got to shape the direction of the session.

NoraActon48267382 (3:31:12 PM): You do, if you choose to take the reins. So far you've been choosing to try to stonewall me instead. And that's fine. But if I gave up at the first sign of resistance, I wouldn't be a very good therapist at all.

thejanethe (3:31:16 PM): Why not? Resistance means the patient doesn't want your help. I thought your big mantra was that you couldn't help anyone who didn't want to be helped?

NoraActon48267382 (3:31:20 PM): That's true. But resistance doesn't necessarily mean the patient doesn't want to be helped.

thejanethe (3:31:22 PM): Um, duh. Yes, it does.

NoraActon48267382 (3:31:28 PM): Not necessarily, Jane. Sometimes resistance is much more about fear than anything else.

thejanethe (3:31:33 PM): Why do you keep inserting my first name everywhere? "Blah blah blah, Jane," "Jane, blah blah blah." Is that some old-lady therapist thing?

NoraActon48267382 (3:31:41 PM): Probably. But getting back to my original question, what made you decide to bring your laptop in today?

thejanethe (3:31:44 PM): What are you, a psychiatric pitbull?

NoraActon48267382 (3:31:48 PM): Quite possibly. How does that make you feel?

thejanethe (3:31:52 PM): ...

NoraActon48267382 (3:31:56 PM): :)

thejanethe (3:31:58 PM): OMG you are messing with me, aren't you?

NoraActon48267382 (3:32:05 PM): I'll confess to using a little humor to break the tension every now and then. What's OMG?

thejanethe (3:32:06 PM): Jesus. LOL

NoraActon48267382 (3:32:08 PM): OMG is Jesus? :)

thejanethe (3:32:10 PM): Sort of.

> **RawKdAsKEEbaLL** (3:32:10 PM):
> WE WON!!!
> !!!!!!!!!!!!!!!!!!!!!!11 2 MORE REGONIAL
> TOURNAMENTS & WERE GOING 2
> REGIONALS!!!!!!!!!!!!!!!!!!!!!!!!!!!!!!!!!!!11
>
> **thejanethe** (3:32:13 PM): Oh, hey,
> Gary!
>
> **thejanethe** (3:32:15 PM):
> Congratulations!

NoraActon48267382 (3:32:17 PM):
Did your computer make that noise just
now, or did I do something?

thejanethe (3:32:20 PM): No, it's
someone else IMing me. Hold on, I'll
get rid of him.

NoraActon48267382 (3:32:25 PM):
Oh, you can do two of these at one
time? That sounds confusing.

> **RawKdaSkEEbaLL** (3:32:26 PM):
> OMG u so shud have been their we
> KICKED ASSSSSSS
>
> **thejanethe** (3:32:28 PM): Awesome!
>
> **thejanethe** (3:32:30 PM): Seriously,
> that's fantastic!
>
> **RawKdaSkEEbaLL** (3:32:34 PM):
> WOOT WOOT next match is in
> farberville can u go?!?!?!!!?!

thejanethe (3:32:36 PM): I can try. I'd like to.

thejanethe (3:32:39 PM): But right now, I should probably go... I'm busy, Gary, sorry. :(

RawKdaSkEEbaLL (3:32:43 PM): yah ur busy on the internet :P

thejanethe (3:32:45 PM): No, really. I'm -- okay, fine, honestly? I'm in a therapy session.

RawKdaSkEEbaLL (3:32:49 PM): waht are u doing on the internet in a threapy session?!? lol

thejanethe (3:32:51 PM): ...that's a long story. But I probably shouldn't chat with other people until the session is over.

RawKdaSkEEbaLL (3:32:55 PM): y who r u chattin w/

thejanethe (3:32:57 PM): ...my therapist.

RawKdaSkEEbaLL (3:33:01 PM): LOL!!!!!! wtf?!?!

thejanethe (3:33:05 PM): Look, I'll explain later, I just should go for now, okay?

RawKdaSkEEbaLL (3:33:07 PM): ok

RawKdaSkEEbaLL (3:33:09 PM): but dude, u so have to explian

thejanethe (3:33:10 PM): Yes, I know.

Later.

thejanethe (3:33:12 PM):
Congratulations again!

RawKdaSkEEbaLL (3:33:13 PM):
WOOT WOOT FARBERBILLE QUACK
IN FEAR OF US

thejanethe (3:33:13 PM): Hi, sorry.

NoraActon48267382 (3:33:15 PM): Don't worry about it. I was picking a "buddy icon".

NoraActon48267382 (3:33:17 PM): Can you see it?

thejanethe (3:33:18 PM): Did you seriously just pick a Pikachu icon?!

NoraActon48267382 (3:33:20 PM): Why not?

NoraActon48267382 (3:33:22 PM): I thought it was cute.

thejanethe (3:33:26 PM): OK, that's from Pokemon and it's for nine-year-olds. Try again.

NoraActon48267382 (3:33:27 PM): Oh. All right.

NoraActon48267382 (3:33:30 PM): How about this? I like cats.

thejanethe (3:33:32 PM): AAAAAAAAAAAACK THAT IS FOR FURRIES AND OMG OMG THAT IS SO NOT ALLOWED

NoraActon48267382 (3:33:34 PM): Goodness. What's a furry?

thejanethe (3:33:36 PM): ...I am not explaining it to you. But go pick another icon. From another category or something. One that does NOT SAY "FURRY PRIDE" ON IT. What are you in, the Humiliating Crap category?

NoraActon48267382 (3:33:39 PM): Well, the one I'm in just says "Cartoons". But in the interest of time, can I just use this smile face?

thejanethe (3:33:40 PM): Yes. Yes, by all means. Please do.

NoraActon48267382 (3:33:42 PM): Well, all right. :)

NoraActon48267382 (3:33:43 PM): So, who were you chatting with? He seemed entertaining.

thejanethe (3:33:45 PM): Hm? Oh. That was Gary. And, yeah, I guess he is pretty entertaining.

NoraActon48267382 (3:33:47 PM): He's a friend of yours?

thejanethe (3:33:50 PM): I don't know what the heck he is. He's... man, it's awfully hard to find words for Gary. Eesh.

NoraActon48267382 (3:33:55 PM): More along the lines of a boyfriend?

thejanethe (3:33:57 PM): ::eyeroll:: Do I look like a girl who has a boyfriend? No.

NoraActon48267382 (3:34:04 PM): Well, I'm not sure what a girl who has a boyfriend looks like, really. But if he's not a friend and he's not a boyfriend, how would you describe him?

thejanethe (3:34:07 PM): Gary... Gary. I guess I would say that Gary is a dyslexic regional Skeeball champion who introduced himself to me by asking whether my math teacher drinks more coffee or more tea.

NoraActon48267382 (3:34:12 PM): You're right, he certainly does sound entertaining. :)

thejanethe (3:34:15 PM): He's a friend of mine, I guess. It's just weird, because I don't really do the whole "friends" thing.

NoraActon48267382 (3:34:19 PM): So chatting with friends isn't how you pass your time online, then? Or do you only chat with Gary?

thejanethe (3:34:31 PM): Online's different.

NoraActon48267382 (3:34:35 PM): How so?

thejanethe (3:34:37 PM): It just is. You can tell.

NoraActon48267382 (3:34:44 PM): I can. And I suspect it's even more different when you're not sitting across the room from the other person.

thejanethe (3:34:46 PM): Uh, yeah. ::eyeroll::

NoraActon48267382 (3:34:50 PM): Yes! See, I saw that eyeroll across the room.

thejanethe (3:34:53 PM): Yes, your perceptive acuity is unparallelled.

NoraActon48267382 (3:35:02 PM): Why, thank you, Jane. At any rate, it's one thing when you can see expressions across a room. But I'm led to wonder what happens when you're typing to a total blank slate.

thejanethe (3:35:05 PM): ...blank slate?

NoraActon48267382 (3:35:11 PM): Yes. What's it like to be typing to a blank screen? When no one can see your reactions?

thejanethe (3:35:13 PM): You type out your reactions. That's the point.

NoraActon48267382 (3:35:16 PM): But do you? Always?

thejanethe (3:35:18 PM): Whatever. Sometimes I don't tell people when I'm rolling my eyes at them.

NoraActon48267382 (3:35:26 PM): Yes, you forgot to mention it just now. ;)

thejanethe (3:35:29 PM): You're really getting the hang of those smileys. Bully for you.

NoraActon48267382 (3:35:39 PM): You're adept at covering your emotions in real life, Jane, and you spend a lot of energy on it. I'm wondering if it isn't that much easier online. And if that isn't important to you.

thejanethe (3:35:41 PM): Whatever. I mostly just talk to Gary. Or random people who are online.

NoraActon48267382 (3:35:45 PM): What sort of random people?

thejanethe (3:35:47 PM): Um, what does the word "random" mean to you?

NoraActon48267382 (3:35:54 PM): Sorry, I phrased that badly. What I mean is, how do you find these random people?

thejanethe (3:35:57 PM): Wherever. Different websites, mostly. Chatrooms occasionally.

NoraActon48267382 (3:36:04 PM): How do those work? I'm sorry to sound so dense, but I'm so new to this.

thejanethe (3:36:07 PM): Jesus. Okay, websites are websites. You know what a website is?

NoraActon48267382 (3:36:11 PM): I think I do...

thejanethe (3:36:16 PM): God, how old ARE you? Websites, like yippee. com, zooooomsearch.com. Stuff that ends in .com, those are websites. Or they end in .org or .net. If you get to it by going in to Internet Explorer or Firefox or Chrome or whatever, that's a website.

NoraActon48267382 (3:36:20 PM): Oh! I know websites.

thejanethe (3:36:22 PM): Congratulations, you win the internet.

NoraActon48267382 (3:36:26 PM): I win the Internet?

thejanethe (3:36:28 PM): JUST AN EXPRESSION. Man.

NoraActon48267382 (3:36:33 PM): Okay, so how do you find people to talk to on websites?

thejanethe (3:36:39 PM): Well, it depends on the website. There are a few that most people use. ReCirclr and FriendsLink are the main ones. For people my age, anyway. :P

NoraActon48267382 (3:36:42 PM): So how do ReCirclr and FriendsLink work?

thejanethe (3:36:44 PM): You've seriously never heard of FriendsLink?

NoraActon48267382 (3:36:48 PM): It sounds a bit familiar, but I'm not sure.

thejanethe (3:36:51 PM): Man, congratulations on being one of like 200 people in this country who don't have a FriendsLink. :P

thejanethe (3:36:53 PM): You give it your real name, and then you can search for people you know by their names. Then you follow them and you can see status updates that they make.

thejanethe (3:36:55 PM): STATUS UPDATES are just short posts about basic stuff that happens in your life.

thejanethe (3:36:57 PM): You can chat like this with friends who are on the site at the same time as you as well.

NoraActon48267382 (3:37:02 PM): Oh, wait, I think I do know about this one. People keep sending me invitations to join.

thejanethe (3:37:04 PM): So why haven't you?

NoraActon48267382 (3:37:07 PM): I suppose it's just not really my thing.

NoraActon48267382 (3:37:12 PM): A friend of mine let me look at hers once and it seemed like most of the people she was friends were either talking about whether they had done their laundry that day or posting pictures of food they were about to eat.

thejanethe (3:37:14 PM): LOL!

thejanethe (3:37:16 PM): Maybe your friend should work on having less boring friends.

NoraActon48267382 (3:37:19 PM): Maybe. :)

NoraActon48267382 (3:37:24 PM): But, wait, I'm confused: I was asking how you found "random people" online, but it sounds like that site is mostly for keeping in touch with people you already know.

NoraActon48267382 (3:37:27 PM): So how do you meet new people on the Internet?

thejanethe (3:37:39 PM): I really don't get why you care about any of this.

NoraActon48267382 (3:37:42 PM): Well, I'm interested in why you

196

care about any of it.

thejanethe (3:37:45 PM): Oh, so now I have to explain or you'll think I'm wasting my life on boring crap. Way to manipulate.

NoraActon (3:37:48 PM): Well, that wasn't my intention at all, but now I'm curious about two things: how you meet new people on the Internet, and why you're trying to avoid explaining it to me.

thejanethe (3:37:51 PM): Jesus.

NoraActon48267382 (3:37:54 PM): You could also have said: ::very large eyeroll::

NoraActon48267382 (3:37:56 PM): Oh! And then you could have said: ::giggles::

thejanethe (3:37:58 PM): ::snort:: This is true. I could have. Take a gold star.

NoraActon48267382 (3:38:02 PM): I won the Internet, I get a gold star, this is great.

thejanethe (3:38:05 PM): Ha.

NoraActon48267382 (3:38:09 PM): And now you could say ::giggles:: again.

thejanethe (3:38:12 PM): I'm sorry, we have no more prizes to give out today.

NoraActon48267382 (3:38:15 PM): No wonder, if your Internet is all gone.

thejanethe (3:38:19 PM): Don't worry, it gets replenished frequently.

NoraActon48267382 (3:38:22 PM): Oh, good.

NoraActon48267382 (3:38:28 PM): But back on my original topic, what are the "ReCirclr" and "chat rooms" that you mentioned above? Are those the places where you meet new people?

thejanethe (3:38:36 PM): ::sigh:: Those are the two main places, yes.

NoraActon48267382 (3:38:39 PM): So what are they like?

thejanethe (3:38:44 PM): Well, chat rooms are kind of like this, only with a bunch of people. You use a program to go into a "room" where there are a bunch of people online and you just talk with them. ReCirclr is a website where people... hm, it's hard to explain.

thejanethe (3:38:52 PM): The big thing about it is that people post all kinds of stuff -- pictures, text posts, video clips, whatever -- and if other people like something you posted they can repost it so all their friends can see it. Or people can post their own responses to it.

NoraActon48267382 (3:38:54 PM): Interesting.

NoraActon48267382 (3:38:57 PM): And how do you find people to talk to in chat rooms and ReCirclr?

thejanethe (3:39:03 PM): You can just search for people who are interested in things you're interested in.

NoraActon48267382 (3:39:06 PM): Ah. What kind of interests?

thejanethe (3:39:12 PM): I don't know, all kinds of things.

NoraActon48267382 (3:39:15 PM): Well, like hobbies?

thejanethe (3:39:17 PM): Sure. Like hobbies. Whatever.

NoraActon48267382 (3:39:20 PM): So do you only talk to people about your favorite hobbies, then, or do you talk about other things too?

thejanethe (3:39:30 PM): Uh, you kind of talk about anything you feel like talking about. Like normal people. :P We're not aliens or something.

thejanethe (3:39:33 PM): Look, isn't time supposed to be up now?

NoraActon48267382 (3:39:51 PM): Actually, you're right. There are about ten minutes left but I wanted to discuss some housekeeping matters with you -- scheduling, appointment frequency, and so on. If you don't mind, I think I'd prefer to discuss that via vocal cords. Talking via computer has been very interesting and you can feel free to bring your computer in next time if you'd like to try it again, but I think it would be good to keep at least part of our session spoken out loud each week.

thejanethe (3:39:56 PM): Whatever you say.

thejanethe has signed off.

river_tammy:

wtf is going on w/jaela lately? two episodes ago she was obsessed w/ rescuing her parents then last week she was slutting it up and creeping on thorin and now she's trying to send luko into a black hole. why can't this show keep track of its plots for like two seconds

#looktotomorrow #ltt

jessamyns_jenna:

Related question -- why is Jaela a total idiot?

#looktotomorrow #jaela #yeahisaidit

racheltessers:

Wow, you guys are being pretty harsh! I find it ironic that a couple weeks ago, when Jaela was trying to save her parents, all anyone could talk about was how terrible she was for endangering her planet and whatever, blah blah blah. So then she backs off from it, and now everyone's on about how she should still be focusing on the thing with her parents. I mean, make up your minds, guys.

Personally, I think what's been going on with Jaela makes perfect sense as an emotional arc. Saureshan's election plunged her back into her grief over her parents, and so she was trying to rescue them -- but then the first attempt failed, and I think she just couldn't bear to keep herself immersed in it anymore. And when people are reeling from grief, they often throw themselves passionately into other things. Thorin is an important emotional support for her (and seriously, "slutting it up"? where on earth are you getting that? What, did she wear too much lipstick for you or something?) and Luko is in alliance with Saureshan and is currently doing horrible things to the planet where Jaela lived for the second half of her childhood. She's not being inconsistent and she's certainly not being an "idiot". She's dealing with things the best way she can.

#rachelcaresaboutthings #rachelexplainstheworld #jaeladefenderforever

200

#awilddramallamaapproaches
#looktotomorrow #ltt

jessamyns_jenna:
Or she's an idiot.

#looktotomorrow #jaela #standingbyit

tardisxroniaotp:
ffs, jenna, why can't you ever lay off for like two seconds? give it a rest. Smh

lttgurl4life:
wtf?!?!! jaelas so not an idiet! she was the smartest in the entire acadamy!!!!!! u just dont want her to get together w/thorin bc u want the rest of us 2 be miserable!!!!!!!!!!!!

#looktotommorow #ltt

jessamyns_jenna:
Wow. Speaking of idiots...

harmony4eva:
pops popcorn

racheltessers has unfollowed the rest of this thread.

Look to Tomorrow: Auction Planning has finished loading.

RachelTessers has entered the chat.

RachelTessers (7:29:08): Hi, guys!

RachelTessers (7:31:02) ...anybody here?

RachelTessers (7:35:33): ::taps mic:: Is this thing on? ;)

RachelTessers (7:36:20): No, seriously, I have no idea if the chat just isn't loading properly, or if I am... talking to myself. I hope I'm not talking to myself. LOL

RachelTessers (7:38:09): Anyway, I'll give it a few. Send me a FL chat if you're here, just so I know.

* * *

Rachel W (7:42:43 PM): Hey, Teresa, what's up?

Teresa L (7:42:49 PM): oh hey rachel

Teresa L (7:42:50 PM): nmh, u?

Rachel W (7:42:53 PM): Oh, I was just checking in because we were scheduled to do that auction planning chat tonight, you know, on the LtT IRC channel?

Teresa L (7:42:59 PM): oh right

Teresa L (7:42:01 PM): crap I'm sry, I totally forgot

Rachel W (7:42:03 PM): Oh, no problem. We're off to a bit of a slow start :), so you're welcome to join now.

Teresa L (7:42:20 PM): yeah the prob is my boyfriend's over now & its not rly a good time

Rachel W (7:42:23 PM): Oh. Well, no problem. I'll email you about whatever we come up with and where we're planning to go from here?

Teresa L (7:42:37 PM): coolbeans

Rachel W (7:42:38 PM): Thanks, T!

Teresa L (7:42:38 PM): later

* * *

Rachel W (7:43:22 PM): Hey, Aimee, what's up?

Aimee J (7:43:22 PM): "Apparently, the Chrononautical Hologrammer is not at this time sensitive enough to detect the presence of large piles of manure in the landing zone. Jaela, could you send headquarters a message to work on that?" --Thorin Lancet, LOL!

Rachel W (7:43:23 PM): LOL Great quote.

Rachel W (7:43:26 PM): Just checking in to see if you were around -- we were going to do that auction-planning chat on IRC, if you felt like popping in...

Rachel W (7:44:02 PM): Well, hope to see you there! Later!

* * *

SaraPear has entered the chat.

SaraPear (7:45:13 PM): hey is anyone here

RachelTessers (7:45:14 PM): Sara! Hey!

SaraPear (7:45:16 PM): where is everyone lol

RachelTessers (7:45:18 PM): I have no idea! They have all mysteriously disappeared.

SaraPear (7:45:20 PM): like the chat crashed?

RachelTessers (7:45:22 PM): No, like no one's shown up yet. LOL

RachelTessers (7:45:27 PM): Maybe you're right and the chat isn't working right, I don't know. Did you have any problem getting in?

SaraPear (7:45:29 PM): no it loaded fine

RachelTessers (7:45:33 PM): Huh. Maybe people didn't get the message? I posted to RC and FL about it earlier today, but maybe I should have posted about it last night too, for the RC night crowd.

SaraPear (7:45:40 PM): yea maybe

RachelTessers (7:45:43 PM): I hope no one's mad at me about the ReCirclr thread from last night -- the one about Jaela's parents.

SaraPear (7:45:55 PM): oh i don't think anyone's mad at u

RachelTessers (7:45:58 PM): I hope not. I felt like it got a little more dramatastic than I wanted it to be.

SaraPear (7:46:04 PM): yea it got kinda nuts but u weren't really in the drama part

RachelTessers (7:46:06 PM): Well, I'm glad you think so.

RachelTessers (7:46:09 PM): I hope everyone else does too. :)

RachelTessers (7:46:14 PM): Anyway. About the auction -- do you want to try to start planning now and see who shows? We couldn't talk donations or anything, but there are a few nuts-and-bolts behind-the-scenes things we could talk about.

SaraPear (7:46:21 PM): well i have a lot of homework rite now so im not sure

SaraPear (7:46:26 PM): can u just message me when ppl come? & ill do my homework until then

RachelTessers (7:46:30 PM): Oh. Yeah, totally. Just leave FL chat on, I'll let you know.

SaraPear (7:46:36 PM): ok, ty

* * *

Rachel W (7:46:03 PM): Hey, Jennie! You up for an auction chat?

Jennie P (7:46:03 PM): BEARFIGHT CONCERT!!!! ^.^

Rachel W (7:46:05 PM): Oh, hey, you got tickets? That's cool.

Rachel W (7:46:07 PM): Drop me a line when you get in, I'll update you on what's up with the auction.

* * *

RachelTessers: @CeruleanCervidae Hey Teal, have you seen Audra around anywhere? We were supposed to meet up in the auction-plan chat but she never showed

CeruleanCervidae: @RachelTessers Nope... sorry. How's that going?

RachelTessers: @CeruleanCervidae Idk. No one's shown up yet. LOL

CeruleanCervidae: @RachelTessers ha, sorry about that

RachelTessers: @CeruleanCervidae You're welcome to drop by if you like -- we really appreciate you donating that fic

CeruleanCervidae: @RachelTessers I'm a little busy right now, but I'll try to make it...

RachelTessers: @CeruleanCervidae Awesome! Thanks! :)

* * *

thejanethe (11:09:32 PM): Hey, Gary, you there?

Auto-Response from **RawKdaSkEEbaLL**: restin up 4 the SKEEBALL REGIONALS WOOWOOWOO GO SQUIRRELS

thejanethe (11:09:43 PM): I still can't believe you guys call yourselves the Squirrels

thejanethe (11:12:21 PM): Gary? Are you there?

thejanethe (11:12:49 PM): I just thought maybe the sound on your IM was on and you might wake up or... I don't know

thejanethe (11:13:37 PM): I just feel sort of... like things are falling apart?

thejanethe (11:14:02 PM): I'm supposed to be running this auction thing for the Lookies contest, I think I told you, and it's not going very well. And I sort of feel like... I don't know, I guess everyone's just busy, but I got to feeling lonely, I guess.

thejanethe (11:14:07 PM): I don't get why NO ONE is helping me with this auction when I'm putting so much work in and everyone knows it's our only shot at the special prizes, but more than that... I don't know

thejanethe (11:14:13 PM): It just feels like people are avoiding me or brushing me off or whatever. Do you know what I mean?

thejanethe (11:16:14 PM): Gary?

thejanethe has signed off.

From: "Elana Landry" <<u>elandry@yippee.com</u>>
To: <u>tennysonlovers@yippeegroups.com</u>
Subject: Re: in memoriam and healing through writing
Date: 4/12/2013

I'm not sure that I understand your premise when you talk about writing
as therapeutic and cite Tennyson as an example. I know he was severely
depressed throughout his life, but I don't agree that he's any kind of an
example that people should follow in trying to deal with depression. To
my mind, and I've written about this a little before in <u>previous posts</u>,
Tennyson's poetry -- particularly "In Memoriam" -- is heartwrenching
and beautifully written, but seems to have been actively keeping him
from healing. I mean, it's like picking at a scab. He wrote about Hallam's
death for *twelve years*, pretty obsessively! Twelve years of deep grieving
does not show great healing, you know what I mean? And take lines
like "He loves to make parade of pain/That with his piping he may gain/
The praise that comes to constancy..." How does that square with your
assertion that he was writing in order to heal?

The site you're linking to, the one about depression and healing through
the written word, is pretty hippie and New Age-looking. I just don't see
the relevance to a scholarly discussion of Tennyson and his work -- which,
if you look at the group info, is what this group is for.

From: "Astrid Moore" <<u>waverflame@yippee.com</u>>
To: <u>tennysonlovers@yippeegroups.com</u>
Subject: Re: in memoriam and healing through writing
Date: 4/12/2013

a. i'm not a newbie & i know what the group is for. so do the mods. when
they tell me to take the post down i will.

b. tennyson wrote "in memoriam" as a bunch of individual poems. not all
at once. so it wasn't like an ongoing project that he obsessed over for 12
years. he just NEVER lost his grief for his friend. because when you lose

someone that close, you NEVER do. you will always remember them. so he wrote about remembering his friend, and grieving for him. which was the healthiest way for him to deal with it.

c. you have a logical fallecy when you assume that b/c he grieved for 12 years and wrote about his grief, his writing caused his grief

d. thanks for the nice "hippie and new age" jab. i'm going to take you so much more seriously now i know you're some conservative suit who thinks little pills of serotonin-boosters prescribed by a billion-dollar drug industry that has a vested interest in people keeping on feeling crappy so they can make more money off their pills is a better way of dealing with GRIEF than actually GRIEVING. this country is so all about not wanting people to feel things. at least in tennyson's era people didn't have all these little pills to substitute for emotions, so they knew how to talk/write about what they were feeling.

From: "Elana Landry" <elandry@yippee.com>
To: tennysonlovers@yippeegroups.com
Subject: Re: in memoriam and healing through writing
Date: 4/12/2013

Whoo, boy! For all your insistence that "I know what this group is for", you sure know how to drag a thread off-topic. For your information, I am not a "conservative suit" and I don't believe in medications for depression either. I believe in people getting on with their lives. THAT is the problem with our country today, and it's the reason both for the "billion-dollar drug industry" AND the hippie-dippie writing-about-your-feelings-will-cure-your-cancer crap that's up on that website you linked

Despite the fact that virtually nothing in your comment had anything to do with Tennyson, I'll be nice and bring this back on topic. It's absolutely not a logical "fallecy" (see also: the part in the comm info where it asks that we use proper spelling and grammar) to say that Tennyson's writing

208

about his grief perpetuated his grief. Come on, we're talking about <u>twelve years</u> here. You can't tell me you think it's normal to keep grieving for that long. Plus, he even talks about how he's not sure why he's writing. I used to love "In Memoriam", but the more I read it the more it seems like he's getting off on grieving. Like he knows that his pain makes for good poetry, so he just keeps clinging to it. What he needed wasn't to record every single thing he was feeling. And it wasn't Prozac either. What people don't get is that there are choices involved here. He made a choice to write about his friend's death constantly, he made a choice to obsess over those feelings rather than eventually getting to a point where he ignored them and let them weaken on their own. What he did was like throwing wood on a fire. You have to starve a fire.

Everyone acts like grief is some sacred emotion and you have to succumb to it before you can heal. Grief isn't sacred. It's just a shitty emotion like every other shitty emotion, and shitty emotions are just like every other shitty thing in life. Why would you want to invite shitty things into your life? Why would you want to fetishize them in 131 poems?

From: "Astrid Moore" <<u>waverflame@yippee.com</u>>
To: <u>tennysonlovers@yippeegroups.com</u>
Subject: Re: in memoriam and healing through writing
Date: 4/12/2013

haha, you're so oblivious i feel sorry for you. come back when someone close to you dies & you actually know what grief/emotion is. until then you're just embarrassing yourself. how old are you? you're so naive and ignorant you sound like you're about 12.

From: "Elana Landry" <<u>elandry@yippee.com</u>>
To: <u>tennysonlovers@yippeegroups.com</u>
Subject: Re: in memoriam and healing through writing
Date: 4/12/2013

What the FUCK makes you think you know a single fucking thing about my life? I'm not 12, I'm 27 and a graduate student working on my dissertation, and you're a fucking asshole. Why don't you go grab one of your crystals you use to align your chakras and say a prayer to the Sacred Goddess while you shove it up your ass.

Asskicker Du Jour (motherabraham@yippeegroups.com) moderated a thread in **tennysonlovers:** MOD NOTE

This thread has been frozen. Both "elandry" and "waverflame" are temporarily suspended from commenting and posting. Read the group info on what is and is not allowed in this group before reapplying for posting access.

thejanethe (3:21:23 PM): I'll do this IM therapy thing again if you want, but I have to warn you I'm not going to be paying much attention.

thejanethe (3:21:27 PM): I'm in a Scrabble tournament on boredgames. net today. I have to win six games by seven pm to qualify.

NoraActon48267382 (3:21:32 PM): Really? Who's in the tournament?

thejanethe (3:21:36 PM): Anyone. It's a pretty new site. I think this is their first official ranking tournament.

thejanethe (3:21:45 PM): Which is why I get to compete at all. :P Scrabble tournaments are fun but usually the really good players are so much better than I am that there's no point.

NoraActon48267382 (3:21:48 PM): You'd rather not play if you're not going to win?

thejanethe (3:21:50 PM): Um, yeah. I'm not stupid.

thejanethe (3:21:53 PM): Anyway, I'm going to go register now.

NoraActon48267382 (3:21:57 PM): So playing for the sake of playing doesn't cut any ice with you.

thejanethe (3:22:00 PM): "Cut any ice?"

NoraActon48267382 (3:22:02 PM): "Dodge the question?"

thejanethe (3:22:05 PM): :P No. Anyway. Going now.

NoraActon48267382 (3:22:10 PM): Wait. Why don't you play against me?

thejanethe (3:22:14 PM): ...

thejanethe (3:22:16 PM): This is a stupid idea.

NoraActon48267382 (3:22:27 PM): Why? I have no familiarity with tournament Scrabble, so you're sure to beat me. With barely any effort, besides. Which means that you and I could continue our chat, and you could win your game, and I could be introduced to the world of tournament Scrabble.

thejanethe (3:22:30 PM): Why would you be interested in the world of tournament Scrabble?

thejanethe (3:22:33 PM): Are you even allowed to spend our therapy time playing games? That's so not therapy.

NoraActon48267382 (3:22:40 PM): Anything that interests you interests me. We've still got a lot of getting to know each other to do, after all. It's only been a few sessions.

NoraActon48267382 (3:22:45 PM): Oh, a lot of people wouldn't. But the way I figure it, if I don't play Scrabble with you, you won't talk to me.

NoraActon48267382 (3:22:47 PM): So what's the point of that?

thejanethe (3:22:49 PM): And what if I still don't talk to you?

NoraActon48267382 (3:22:52 PM): Then I get to play Scrabble. ;-)

thejanethe (3:22:54 PM): Dude, you are the stubbornest doctor ever.

NoraActon48267382 (3:22:58 PM): But I've learned my emoticons! (:-))

thejanethe (3:23:02 PM): How did you know they were called that?

thejanethe (3:23:04 PM): And what about boundaries?

NoraActon48267382 (3:23:07 PM): I do my research.

NoraActon48267382 (3:23:09 PM): What about boundaries?

thejanethe (3:23:12 PM): You're acting more like my friend than my therapist.

NoraActon48267382 (3:23:18 PM): There's no rule that says our therapeutic relationship can't be friendly, Jane. Oh, some schools of therapy would say so, but I don't adhere to one of those schools.

NoraActon48267382 (3:23:26 PM): Right now I think the most important things are giving you a chance to learn to trust me, and giving me a chance to get to know you. Anything that helps with that is okay in my book.

NoraActon48267382 (3:23:32 PM): Of course, there are certain standards of professionalism. But to my mind, playing Scrabble doesn't breach them at all.

thejanethe (3:23:35 PM): Hahahaha! You keep shooting for the moon, there, Nora.

NoraActon48267382 (3:23:38 PM): When did you get so concerned about boundaries?

thejanethe (3:23:40 PM): I do my research too.

NoraActon48267382 (3:23:43 PM): We're well matched, then. :)

NoraActon48267382 (3:23:45 PM): What do you mean, shooting for the moon?

thejanethe (3:23:47 PM): "Giving you a chance to learn to trust me." HAHAHAHAHAHA.

NoraActon48267382 (3:23:49 PM): Why is that such an outlandish idea, Jane?

thejanethe (3:23:50 PM): For starters, you haven't stopped calling me Jane every other word.

NoraActon48267382 (3:23:53 PM): Oops! You're right, perhaps I do do that too frequently.

NoraActon48267382 (3:23:56 PM): Why is that an impediment to trust, though?

thejanethe (3:23:58 PM): It's so *therapeutic*.

NoraActon48267382 (3:24:01 PM): I assume the italics make that a dirty word?

thejanethe (3:24:02 PM): Pretty much.

NoraActon48267382 (3:24:07 PM): So I'm a bad therapist because I'm therapeutic?

thejanethe (3:24:09 PM): In the sense that you act like a therapist, yeah.

NoraActon48267382 (3:24:13 PM): So you don't trust therapists in general.

thejanethe (3:24:15 PM): Um, no. LOL This is not news.

NoraActon48267382 (3:24:19 PM): Hm. What's so wrong with therapists?

NoraActon48267382 (3:24:23 PM): Besides the fact that we use first names too much.

thejanethe (3:24:27 PM): I don't need people prying around inside my head, thanks.

NoraActon48267382 (3:24:40 PM): But that's circular. What you're saying is that you don't trust people enough to let them inside your head, so you don't trust therapists because that's what they do. But that begs the question of why therapists in general are not worthy of your trust.

thejanethe (3:24:44 PM): ...talk about circular. You totally lost me.

NoraActon48267382 (3:24:48 PM): Boiled down: it's not therapists you don't trust. You don't trust people.

thejanethe (3:24:50 PM): This is also not news.

NoraActon48267382 (3:24:54 PM): But that's my point. You keep assuming that a lack of trust in other people is completely unsurprising, a done deal.

NoraActon48267382 (3:24:55 PM): Why?

thejanethe (3:24:59 PM): That's not true. I trust some people. Just not most people.

NoraActon48267382 (3:25:02 PM): Whom do you trust?

thejanethe (3:25:10 PM): I trust Gary. I guess.

NoraActon48267382 (3:25:13 PM): Your friend from school.

thejanethe (3:25:18 PM): Yeah. I can talk to him about stuff I wouldn't talk to most people about.

thejanethe (3:25:24 PM): It's just that people have to earn my trust. Why is this so revolutionary?

NoraActon48267382 (3:25:27 PM): But that's what I said I'd like to do, and you dismissed the possibility.

thejanethe (3:25:30 PM): Yeah, well, people don't have a very good track record thus far. And especially not therapists.

NoraActon48267382 (3:25:35 PM): I've looked at your medical record, and it seems like most of your therapeutic relationships were very short-lived. The longest one seemed to have lasted a few months.

thejanethe (3:25:38 PM): Like I said, I didn't trust them. No point in seeing them.

NoraActon48267382 (3:25:40 PM): Here's the thing, though. You shut people down.

NoraActon48267382 (3:25:42 PM): You've been trying very hard to do that ever since you set foot in here.

thejanethe (3:25:44 PM): What, are you going to tell Spectrum on me?

NoraActon48267382 (3:25:49 PM): Even though we can see each other's expressions, the lack of tone of voice fails us sometimes over the computer, doesn't it? You're not in any kind of trouble for your resistance. It's the way you approach this. We work with it. Your job isn't to make your therapy easy for me.

thejanethe (3:25:54 PM): Good. I wasn't really planning on it. :P

NoraActon48267382 (3:25:59 PM): So it doesn't make me angry when you attempt to short-circuit our therapy sessions. But it makes me wonder what's made you so mistrustful of people in general.

thejanethe (3:26:05 PM): If you get screwed over enough times, you don't want to get screwed over any more. I mean, a baby can learn not to touch a hot stove if it gets burned enough times.

NoraActon48267382 (3:26:07 PM): So you see trusting other people as touching a hot stove.

thejanethe (3:26:12 PM): I've gotten burned.

NoraActon48267382 (3:26:14 PM): How so?

thejanethe (3:26:19 PM): Just... people you're supposed to rely on aren't reliable.

thejanethe (3:26:24 PM): Everyone has their own life, and everyone's wrapped up in their own life, and no one's there for you when you need them. People make big speeches about how you should trust them and lay your life in their hands or whatever the hell, and then they're not there.

thejanethe (3:26:26 PM): You know those trust exercises where you fall backwards? People drop you.

NoraActon48267382 (3:26:28 PM): On purpose?

thejanethe (3:26:32 PM): Sometimes, and sometimes they're not strong enough, and sometimes they're falling-down drunk and you topple them over too, but anyway it doesn't matter because you're on the floor.

NoraActon48267382 (3:26:35 PM): By "falling-down drunk" you're referencing your father.

thejanethe (3:26:38 PM): Of course. Though I'm sure he told you he "doesn't drink anymore", that time he called you.

NoraActon48267382 (3:26:41 PM): You put "doesn't drink anymore" in quotes.

thejanethe (3:26:46 PM): Yeah, he's quit for like two weeks. He's all on about how his life has changed completely, and, well, whatever, Dad.

thejanethe (3:26:47 PM): Look, weren't we going to play Scrabble?

NoraActon48267382 (3:26:49 PM): Well, I'm not sure we'll have time for a full game at this point.

NoraActon48267382 (3:26:52 PM): Let's stay with this a moment. How do you react when you see your father drunk?

thejanethe (3:26:53 PM): Dude, I told you RIGHT OUT at the beginning

216

of the session that I have to win six games by seven o'clock. I'm not interested in staying with this a moment.

NoraActon48267382 (3:26:56 PM): Just the one question -- short answer? When you come home and find your father drunk, what do you do?

thejanethe (3:26:57 PM): I go up to my room. Come ON.

NoraActon48267382 (3:26:59 PM): Where the computer is.

thejanethe (3:27:01 PM): Where the computer is, yes. Is this supposed to be some sort of revelation?

NoraActon48267382 (3:27:03 PM): Is what supposed to be some sort of revelation?

thejanethe (3:27:05 PM): That I use the computer a lot because my dad's a drunk. I know that.

NoraActon48267382 (3:27:09 PM): Well, I'm not sure. I'm not sure that's necessarily the conclusion.

thejanethe (3:27:11 PM): Of course it is. Look, my home life is crappy, so I find a way out of it. It's sensible, not crazy.

NoraActon48267382 (3:27:14 PM): Goodness, I never thought it was crazy. Coping mechanisms are rarely crazy.

thejanethe (3:27:16 PM): My dad's drinking is a coping mechanism, right? Does that make it normal?

NoraActon48267382 (3:27:20 PM): Normal is a tricky term. Is it understandable? I think so. Is it healthy? No.

thejanethe (3:27:22 PM): So now you're going to tell me my computer use is unhealthy. I happen to think it's the only healthy thing IN my life.

NoraActon48267382 (3:27:23 PM): Tell me about how it's healthy.

thejanethe (3:27:25 PM): We just went over this! My dad is -- weird. My mom is dead. I'm socially awkward and I need some sort of escape.

thejanethe (3:27:26 PM): Name one thing that would be healthier, given all that.

NoraActon48267382 (3:27:28 PM): Maybe what you're doing right now.

NoraActon48267382 (3:27:29 PM): Talking about it. Feeling it.

thejanethe (3:27:31 PM): So I should just go to therapy all the time? I don't know if you noticed, but talking about it makes me FEEL SHITTY.

NoraActon48267382 (3:27:33 PM): Feeling shitty things... well, it feels shitty.

NoraActon48267382 (3:27:35 PM): Unfortunately, it's also necessary.

thejanethe (3:27:36 PM): Says the woman who makes a living off other people feeling shitty.

NoraActon48267382 (3:27:40 PM): Well, it's true I'd be out a job in a world where everyone's lives were perfect. However, it's also true that if we lived in that world, I'd be thrilled to take up a job in interior decorating.

thejanethe (3:27:42 PM): ::snort::

NoraActon48267382 (3:27:46 PM): My job isn't to keep you feeling shitty, Jane; it's to help you through the shitty feelings.

NoraActon48267382 (3:27:49 PM): And I wonder. Have you been happy in the last year or so, since you've delved so much into the Internet?

thejanethe (3:27:54 PM): More than I would be without it.

thejanethe (3:27:55 PM): Seriously, ARE WE GOING TO PLAY SCRABBLE?

NoraActon48267382 (3:27:59 PM): Well, we could give it a try, but I'm a little worried that we don't have quite enough time for that.

thejanethe (3:28:02 PM): Oh, man, you are SO not screwing up my tournament score. Let's go to boredgames.net, I'm starting a game with you and then you're forfeiting it.

218

NoraActon48267382 (3:28:04 PM): Oh, will that work? Great!

thejanethe (3:28:06 PM): I'll talk you through the registration. Let's go.

thejanethe has signed off.

brad memphis7 has requested a guest chat.

brad m (10:58:57 PM): hi

Rachel W (10:59:20 PM): Uh, hi. Do I know you?

brad m (10:59:06 PM): yea im brad memphis

brad m (10:59:15 PM): suck my cock

Rachel W has blocked **brad memphis7**.

jane shiling has requested a guest chat.

jane s (11:01:00 PM): hear i am back again

Rachel W (11:01:19 PM): Who the HELL is this?

jane s (11:02:14 PM): ur dream guy w/ a fat 12-inches 2 shove down ur throt

Rachel W *(11:03:12 PM):* 192.80.65.234

jane s (11:03:17 PM): ?

Rachel W (11:03:40 PM): That's your IP address, you jerkoff, and it'll take me about another five seconds to track it down to your house, so you want to go ahead and tell me who you are before I report you for harassment?

jane s (11:03:48 PM): oooooim scarred

Rachel W (11:04:13 PM): Never get over that botched circumcision, do you?

jane s (11:04:17 PM): huh

Rachel W: One more time: WHO IS THIS?

jane s (11:04:28 PM): i told you im brad mempis

jane s (11:04:48 PM): just like ur a 20yrold named rachel lololololololol

Rachel W (11:05:35 PM): what???

jane s (11:05:46 PM): Hi. I'm Rachel. I'm a 20-year-old English major at a small college in western Massachusetts whose name I'm not going to tell you, because I'm so phenomenally sexy that if I told you where I am I'm sure you wouldn't be able to resist stalking me. I'm a big-time fangirl for Brad Memphis. I spend most of my time writing fanfiction, getting my ass kicked by various classes, wasting way too much time online, being really terrible at intramural volleyball, and reading books that are not among my school assignments while ignoring the ones that are. Consequently, I'm a Red Bull addict, and I can pull more consecutive all-nighters than you, hands down. If there's anything more you want to know, feel free to message me to ask. I'm friendly. :)

Rachel W (11:05:55 PM): It's my profile info, so what?

jane s (11:07:39 PM): yeahkeep talkin JANE

Rachel W (11:07:46 PM): I have no idea what you're talking about.

jane s (11:08:09 PM): lololololol thats y u acepted the chat wen i changd my name to janeshiling lolol

Rachel W (11:08:14 PM): She's my cousin.

jane s (11:08:21 PM): HAHAHAHAHAHAHAHAAHAHAHA

jane s (11:08:39 PM): ur such a fuckin retard

Rachel W (11:09:00 PM): Meanwhile you still haven't said WHO THE HELL THIS IS

jane s (11:09:20 PM): i keep tellin u im brad

jane s (11:09:39 PM): i read all the storrys u rite abt me in eng class

jane s (11:09:44 PM): their sooooooooooo sexyyyy

Rachel W (11:09:55 PM): Whose English class?

Rachel W (11:10:28 PM): How did you get a hold of my name?

jane s (11:11:06 PM): you sined in on a scool comp u fuckin tard

Rachel W (11:11:45 PM): I told you I'm Jane's cousin. I was visiting her at school.

jane s (11:12:02 PM): He tried to pull back. His brain attempted to send a signal to his hands, his torso, his mouth -- this isn't a good idea, this should not be happening this way, stop! But her lips tasted of Palietan jasmine, coated with fine silver dust and undercut with the salty tang of drying tears -- traces of windblown pollen from a planet foreign to them both, and who knew that could be so erotic could be so mind-scrambling as she pulled him back in, kissed him harder, deeper, and he wanted her more than he'd ever wanted anything in his life --

Rachel W (11:12:04 PM): oh you SHIT

jane s (11:12:16 PM): HAHAHAHAHAHAHAHAHA

jane s (11:12:37 PM): shoudent put links to ur pornos in ur userinfo bitch

Rachel W (11:13:40 PM): what the fuck are you talking about, pornos? you and your right hand ought to know the difference

Rachel W (11:13:43 PM): or is it your index finger and your thumb?

jane s (11:14:10 PM): hahahahahahah we shd askthe kids @ scool if its porno or not ill print some coppies

jane s (11:14:14): we can red them allowed nxt time ms f is aslep

Rachel W has blocked **jane shiling**.

yousuck bradscock has requested a guest chat.

yousuck b (11:16:30 PM): hey wut hapned 2 all ur storys that were there

Rachel W (11:17:48 PM): What stories?

Rachel W (11:18:04 PM): You must have imagined them.

yousuck b (11:18:21 PM): oh well luckey i saved them

Rachel W (11:18:28 PM): Oh, right. You didn't save shit, you dumbass.

yousuck b (11:18:48 PM): hahah well have 2 wait 4 tommorow 2 c

Rachel W (11:18:56 PM): tomorrow's SATURDAY

Rachel W (11:19:16 PM): Let me lay it out for you real clear, dude:

yousuck b (11:21:08 PM): yea lay it out 4 me good lol

Rachel W (11:21:20 PM): a. I've never written any stories about Brad Memphis or anybody else

Rachel W (11:21:24 PM): b. I have no idea who Jane Shilling is or what you're talking about

Rachel W (11:21:25 PM): c.

yousuck b (11:21:38 PM): wuts c

Rachel W (11:21:44): oh, don't worry, it's coming

yousuck b (11:21:46): LOLOLOLOLOLOL I BET ITIS

Rachel W (11:22:01 PM): www.takemethere.cc

yousuck bradscock has left the chat.

http://www.diarynow.com/users/thejanethe/4350.html
Date: 4/13/2013
Security level: Private

oh god oh god oh god
NO! This is NOT HAPPENING, it just
Okay, it's okay. I have to calm down, I just have to
OKAY, jesus
Okay. I am not going to cry and scream and be hysterical anymore. I
-- no. I don't have *time* for that. This doesn't have to be a catastrophe
-- no, it DOESN'T have to be one, I AM NOT GOING TO LET THIS BE A
CATASTROPHE -- but I just have to do some stuff, I mean, figure out what
to do now. And then I'll do it. And -- good.

Right. I am breathing. I am thinking. I will make this okay.

I am making a list of all the things that will fix this and I am crossing
off the ones I have done and then I will keep crossing off as I do them
because that is organized and rational and stuff

1. ~~Emergency deletion of all of Rachel's fanfiction from all public sites~~
2. ~~Knock Jason offline before he can print any fics that might have been open/cached in his browser~~

I think I did this, oh, God, I hope this worked -- that's the crashout
shock site that the assholes at 69hackerz always use on newbies and trolls,
or I think it is, I don't even know, I know someone used it on Teal and she
lost a lot of her writing in a computer crash but that was a long time ago
and anyway I think it's just supposed to crash your computer with tons
of .gifs and browser windows that auto-open or something, I don't think
it's a virus or anything, and what if computers don't overload from that
stuff anymore? but the guest-connect infocheck said he was running IE6
(Jesus, IE6!) which means his computer is really really old, and anyway he
left right away without saying anything, so his computer probably crashed,
right? and if he was using IE6 there won't be any browser auto-save or
cache, so he can't have any of my fics anymore, except what if he DOES and
OH MY GOD I'M PANICKING AGAIN I WILL NOT PANIC I WILL NOT

It's going to be fine. I'm like 99% sure I kicked him offline before he
could do anything. I'll deal with the 1% chance if/when I need to.

224

Starting over:

1. ~~Delete of all Rachel's fanfiction from all public sites~~
2. ~~Knock Jason offline~~
3. ~~Create new email for Rachel & change all profiles to reflect new email~~
4. ~~Change DN username -- DO NOT forward from racheltessers~~
5. Repost all fanfic to a FLOCKED, SEPARATE DN
6. Send email to LtT Yippee group about switch in username/email/ fanfic posting

That's everything I can do online, I think. I'll do the last few things when I'm feeling more pulled together. I... oh God, I have to know if Jason managed to save my fanfic, I just have to know -- how can I find out? He's so stupid you can tell within like two seconds if he's bluffing, but I CAN'T wait the weekend to find out, and I can't chat him either, christ i'm falling apart AGAIN

Okay. I'll email Gary. Or call him. That's what I'll do. I'll get Gary to chat with Jason pretending to be someone at school, I don't know, whoever, or he can even be himself, and if Jason doesn't bring the fanfic thing up within like two seconds he probably hasn't got shit, but Gary can bring it up too, whatever, the point is that Jason WANTS to spread the word on this as fast as possible so if he doesn't C&P big sections of fanfic into the chat immediately it probably means he's got nothing. I was so horrified when Gary found out I write fanfic but thank God he knows, after all.

okay sending a text message

Gary, where are you

oh SHIT Jason just got back on FL, I SO can't deal with him, staying invisible, but I HAVE to know -- GARY WHERE ARE YOU

okay, okay, Gary's on it, okay

He hasn't got anything. He didn't answer Gary when Gary chatted him, which was suspicious enough because he'd totally have been crowing about it if he'd had anything. But Gary had Andrew Schmidt's password from back when they both used to hang out with Louie Vitelli & crew -- I think he found it out by accident or something, I didn't quite get that, but whatever, he had it and it saved my ass -- so he messaged Jason as Andrew (which was really pretty ballsy of him, and I'm going to have to thank him when I can think straight again) and Jason chatted with him for awhile but didn't say anything about the fics. If he had them there's *no way* he wouldn't have pasted it into the chat. He's always trying to impress Andrew. And everybody else at the entire school.

He's got nothing.

And I can't stop thinking "so do I..." but I WON'T. He is NOT going to take everything from me, he can't! This is MY life, Rachel is MY life, and Jason Malone is NOT FUCKING GOING TO WRECK IT. Okay, all the name-recognition-building stuff I was doing for the Lookies is sort of out the window, but it'll be okay, really, people know *me* not the name, right? Okay, so omgbradomgbrad is not the most creative handle in the world, but I had to come up with something fast and it couldn't have the word "Rachel" in it -- "Rachel" has got to disappear from the fandom. But I sent a message to the LtT boards/group letting them know I switched screen names (who knows, maybe I'll get floods of sympathy for having had my computer hacked -- that's what I told them -- and it'll actually be good for me) and telling them I'm going by "Maya" now in public instead of Rachel. The only really scary part is I deleted Rachel's ReCirclr right away because I had just backed it up on rcbook, but I forgot that that doesn't back up comments, which means the auction... is gone. Like, I don't have anyone's bids anymore. But I can probably reconstruct that from comment notifications? Or something. I can do that. When I have time.

I just have to start getting omgbradomgbrad settled into the fandom. Make sure all the fics are reposted properly, write some new ones to put on a new ff.com profile that'll link to omgbradomgbrad (igh, already I'm tired of typing that -- maybe I'll get used to it?). I have to email Audra and tell her what happened and write some new drabbles to put up on her site under the new name. I can get name recognition for omgbrad and carry over Rachel's fans, too. It'll be okay.

I'm afraid if I think too much about Jason Malone I might literally kill him. So... I won't.

He's got nothing on me. He *is* nothing. He's a NOTHING of a person who has NOTHING to do with me. And when I move to California and write for LtT I'm going to send him a letter with a nice autographed photo and a giant nest of California cockroaches, or something. Everything's fine.

226

Maya B has requested a guest chat.

Maya B (8:19:26 PM): Hi, Audra!

Audra S (8:19:32 PM): Hey, who's this?

Maya B (8:19:37 PM): It's Rachel -- this is the name I changed to because I got hacked.

Audra S (8:19:47 PM): Oh, Rach! Sorry! I didn't place the name at first.

Maya B (8:19:51 PM): It's OK. It feels kind of weird being Maya.

Audra S (8:19:59 PM) I bet!

Maya B (8:20:03 PM): How are you?

Audra S (8:20:10 PM): Oh, I'm fine.

Maya B (8:20:12 PM): Sure? Everything from the other night straightened out?

Audra S (8:20:19 PM): Hmm?

Maya B (8:20:21 PM): From Tuesday? You just seemed a little upset.

Audra S (8:20:27 PM): Oh, that's right. No, I'm totally cool.

Maya B (8:20:30 PM): Oh, good. :)

Maya B (8:20:35 PM): Oh, so, hey, did you get my email?

Maya B (8:20:38 PM): With my new site addresses and stuff?

Audra S (8:20:48 PM): Oh, yeah. I got it, sorry.

Maya B (8:20:54 PM): No, it's OK. I'm just being stupid and spazzy -- I don't know if people haven't checked their emails or if my email got spam-killed or what, but it seems like hardly anyone's friended me over at the new ReCirclr.

Maya B (8:20:57 PM): Hence my wandering around pestering people to make sure they got the email. ;)

Audra S (8:20:40 PM): Aw, hon. Sorry I hadn't friended you back yet. I just haven't been on RC or DN much. I'll go do that now.

Maya B (8:20:41 PM): Thanks. :)

Maya B (8:20:46 PM): I'm sorry I'm being such a pest, but I'm kind of shaken by this whole thing. I guess I'm just feeling a little insecure.

Audra S (8:20:48 PM): Yeah, I can see why. What a shitty thing to have happen. ::hugs::

Maya B (8:20:54 PM): Yeah... it was so random, you know? It just kind of came out of nowhere. I don't even know what happened exactly -- this random guy just sent me a guest chat and next thing I knew he was spouting all this horrible verbal abuse and listing the passwords for all my accounts.

Maya B (8:20:56 PM): I spent half the night trying to get them all shut down so he couldn't use them.

Audra S (8:20:59 PM): Uch, that's awful. Did he get any credit card info or anything like that?

Maya B (8:21:02 PM): No, nothing like that.

Audra S (8:21:04 PM): Well, that's lucky. Still, super-creepy. Ugh.

Maya B (8:21:09 PM): Mostly though what I'm worried about is the auction.

Maya B (8:21:12 PM): I lost all my records of who had donated what, and now I'm totally confused. I mean I had most of it in email notifications and stuff, but you know how RC went on the fritz and wasn't emailing comments for a few days there?

Maya B (8:21:16 PM): Now half the people in the auction are claiming they did a buy-it-now and posted a PayPal confirmation in that period, and I KNOW a bunch of them are lying, but I can't prove anything because the donations were set to go straight to the charity.

Maya B (8:21:18 PM): Jenna just sent me the bitchiest email.

Maya B (8:21:20 PM): I don't even know why she cares -- none of her fics are involved in the mess.

Audra S (8:21:22 PM): Oh, well, Jenna. Has she ever sent an email that *wasn't* bitchy? :)

Maya B (8:21:23 PM): True. :)

Maya B (8:21:25 PM): She's not the only one sending me mean emails, though.

Maya B (8:21:33 PM): I mean, to be fair, some people are being mean, but most of them are just freaked out -- and I guess it would suck to have actually donated money and then have the record of it lost. Though, FFS, it's donations to *charity*.

Maya B (8:21:35 PM): I sort of feel like people should just suck it up. LOL

Maya B (8:22:04 PM): Aud? Everything OK?

Audra S (8:22:07 PM): Yeah, I'm really sorry.

Audra S (8:22:08 PM): I'm chatting back and forth with somebody else, too. It's a school project thing.

Maya B (8:22:09 PM): Well, I certainly know what that's like!

Audra S (8:22:10 PM): I know! :)

Maya B (8:22:13 PM): Anyway, I know I've probably been asking like way too much of you, but I thought maybe sometime this weekend, maybe, if you weren't too busy, we could chat about auction stuff? I'm just really freaked out right now.

Maya B (8:22:15 PM): Your beta service is one of the contested items right now, so I thought maybe you could help straighten that out?

Maya B (8:22:17 PM): Plus, I thought maybe because you're so popular in the fandom you might be able to use your charms to worm the truth out of some people where I can't. ;)

Audra S (8:22:20 PM): Oh, I don't think I'm that popular!

Maya B (8:22:21 PM): Oh, you know you are! ;)

Audra S (8:22:22 PM): Ah, you're just as popular as I am. :)

Maya B (8:22:23 PM): No I'm not! ROFLMAO

Audra S (8:22:25 PM): Well, we won't quibble over it. :) I just don't think people would really talk to me about that sort of thing, though, you know?

Maya B (8:22:27 PM): Fair enough. What should I do about the beta thing, though?

Audra S (8:22:29 PM): Oh, you can give it to whoever you think is fair. I wasn't paying attention to the bidding, so I really have no idea.

Maya B (8:22:31 PM): I think it was either Quicksilver92 or Jennie Page? Does that sound right?

Audra S (8:22:32 PM): Sure. Just let me know.

Maya B (8:22:33 PM): Oh, absolutely. :)

Maya B (8:22:39 PM): I just wish people would stop sending me these awful emails. Like I'm not even more freaked out than they are, you know? I'm the one whose fucking accounts got hacked.

Audra S (8:22:42 PM): Yeah, I'm really sorry about that. That totally sucks. I can't even imagine. :(

Maya B (8:22:47 PM): It's pretty scary not to feel safe online, you know?

Maya B (8:22:51 PM): I mean, with hackers and stuff. I never got hacked before.

Audra S (8:22:53 PM): Yeah, it's never happened to me either. That really is creepy. I'm sorry.

Maya B (8:23:05 PM): So, hey, did you catch Brad in Wrangling the Wild Steed last night? I was totally psyched, they never show it on basic cable.

Audra S (8:23:07 PM): Oh, no, I missed it.

Maya B (8:23:08 PM): That sucks! :(

Audra S (8:23:10 PM): Yeah. :(

Audra S (8:23:12 PM): Hey, Rach, I'm sorry -- I'm going to have to go,

OK? I just realized how late it's getting -- have to get this project done.

Maya B (8:23:14 PM): Oh, no, absolutely. Like I said, I know where you're coming from there. :)

Audra S (8:23:15 PM): We'll talk soon, OK?

Maya B (8:23:16 PM): Great!

Maya B (8:23:17 PM): Talk to you later!

Audra S (8:23:18 PM): Later!

Audra S has signed off.

http://www.diarynow.com/users/thejanethe/85260.html
Date: 4/16/2013
Security level: Private
Mood: numb

What just happened? I... what?

I mean maybe she was just distracted by something that was going on around her or something, obviously that happens sometimes... but...

and I know that isn't it, I know it's me

why is it ALWAYS me? What do I always do wrong?

From: omgbradomgbrad@yippee.com
To: looktotomorrowfans@yippeegroups.com
Date: 4/17/2013
Subject: Auction

Hi guys!

So here's the deal with the auction, since a lot of you have been asking. As most of you probably know, the auction site had to be relocated after all my accounts got hacked. The auction is now at www.recirclr.com/users/ omgbradomgbrad/287323438.html. A couple of things:

First -- **no one's credit card or PayPal information could possibly have been stolen or accessed in any way by the hacker.** I never had anyone's credit card or PayPal information: the only information regarding payment that I ever had was the payment confirmations from the Hannah J. Christiansen site, and those DID NOT AND DO NOT list any personal information. Even if they had, the person who hacked me WAS NOT after credit card numbers or anything like that. It was a personal thing. The hacker was an asshole that I reported to university administration for harassing me, so he decided to mess with my online accounts to get back at me. **YOU HAVE NOTHING TO WORRY ABOUT. THERE IS NO NEED TO FREAK OUT.** So you can stop emailing me about that. LOL

Second thing: Yes, I lost a lot of records on the auction when my ReCirclr got taken out. I had to shut down all my accounts as fast as I could after I got hacked and there was no way to save anything. I got some of the information back via ZoomCache but it *was* out of date and my records of your bids *may have been* lost. But look, I'd like to skirt around this but I can't: a lot of people are claiming they bought and paid for items already with the Buy It Now option, and some of those people are lying. You know who you are; I have suspicions but I can't prove them because I don't have the records. But seriously, guys, just cut it out and be honest, okay? Lying about this is really stupid. You're cheating a charity organization and you're endangering the whole fandom's chances of meeting the $15,000 goal. If we don't meet that goal there's no read-through sit-in, there's no personalized autographs -- all of the awesome prizes are gone. Getting a free beta or piece of fanart is NOT WORTH screwing a charity out of money and the fandom out of good prizes.

Third: Everyone's messaging me about the above two things (guys, please, I got HACKED, it wasn't on purpose and I couldn't help it, so PLEASE stop yelling at me!) and I think a lot of people have decided that because of all of that, the auction is dead. THE AUCTION IS NOT DEAD, AND WE NEED YOUR PARTICIPATION MORE THAN EVER!!!! I don't have exact numbers, but there were AT LEAST $1,200 worth of bids that had been posted already, and most of the items were still active. With a little more help from everyone, we could have made the goal. But right now the donations to the Hannah J. Christiansen foundation are at $5,700, and they've really slowed down in the last couple of weeks. We can't afford to let the auction die, guys - especially not now, with just five weeks left! Please don't back out now! My accounts can't possibly get hacked again, I've made sure of it. We just need to pick up where we left off and keep getting stronger!

Once again, the auction has been relocated to www.recirclr.com/users/omgbradomgbrad/287323438.html. There are two simple things all of you who had been participating need to do:

- Everyone who had posted an item for auction, please repost it there.
- Everyone who was bidding on an item, post your MOST RECENT bid on it. If you look at an item and see that someone else has already posted a higher bid, you can either outbid them or let it be. If someone posts an item that you already bought via Buy   w, email me the payment confirmation that you got from HJC and I'll take care of it. DO NOT LIE ABOUT THIS. IT'S COMPLETELY IMMORAL AND IT CHEATS EVERYONE -- and on a personal note, I can't deal with it anymore, guys. Getting hacked was stressful enough. I can't fight about this anymore.
- Keep bidding and keep positive! This is a setback, not a defeat! If everyone pitches in, we can totally hit the $15,000 mark. There are tons of great items up for auction, so bid on what you like and keep this alive!

Love,

Rachel ("Maya" in public now)

Spectrum High School Email
"Where achieving potential is just the beginning"
Compose Mail
1 - 16 of 43 Older › Oldest »
Mark Unread As: Bold
Check to Delete

	Paul Sheehan	**Urgently needed guidance meeting -- please respond** -- Dear Jane, Of late there's been a great deal of concern expressed about your attendance in particular and emotional…
☑	**Amy Downing**	**Is everything all right?** -- Sweetie, is everything okay? I've been trying to call you for a few days now, but I keep getting a message saying your voicemail inbox is full…
☑	**Margaret Baker**	**Missing assignments** -- Jane -- You have not yet responded to my previous email, nor turned in any of your late assignments. In addition, you have repeatedly avoided…
☐	Gary Huang	skeeball match against farbervill:) -- hi jane heres the flier 4 the fvill skeeball match like i said id send :) u cn print it out & papper ur nheiborhood w/ it!!! lol…
☑	**Lorilynn Meisner, LICSW**	**Meeting** -- Hi Jane, I wanted to let you know I've been concerned about you lately. Last week when I called you out of class, Ms. Montoya said you left, but you didn't come…

☑	**Laine Elsing**	**Missing you around the library!** -- Hi Jane, I just wanted to check in because I haven't seen you around in a few weeks. Is everything all right? Don't feel pressured to come if…
☑	**Eileen Frolich**	**Book list** -- Dear class, Here is the list of books from which you may select two books to report on in the coming months -- one from group A, which will be…
☑	**Paul Sheehan**	**IMPORTANT: IEP Signature** -- Hello Jane, We still do not have a copy of your individualized education plan signed by your parent/guardian. At this…
☑	**Margaret Baker**	**Makeup test** -- Dear Jane: As you are no doubt aware, you missed the makeup exam you were scheduled to take this afternoon, which was your second and final…
☑	**Julia Koren**	**End-of-term thesis** -- Jane, Sorry we missed each other after class today. As I said before, a term-end thesis is fine, but we need to meet after class to…
☑	**Lorilynn Meisner, LICSW**	**Weekly progress reports** -- Hi Jane! I'm sorry we haven't connected in a few weeks. Please do stop by my office during homeroom when you have a chance -- your…
☑	Gary Huang	movies 2nite? -- hay jane u cut geog AGAIN 2day what r u crazey?! :) neway so heres the movie times 4 lev. rising if u still want to go tonite movies.yippee.com/leviathanrising call…

✓	**Chris Montague**	**Missed Labs** -- Jane: You left class too fast for me to talk to you today, but your lab partners asked that I talk to you about your missing labs. They're shouldering all the...
✓	**John Palin**	**Weekly class notes** -- Dear class: This week's class notes and study sheets are attached to this email. The bonus take-home questions for the test are...
✓	**Alan Dumott**	**Make up papers** -- Hi Jane Here are the 6 make up assignments that we had discussed I would email to you after class last week. You can turn...
✓	**Amy Downing**	**Movies?** -- Hi Jane! I'm sorry we never got to firm up our plans to see a movie last week -- I was really looking forward to it. Can we catch up next...

Date: 4/19/2013
Security level: Private

Audra's in the hospital. Apparently.

I have no idea why.

She disappeared from the fandom a few days ago -- suddenly she wasn't on FL, RC, DN, email, IRC, anywhere. To be honest I thought she had blocked me or something. Which I could barely stand to think about to begin with. But then word started filtering around the fandom that she was in the hospital, and finally someone mentioned it in the LtT chat. Now it's all total drama because Jennie was the only one Audra told but Jennie can't keep a secret for shit (*why* would Audra tell *Jennie* of all people? *why*?) and now the whole fandom is gossiping about it.

And Audra's still hospitalized. No one knows why. Even Jennie says she doesn't know. I don't know if she's lying or not.

I don't know anything.

I'm so scared it's making me sick. What if it's something serious -- I mean it can't be something *fatal* or anything, she'd have *told* me if it were something like that -- but would she? She's seemed so distant lately... I don't know, how can you be friends with someone and not know about something like this?

and I can't deal with this, I JUST CAN'T DEAL WITH IT, not on top of everything else

I have to stop my brain. I have to stop it.

RawKdaSkEEbaLL (7:04:25 PM): hi three

thejanethe (7:04:27 PM): Thank God SOMEONE'S online.

RawKdaSkEEbaLL (7:04:30 PM): uh.... takinhg that as a complement

thejanethe (7:04:32 PM): sorry

thejanethe (7:04:33 PM): I'm just completely flipped out

RawKdaSkEEbaLL (7:04:36 PM): y wats wrong

thejanethe (7:04:37 PM): My friend Audra's in the hospital and I have no idea why and no one will tell me anything.

RawKdaSkEEbaLL (7:04:40 PM): woah

RawKdaSkEEbaLL (7:04:43 PM): calm down

RawKdaSkEEbaLL (7:04:48 PM): this is the internet friend rite

thejanethe (7:04:49 PM): yeah, one of them

RawKdaSkEEbaLL (7:04:52 PM): well wat is it? is it sumthing serius

thejanethe (7:04:53 PM): I don't know! I just told you, no one will tell me anything!

RawKdaSkEEbaLL (7:04:56 PM): ok ok sry

RawKdaSkEEbaLL (7:04:58 PM): how did u find out shes in the hospitel

thejanethe (7:05:01 PM): She told someone else in the fandom and the someone else turned it into chatroom gossip.

thejanethe (7:05:04 PM): I don't know why she'd do that.

RawKdaSkEEbaLL (7:05:07 PM): yea ppl who gosip like that suck

thejanethe (7:05:09 PM): No, not Jennie. I mean Audra.

RawKdaSkEEbaLL (7:05:12 PM): y shed do what? get hospitelized? lol

thejanethe (7:05:15 PM): NO. I just mean I don't know why she'd tell Jennie and not anyone else.

thejanethe (7:05:17 PM): Jennie's a horrible gossip.

RawKdaSkEEbaLL (7:05:20 PM): well she probly thot she cd trust her

thejanethe (7:05:22 PM): But WHY, though?

thejanethe (7:05:25 PM): I just... never mind.

RawKdaSkEEbaLL (7:05:28 PM): r u upset she dident tell u

thejanethe (7:05:29 PM): Maybe I am, okay?

thejanethe (7:05:32 PM): I know it's totally unfair and I know it's not the point but I don't CARE, I don't like it when people I thought were my friends keep secrets from me.

thejanethe (7:05:35 PM): Like, what, she thought I was less trustworthy than Jennie? It just -- oh, I don't know, I don't even know why I care, and I wish my brain would SHUT UP about it

RawKdaSkEEbaLL (7:05:37 PM): hey its ok

RawKdaSkEEbaLL (7:05:39 PM): ur woried & u wish shed talked 2 u, its not a bad thing

thejanethe: But it is! I *am* worried about her, I'm totally worried, and what does it matter who she told? I mean what if she's really sick?

thejanethe (7:05:40 PM): Seriously, Gary, she could be friggin' dying, and I STILL wouldn't know

RawKdaSkEEbaLL (7:05:43 PM): woah woah woah

RawKdaSkEEbaLL (7:05:45 PM): hold on

thejanethe (7:05:50 PM): You're always saying that. "Whoa hold on." I am NOT going to hold on, this is someone I used to consider a really good friend and now not only is she acting like a stranger she's in the hospital and no one will tell me why!

RawKdaSkEEbaLL (7:06:53 PM): ok

RawKdaSkEEbaLL (7:06:55 PM): so have a panick attack but its not gunna help ne1

thejanethe (7:06:57) PM): I just don't know where to go from here.

RawKdaSkEEbaLL (7:06:58 PM): did u call her?

thejanethe (7:07:00 PM): No.

thejanethe (7:07:02): I don't know the number.

RawKdaSkEEbaLL (7:07:04 PM): do u know wat hospitel shes in

thejanethe (7:07:06): I don't know. Someone said it was St. Elizabeth's in Ellery but that could be just a rumor.

RawKdaSkEEbaLL (7:07:08 PM): well u can call the hosp main line & ask 4 her room #, theyll probly put u thru if shes there

thejanethe (7:07:24 PM): The thing is... well, it doesn't matter in this context, I guess.

RawKdaSkEEbaLL (7:07:27 PM): what>

thejanethe (7:07:35 PM): It's just weird.

thejanethe (7:07:40 PM): I've never talked to her on the phone before.

RawKdaSkEEbaLL (7:07:43 PM): yah that could b a lil weird

thejanethe (7:07:49 PM): I... kind of draw a sharp line between who I am on the Internet and who I am in real life, you know?

RawKdaSkEEbaLL (7:07:53 PM): like how?

thejanethe (7:07:58 PM): I don't know.

thejanethe (7:08:04 PM): It's just...

thejanethe (7:08:17 PM): Okay. This isn't something I talk about with most people.

RawKdaSkEEbaLL (7:08:18 PM): ok

thejanethe (7:08:21 PM): In fact, you're the first person I've told.

RawKdaSkEEbaLL (7:08:23 PM): thanx

thejanethe (7:08:26 PM): ...you're welcome.

thejanethe (7:08:31 PM): I mean, not that it's a big deal.

thejanethe (7:08:51 PM): Audra just... doesn't exactly know me the way I am in real life.

RawKdaSkEEbaLL (7:08:53 PM): well sure

RawKdaSkEEbaLL (7:08:55 PM): i figured

thejanethe (7:08:58 PM): What do you mean?

RawKdaSkEEbaLL (7:09:02 PM): ur pretty quiet in school & stuff

RawKdaSkEEbaLL (7:09:07 PM): & dont have 2 many freidns there

RawKdaSkEEbaLL (7:09:11 PM): but ur always talking abt ur friends online

thejanethe (7:09:13 PM): Yeah, but I don't just mean I'm more outgoing online or something.

thejanethe (7:09:16 PM): You ever use an alternate name online, like for a message board or something?
RawKdaSkEEbaLL (7:09:19 PM): well yah evry1 does :)

thejanethe (7:09:24 PM): Well, I don't mean a username or whatever. Audra thinks my name's Rachel.

RawKdaSkEEbaLL (7:09:26 PM): ok

RawKdaSkEEbaLL (7:09:29 PM): so when u call her say its rachel :)

thejanethe (7:09:35 PM): She also thinks I'm in college, and that I have a boyfriend, and a bunch of friends, and... basically, she thinks I'm someone totally different.

RawKdaSkEEbaLL (7:09:38 PM): rly?

RawKdaSkEEbaLL (7:09:40 PM): how come?

thejanethe (7:09:44 PM): I don't know. I guess I just started with a different name, and then before I knew it it just sort of... evolved.

RawKdaSkEEbaLL (7:09:46 PM): oic

thejanethe (7:09:54 PM): I'm not sure what reaction I expected, I guess I expected you to be more surprised or something.

RawKdaSkEEbaLL (7:09:55 PM): y?

thejanethe (7:09:59 PM): Um, I don't know.

RawKdaSkEEbaLL (7:09:06 PM): so wats rachel like? like, her personnality

thejanethe (7:10:09 PM): Um... She's smarter than I am, I think, and funnier.

RawKdaSkEEbaLL (7:10:12 PM): how can she b smarter & funnier then u

RawKdaSkEEbaLL (7:10:14 PM): ur the 1 that writes her emails n sytuff :)

thejanethe (7:10:14 PM): I don't know, she just is.

thejanethe (7:10:16 PM): She's prettier than I am, too.

RawKdaSkEEbaLL (7:10:19 PM): u made up what she looks like?

thejanethe (7:10:22 PM): Please don't call me crazy. I'm not in much of a state to deal with it right now.

RawKdaSkEEbaLL (7:10:25 PM): i didnt say ur crazy

RawKdaSkEEbaLL (7:10:27 PM): just cureous about wat she looks like
thejanethe (7:10:30 PM): Um... hold on. I have a picture of her.

RawKdaSkEEbaLL (7:10:33 PM): howd u get a picture of her??!!!!??

RawKdaSkEEbaLL (7:10:34 PM): lol

thejanethe (7:10:37 PM): It's just some random person off an image search who looked the way I pictured her. One sec.

RawKdaSkEEbaLL (7:10:40 PM): ok

thejanethe (7:10:45 PM):

RawKdaSkEEbaLL (7:10:47 PM): shes pretty

thejanethe (7:10:49 PM): Told you so.

RawKdaSkEEbaLL (7:10:51 PM): ur pretty 2 tho

thejanethe (7:10:53 PM): ::snort:: please.

RawKdaSkEEbaLL (7:10:56 PM): what? u r

thejanethe (7:10:59 PM): Well, whatever, not going to bother debating that now. The point is that I certainly look nothing like her.

RawKdaSkEEbaLL (7:11:03 PM): yah u don't

RawKdaSkEEbaLL (7:11:07 PM): how come she has 2 look so diffrent

thejanethe (7:11:11 PM): Because I don't think I'm pretty, and we're going in circles.

thejanethe (7:11:14 PM): What she looks like isn't the point anyway. She's just... really different from me.

RawKdaSkEEbaLL (7:11:15 PM): ok

RawKdaSkEEbaLL (7:11:17 PM): so audra thinks ur Rachel

RawKdaSkEEbaLL (7:11:20 PM): does whastername think so 2?

thejanethe (7:11:22 PM): What's whose name?

RawKdaSkEEbaLL (7:11:25 PM): sry, the 1 who she told abt being in the hospitel

RawKdaSkEEbaLL (7:11:25 PM): the gosipy 1

thejanethe (7:11:29 PM): Oh, Jennie. Yeah, everyone in the LtT comm knows me as Rachel.

thejanethe (7:11:31 PM): She has a ReCirclr and stuff.

RawKdaSkEEbaLL (7:11:33 PM): who does?

thejanethe (7:11:34 PM): Rachel.

RawKdaSkEEbaLL (7:11:36 PM): oh

RawKdaSkEEbaLL (7:11:40 PM): can i see?

thejanethe (7:11:42 PM): Not right now.

RawKdaSkEEbaLL (7:11:45 PM): ok

thejanethe (7:11:59 PM): Anyway, so that's why it's weird for me to call her.

RawKdaSkEEbaLL (7:11:03 PM): u wouldnt want to play rachel on the phone?

thejanethe (7:11:06 PM): Pretty much.

thejanethe (7:11:09 PM): I've never done it in person before, you know, I just don't know how it would go.

RawKdaSkEEbaLL (7:11:12 PM): right

thejanethe (7:11:14 PM): But meanwhile I'm flipping out.

RawKdaSkEEbaLL (7:11:17 PM): im sorry

thejanethe (7:11:20 PM): And I really, really wish I could visit her.

RawKdaSkEEbaLL (7:11:24 PM): u dont even know if shell be in the hosp. long

thejanethe (7:11:27 PM): Yeah, but if she is, it's been bugging me that I never could visit her, you know?

thejanethe (7:11:29 PM): I never really wanted to take it into real life before, but... I don't know.

thejanethe (7:11:31 PM): I'd love to give her a surprise visit

RawKdaSkEEbaLL (7:11:35 PM): wheres she live?

thejanethe (7:11:37 PM): Upstate New York.

RawKdaSkEEbaLL (7:11:41 PM): like a 5 hr drive

RawKdaSkEEbaLL (7:11:46 PM): if she winds up in the hosp. 4 a long time mayb we cn drive up in my sisters car

thejanethe (7:11:49 PM): No, we really can't. She's seen the picture of Rachel too.

thejanethe (7:11:51 PM): And I'm sure she wouldn't want to see me even if I were Rachel.

RawKdaSkEEbaLL (7:11:54 PM): well if u change ur mind

RawKdaSkEEbaLL (7:11:57 PM): a road trip woud b fun :)

thejanethe (7:11:59 PM): Yeah, we talked about that.

thejanethe (7:12:02 PM): All the same I think I'd rather do a little more local driving with you first, if that's all the same to you.

RawKdaSkEEbaLL (7:12:05 PM): u dont think i can drive??!!

thejanethe (7:12:07 PM): ...I think it would be prudent to get in a bit more practice first.

RawKdaSkEEbaLL (7:12:11 PM): ok so what r u doing 2nite

thejanethe (7:12:15 PM): You always ask me out for the same night. I'm not at all sure that's proper protocol.

RawKdaSkEEbaLL (7:12:18 PM): propper what?

thejanethe (7:12:22 PM): Never mind. I was planning on sitting at home and stressing about Audra.

RawKdaSkEEbaLL (7:12:27 PM): well i can see thats a ton of fun but wanna go 2 the drivein instead>?

thejanethe (7:12:30 PM): What's showing?

RawKdaSkEEbaLL (7:12:33 PM): gostbusters i think

thejanethe (7:12:36 PM): Ghostbusters?!

RawKdaSkEEbaLL (7:12:40 PM): yah they show old stuff

RawKdaSkEEbaLL (7:12:45 PM): i think there showing 1 and 2 but 2 kinda sux so we coud just see 1 & come back

thejanethe (7:12:47 PM): I've never seen either one.

RawKdaSkEEbaLL (7:12:50 PM): u shoud! its funny
RawKdaSkEEbaLL (7:12:52 PM): so u wanna go?

thejanethe (7:12:55 PM): Okay, sure. Get my mind off this whole situation, anyway.

RawKdaSkEEbaLL (7:12:57 PM): k :)

RawKdaSkEEbaLL (7:13:01 PM): pick u up in 1/2 hr

thejanethe (7:13:06 PM): Try not to run anyone over on the way.

RawKdaSkEEbaLL (7:13:07 PM): haha

RawKdaSkEEbaLL has signed off.

thejanethe (7:13:10): ...this is just a friends thing, right?

I'm going to scream. I'm going to die. I'm going to not know how to handle this at all because MRS. BAKER IS RUINING MY LIFE AND I AM SO NOT KIDDING, she is seriously wrecking EVERYTHING, it's totally like she's planning it, and I don't get why she hates me so much and I don't know what to do from here and I just don't know how to --

-- I am not going to calm down if I keep up the screamyranting, am I?

But I can't help it. Mrs. Baker gave me a warning notice. She mailed a warning notice to my dad. She mailed a warning notice to my dad saying that my math average at midterm was 22% and my dad has completely. flipped. out. What the HELL is she doing sending home WARNING NOTICES?! The whole POINT of Spectrum is that they don't do things like warning notices. Most of the teachers don't even do numeric *grades*, for crying out loud. It's all about how school isn't about competition and measuring achievement against an arbitrary standard, it's about encouraging students to live up to their full potential no matter what that is and that's not quantifiable and now she's SENDING HOME WARNING NOTICES TO STUDENTS WHO ARE "FLUNKING"?! I don't believe this. I seriously do not even know how to CONCEIVE OF BEGINNING TO COMPREHEND the fact that she has sent me home a warning notice and my dad has flipped his shit. And you want to know the best part? The best part of this whole awesome business? She's flunking me for not doing my HOMEWORK. My homework?! What kind of fascist satanic teacher averages homeworks in like they're quiz scores?! I mean, God, she already basically forced me to get into counseling -- isn't the point of that to help me through my problems with authority and compliance with -- with -- I don't know, homework-doing? What am I supposed to *do*?

And my dad, my dad has lost it. He's completely... just... lost it. Obviously Mrs. Baker is totally smug about this whole thing, she thinks she is Teaching Me a Lesson and Refusing To Accept Excuses, but really what she is doing is Wrecking My Life Completely. I don't mean my school life, I don't give a shit about that, but my dad. He just... he's still not drinking,

248

I guess, but he's wandering around all the time with his hands bunched up into white-knuckled fists at his sides, and he keeps licking and smacking his lips, like it's a tic. I don't get it. Before he was doing those things but he kept trying to act all cheerful and chipper, which was painful to watch, sure, because it was so totally faked, and anyway the facade kept cracking all over the place. But since he got the warning notice... It's like it just cemented everything in his head, that he's a horrible parent and this would never have happened if Mom hadn't died and he should have died instead of Mom because he's completely failed me and GOD, IT'S JUST A MATH CLASS, DAD, and PLEASE STOP TALKING ABOUT MOM BECAUSE IT'S HORRIBLE AND EMBARRASSING, but he won't. He's in like a perpetual state of breakdown. And what am I supposed to do, take care of him? How do I do that? I don't know how to do that, he's my dad! It's like, how do you tell your dad that even though you're a huge and total letdown and a failure at everything, that's your fault, not his?

I don't know what to do. I tried to rent a Drew Barrymore movie for us to watch together last night because I hoped it would cheer him up but he stared at it kind of blank-eyed and then threw it across the room. And then he stood there with his fists clenched for a really long time, and then he said "How about some dinner?!" in this crazy-bright-cheerful voice, and then he made chicken and corn and boiled the corn into a huge soggy mess and burned the chicken. I just... what am I supposed to *do*?!

It's a *math class*. My dad is losing his mind because I got a *warning notice in a math class.*

I almost wish he would just start drinking again. Or at least go back to drinking and ease back out of it again. I don't think this cold turkey thing works. Clearly the alcohol was the only thing keeping him from a complete meltdown. And I... I don't know, I didn't like it when he was drinking, obviously... but this is like even scarier. When he was drinking I knew what to expect, he didn't pay me any attention and he was all glazey and fogged-over, but it was predictable, right? And now he hates himself so much, and he's so miserable and so angry at himself, and I'm not afraid that he'll lash out at me, but what if... I don't know...

Fuck Mrs. Baker. Fuck her. This is all her fault.

distrasbitch:

ack, Jaela rescuing her parents is the stupidest fucking plotline ever. It totally screws up how angsty Jaela's been since the show began because her parents' murder was such a huge part of who she was. So what, now she's going to be all healed and happy? how is that interesting?

#looktotomorrow

slytherclaw1997:

maybe the writers will kill her parents off again. that would be good.

jessamyns_jenna:

I'd watch that. I can't even with the actress who plays her mom. She has chunks of scenery between her teeth in every scene.

distrasbitch:

actually maybe you're right. Maybe that is where they're going? She brought them to Taleswa and they said something a few episodes ago about dormant volcanos there...

clearlycanadian:

EVERYONE WHO WANTS JAELA'S MOM THROWN INTO A VOLCANO, RAISE YOUR HANDS

jessamyns_jenna:

raises both hands

omgbradomgbrad:

What the FUCK is wrong with you people?! Are you fucking sadists?!?! Oh, yeah, let's just go kill off Jaela's parents AGAIN, she's not tragic enough anymore! Characters are just NO FUN when they're not completely destroyed by their parents' murders! It's not like she needs a mother or like she's an actual character who anyone CARES about whether she's happy or not, right? Let's just shove her through a fucking meat grinder, because

250

I don't like the actress who plays the mother! How can you even pretend you like this show when you just want to kill characters' parents so you can watch them cry or fall apart or something? I mean could you even pretend to imagine for two fucking seconds what losing your parents would be like? You're getting off on someone else's pain and you're fucking sick. GTFO and DIAF

omgbradomgbrad has unfollowed this thread.

omgbradomgbrad has turned off comments.

omgbradomgbrad has closed their askbox.

omgbradomgbrad has blocked private messages.

Date: 4/21/2013
Security level: Private

He did it. He started drinking again.

And a social worker came today.

Do you know why a social worker came today? A social worker came today because I overslept.

I stayed up last night writing fic, and I slept through my alarm. Because I was sleeping, I did not wake Dad up so he could drive me to school. Dad did not wake up either.

Dad must have felt very bad about all of this, because instead of waking me up and driving me to school late, he drove to the liquor store and got a six-pack of beer and a bottle of vodka.

I was still sleeping when Ms. Meisner called the house. Ms. Meisner. That WHORE Ms. Meisner called the house and talked to Dad, because she was "concerned about me", because I was absent but also because, due to the warning notice and the fact that several of my teachers report that my attitude is "withdrawn" at school, she has been concerned about me. As she is still officially my caseworker at school, she felt it her duty to call. So she called. And Dad answered the phone. And he was shitfaced. And she could tell. And she called the Department of Social Services.

I was not sleeping when the social worker got here. Dad was passed out, and I answered the door. The social worker looks like Ms. Meisner. I hate her.

I did not let the social worker in. I told the social worker Dad was not home, and I did not let her in. She asked how long he had been gone and how long he would be gone and I said he had left five minutes ago to go to the supermarket and would not be home for an hour, and I would not let her in. She said she could not legally force me to let her in but she said that if I did not let her in it would "be a factor in the decisions they make regarding my case." I asked her if she was going to take me to foster care right then, and she said no, and I told her to go away, and she asked me if we could schedule an appointment, and I, I had to schedule an appointment with her because if she didn't she would make me go to foster

252

care and I don't, I can't, it so I told her to come back Saturday and she said TOMORROW because social workers don't WORK weekends, they only destroy your life MONDAY TO FRIDAY NINE TO FIVE and she is going to come back tomorrow at three-thirty.

She gave me a very nice professional little card saying that her name is Kristine Bainsbridge, LICSW. ZoomSearch says she was on the dean's list at Lesley College. I left her card on the kitchen table with a note telling Dad who she was, when she was coming, and telling him not to have anything to drink until she was gone.

I started to pour out the little bit of vodka that was left in the bottle in the sink, and then I took it to my room instead.

Audra is still in the hospital.

The Lookies are still going up in flames.

Gary is at Skee-ball practice. They have a tournament coming up.

I tried to watch LtT torrents but I kept bursting into tears.

I tried to drink the rest of the vodka but it was horrible and I threw up.

I feel like a zombie. I can't think. I don't want to think.

http://www.twistedart.net/blackwingedsoul/329721.html
Date: 4/21/2013
Mood: blank
Security: Public

i have a razor

give me a reason not to use it

Leave a Comment   18 Comments

http://www.diarynow.com/thejanethe/98672.html
Date: 4/22/2013
Security level: Private

Social worker came.

Dad was not drunk. But when I got home from school he just stared at me with hollow red-rimmed eyes and his face was gray and saggy and he looked a hundred and ten and he was shaking all over, and I knew it was not going to go well. And when the social worker came he cracked like a dropped egg.

He cried, and he told her he was an alcoholic and a terrible parent, and he loved me more than *anything in the world* but he couldn't take care of me. The social worker asked if Dad was saying he wanted to *give me away*, she *asked* that, and Dad... he paused. He paused like he didn't know the answer. And then he really started sobbing.

He said no eventually. He did say no. He... he said no.

The social worker said she could help us find "resources" and Dad asked what those were. She said she thought he needed to go to rehab, or possibly a dual-diagnosis inpatient psychiatric program where they treat people with addictions and a mental illness diagnosis. Because, she said solemnly, it seemed to her that Dad was *very depressed*. Dad said but what about Jane, and she said part of what DSS does is finding placements for children in those circumstances, and then I lost it and I yelled NO, I am NOT GOING TO FOSTER CARE and she asked if there was anyone else I could stay with and I said Auntie Amy, and she asked if Aunt Amy had a criminal record and I said NO, and she asked if Aunt Amy drank or used any substances and I said NO, and then pointedly said she's MOM's sister. That was mean. But it also made the social worker's face relax a little, the fucking bitch. She said I could stay there for a few days if Dad said okay, and he did, and they're going to run some paperwork and talk to Aunt Amy and if everything checks out Aunt Amy will be some kind of approved care provider for me or something.

Dad has to go to his psych ward/rehab/wherever on Monday. They're finding him a spot. But they said I had to go to Aunt Amy's tonight. They called her and she was horrified and said I could stay with her indefinitely,

255

and they made me pack and the social worker drove me. The house is so nice and neat and everything smells fresh and there are calla lilies on the end table like Mommy used to have, and I almost broke when I saw them. Auntie Amy hugged me for a long, long time, and I stared at her like a zombie and then I asked her where I was staying. She said the guest room, and I came here and locked myself in. Besides telling me she'd made me supper, and then later saying she'd put it in plastic wrap and left it in the fridge, she hasn't bothered me.

And I'm here. And I can't leave the room. I have to be alone. But there's nothing I can do. I can't focus on LtT and no one is online and everything is so wrong. And there's... there's nothing I can do. I tried to write fanfiction, and I can't concentrate. I tried going online as Zelda, but I blew up immediately over nothing at all and instead of letting off steam I just started sobbing, and I had to sign off. And I tried writing a post as Ethan, but I got so deep into the suicide talk that I scared myself. And I tried posting as Rachel and I couldn't even make my fingers hit the keys. And now I'm sitting here, just Jane, sitting here in my aunt's house, and you want to know the worst thing, you want to know the most horrible thing, I'm *relieved* to be here. I'm relieved that I'm here and everything is clean and tidy and Auntie Amy made me a supper that's not a TV dinner and I don't have to worry about Dad knocking on my door and stumbling in drunk to tell me all weepy that he's so sorry he's such a terrible father, and I don't have to hear him throwing up in the bathroom, and I don't have to see him passed out in front of the TV while Drew Barrymore kisses some guy in the middle of a baseball field. I don't have to see him at all, I don't have to see the crags in his face or smell the pajamas he's been wearing for three days or hear the tremble in his voice. I love my dad, and I hate my dad, and I don't have to see him anymore.

And now I'm crying. I wrote it all, every single *horrible* detail, because talking about things and writing about them is supposed to make you feel *better*, that's what Nora says, and NORA IS FULL OF SHIT. Actually, I take that back. Nora *doesn't* say it's supposed to make you feel better. She says it's supposed to make you feel WORSE, but you're supposed to do it anyway! Because she's a freaking basket case! Well, here you go, Nora. I'm "working through my feelings", and writing down every sucky thing

256

that happens to me, and I feel absolutely shit-awful. In fact I've never felt worse in my life. That's some bang-up therapy you're doing; you got me to the point where I make myself feel terrible all on my own, when you're not here to do it for me. Maybe one of these days I'll feel so bad I'll kill myself and then you can call me cured.

Hello, ZeldaStar519! Thank you for your edits to this page

Article   Discussion   Edit this page   History   Watch

Man (Redirected from Men)
This article is about adult human males. For humans in general, see Human. For the word "man", see Man (word). For other uses, see Man (disambiguation).

THEY ARE ASSHOLES!!!!!!!!!!!!!!!!!!!!!!!!!!!!!!!!!
you have to watch out for them
they are BIOLOGICALLY IMPELLED to BETRAY YOU and HURT YOU and ABANDON YOU WHEN YOU NEED THEM
they say they care about you but all they care about is THEIR OWN SELFISHNESS
they say they'll take care of you and THEY LEAVE YOU TO ROT
THEY ABANDON THEIR CHILDREN
THEY ARE NOTHING WITHOUT WOMEN
WATCH OUT FOR MEN!!!!!!!!!!!!!!!!!!!!
they will always betray you
they will always hurt you
they will always always abandon you
it is SCIENTIFIC FACT!!
NEVER TRUST THEM
never trust

Categories:

Articles with limited geographic scope | Gender | Men

NoraActon48267382 (3:21:56 PM): I see you're giving me the silent treatment. Any chance you'll respond if I talk to you this way instead?

NoraActon48267382 (3:22:38 PM): You can explain more points of Internet grammar to me. I'm still woefully Internet-illiterate, I know. :)

NoraActon48267382 (3:23:17 PM): Or you could explain to me what you meant when you said your friend Gary participated in "competitive Skee-ball". I've been wondering ever since.

NoraActon48267382 (3:27:45 PM): No small talk either, huh? Then I'll cut the crap.

NoraActon48267382 (3:27:58 PM): I can't imagine how badly you must be hurting right now. I would very much like to help.

NoraActon48267382 (3:28:16 PM): You may already know this, but I wasn't the one who called DSS.

NoraActon48267382 (3:28:35 PM): I won't lie to you and say that I hadn't thought about it. But I wasn't convinced that it would be the most helpful option for you. I had decided to hold off and see if your father started drinking again, and if he did, then I would consider calling.

NoraActon48267382 (3:30:02 PM): What I want you to know is that I would never have called and made a report without discussing it with you first. I'd have asked for your opinions first, and taken them seriously; and if I had to report against your wishes, I would tell you that as well.

NoraActon48267382 (3:30:19 PM): I know you're not in a mood to trust therapists right now. But you and I have made some progress in previous sessions, and on occasion, you've opened up.

NoraActon48267382 (3:30:43 PM): And I can picture the things that must be running through your head right now, the confusion and the anger and the hurt, and it must be brutal to keep it all locked in.

NoraActon48267382 (3:31:06 PM): What I'm asking you to do -- just to talk -- is very much like those trust exercises you described in a previous session. You told me then that you don't do those. People drop you, you said.

NoraActon48267382 (3:31:22 PM): But I want you to think about what it's costing you to keep all of your feelings to yourself right now. And then I want you to think about our sessions, and ask yourself whether I'm likely to drop you.

NoraActon48267382 (3:36:04 PM): Jane?

thejanethe (3:36:55 PM): You know something, Nora?

thejanethe (3:36:59 PM): I don't dislike you, exactly. For a therapist, you're not half-bad.

NoraActon48267382 (3:37:07 PM): Thank you. I know you well enough to know that's high praise.

thejanethe (3:37:15 PM): No. You shouldn't thank me, and it's not high praise, and you don't know me. And do you know why?

NoraActon48267382 (3:37:18 PM): Tell me.

thejanethe (3:37:22 PM): Because you're still a therapist. And I still don't trust you. And sometimes, and now would be one of those times, you just need to shut the fuck up.

thejanethe has signed off.

thejanethe (8:12:04 PM): Gary! You there?

Auto-response from **RawKdaSkEEbaLL**: waitin 2 CRUSH @ FARBERVILLE WOOT WOOT YEAAAAAAAAAAA

thejanethe (8:12:08 PM): Oh, come on. You've gotta be there. Please?!

RawKdaSkEEbaLL (8:12:19 PM): yea, hi, sry

RawKdaSkEEbaLL (8:12:25 PM): was away 4 a min

thejanethe (8:12:28 PM): GARY.

RawKdaSkEEbaLL (8:12:31 PM): thats my name :)

thejanethe (8:12:32 PM): You remember that time when you said we should drive up to visit Audra?

RawKdaSkEEbaLL (8:12:34 PM): ummmmm... sorta

RawKdaSkEEbaLL (8:12:37 PM): audras the 1 in the hospetel, rite? hows she doing?

thejanethe (8:12:50 PM): I don't know, but we're going to find out.

RawKdaSkEEbaLL (8:12:56 PM): we r?

RawKdaSkEEbaLL (8:13:00 PM): whaht do u mean we?

thejanethe (8:13:05 PM): I mean that you and I are going to drive to upstate New York to see Audra in the hospital.

RawKdaSkEEbaLL (8:13:09 PM): r u serius?

thejanethe (8:13:13 PM): Dead serious. Come on, weren't YOU serious when you suggested it?

RawKdaSkEEbaLL (8:13:17 PM): yea but'

RawKdaSkEEbaLL (8:13:19 PM): wait

RawKdaSkEEbaLL (8:13:22 PM): when did u want 2 go?

thejanethe (8:13:23 PM): Tonight.

RawKdaSkEEbaLL (8:13:26 PM): tonite?!?!!

thejanethe (8:13:28 PM): Tonight!

RawKdaSkEEbaLL (8:13:30 PM): did u loose ur mind?! lol

thejanethe (8:13:33 PM): Why would I have lost my mind? You have to be in town for the weekends to prep for the Farberville match. So we cut school for a few days, so what?

thejanethe (8:13:36 PM): And, dude, you JUST got your new car AND your license. TELL ME this is not perfect.

RawKdaSkEEbaLL (8:13:41 PM): uhhh it isnt a new car

RawKdaSkEEbaLL (8:13:43 PM): its way old

thejanethe (8:13:46 PM): Oh, come on, it can't be in *that* bad shape, can it? I just rode in it last weekend, for crying out loud, it's fine.

RawKdaSkEEbaLL (8:13:49 PM): yea but

RawKdaSkEEbaLL (8:13:51 PM): wait

RawKdaSkEEbaLL (8:13:55 PM): did she get wurse or sumthing

thejanethe (8:13:57 PM): DUDE I DON'T KNOW

thejanethe (8:13:58 PM): If I knew we wouldn't have to go!

RawKdaSkEEbaLL (8:14:05 PM): soooooooooooooooooooooo....... u just want 2 go cuz u cant find out whats up

thejanethe (8:14:07 PM): Sure.

RawKdaSkEEbaLL (8:14:10 PM): sure?

thejanethe (8:14:13 PM): I want to go because I'M SICK OF WAITING, is why I want to go. This is getting ridiculous.

thejanethe (8:14:16 PM): Everything is just -- I've just been freaking out about everything for too long, and I need to get out of here. I need to actually *do* something, not just freak out.

RawKdaSkEEbaLL (8:14:21 PM): wait do something? whaht do u mean

thejanethe (8:14:26 PM): I mean go to New York!

RawKdaSkEEbaLL (8:14:29 PM): no but i mean

RawKdaSkEEbaLL (8:14:32 PM): how does that help ur freind

thejanethe (8:14:34 PM): What, wouldn't you want to know your friends cared about you if you were in the hospital?

RawKdaSkEEbaLL (8:14:39 PM): i gess

thejanethe (8:14:43 PM): Sheesh, if that's the way you feel about it, remind me not to waste my time visiting you the next time you get hit by a car. :P

RawKdaSkEEbaLL (8:14:48 PM): lol well im not gunna get hit by a car

thejanethe (8:14:50 PM): Oh good.

RawKdaSkEEbaLL (8:14:55 PM): but seriusly im just confussed

thejanethe (8:14:58 PM): Man, how much persuading do you need? I didn't think *you'd* be a chicken about this!

RawKdaSkEEbaLL (8:15:02 PM): dude its not chickening

RawKdaSkEEbaLL (8:15:04 PM): just like

RawKdaSkEEbaLL (8:15:08 PM): sooo............u want 2 go to ny tonite

thejanethe (8:15:10 PM): What have we been TALKING about?! aieee!

RawKdaSkEEbaLL (8:15:13 PM): ok

RawKdaSkEEbaLL (8:15:18 PM): where r we foing?

thejanethe (8:15:22 PM): We're going to upstate New York. St. Elizabeth's Hospital in Ellery. I checked it out on MapFinder. It doesn't look too hard to find.

RawKdaSkEEbaLL (8:15:25 PM): r u sure it cant wait?

RawKdaSkEEbaLL (8:15:32 PM): y not wiat til tommorrow morning @ least>? wed have 2 stay overnite if we went now?

thejanethe (8:15:36 PM): I don't want to wait. I have no idea what's going on with Audra, no one will tell me -- for all I know she's in crisis and may not even make it until the weekend.

RawKdaSkEEbaLL (8:15:40 PM): where wd we stay?

RawKdaSkEEbaLL (8:15:43 PM): is she rilly that sick?

thejanethe (8:15:45 PM): We'd stay in a motel. They're way cheap up there, like thirty bucks a night per room. I've got plenty for that, plus gas money, money to eat, stuff like that. I've always been a miser. It pays off.

thejanethe (8:15:47 PM): Dude, I have NO IDEA if she's that sick and I'm TIRED of waiting for someone to tell me. I'M GOING.

RawKdaSkEEbaLL (8:15:50 PM): stay in a motel?

thejanethe (8:15:50 PM): If you don't want to go with me I'll have to take a bus, but it will take forever, and I don't really like that idea. Come on, don't you think a road trip would be exciting?

thejanethe (8:15:52 PM): Oh, get your mind out of the gutter! LOL Yes, a motel. With two twin beds. :P

RawKdaSkEEbaLL (8:15:55 PM): my mind wasent in the gutter :P:::::

RawKdaSkEEbaLL (8:15:59 PM): i just didnt know if theyd let us regester w/ no adult id

thejanethe (8:16:05 PM): I already booked a room in one of the motels online with my dad's credit card. I'll bring it with us and make up some story when we get there for why he's not checking in with us. They'll buy it. I mean, it's a cheap motel, not CIA headquarters.

RawKdaSkEEbaLL (8:16:08 PM): hmmmmmmmmmmmm

RawKdaSkEEbaLL (8:16:12 PM): a plan feendishly simple in its intriccasies ;)

thejanethe (8:16:14 PM): OMGSIMPSONSREFERENCE! LOL

RawKdaSkEEbaLL (8:16:17 PM): yah i started watching it after u said u liked it

thejanethe (8:16:18): Trust you for that. LOL

thejanethe (8:16:19 PM): So are you in?

RawKdaSkEEbaLL (8:16:21 PM): i dunno

RawKdaSkEEbaLL (8:16:24 PM): it seems realy..... uh.... sudden?

RawKdaSkEEbaLL (8:16:29 PM): i mean u just told me like 2 mins ago that were goin 2 ny

RawKdaSkEEbaLL (8:16:32 PM): & whne do we leave?

thejanethe (8:16:34 PM): As soon as possible.

RawKdaSkEEbaLL (8:16:38 PM): c waht i mean?! lol

thejanethe (8:16:40 PM): I know, it is sudden. But I am JAZZED, dude. I am READY TO GO.

RawKdaSkEEbaLL (8:16:42 PM): y?

RawKdaSkEEbaLL (8:16:44 PM): what hapened?

thejanethe (8:16:47 PM): What do you mean, "what happened"? I told you, Audra's in the hospital. She's a friend of mine and I'm sick of waiting around. I have no idea how sick she is, I have no idea what happened to her. What if she's been in a car wreck? Or if she has cancer or something crazy like that? I'm just fed up with the waiting.

RawKdaSkEEbaLL (8:16:50 PM): yea but shes been in the hospietel for days now?

RawKdaSkEEbaLL (8:16:53 PM): y now?

thejanethe (8:16:55 PM): Sometimes you just get fed up. You know?

RawKdaSkEEbaLL (8:16:58 PM): i gess

RawKdaSkEEbaLL (8:17:02 PM): buut what abt the rachel thing

thejanethe (8:17:04 PM): "the Rachel thing"?

RawKdaSkEEbaLL (8:17:08 PM): yea ur other personallity

RawKdaSkEEbaLL (8:17:15 PM): i thot u didnt want 2 visit her cos shed find out or something

thejanethe (8:17:19 PM): I'm just going to tell her I use a fake picture online because I'm ugly. :P

RawKdaSkEEbaLL (8:17:22 PM): ur not ugly

thejanethe (8:17:25 PM): Man, we are not having this conversation again. LOL

RawKdaSkEEbaLL (8:17:28 PM): but wiat, rachel's in colledge rite

thejanethe (8:17:29 PM): So?

RawKdaSkEEbaLL (8:17:31 PM): no offence but u dont rly look like ur in colledge

thejanethe (8:17:33 PM): Oh, whatever. People look younger than they are all the time.

thejanethe (8:17:34 PM): I'll put on makeup or something.

RawKdaSkEEbaLL (8:17:36 PM): i nevr saw u in makeup, u nevr wear it

thejanethe (8:17:38 PM): So we stop at some 24-hour drugstore and buy some. I'll look up some instructions online for how to put it on.

RawKdaSkEEbaLL (8:17:41 PM): lol, ok

RawKdaSkEEbaLL (8:17:45 PM): but if u nevr saw her in person b4 it coud be akwerd to see her for the 1st time in the hospetel?

thejanethe (8:17:49 PM): If it seems awkward, I'll turn right back around. But I don't think it will be.

thejanethe (8:17:51 PM): Really. I know Audra.

RawKdaSkEEbaLL (8:17:54 PM): i dunno

thejanethe (8:17:56 PM): Come on, dude. TELL ME a road trip doesn't sound like the greatest thing ever. TELL ME you aren't dying to try out your new wheels on a long trip.

RawKdaSkEEbaLL (8:18:00 PM): that part does sound kinda fun

RawKdaSkEEbaLL (8:18:03 PM): like adventurrous!

thejanethe (8:18:04 PM): And we'll get to stay in a motel!

RawKdaSkEEbaLL (8:18:08 PM): yea...............

RawKdaSkEEbaLL (8:18:13 PM): ok

RawKdaSkEEbaLL (8:18:16 PM): count me in

thejanethe (8:18:17 PM): YAY!!!

thejanethe (8:18:20 PM): Go pack and then take a nap so you'll be ready to do some driving tonight. Can you pick me up at eleven-thirty?

RawKdaSkEEbaLL (8:18:25 PM): 11:30..ok

RawKdaSkEEbaLL (8:18:29 PM): yea i can get sum sleep n then we cn drive for like 3 or 4 hrs?

thejanethe (8:18:32 PM): Exactly. In the middle of the night. with no traffic, we'll totally make good enough time on the roads to be in Ellery in four hours or so. We'll be in bed again by 3:30, and we can sleep in and then go to visiting hours at noon.

thejanethe (8:18:34 PM): I've got the whole thing mapped out. Dude, this is AWESOME.

RawKdaSkEEbaLL (8:18:37 PM): yea, it is kinda :-)

thejanethe (8:18:38 PM): XD

thejanethe (8:18:40 PM): Okay, you go pack and get sleep. I'll do the same.

RawKdaSkEEbaLL (8:18:44 PM): ok

thejanethe (8:18:49 PM): Oh, and by the way, I'm not at my dad's. I'm staying with my aunt for awhile. She lives at 137 Chicopee Street, on the west end of town. When you get here, don't honk or anything. Pull up to the front. I'll be on the lookout.

RawKdaSkEEbaLL (8:18:55 PM): wait, ur @ ur aunts? y?

thejanethe (8:18:58 PM): My dad's out of town at a conference.

RawKdaSkEEbaLL (8:19:03 PM): a confrence? i thot he was retired?

thejanethe (8:19:10 PM): He is, but he still likes to keep up with what's going on in his field.

RawKdaSkEEbaLL (8:19:14 PM): wat did he do, neway

thejanethe (8:19:16 PM): THIS IS NOT HELPING US TO GET TO NEW YORK TONIGHT. Go pack and then go sleep. LOL

RawKdaSkEEbaLL (8:19:20 PM): ok

RawKdaSkEEbaLL (8:19:23 PM): see u in a few hrs!

thejanethe (8:19:24 PM): YES!

thejanethe has signed off.

Maya B (2:56:13 AM): Jennie?

Jennie P (auto-response) (2:56:14 AM): zzzzzzzzzzzzzzzzzzz....nite :-)

Maya B (2:56:22 AM): Jennie, it's Rachel. I guess you're asleep, or maybe just in bed? but if you're there I'd really appreciate your coming to the computer... I know you live in New York somewhere, and I think you know Audra better than most people, so maybe you'd know more about this, but... I'm not making any sense, am I? LOL

Maya B: It would just be really helpful if you were there. Are you?

Maya B (2:57:02 AM): Look, okay, I'm going to keep talking, because maybe you'll come back or something. I'm really sorry, I hate to be so obnoxious, I'm just... kind of desperate.

Maya B (2:57:08 AM): I... huh, this sounds so dumb. :(And kind of funny, I guess! I was trying to visit Audra -- like, as a surprise?

Maya B (2:57:17 AM): Only I, um, well, I guess I sort of got lost along the way. The GPS in my phone got all fouled up somehow and it sent me driving around in circles, and now the battery's almost dead and I'm in the middle of nowhere. I tried to get the directions on MapFinder and I've used Yippee Maps and even the ZoomMaps satellite pictures and stuff, but none of them are helping -- I think some of the signs are mislabeled or something, maybe?

Maya B (2:57:28 AM): But I'm sort of stranded on the side of the road. I'm running low on gas and I don't want to just keep driving around randomly until I know where I'm going, because I have no idea where there's a gas station or anything. All the local gas stations that I could find aren't 24 hours.

Maya B (2:57:41 AM): So I'm just sitting next to the curb near some random person's house. I'm stealing someone's unsecured wireless connection to be on the Internet right now, but it's sort of going in and out, and my laptop battery is running down fast too. And obviously it's the middle of the night, and I don't want to wake up some stranger and be like "Excuse me, can I use your phone?"

Maya B (2:57:52 AM): But it's -- well, it's pretty creepy being stranded here in the middle of nowhere. It's some crazy dark suburban town where there aren't even, like, streetlights. And it's called Elm Street. I mean, SERIOUSLY, ELM STREET?! lol

Maya B (2:58:01 AM): I don't even know what town I'm in. But I thought maybe Audra, being from around here, would know, and maybe you could call her and see? or else you might know, since you're from upstate NY somewhere?

Maya B (2:58:17 AM): I don't know... I'm just a little lost, I guess.

Maya B (2:58:17 AM): I mean, yeah. I sort of made that clear. LOL

Maya B (2:58:20 AM): Um, I'm really sorry to have bothered you... no one else was online... but I'm sorry. Stupid, I know. It'll totally be fine, I'll just see if I can find a different map site or something.

Maya B (2:58:20 AM): Anyway, no worries! You can just delete this when you get it.

Maya B (2:58:21 AM): I'm really sorry. Bye

* * *

Maya B (3:03:57 AM): hey Carol!

Auto-Response from **Carol C-P** (3:03:58 AM): Slowly, gently, night unfurls its splendor... grasp it, sense it, tremulous and tender...

Maya B (3:04:03 AM): ah, your new fandom. :)

Maya B (3:04:10 AM): Sorry to chat you so randomly (and so late), but I wanted to ask -- you live somewhere in upstate NY, right?

Maya B (3:04:19 AM): Hm, well, I'm guessing you're probably asleep

Maya B (3:04:21 AM): talk to you later...

From: janeshilling@spectrum.org
To: eleanor.acton@firstgroupnet.com
Date: 4/24/2013
Subject: Hi

Nora,

I am having an official Crazy Patient Crisis and if you are online you should email me back immediately. I will pay you for your time.

Jane

P.S. I am sorry I told you to shut the fuck up at our last session. Please email me if you get this.

From: thejanethe@yippee.com
To: jessieshill@owletpublishers.com
Date: 4/24/2013
Subject: (none)

Mommy?

Has your email address died yet?

I'm scared, Mom

From: MAILER-DAEMON@owletpublishers.com
To: thejanethe@yippee.com
Subject: Returned mail: User unknown

 *** ATTENTION ***
----- The following addresses had permanent
fatal errors -----
<jessieshill@owletpublishers.com>
   ----- Transcript of session follows -----
... while talking to air-xa04.mail.
owletpublishers.com.:
>>> RCPT To:<jessieshill@owletpublishers.com>
<<< 550 MAILBOX NOT FOUND
550 <jessieshill@owletpublishers.com>... User
unknown
Message/delivery-status
Reporting-MTA: dns; rly-xa04.
mx.owletpublishers.com
Final-Recipient: RFC822; jessieshill@
owletpublishers.com
Action: failed
Status: 5.1.1
Remote-MTA: DNS; air-xa04.mail.owletpublishers.
com
Diagnostic-Code: SMTP; 550 MAILBOX NOT FOUND
Message-ID: <20050214005340.5571.qmail@
web53208.mail.yippee.com>
Received: from [209.6.220.18] by web53208.mail.
yippee.com via HTTP
From: thejanethe@yippee.com
Subject: (none)
MIME-Version: 1.0
Content-Type: multipart/alternative;
boundary="0-638409771-1108342419=:4176"
X-OWLETPUBLISHERS-IP: 206.170.11.601
X-OWLETPUBLISHERS-SCOLL-SCORE: 0:0:0:
X-OWLETPUBLISHERS-SCOLL-URL_COUNT: 0

Stars May Fall
Chapter 23

This was not a game now, no grinning monkey at the controls to suck them back in; no second chances and no maybes.

One oxygen tank, two people. The eternal blackness of deep space.

How many breaths in an oxygen tank, he wondered? They were gasping now; Jaela was screaming. One of these oxygen tanks, the small ones, designed for the shortest of expeditions on planets with the strongest gravity, might last a half an hour in ideal circumstances. These were not ideal circumstances. So; twenty minutes. Ten if they split it. Less, because small amounts of oxygen were venting from the second hose, jammed awkwardly into a socket meant for one.

Meant for one.

Thorin made up his mind.

He reached out, grabbed for his oxygen tube. Pulled. Hard.

For a few breaths -- one, two, three -- nothing happened. Jaela's eyes widened; she was screaming words now, screaming at him to put it back -- he knew, though he couldn't hear her; knew she was screaming at him to put it back, Jordana would learn what had happened to them, she would send someone back through time to rescue them, the paradoxes would be fixable, they had a chance, but put it back, Thorin, please put it back - and though he pinwheeled head over feet, floating away, away, each second pushing him farther away, he knew what she would be saying. His own brain had screamed the same things in those first few desperate seconds, those seconds when he had wanted to believe it would be okay.

Three and a half breaths in the abyss hit him, knifing into his lungs, leaving him doubled up, gasping at the last few remnants of oxygen, spinning off into blackness. The stars loomed before him, impossibly bright, impossibly close; as his eyes exploded with starburst hemorrhages and darkness descended he felt the red imprint of Sirius against his skull, wondered if he would be drawn in, burned. He was dying and he wished he could have died staring into Jaela's eyes. He felt her screams closing in on his crumpling brain, and yet he knew, his last snatches of thoughts clear and sharp, that he had done the right thing. Jordana might have saved them but she might not have and twenty minutes was a bigger window than six or seven, the paradoxes of saving one life much easier to correct for than two; he might have lived but he might not have and in the end we all die, and in a way the certainty was a relief, knowing that he had given his life for Jaela, knowing that what awaited him was mere blackness, mere ending. The uncertainty and the pain were left to Jaela, and a faint shred of doubt crept into his certainty, wondering if the gift he had given her might not be more of a curse after all, wondering --

Blind, he thought of her green eyes, and died.

RawKdaSkEEbaLL (5:45:26 PM): hi jane

thejanethe (5:45:47 PM): Hey, Gary.

RawKdaSkEEbaLL (5:45:53 PM): whats up

thejanethe (5:46:03 PM): Not too much.

RawKdaSkEEbaLL (5:46:23 PM): so.....

thejanethe (5:46:30 PM): ?

RawKdaSkEEbaLL (5:46:36 PM): nothin

RawKdaSkEEbaLL (5:46:40 PM): lol

thejanethe (5:46:50 PM): Uh, okay. LOL

RawKdaSkEEbaLL (5:47:00 PM): no i was just wondrin how ur doing

thejanethe (5:47:05 PM): I'm fine.

thejanethe (5:47:10 PM): Why wouldn't I be?

RawKdaSkEEbaLL (5:47:12 PM): uhh....

RawKdaSkEEbaLL (5:47:15 PM): like just wonderin if u ghot in trouble or w/e?

thejanethe (5:47:19 PM): Oh, that. No, I'm fine.

thejanethe (5:47:27 PM): I mean, my aunt got all freaked out. I have to write a letter to Ms. Meisner and some DSS person and I don't know who all else, explaining what happened. But whatever.

RawKdaSkEEbaLL (5:47:29 PM): a leter?

thejanethe (5:47:35 PM): Yeah, about how I understand the consequences of my actions and I'm not going to do it again, blah blah blah. Don't worry, I'm going to tell them it was all my idea.

RawKdaSkEEbaLL (5:47:37 PM): i wasent worried

RawKdaSkEEbaLL (5:47:39 PM): i mean not abt that

RawKdaSkEEbaLL (5:47:41 PM): im alredy grounded 4 like a million yrs anyway

thejanethe (5:47:46 PM): So what were you worried about?

thejanethe (5:47:47 PM): Ugh, sorry about that.

RawKdaSkEEbaLL (5:47:52 PM): i dunno

RawKdaSkEEbaLL (5:47:57 PM): just how you were upset & stuff

thejanethe (5:48:04 PM): Oh. No, I'm fine. Sorry I fell apart.

thejanethe (5:48:07 PM): It was stupid. Just, my dad and everything... whatever. I'm fine.

RawKdaSkEEbaLL (5:48:11 PM): u keep saying that?

thejanethe (5:48:14 PM): What?

RawKdaSkEEbaLL (5:48:16 PM): im fine, whatevr

thejanethe (5:48:18 PM): Well, I am fine.

thejanethe (5:48:21 PM): Stuff kind of sucks, I had a stupid idea, I'm sorry I dragged you into it.

RawKdaSkEEbaLL (5:48:34 PM): hey i told u my dad used to drink rite

thejanethe (5:48:39 PM): ...yes?

RawKdaSkEEbaLL (5:48:43 PM): i mean stuff used to get rly rouf 4 me too back then

thejanethe (5:48:47 PM): Right. Well, yeah, it does.

thejanethe (5:48:48 PM): I'm sorry.

RawKdaSkEEbaLL (5:48:53 PM): i ran away 1 time

thejanethe (5:48:56 PM): You did?

thejanethe (5:48:58 PM): Where?

RawKdaSkEEbaLL (5:48:59 PM): not far

RawKdaSkEEbaLL (5:49:02 PM): like to the end of the street lol

thejanethe (5:49:04 PM): Huh?

RawKdaSkEEbaLL (5:49:09 PM): well my parents used to fight all the time b4 my dad left, rite

RawKdaSkEEbaLL (5:49:13 PM): & this 1 time it was worse then usual

RawKdaSkEEbaLL (5:49:15 PM): like I thot he was gunna beat my mom up or sumthing

thejanethe (5:49:16 PM): Oh, shit.

thejanethe (5:49:20 PM): Um... did he?

RawKdaSkEEbaLL (5:49:24 PM): no he nevr actully did it but he was.. sorta scarey

RawKdaSkEEbaLL (5:49:31 PM): i dunno

RawKdaSkEEbaLL (5:49:35 PM): neway it was all kinda crazey & i ran out of the house

RawKdaSkEEbaLL (5:49:37 PM): but i dident rly have anywere to go

thejanethe (5:49:39 PM): Yeah, I hear that.

RawKdaSkEEbaLL (5:49:41 PM): neway i wound up in the playground

RawKdaSkEEbaLL (5:49:42 PM): in the slide

thejanethe (5:49:44 PM): ...what? LOL

RawKdaSkEEbaLL (5:49:46 PM): like the kiddy slide thats like a tunnal?

RawKdaSkEEbaLL (5:49:48 PM): i hid in the bendey part 2 go 2 sleep

thejanethe (5:49:50 PM): In the slide?! Wait, how old were you?!

RawKdaSkEEbaLL (5:49:51 PM): like 10 or sumthin

thejanethe (5:50:54 PM): Jesus, and you were out all night?

RawKdaSkEEbaLL (5:50:57 PM): no not all nite cuz after i fell asleep i started slideing down

RawKdaSkEEbaLL (5:50:59 PM): & i woke up slideing

thejanethe (5:51:00 PM): OMG! LOL

thejanethe (5:51:02 PM): Sorry, I know it's not funny, but...

RawKdaSkEEbaLL (5:51:04 PM): no its funney now u cn laugh :)

thejanethe (5:51:06 PM): Waking up in a slide. Man, Gary.

RawKdaSkEEbaLL (5:51:09 PM): almost out of the slide

thejanethe (5:51:10 PM): Right. LOL

thejanethe (5:51:13 PM): So what did you do then?

RawKdaSkEEbaLL (5:51:15 PM): just went home

RawKdaSkEEbaLL (5:51:18 PM): but i dident want to go inside so i sleped in the garrage

thejanethe (5:51:19 PM): Ah.

thejanethe (5:51:07 PM): So you ran away... to your garage.

RawKdaSkEEbaLL (5:51:08 PM): yepo

thejanethe (5:51:10 PM): Well, I'm sorry that happened.

RawKdaSkEEbaLL (5:51:12 PM): no its ok now

RawKdaSkEEbaLL (5:51:14 PM): but u know like

RawKdaSkEEbaLL (5:51:22 PM): i totaley had 2 to get out of the house rite

RawKdaSkEEbaLL (5:51:25 PM): i just....... idk

RawKdaSkEEbaLL (5:51:32 PM): i coudent be in a house w/them

thejanethe (5:51:35 PM): Well, right. Hence running away?

RawKdaSkEEbaLL (5:51:38 PM): hence :)

RawKdaSkEEbaLL (5:51:49 PM): look its just u dont have 2 pretend its all ok

thejanethe (5:51:52 PM): ...except it is.

thejanethe (5:52:55 PM): Look, I'm sorry your dad was angry or abusive or whatever, but I'm fine at my aunt's. She's really nice.

RawKdaSkEEbaLL (5:52:57 PM): no thats not wat i mean

RawKdaSkEEbaLL (5:52:59 PM): & i just told u, he wasent abusive

thejanethe (5:53:02 PM): Well, verbally abusive.

RawKdaSkEEbaLL (5:53:04 PM): i dident say that either, they just fought alot

thejanethe (5:53:06 PM): OK, well, anyway, that's not what's going on here.

RawKdaSkEEbaLL (5:53:08 PM): i dident say it was

RawKdaSkEEbaLL (5:53:10 PM): i just said i know wat it's like 2 have 2 get away

thejanethe (5:53:13 PM): But I *don't* have to get away. Are you listening to me?

thejanethe (5:53:15 PM): My aunt's really sweet.

RawKdaSkEEbaLL (5:53:19 PM): jane ur in foster care

thejanethe (5:53:23 PM): I'm not in foster care! That is specifically NOT where I am!

RawKdaSkEEbaLL: (5:53:26 PM): u said social workers came 2 ur house & said u coudent live with ur dad

thejanethe (5:53:29 PM): He's at a *rehab*. For like a month.

thejanethe (5:53:32 PM): What, I'm supposed to follow him to rehab? Sleep on a cot in his room?

RawKdaSkEEbaLL (5:53:35 PM): no but u know what i mean

thejanethe (5:53:37 PM): Yes, and you're completely missing the point!

RawKdaSkEEbaLL (5:53:41 PM): ok

RawKdaSkEEbaLL (5:53:44 PM): look i gess im not saying this rite

RawKdaSkEEbaLL (5:53:49 PM): but i was the one in ny w/ u, ok

RawKdaSkEEbaLL (5:53:53 PM): & u were talking to me last nite

thejanethe (5:53:56 PM): I was stressed!

RawKdaSkEEbaLL (5:53:59 PM): but thats what im saying

thejanethe (5:54:02 PM): I shouldn't have gone in the first place, it was a dumb idea, we were lost, whatever!

RawKdaSkEEbaLL (5:54:05 PM): yea but

thejanethe (5:54:06 PM): But nothing! What the hell, Gary!

RawKdaSkEEbaLL (5:54:10 PM): all i was trying 2 say is i know were ur comming from

thejanethe (5:54:12 PM): Oh for God's sake, where exactly do you think I'm "coming from"?!

thejanethe (5:54:13 PM): I was wound up last night. That's ALL.

RawKdaSkEEbaLL (5:54:15 PM): so wat u made up all that stuff

thejanethe (5:54:17 PM): No, of course not, but I was just, I don't know, stressed!

thejanethe (5:54:19 PM): The social workers getting involved is ridiculous, Ms. Meisner is being a total bitch, and it's just -- it's fine!

thejanethe (5:54:20 PM): The only problem is NO ONE WILL LEAVE ME ALONE

RawKdaSkEEbaLL (5:54:21 PM): woah

RawKdaSkEEbaLL (5:54:23 PM): dude im ttly not trying to ofend u or nothing

RawKdaSkEEbaLL (5:54:25 PM): i gess this is comming out all rong or w/e

thejanethe (5:54:26 PM): Then maybe you ought to LET IT GO.

RawKdaSkEEbaLL (5:54:27 PM): but wat am i suposed to do

RawKdaSkEEbaLL (5:54:28 PM): ignore all the stuff u said

thejanethe (5:54:30 PM): What you're supposed to DO is give me some goddamn space on this!

thejanethe (5:54:33 PM): Christ, I have every other human being in my life jumping all over me and harassing me about -- about EVERYTHING, and now you're trying to make this all about you and your problems from like six years ago all because my dad actually got into rehab???

RawKdaSkEEbaLL (5:54:34 PM): wait wut?

RawKdaSkEEbaLL (5:54:35 PM): dude no

RawKdaSkEEbaLL (5:54:38 PM): this has nothing 2 do w/ my dad

thejanethe (5:54:39 PM): Then why the fuck did you bring him up!

RawKdaSkEEbaLL (5:54:41 PM): look just cool off & quit swaring @ me

RawKdaSkEEbaLL (5:54:45 PM): i brout him up b/c i just thot u cd use some1 to talk 2

thejanethe (5:54:48 PM): Oh, okay, so if you come after me with stories about your drunk dad I'll spill stories about my drunk dad and then we can like cuddle around an open fire or something?

thejanethe (5:54:50 PM): WTF!

RawKdaSkEEbaLL (5:54:52 PM): ok srsly this has NOTHING 2 DO W/ MY DAD

RawKdaSkEEbaLL (5:54:54 PM): I WAS TRYEING 2 GDET U TO TALK

RawKdaSkEEbaLL (5:54:56 PM): b/c u DONT TALK 2 ANYONE

RawKdaSkEEbaLL (5:54:58 PM): u dident even come 2 scool 2day

thejanethe (5:55:00 PM): Oh, yeah, that would've been a great idea, come into school so I could get called into Ms. Meisner's office to "discuss" everything. That would have been awesome.

RawKdaSkEEbaLL (5:55:01 PM): ur gonna get kicked out if u keep skiping

thejanethe (5:55:02 PM): They're not going to KICK ME OUT. It's SPECTRUM.

RawKdaSkEEbaLL (5:55:04 PM): or sumer scool, w/e

thejanethe (5:55:06 PM): Whatever! They're not going to send me to summer school, I'll have Nora talk to them or something, and why the HELL do you care, anyway?!

RawKdaSkEEbaLL (5:55:08 PM): b/c ur my FREIND

thejanethe (5:55:10 PM): Then why don't you try acting like one? I have plenty of counselors to pry around in my head and bug me about personal shit all day long, I really do not need it from you. As I've said like TWENTY FUCKING TIMES IN THIS CONVERSATION ALREADY.

RawKdaSkEEbaLL (5:55:13 PM): ok seriusly jane lay off

RawKdaSkEEbaLL (5:15:15 PM): im not trying to get u mad

thejanethe (5:55:16 PM): Oh, brilliant!

RawKdaSkEEbaLL (5:55:19 PM): i dident mean 2 bring up stuff thats 2 sensetive or w/e

RawKdaSkEEbaLL (5:55:22 PM): but like last nite?

RawKdaSkEEbaLL (5:55:25 PM): wtf, im supossed to pretend that nevr hapened?

thejanethe (5:55:26 PM): Oh FFS, Gary, what do you think DID happen?

thejanethe (5:55:27 PM): I made a stupid decision to try to visit a friend in New York, we got lost, I got panicked, we came home!

RawKdaSkEEbaLL (5:55:30 PM): jane u were way more then panicked

RawKdaSkEEbaLL (5:55:33 PM): @ the end u coudent even talk, i had to get us all the directons & stuff

RawKdaSkEEbaLL (5:55:36 PM): all u coud do was write ur fanfictons

thejanethe (5:55:37 PM): Jesus, DON'T EVEN START

thejanethe (5:55:39 PM): So writing helps me relax, what the fuck do you care?

thejanethe (5:55:40 PM): at least I wasn't running around in the middle of the night trying to find a fucking Skee-ball alley

RawKdaSkEEbaLL (5:55:43 PM): uh i dident go lookinjg for a skeeball alley, i found a gas station & got a map

RawKdaSkEEbaLL (5:55:47 PM): you woudent even let me use the comp to look up maps online

thejanethe (5:55:49 PM): I told you, I already looked at every single goddamn map site I could find!! What did you want to do, run down the gas idling on street corners and messing with the same screwed-up maps all night?

RawKdaSkEEbaLL (5:55:52 PM): i toled u i think we got the wrong street adress

RawKdaSkEEbaLL (5:55:53 PM): but w/e

RawKdaSkEEbaLL (5:55:55 PM): i dont even know what were fighting abt rite now

thejanethe (5:55:56 PM): We wouldn't be fighting if you had just SHUT UP TEN MINUTES AGO

RawKdaSkEEbaLL (5:55:58 PM): i just dont get what hapened is all

thejanethe (5:55:59 PM): NOTHING HAPPENED.

RawKdaSkEEbaLL (5:56:03 PM): ur like crying all over me & telling me all this stuff last nite & now ur just oh nothing hapened

thejanethe (5:55:04 PM): I DO NOT WANT TO TALK ABOUT IT.

thejanethe (5:56:05 PM): Is that clear enough? I DO NOT WANT TO TALK ABOUT IT

RawKdaSkEEbaLL (5:56:08 PM): uh i got that now

thejanethe (5:56:09 PM): then WHY ARE WE STILL TALKING ABOUT IT?!

RawKdaSkEEbaLL (5:56:12 PM): i have no iudea exeped u keep geting mad & yelling @ me & i totaley dont know waht im suposed 2 say

RawKdaSkEEbaLL (5:56:14 PM): im sorrey i upset u

RawKdaSkEEbaLL (5:56:15 PM): just quit yelling

thejanethe (5:56:15 PM): Yeah, you and everyone else.

thejanethe (5:56:16 PM): Sit back, be quiet, let everyone pry as much as they want to, fuck around with my head as much as they want to, do whatever they want to ruin my life and just be a good girl!

RawKdaSkEEbaLL (5:56:19 PM): ok i dont even know what were talking abt anymore

thejanethe (5:56:20 PM): You know what? We're not. We're not talking anymore.

RawKdaSkEEbaLL (5:56:21 PM): what?

thejanethe has signed off.

Maya B (3:32:27 PM): AUDRA! OMG YOU'RE BACK.

Maya B (3:32:31 PM): Are you all right? I was so worried!

Maya B (3:32:43 PM): Oh my God, it's seriously so good to see you online.

Maya B (3:32:58 PM): Unless... is this Audra?

Maya B (3:33:04 PM): If it's Audra's mom or something, just let me know, just -- is she okay?

Audra S (3:33:18 PM): Hi, Rachel. Yeah, it's Audra.

Maya B (3:33:20 PM): Hi!

Maya B (3:33:23 PM): Um, what's up?

Maya B (3:33:28 PM): Jennie said you were in the hospital. I was pretty worried. I thought -- well, never mind.

Audra S (3:33:32 PM): That I was dead? :) No, I'm fine.

Maya B (3:33:36 PM): Well, maybe.

Audra S (3:33:49 PM): I'm sorry you were so worried.

Maya B (3:33:52 PM): NO. I mean, really, don't be worried. It's not about me.

Audra S (3:33:58 PM): I didn't want to worry people. I thought you might worry more if I just disappeared.

Maya B (3:34:05 PM): Well, it's okay, either way, as long as you're okay. Are you okay?

Maya B (3:34:27 PM): ...Aud?

Audra S (3:34:32 PM): Sorry. I'm -- I guess I'm distracted.

Maya B (3:34:35 PM): It's okay.

Maya B (3:34:54 PM): You're all right, though?

Maya B (3:35:08 PM): Okay, I guess you're probably busy. I hope you're feeling all right. I'll talk to you later or something.

Audra S (3:35:11 PM): No, wait, Rach. I'm sorry.

Maya B (3:35:14 PM): For what?

Audra S (3:35:19 PM): I can tell you're pissed. I didn't mean to piss you off. I'm... well, I'm sorry.

Maya B (3:35:26 PM): Wait, Audra, what's going on? I'm not pissed, I'm just confused.

Maya B (3:35:39 PM): I mean like I'm not trying to pry or anything. I was just, well, worried.

Maya B (3:35:47 PM): Audra? Are you still there?

Maya B (3:39:19 PM): Look, I still don't know what's going on, and there keep being these big pauses, so I'm just going to put it out on the table, I guess. I really care about you, and I really value our friendship. And lately, things have felt... sort of off. And I don't know why. And I guess that's why I got snappy -- I'm sorry about that. I know you don't need it right now. I just felt sort of shut out, when you were in the hospital, because Jennie obviously knew what was going on, but she wouldn't tell me, and you were out of commission. And I'm not trying to make this into a "you like Jennie more than you like me!" thing, or to be all super-dramatic. Really, I'm not. And if this is all too much for you to deal with right now, it's really okay for you to just say so. Really. Mostly I just... I want to understand. And I really do want you to know that I care about you. Okay?

Maya B (3:39:27 PM): Wow, that must be the longest message ever sent in the history of FL. LOL

Audra S (3:39:41 PM): Oh, Rach.

Audra S (3:39:46 PM): I'm really sorry.

Audra S (3:39:58 PM): Um... I'm just sorry you've been feeling that way.

Maya B (3:40:05 PM): It's all right. You don't need to apologize so much, I'm not mad.

Audra S (3:40:19 PM): I'll try to explain. But... it's sort of hard to put words to.

Maya B (3:40:23 PM): Well, I'm listening.

Audra S (3:40:46 PM): Okay.

Audra S (3:40:55 PM): Um, for starters... what my mom said about the hospital, that wasn't really 100% true. Well, I mean, it was true as far as it went.

Maya B (3:41:04 PM): Okay...

Audra S (3:41:19 PM): But it wasn't really... like, a medical hospital, or what you think of as one. I was on the psych ward.

Maya B (3:41:45 PM): Wow. God, I don't know what to say.

Audra S (3:41:53 PM): It's all right, no one really does.

Maya B (3:42:07 PM): I will TOTALLY understand if this is too personal, but if you want to talk about why, I'm here.

Audra S (3:42:18 PM): Yeah. I'm, well, a cutter.

Audra S (3:42:26 PM): I don't know if you know much about it.

Maya B (3:42:36 PM): A bit. I know a couple of kids at school who do it. But not that well.

Maya B (3:42:51 PM): I'm really sorry.

Audra S (3:43:07 PM): It's all right. It's sort of hard to explain to someone who hasn't experienced it... I know it sounds gross, probably.

Maya B (3:43:16 PM): No. It doesn't, really.

Audra S (3:43:29 PM): It sounds gross to me, when I try to think about it the way someone else must. Usually people either get grossed out, or they make fun of it, like it's a fake emo thing.

Maya B (3:43:35 PM): People make fun of it?! God, how awful can people be?

Audra S (3:43:44 PM): It's just that... I know I can't explain it... I don't even know why I'm trying. I'm sorry.

Maya B (3:43:58 PM): If you want to talk about it, please do. And please don't apologize. I feel like the jerk. I feel like I should have asked, or something.

Audra S (3:44:12 PM): It's not usually how you start conversations. "Hey, Aud, how you doing? Engaged in any self-mutilation today?"

Maya B (3:44:14 PM): LOL!

Maya B (3:44:17 PM): I'm sorry, should I not laugh?

Audra S (3:44:23 PM): It was a joke. You should laugh. :)

Maya B (3:44:31 PM): Okay. :)

Audra S (3:45:03 PM): I don't know. The thing about cutting is that it's not like I *like* pain, or blood, or any of that stuff. It's not like it's a fetish or something. A lot of people seem to think that it's all about, like, reveling in exquisite pain or something. It's not that.

Audra S (3:45:11 PM): It's just that sometimes things get to be too much. And I don't know how to handle them, and I get panicky and freaked-out and I just... I can't cope. And cutting centers my thoughts again, gets them focused.

Audra S (3:45:19 PM): I know that probably doesn't make sense.

Maya B (3:45:37 PM): No. I think I get it.

Maya B (3:45:44 PM): Really, I know that sounds stupid or like a lie. But it just... I think I get it.

Audra S (3:46:02 PM): Well, anyway, my mom didn't know about it for a long time. But she is not exactly the most respectful person in the world when it comes to privacy, so she barged in on me in my room the other day, and I was in just a bra, so my arms were showing.

Maya B (3:46:05 PM): AAAAAGH.

Audra S (3:46:07 PM): I know, right?

Audra S (3:46:16 PM): In addition to her tendency to not understand the concept of privacy, she also does not tend to understand the concept of "reacting sanely and sensibly to stressors". She's pretty all-or-nothing. So she had a huge freakout attack and dragged me to the ER and told the doctors I was suicidal, which I was not, may I add, but she wanted me admitted and as I am not quite 18 yet, presto-chango, I was in a locked ward a few hours later.

Maya B (3:46:18 PM): God.

Maya B (3:46:19 PM): What a crazy thing to have happen.

Maya B (3:46:22 PM): I mean... horrible.

Audra S (3:46:31 PM): ::laughs:: Rachel, honey, it's okay. I'm not going to freak out and slice my arm open with a vegetable peeler because you said the word "crazy".

Maya B (3:46:37 PM): LOL! I'm glad to see your sense of humor is still intact.

Audra S (3:46:45 PM): I guess it is. Funny, I hadn't actually thought it was.

Audra S (3:46:49 PM): I guess talking helps.

Audra S (3:46:58 PM): Well, anyway. It wasn't that big of a deal. They might have even let me go -- I think everyone could see my mom is crazier than I am ::eyeroll:: except they have this mandated hospitalization period for people who are suicidal, and, well, there were the cuts on my arms. I kept telling them I wasn't trying to kill myself. But I guess they figured better safe than sorry.

Audra S (3:47:05 PM): It wasn't so bad. Not much like *Girl, Interrupted*. But not so bad.

Maya B (3:47:09 PM): Want to talk about it?

Audra S (3:47:14 PM): Not right now, I don't think. I'm a little drained. I'm glad I talked to you about what happened, but I think I'd rather change the subject.

Maya B (3:47:18 PM): Okay, sure.

Maya B (3:47:33 PM): So, um, did they have a TV on the ward? Did you catch the last episode of LtT? :)

Audra S (3:47:37 PM): They did, but I didn't watch it.

Maya B (3:47:40 PM): Oh, man! You passed up an opportunity to swoon over Brad?

Audra S (3:47:52 PM): The thing is...

Maya B (3:48:12 PM): Yeah?

Audra S (3:48:17 PM): The thing is, all of that's just... sort of hard to focus on in a situation like that.

Maya B (3:48:23 PM): Oh. Makes sense.

Audra S (3:48:28 PM): Well, not the way you're probably thinking.

Audra S (3:48:33 PM): The thing is that I kind of dove into the whole fandom thing as an escape mechanism.

Audra S (3:48:39 PM): And once I was hospitalized... well, I was really scared and all that, but also I felt like -- it's hard to explain.

Maya B (3:48:47 PM): Yeah?

Audra S (3:49:13 PM): I just felt like I'd hit a turning point. And I didn't want to go back. It's funny, I'd have thought I would.

Audra S (3:49:20 PM): But it almost made me sick, if I'm telling the truth, almost made me sick to think about diving back in. It was like -- it's all on the table now. The shit has officially hit the fan. No more pretending. And no more hiding.

Maya B (3:49:37 PM): Wow. That sounds really hard.

Maya B (3:49:41 PM): ::laughs:: Things must be really rough when Brad Memphis makes you sick!

Audra S (3:49:44 PM): Sort of!

Audra S (3:49:49 PM): I just -- maybe it won't last, but right now I hate the thought of all of that. Of burrowing into fandom to try to escape what's really going on.

Audra S (3:49:55 PM): Maybe it'll change. I'm sure this burst of determination or whatever won't last forever.

Maya B (3:50:01 PM): I'd miss having you to talk LtT with!

Audra S (3:50:07 PM): But if I don't want to talk about LtT, can we still talk?

Maya B (3:50:12 PM): Oh God, am I making it sound like we couldn't? Of course we can.

Maya B (3:50:19 PM): I'm really sorry if I've given that impression. Like I said, I really value our friendship.

Audra S (3:50:31 PM): I'm glad. I guess... well, as long as I'm spilling my guts!

Maya B (3:50:33 PM): Yeah?

Audra S (3:50:39 PM): I guess that's why I pulled away from you before I was hospitalized.

Maya B (3:50:42 PM): Oh?

Audra S (3:50:46 PM): I'm sorry, I know this is going to sound bitchy.

Maya B (3:50:49 PM): STOP APOLOGIZING. LOL Seriously, I want to know.

Audra S (3:50:53 PM): Okay, then.

Audra S (3:51:08 PM): I was just going through a rough time. Like I said, my mom -- she's difficult. And things have been difficult. Well, witness my little problem.

Audra S (3:51:16 PM): But when I tried to make our conversations a little more personal, a few times, you didn't seem to want to get too personal. Or...

Audra S (3:51:32 PM): I don't know. I had a hard time opening up. I didn't think you'd be able to relate.

Audra S (3:51:40 PM): Things seemed to be so perfect for you.

Audra S (3:51:47 PM): And *please* don't get me wrong -- I'm really thrilled that they're so good! I'm thrilled that you have your Boy and that your program at school is so exciting and all that. Really. The world has enough shit in it, you don't deserve any.

Audra S (3:51:54 PM): But I just had a hard time talking about how messed up things were for me. Partly I didn't want to depress you. But partly I just wasn't sure you'd understand.

Audra S (3:52:02 PM): It's why I gravitated more to Jennie. Although if I'm being honest I have more in common with you, in some ways. But Jennie's had a rough time herself. I don't want to get into the details, it wouldn't be fair.

Audra S (3:52:09 PM): With Jennie, though, it sort of felt more like give-and-take. Like I could dump on her and she could dump on me.

Audra S (3:52:34 PM): Rach? You still there?

Maya B (3:52:48 PM): Yeah, I'm still there. Sorry. I've been reading.

Audra S (3:52:54 PM): It's all right. Are you mad?

Maya B (3:52:58 PM): No, not mad.

Maya B (3:52:59 PM): Really.

Maya B (3:53:03 PM): I'm not really sure what to say. But I'm not mad.

Audra S (3:53:11 PM): You sound kind of stiff. I didn't mean to upset you.

Maya B (3:53:27 PM): You didn't upset me.

Maya B (3:53:34 PM): Just -- can I get back to you? I'm not mad. I just need to think.

Audra S (3:53:39 PM): Oh, God, I really didn't want to upset you. I don't know why I got into it.

Maya B (3:53:42 PM): No, I'm glad you got into it. I just need to go.

Audra S (3:53:44 PM): Rach, wait.

Maya B has signed off.

From: omgbradomgbrad@yippee.com
To: stormgoddess72@yippee.com
Date: 4/28/2013
Subject: (no subject)

Dear Audra,

My name isn't Rachel. It's Jane. I'm not in college, I don't have a Boy, and my life is so far from perfect it's just... well. My mom died last year and my dad is an alcoholic, and I'm basically in foster care. And everything is so fucked up. I made up an online personality because I'm really sick of all the shit that is wrong in my real life. And I'm really sorry.

I'll be on FL. I'll be invisible, but I'll be there, so if you get this and can stand the thought of ever talking to me again, chat me. I'll probably freak the hell out once I send this but I know I have to send it, I have to. I'll explain more later, but I HAVE TO do this because this is all just out of control. Sending now before I lose my nerve.

-Rachel/Jane

* * *

From: omgbradomgbrad@yippee.com
To: stormgoddess72@yippee.com
Date: 4/28/2013
Subject: Hey

Hey Aud,

So... I know that email I sent you was really weird. Like... really weird. I was hoping you'd get online, which was probably stupid, because I know it makes total sense for you not to want to talk to me. Especially because I just said it all out of the blue, like that. I'm sorry I did it that way -- I just knew I would chicken out if I didn't, you know? And I wanted you to know.

I guess I need to explain. I really hope you're reading this, that you didn't just delete it.

I know I should make this pretty short, but I don't know how. I want to say it so you can maybe understand why I did it. Even if you're still mad.

Okay. So, as you know, I had this Rachel persona going on from long before I met you. Like, years. She was around even before my mom died -- that was last year, I'll tell you about it if you ever want to talk to me again -- but when Mom died, everything in my real life just went to hell. So I started going online as Rachel all the time. When I was being Rachel, all wrapped up in fandom -- it was like a high, it was such an escape from everything "real". I never wanted it to be real. That would have ruined the whole point.

But our friendship felt real to me -- one of the first things that had felt both real *and* good in I don't know how long. All the other friendships I've had as Rachel, they've been totally LtT-based. And that shiny cheerful persona was really easy to keep up with everyone else. But with you -- I mean, I kept on almost slipping up with details about my real life all the time. I even almost told you about Rachel -- I mean, about Jane -- a few times. Because I *wanted* to be real with you. I wanted you to know me, Jane-me. The falseness was getting in the way for me too. But I didn't know how to get out of it. I thought you'd hate me, not just for putting you on about Rachel but for not *being* Rachel. Because, I mean, I wouldn't want to be friends with Jane. I am really not the sort of person anyone wants to be friends with. I have exactly one friend, and I don't even know why he likes me. I mean, I'm pretty sure he has a crush on me, but I don't know why that's true either. I'm not pretty. If you ever want to talk to me again I'll show you pictures of the real me. I'm incredibly plain. And boring. And I can be really bitchy in real life. And... trust me, I just couldn't see any reason why you'd want to be friends with me. I figured Rachel was a much better bet.

I guess I told you now because I'd just found out it wasn't Rachel you'd wanted to be friends with all along. I felt like, if we couldn't be friends as Audra and Rachel, then I needed to tell you about Jane. Probably we can't be friends as Audra and Jane either. I know what I did was shitty and probably unforgivable. But I owed you the truth.

This is all so stupid. You're just out of the hospital and I'm laying all this on you. I'm so sorry you never felt like you could talk to me about all of that stuff, if it would have helped. And I'm so damn sorry I lied. You deserve better.

296

I hope you're all right. I really, really do. I... whatever happens, just please take care of yourself. Please.

If you want you can message me or email me, whenever. Actually, instead of messaging me as Rachel on FL, you can message me at Jane Shilling. I'm the one from Denton, MA. I'm just... not really wanting to be online as Rachel right now. But if I'm not online as Jane send me a message anyway -- I have FL chat notifications set up to go to my phone, and I'll get online as soon as I get a message.

Maybe I'll talk to you soon. I hope?

-Jane

* * *

From: omgbradomgbrad@yippee.com
To: stormgoddess72@yippee.com
Date: 4/28/2013
Subject: Please open this -- it's short and painless, promise

Hey Audra,

I know all of this is way shitty and I totally know I should be giving it some time, but I'm just sort of freaking out, and... I mean like I figured you probably went to bed early tonight but I usually see you online when I get home from school and you're not here and, well, look

I AM PUTTING THIS IN A NEW PARAGRAPH SO IT STANDS OUT Can you just email me to tell me if you're never going to be able to talk to me again, or if you need some time, or if you're willing to talk it out but you just haven't been able to get to the computer? Or if you just have other things on your mind because, wow, I know you absolutely do and this is not what you need right now, but you can say that too -- just so I know. Just a few words, seriously, and if it's "I have my own problems to deal with, I don't need yours too" or even "I am never going to talk to you again" that's TOTALLY okay, I just... I'm really freaking out. I'm really sorry. I know after everything there's no reason for you to want to deal with me, but if you knew how completely freaked I am, not knowing -- look at it this way, if you hate me, you can tell me so and I won't feel *good* about that, but at

297

least I won't be having a panic attack. But since I won't be happy about it won't be like you did me any favors, because I will be... not happy about it. In fact it will probably be WORSE than a panic attack so if you hate me you should totally email me to tell me, so I'll know. Please? Seriously, just like three words. Two seconds. Then I'll shut up. I promise.

I'm so so so so so so sorry,

Jane

* * *

To: RawKdAsKEEbaLL@yippee.com
From: thejanethe@yippee.com
Date: 4/28/2013
Subject: I'm sorry

Gary --

I'm so sorry. You were right about everything. I've been trying to hide from everything and I don't know how anymore and everything is so fucked up and I'm just -- I'm really sorry I yelled at you, I was totally out of line and... I don't even know, I'm just such a mess. You probably don't want to IM me because I've been so mean lately and I still don't know how to talk about stuff because every time I try I wind up flipping my shit instead, but just -- please don't hate me, okay? I'll talk to you as soon as I can, I promise. I just feel so lost now and -- whatever. I don't know. But please don't be mad? You're like the only person I have left. Please don't be mad. I'm so sorry.

Your friend-I-hope

Jane

thejanethe (3:08:08 PM): I'm not doing any talking-out-loud time today. And if I get an IM from someone, I'm talking to them and ignoring you. Basically my computer isn't closing.

NoraActon48267382 (3:08:11 PM): All right. May I ask why?

thejanethe (3:08:12 PM): You just did, but I'm not going to answer.

NoraActon48267382 (3:08:14 PM): All right.

NoraActon48267382 (3:08:22 PM): I should let you know that your father called me the day after you sent me the email about your Official Crazy Patient Crisis. Did you send that email on the road to New York, by the way?

thejanethe (3:08:28 PM): More like stuck in the middle of New York. I really wish Auntie Amy had kept her mouth shut. Like he needs to hear that shit.

NoraActon48267382 (3:08:31 PM): He seemed quite upset, though he was very relieved you'd gotten home safely.

NoraActon48267382 (3:08:34 PM): As was I.

thejanethe (3:08:45 PM): Whatever.

NoraActon48267382 (3:08:52 PM): He wanted to know whether I had any idea why you'd run away, but I told him I couldn't discuss it with him due to doctor-patient privilege.

thejanethe (3:08:54 PM): I didn't run away.

NoraActon48267382 (3:09:00 PM): I didn't tell him that even if it weren't for doctor-patient privilege, I couldn't have told him, because in all honesty I didn't have any idea why you'd left.

NoraActon48267382 (3:09:04 PM): If you wouldn't call it running away, what would you call it?

thejanethe (3:09:11 PM): I wasn't, like, leaving forever or whatever. It was just a road trip.

NoraActon48267382 (3:09:14 PM): So late at night, though? And on a school night?

NoraActon48267382 (3:09:16 PM): Why the secrecy?

thejanethe (3:09:28 PM): I don't feel like dealing with this right now.

NoraActon48267382 (3:09:56 PM): All right. What would you prefer to talk about instead?

thejanethe (3:10:02 PM): I would rather not talk. I just want to sit here and work on my story and check my email and not be bothered.

NoraActon48267382 (3:10:06 PM): Well, of course I can't make you talk to me. But I'm afraid I'm going to keep bothering you.

thejanethe (3:10:14 PM): Whatever.

NoraActon48267382 (3:10:22 PM): You know, Jane, I was very happy to get that email from you the other night.

thejanethe (3:10:26 PM): You were happy I was having a crisis?

NoraActon48267382 (3:10:31 PM): No, not at all. What I was happy about, though, was that you chose to email me and to let me in on whatever was troubling you.

thejanethe (3:10:37 PM): I didn't exactly have much choice. As I'm sure my dad told you, I was stranded in the middle of nowhere and I had no way of getting home.

NoraActon48267382 (3:10:41 PM): I can certainly see that it was an emergency. That being said, though: why didn't you call or email your aunt?

thejanethe (3:10:50 PM): I knew she was asleep. I didn't want to get in trouble. And I didn't want her to tell my dad.

NoraActon48267382 (3:10:55 PM): You keep coming back to that -- that you didn't want him to know. Were you worried he would punish you?

thejanethe (3:11:08 PM): No. No, I was not worried he would punish me. In the first place, you will recall, I am living with Auntie Amy, and

300

although I suppose he could tell her to punish me, in the second place he is so far gone beyond the point where he is capable of thinking about things like punishment that if he were to punish me I would sink to my knees in grateful prayer because it would mean he was capable of being a father again. DON'T respond, I'm still ranting.

thejanethe (3:11:19 PM): You see, though it may have escaped your notice, the thing about my father is that he is not a father right now. He is a wreck. The last time I made a mistake, and that one was just a *little* mistake -- I skipped some math homework and slept through my alarm! -- he fucking STARTED DRINKING AGAIN, and a fucking social worker landed on my doorstep. And now he is in a psych ward for alcoholics. Under the circumstances, the fact that you are asking why I do not want to worry him makes me think that maybe you should be the one sitting over here in the crazy person's chair.

NoraActon48267382 (3:11:25 PM): Hard stuff. Very hard.

thejanethe (3:11:28 PM): Yes. Yes, it is. Thank you for saying that, that fixes everything.

NoraActon48267382 (3:11:48 PM): I find it interesting that you say he's "not a father anymore". It seems to me that you could add to that thought: you're not the kid anymore, either. The parent/child roles have been reversed, in a sense. You're the one who worries about your father and tries to protect him, rather than the other way around. You've had to be the adult.

thejanethe (3:11:53 PM): I don't think I'm being an adult. I think basically there's just two kids.

NoraActon48267382 (3:11:57 PM): Yourself and your dad.

thejanethe (3:11:59 PM): No, myself and Giggles the monkey. Of course me and my dad.

NoraActon48267382 (3:12:03 PM): What about your mother? Was she another kid?

thejanethe (3:12:11 PM): ...

NoraActon48267382 (3:12:13 PM): Jane?

thejanethe (3:12:21 PM): You know what, I am so not dealing with you on this. You KNOW that my mom wasn't anything like that, you KNOW she held the whole family together, and you know everything's fucking collapsed since she died, so STOP asking dumbass questions that you already know the answer to just because you're hoping I'll sob and collapse and "grieve" because I already did all of that and at the end, you know what? SHE'S STILL DEAD. And I am SICK of everyone telling me I need to "deal with it", like you CAN deal with the fact that your mother's dead and your father's in a psych ward rehab and you're -- I'm -- this is not shit I can handle and that is why I spend all of my time on the INternet and I didn't need to come here for you to tell me that so SHUT THE HELL UP ALREADY.

thejanethe (3:12:22 PM): I'm not talking any more.

NoraActon48267382 (3:12:25 PM): I'm sorry to have upset you.

thejanethe (3:14:52 PM): Gary?

Auto-Response from RawKdAsKEEbaLL (3:14:52 PM): squirrels r00l, our nutz r bigger then urs :)

NoraActon48267382 (3:14:54 PM): Did that sound mean the person you wanted to talk to is talking with you?

thejanethe (3:14:59 PM): No. He's not there. I guess.

NoraActon48267382 (3:14:54 PM): I must be confused -- I thought that was the little sound the computer makes when someone sends you a reply.

thejanethe (3:14:59 PM): No, it is, but he's away.

NoraActon48267382 (3:15:02 PM): What does that mean, he's "away"?

thejanethe (3:15:08 PM): ::sigh:: It means you put a message up that says you're not at your computer. Then you go away and leave the program running, or you do something else on your computer and leave ZIM up in the background, and it takes messages.

thejanethe (3:15:09 PM): Here.

NoraActon48267382 (3:15:10 PM): Here?

Auto-Response from **thejanethe** (3:15:10 PM): I am away from my computer right now.

NoraActon48267382 (3:15:12 PM): Oh, I see -- that little red circle means someone is away?

thejanethe (3:15:13 PM): Yes.

NoraActon48267382 (3:15:15 PM): But now you have a little red circle, and you're talking to me.

thejanethe (3:15:17 PM): Yes. I am demonstrating for you what an away message looks like.

NoraActon48267382 (3:15:19 PM): Yes, thank you. :) But you can put up an away message without actually being away, then?

thejanethe (3:15:21 PM): Yes.

NoraActon48267382 (3:15:24 PM): So that's a little bit like call screening, then.

thejanethe (3:15:25 PM): Yeah, I guess so.

NoraActon48267382 (3:15:32 PM): What's going on for you right now, Jane?

thejanethe (3:15:36 PM): What? Nothing.

NoraActon48267382 (3:15:39 PM): You seem like you're fighting for control.

NoraActon48267382 (3:15:44 PM): I feel as though I'm feeling around the edges of something that's causing you a lot of pain. Without knowing what it is, though, I'm not quite sure how to handle it.

thejanethe (3:15:48 PM): Nothing, okay? It doesn't need handling. I just -- whatever, like I said, I'm waiting for some people to show up online because I have to talk to them, and they're not here.

thejanethe (3:15:52 PM): And I guess I didn't like you talking about call screening because Gary and I had a fight, and I apologized and he said it was okay and he seemed to understand, but I'm not sure I believe him and I just want to talk to him.

NoraActon48267382 (3:15:57 PM): A fight after you got back from New York, you mean?

thejanethe (3:15:59 PM): Yesterday.

thejanethe (3:16:04 PM): It was stupid, whatever, I don't want to get into it. I just... sort of blew my top at him. I mean, I was mad. But whatever, I'd apologize if he'd let me.

NoraActon48267382 (3:16:08 PM): It must be tough, fighting with him while another one of your close friends is in the hospital. And with your dad being hospitalized, too.

NoraActon48267382 (3:16:11 PM): That's a lot of supports that must be feeling unsteady right now.

thejanethe (3:16:19 PM): I guess.

NoraActon48267382 (3:16:21 PM): That was a lot of typing you just erased. :)

thejanethe (3:16:24 PM): Yep, it sure was! I erased it because I didn't want to send it! Imagine that.

NoraActon48267382 (3:16:28 PM): I think I'm starting to see one of the drawbacks of IM therapy...

thejanethe (3:16:33 PM): Oh, bull. Drawback for you, maybe. I suppose your practice thrives on people blurting out private stuff that they never wanted you to know but they can't take back.

NoraActon48267382 (3:16:39 PM): I don't know; I wouldn't say it affects "my practice", really. But you're right, I like it when my patients are able to let down their guard and talk to me openly.

NoraActon48267382 (3:16:42 PM): I try to make that feel safe. But the first plunge is always the hardest.

thejanethe (3:16:46 PM): Great. So why don't you go twiddle the temperature knobs on your little metaphorical swimming pool so it will be nice and warm for your next patient to plunge into, and I will go write my fanfiction.

NoraActon48267382 (3:16:49 PM): Is that what you'd like me to do?

thejanethe (3:16:51 PM): ...?!

NoraActon48267382 (3:16:55 PM): You never did explain to me what "..." means all on its own like that, but we'll leave that for later. :) Let me tell you how this session has felt to me, over here in my chair.

NoraActon48267382 (3:17:02 PM): You've asked me a few times to back off, and I'll be honest, I'm not sure that I shouldn't do what you're asking -- let it go for now, give you some space and time. But I've also been getting some mixed signals from you, and I want to explore that a little bit.

NoraActon48267382 (3:17:08 PM): On the one hand, you're more overtly resistant than you've been in weeks. Your defensive posture is back, you're being rude off-the-cuff, and so on.

NoraActon48267382 (3:17:11 PM): But you emailed me the other night, and that took a lot of trust.

thejanethe (3:17:13 PM): Desperation.

NoraActon48267382 (3:17:17 PM): That too, I suppose. Still and all, though: you do know I couldn't have helped you in any practical way.

NoraActon48267382 (3:17:20 PM): I couldn't have given you any practical help, or found you any information that you couldn't have found for yourself on the Internet.

thejanethe (3:17:25 PM): I guess I just wanted advice.

NoraActon48267382 (3:17:30 PM): And that makes sense. I'd have been scared too. But in asking for advice, you opened up and admitted that you were in a tough, scary place.

thejanethe (3:17:33 PM): Yeah, well, I was.

NoraActon48267382 (3:17:37 PM): And now you've come in today, and on the one hand you're screaming "get away from me! I don't want you in my life!" Which is an understandable reaction to having opened up like that.

thejanethe (3:17:38 PM): It is?

NoraActon48267382 (3:17:45 PM): It sure is. I was expecting you to be a bit defensive today, to be honest. But I also knew that everything that's going on for you must be causing you a tremendous amount of pain, and I can tell that's true too. I can see it all over your face. I know how hard you try to keep things locked down, I know how hard to fight to keep your emotions from showing. But I know, and you know that I know, that you've been on the brink of tears for most of the session. And I'm hoping now that you can trust me enough to tell me about it.

NoraActon48267382 (3:17:47 PM): You don't have to. If you stop here, I won't push right now. But I get the sense that part of you wants to talk to me.

thejanethe (3:17:49 PM): The problem with you is you keep ignoring the other part.

NoraActon48267382 (3:17:52 PM): Once more, we've come around to how the problem with me is that I'm a therapist. :)

NoraActon48267382 (3:17:54 PM): Hey! I saw that smile!

thejanethe (3:17:56 PM): Involuntary lip twitch.

NoraActon48267382 (3:17:59 PM): You trusted me enough to email me this week, Jane. Do you think you can trust me enough to tell me a little bit about what's on your mind now?

NoraActon48267382 (3:18:04 PM): ...

thejanethe (3:18:07 PM): Fine. You want to know why I went to New York? You want to know who I'm waiting for online? You want to know just how crazy I am? Here.

thejanethe (3:18:13 PM): I have five different personalities on the

Internet. More than five. I don't even know how many. I go on the Internet and I have all these personalities and I can be any of them and I never have to be Jane. How's that for crazy? Multiple personality disorder, voluntarily chosen! On the Internet, no less! You can write a paper on me.

thejanethe (3:18:17 PM): I have five personalities and mostly I'm just one of them, a girl named Rachel who is so much nicer and funnier and sweeter and all-around better than I am and don't you wish she were your patient instead? And Rachel made some friends, only Rachel never talked about her real life, because Rachel didn't have a real life, Rachel just had a cute way of writing and an obsession with Brad Memphis.

thejanethe (3:18:22 PM): And then Rachel's best friend cut her wrists and never said a word about it to Rachel, because Rachel couldn't relate because Rachel never had an ounce of lousy shit in her life! Ever! At which point Jane basically lost her fucking mind and thought it was a good idea to drive to New York and be like "hey, I'm Jane! Also Rachel! How's the loony bin?", but you already know what a fantastic ending that story had. And now Rachel doesn't have any friends at all. Rachel doesn't, and neither for that matter do Zelda or Elana or Heather or Ethan or Callie or Paul or Jesse because THEY ALL SUCK, and THEY ARE ALL ME. I tried to make a bunch of personalities so I could have a life where I didn't suck, and now all that happened is that my life sucks FIVE TIMES AS MUCH.

thejanethe (3:18:25 PM): And... you're just staring at me. Say something, give me your professional diagnosis, tell me exactly how many ways of crazy and fucked-up I am in the DSM-V.

NoraActon48267382 (3:18:35 PM): According to the DSM-V? Who knows. According to me? You're not crazy at all.

thejanethe (3:18:37 PM): ...Did you READ all of that?

NoraActon48267382 (3:18:40 PM): I sure did. I didn't respond until you were done because it seemed like another rant that I shouldn't interrupt.

thejanethe (3:18:43 PM): You read all that and you don't think I'm crazy.

NoraActon48267382 (3:18:47 PM): No, I don't. In fact, I think it's one of the more ingenious ways of dealing with an unbearable life situation that I've heard in awhile.

thejanethe (3:18:48 PM): It's not ingenious. It's a fucking nightmare.

NoraActon48267382 (3:18:50 PM): I know. I can see as much written on your face.

NoraActon48267382 (3:18:52 PM): It looks like it's made you pretty miserable.

thejanethe (3:18:53 PM): It has! I'm totally miserable!

thejanethe (3:18:54 PM): And it was supposed to STOP me being miserable!

NoraActon48267382 (3:18:57 PM): Unfortunately, that's the trouble with defensive mechanisms like this -- tactics designed to keep you from feeling bad things.

NoraActon48267382 (3:19:02 PM): They work for awhile. But the stuff underneath always pushes through in the end. And in the meantime, the defensive mechanisms have usually dragged in some problems of their own.

thejanethe (3:19:04 PM): Then what the hell do you do? What does anybody do when shit is wrong in their lives that is never going to be fixed?

NoraActon48267382 (3:19:06 PM): Do you think it can never be fixed?

thejanethe (3:19:07 PM): You take a look at my life and tell me that it can!

thejanethe (3:19:11 PM): You get Audra and Gary to talk to me again, and you make Dad sane again, and you get DSS off my back, and you fucking undo the car crash that killed my mom! Then you can take away my "defense mechanisms"! Then you can talk about getting stuff fixed!

NoraActon48267382 (3:19:13 PM): I can't do any of those things, Jane.

thejanethe (3:19:15 PM): That's the POINT.

NoraActon48267382 (3:19:19 PM): But you know what I'm going to say.

thejanethe (3:19:20 PM): No. No, I don't.

NoraActon48267382 (3:19:22 PM): It's what I've been telling you all along, and you either argue with me or pretend not to hear. Because it's hard as hell.

thejanethe (3:19:24 PM): What?

NoraActon48267382 (3:19:26 PM): Jane, what was your mother like? What was your life like when she was alive?

thejanethe (3:19:27 PM): `";',,]\\\

thejanethe has signed off.

Dear Mom:

I don't really know how to start this letter. I guess I'll start it anyway.

It was my therapist who told me I should write you a letter. I should say -- I have a new therapist. If you judge how good a therapist is by how much she pisses you off and makes you cry, this one is great. :P But she's the first person I've been able to talk to about stuff since you died. And I guess in our last session, she was trying to get me to talk about you, and I kind of flipped. I threw some stuff, started making a big scene, etc., etc., but while I was yelling at her one of the things I was trying to tell her was that it was pointless to talk about you because NOTHING is going to make it better that you're gone and anyway I didn't want to talk to HER, I wanted to talk to YOU. But you're gone, so I can't, and... well, you see where this is going. Anyway, Nora suggested that I write you a letter, in place of talking to you. It isn't the same thing. But I thought I would try.

I don't know if you already knew all of the stuff I just said. Did you? I mean, are you in some heaven looking down on me and watching everything that happens to me and everything I do? Or do you sort of check in from time to time? Or are you not you at all anymore -- are you changed, reincarnated as someone else or something else? Or are you just... gone?

I really really want you to be out there somewhere, still you, still my mom. But I don't know if I want you to have been watching me all the time since you died. I don't think you'd like the way I've been acting a lot of the time.

I miss you, Mom. That's what I really want to say.

I miss you all the time. I thought before you died that grief went away over time -- that it had, like, a half-life, very neat and orderly, and as time progressed at recurring intervals your grief would be half of what it was the period before, until eventually it was dim and faint and you hardly noticed it. It's not like that at all. I still have moments where I read a really good line in a book, or something funny happens at school, or whatever, and I'm on my way to tell you about it before I remember. And the sick pang I get in my gut never gets any less when that happens. I still want you to kiss me on the cheek at bedtime and to make lemon chicken over pasta (did you know Dad can't cook at *all?* I used to think it would be nice to order pizza every night. It isn't. But it's nicer than eating the stuff Dad cooks.) I just miss you, all the time, and even if I forget a little bit sometimes it's always underneath and it always comes *back*. It's like sleeping. You always wake up.

And I think what's worst is that whenever anything hurt, before, whatever it was, you were always the one I came to -- you were the person I could trust with that stuff, and because my life was what it was and nothing really horrible ever happened, you could always make it better. You could, really. Before you died, I never had anything wrong in my life that you couldn't make better with a long talk and a long hug. And now there's no one I can talk to at all. I don't really *do* friends, as you know. You were always the one I talked to instead. And Dad... Mom, you know how Dad is. I love him so much, but he's so... he's never been strong. He can't handle my pain and his too. I don't really think he can even handle his. So there just isn't anyone for me to talk to. Missing you is the worst hurt of my entire life, and the only person I could talk to about it, who could help me with it, isn't there to help me. Because she's you.

Nora wanted me to tell you I'm angry at you. I could tell. She wouldn't say it outright but she hinted around about how it's okay to be mad at you for dying and leaving me and blah, blah, blah. Whatever. Maybe I am a little angry. But I don't think I need to write about it. If I ever need to get it out of my system, I'll just yell at Nora. She deserves it. If it weren't for her I wouldn't be having to write this letter in the first place. :P

I think that's enough heavy stuff. Because, you know, your being gone, it's not all about me being weepy and moany about the woe and tragedy of a motherless existence. So much of it is just stupid day-to-day stuff. I could write this letter to be twenty pages longer than it is right now, and not get to the end of what I want to say. I want to tell you about how I read *A Tree Grows in Brooklyn* for the first time last week and loved it as much as you said I would. And about how Jim's Convenience Store on the corner put up a huge new sign, really colorful and snazzy and obviously expensive, and it says they sell GROCERIE'S in big blue letters. And I want to tell you about the Scrabble documentary I watched and how someone scored like a 370-point word and broke the record for highest-scoring word ever, but the

Scrabble pros are debating whether it should be counted as official because the guy got lucky instead of using conventional Scrabblic wisdom. And... you see what I mean. You'd be interested in all of this stuff, and I don't know anyone else who would be. Why would anyone but you and me care that the convenience store sign says GROCERIE'S?

I just miss you, Mom. I miss you so much.

Nora says if I keep doing this, keep writing to you or writing about you and talking about you and thinking about you and working through my grief, I'll make peace with it. She says the reason it still hurts so much when I think about it is that I've been pushing it all down, so I haven't worked through any of it. Nora has an answer for everything. But what the hell.

So maybe I will write more, and if I can write more another time, then I think this is enough for now.

The only real problem with this letter was that I wanted to "send" it to you somehow. I didn't just want to write it or leave it on my computer, or print it off and bury it in a desk drawer. I want *you* to have it. Nora suggested I tie it to a balloon string and let the balloon go, but I laughed at her pretty hard for that one. First of all we don't have a helium tank, and second of all, I know you're not *actually* up in some cloud in the sky peering down at me. If I tied it to a balloon string it would either get caught up in electrical wiring or run out of helium and fall into the sewer halfway across the country or something. No thanks.

So what I'm going to do is print this off and gather it together with a few other things that I think you would like. Some autumn leaves I saved -- fall was always your favorite season. A picture of you, me, and Dad. A ticket stub to a movie I saw a few weeks ago that you would have loved. Some poetry. I wish I could give you some petals from some of the early roses from your garden, but no one's been taking care of them this year, and there are no early roses. I'll take care of your garden next year, I promise.

But I'm going to get all those things, and I'm going to have Gary drive me to the lake this weekend. He's under strict orders to drop me off and then drive away and leave me alone until I call him to come get me. And I'm going to burn them -- this letter and everything else. Where we used to have campfires on Labor Day weekend. And where your ashes are scattered. Unlike at our campfires, I will NOT sing -- my voice is as horrible as it ever was and you're not around anymore to make me. :P But maybe I'll bring some music you liked. Peter, Paul, and Mary, or whatever. Some of your goofy hippie music. And I'll burn the things and let them turn to ashes, and listen.

I really hope it will feel like you're there. If you're watching me type this now, please make a note to show up. Be a ray of sunshine or a gentle breeze or something, or maybe you can possess the body of a cute little bunny rabbit and hop up on my knee. Send a damn rainbow, whatever, I don't care. Just... be with me.

Anyway, when I'm done I'll scatter the ashes where your ashes are scattered. It's not perfect, but it's better than a balloon.

I love you, Mom. I'll write to you again.

Love forever,
Jane

Jane S (8:23:32 PM): Audra?

Audra S (8:23:39 PM): Oh, hey, Jane!

Jane S (8:23:42 PM): Hi! :)

Jane S (8:23:43 PM): What's up?

Audra S (8:23:46 PM): Not too much.

Audra S (8:23:50 PM): It feels so funny to call you Jane. LOL

Jane S (8:23:53 PM): Oh. Right. :-)

Audra S (8:24:07 PM): Do you have any nicknames or anything?

Audra S (8:24:12 PM): Like, I used to call you Rach, but now I don't know if you go by something different...

Jane S (8:24:14 PM): Oh. No, not really.

Jane S (8:24:16 PM): There aren't that many nicknames for Jane, really.

Audra S (8:24:18 PM): Oh. I guess not.

Audra S (8:24:49 PM): It's funny because Jane is my middle name.

Jane S (8:24:42 PM): Oh, is it?

Jane S (8:24:44 PM): I didn't know that.

Audra S (8:24:50 PM): Yeah. There was never really any reason to mention it.

Jane S (8:24:53 PM): I guess not.

Jane S (8:25:17 PM): My middle name is Christine.

Jane S (8:25:19 PM): Which... is really not relevant to anything. LOL

Audra S (8:25:23 PM): Well, hey, now I know. :)

Jane S (8:25:48 PM): ...

Jane S (8:25:51 PM): You know what?

Audra S (8:25:56 PM): What?

Jane S (8:25:59 PM): This is the most *fucking* awkward conversation I've ever had in my entire life.

Audra S (8:26:01 PM): ROFLMAO

Jane S (8:26:09 PM): I'm sorry. Obviously I am not doing this first-conversation-as-Jane very well.

Audra S (8:26:13 PM): Is Jane that different from Rachel?

Jane S (8:26:21 PM): ...I don't know. It's sort of a complicated question.

Jane S (8:26:23 PM): Before I answer, can I apologize?

Audra S (8:26:26 PM): For what?

Jane S (8:26:30 PM): Well, apart from, you know, everything... LOL

Audra S (8:26:34 PM): I think you apologized pretty thoroughly in the series of emails you sent me. ;)

Jane S (8:26:36 PM): That's actually what I wanted to apologize for.

Audra S (8:26:39 PM): Oh brother. LOL

Jane S (8:26:44 PM): No, I'm serious. I... I don't know, I felt like those emails came off kind of stalkery, or something.

Audra S (8:26:50 PM): Stalkery! No one has ever implied I was interesting enough to have a stalker before!

Jane S (8:26:54 PM): LOL No, but you know what I mean. I know the emails were a little... uh... overboard.

Jane S (8:27:01 PM): I was just really anxious, I guess -- and about more stuff than just what was in the email. I think I was sort of channeling all of my anxiety into the emails?

Audra S (8:27:05 PM): Right, I got that.

Audra S (8:27:09 PM): Maybe I recognized it from the way that I get.

Audra S (8:27:16 PM): When things are bad at home I am six thousand percent more prone to having panic attacks about school.

Jane S (8:27:20 PM): Whereas I have never in my life been known to panic about school ;), so I have to find something else to occupy myself!

Jane S (8:27:25 PM): But, yeah. I didn't want you to think that on top of everything else I was some sort of total obsessive wackjob.

Audra S (8:27:29 PM): No, I didn't think that.

Audra S (8:27:36 PM): Though I did wonder if... well, it was probably stupid.

Jane S (8:27:39 PM): No, what?

Audra S (8:27:44 PM): Well... Rachel-you is the only you I know, right?

Jane S (8:27:47 PM): ...what? LOL

Audra S (8:27:52 PM): Well, like, it's not like you invented the concept of fake online personas, you know. ;) And I was thinking of Kelsey-Sara-Denise...

Jane S (8:27:55 PM): OMG! ROFLMAO No, no, I'm not a KSD!

Audra S (8:27:59 PM): You're not, like, Teresa or Jenna or someone?

Jane S (8:28:01 PM): AUGH NO! Why would you think I was JENNA?! >:-S

Audra S (8:28:05 PM): I don't know! I'm sorry.

Jane S (8:28:08 PM): No, don't be sorry! Just... NO, I'm not Jenna. LOL Or Teresa.

Jane S (8:28:12 PM): I, um. May have used a few other usernames online at times...

Audra S (8:28:13 PM): Ah.

Jane S (8:28:19 PM): No, no, it was different, and I swear, I never... well, only one of them was in the LtT fandom, and... oh, Christ, every time I think I can say something definite that will make me sound less crazy, like "but I was never anyone else!" or "but none of the others were in LtT fandom!"... none of them are true. ::facepalm::

Audra S (8:28:28 PM): Wait, wait, back up, who else in the LtT fandom were you?

Jane S (8:28:32 PM): Ummm... I don't think you know him.

Audra S (8:28:34 PM): A boy?

Jane S (8:28:37 PM): Yeah. He only wrote a couple of fanfics -- Ethan? blackwingedsoul?

Audra S (8:28:43 PM): ...OMFG ROFLMAOOOOOOOOOOOOOOO

Jane S (8:28:46 PM): What's so funny?

Audra S (8:28:54 PM): Wait wait wait, I'm sorry, really, but are we talking about that crazy emo boy with the fanfics where everyone kills themselves and the Diarynow that's like dark gray text on a black background and in his icon he's wearing eighteen pounds of eyeliner?

Jane S (8:28:56 PM): ...yes

Audra S (8:29:00 PM): ROFL ROFL ROFLMAO

Jane S (8:29:03 PM): Whoa there, dude.

Audra S (8:29:06 PM): I'm sorry, I know I shouldn't laugh, I just - ::dies::

Jane S (8:29:07 PM): I didn't know it was that funny.

Audra S (8:29:12 PM): I know, but he just -- God, those are the most emo fics EVER in the history of the WORLD.

Audra S (8:29:15 PM): Well-written and all, but... OMG! Wasn't there some fic where, like, four of the characters made suicide attempts? It was, like, a chain reaction, right?

Jane S (8:29:18 PM): Three of them, not four.

Audra S (8:29:25 PM): Oh, man. And his journal! Like, I never read any of the entries -- how could anyone read that color text on that background?! - but with the layout, and the icon, I swear to God, I was like "this guy is like a parody of himself!" And now... HAHA HE TOTALLY IS. ROFLMAO

Jane S (8:29:30 PM): Okay, um, I think maybe I'm going to sign off and come back when you're done laughing, okay?

Audra S (8:29:32 PM): Wait, don't leave. Look, I'll stop, seriously.

Jane S (8:29:35 PM): No, whatever. I know it's ridiculous, I just -- look, you really want to know?

Audra S (8:29:37 PM): Yes.

Jane S (8:29:54 PM): Because when your mom is dead and your dad is an alcoholic and you spend every day wondering if you're going to wake up and find him dead in a pile of his own puke or maybe floating in bloody bathwater and you don't know what the fuck will happen to you then, sometimes *you just get to feeling emo about it.* That's why Ethan, okay? Because my life is seventeen different kinds of fucked up and I know perfectly well it's really funny, it's really hilarious that sometimes I feel like being this emo boy who's all morbid and pondering suicide and death constantly, well, you know, that's just what it is and I am sending this before I lose my nerve.

Jane S (8:29:59 PM): ::deep breaths::

Audra S (8:30:04 PM): Wow.

Audra S (8:30:06 PM): I'm really sorry, J.

Audra S (8:30:07 PM): (Can I call you J?)

Jane S (8:30:09 PM): Whatever.

Audra S (8:30:13 PM): I'm really, really sorry I laughed so hard. Like... really.

Audra S (8:30:16 PM): I can't believe I was so insensitive.

Jane S (8:30:20 PM): ::sigh:: It's okay.

Audra S (8:30:24 PM): No, it isn't. Really, I don't believe I was such an asshole.

Jane S (8:30:27 PM): Seriously. Don't worry about it. First of all I earned it, and second of all, I definitely know that Ethan's ridiculous.

Jane S (8:30:31 PM): I mean, that's the point of making him. If I pretend he's just a parody of emo kids, I don't have to admit to... actually feeling that way. Or whatever.

Audra S (8:30:32 PM): You didn't earn it.

Jane S (8:30:34 PM): Oh hell yeah I did!

Audra S (8:30:36 PM): ...okay, maybe you did. A little.

Jane S (8:30:38 PM): LOL Okay.

Jane S (8:30:39 PM): Really, it's cool.

Audra S (8:30:43 PM): Still, I should be more sensitive about... people's ways of being fucked up. And I'll try to in the future.

Audra S (8:30:46 PM): Given the manifold ways in which I am fucked up... I should know better.

Jane S (8:30:48 PM): Well, okay.

Jane S (8:30:53 PM): Sometimes I wonder if everyone in fandom is doing shit like this.

Jane S (8:30:55 PM): I mean, if everyone is hiding.

Audra S (8:30:58 PM): I don't know.

Audra S (8:31:03 PM): I don't think so, actually.

Jane S (8:31:04 PM): No?

Audra S (8:31:06 PM): I mean, I suspect we're not the only ones, but I think... I don't know, I think some people are less immersed.

Jane S (8:31:08 PM): They'd have to be! LOL

Audra S (8:31:09 PM): LOL! True.

Audra S (8:31:11 PM): But, like, people like Teal or Allie or Maxxi... I don't know.

Audra S (8:31:13 PM): I just get a different vibe off of them. They seem -- I don't know how to phrase it... I guess they just seem like fandom is a thing in their lives, but not the only thing, you know?

Jane S (8:31:24 PM): So with Rachel, you got a vibe that fandom was the only thing for her?

Audra S (8:31:26 PM): At the time, actually, no. But looking back... I don't know.

Audra S (8:31:29 PM): You talked a lot about Rachel's life offline, but I never saw a lot of evidence of it, I guess?

Audra S (8:31:31): I mean, you're kind of online about 18 hours a day. :)

Jane S (8:31:32): LOL! OK, no argument. :)

Audra S (8:31:37 PM): But that's really only in retrospect. Still, though, looking at people in fandom from that angle, I basically think some of them are okay and some of them are... not so much.

Jane S (8:31:38 PM): "Not so much" is a very kind way of describing the shitshow that is my life right now. LOL

Audra S (8:31:40 PM): And mine, I guess!

Jane S (8:31:43 PM): How are things going with that, by the way?

Audra S (8:31:46 PM): Oh, fine. It's settled down a lot.

Jane S (8:31:49 PM): Is your mom still being nuts?

Audra S (8:31:51 PM): Well, you know. She's my mom.

Jane S (8:31:58 PM): Are you... I mean, have you been okay?

Audra S (8:32:02 PM): Heh. Your status just went back and forth between "Jane S is typing" and "Jane S has deleted text" about seventeen times.

Audra S (8:32:05 PM): Was that going to end "Have you been cutting?"

Jane S (8:32:11 PM): I don't know. Maybe.

Audra S (8:32:14 PM): Not in the last hour.

Jane S (8:32:19 PM): Oh.

Audra S (8:32:22 PM): I'm working on it, okay? It doesn't just stop all at once.

Jane S (8:32:25 PM): No, I know. I'm sorry, I didn't mean to imply you weren't doing enough.

Audra S (8:32:27 PM): It's all right. I'm sorry I yelled.

Jane S (8:32:29 PM): You didn't yell. No need to apologize.

Audra S (8:32:33 PM): I guess I felt like yelling.

Jane S (8:32:36 PM): I'm sorry.

Audra S (8:32:45 PM): I just... like, my mom strips off my shirt every night and examines my arms, like she has some fucking right. And like it's that easy, like you can just... stop. It just makes things so much worse.

Audra S (8:32:47 PM): So I'm sensitive about it.

Jane S (8:32:50 PM): I don't blame you.

Jane S (8:32:54 PM): I don't know how this will go over, so I'll just say it... if you're ever, you know, thinking of doing that, and you want to talk instead, you can call me. 978-555-0674. I'm up late, and it's a cell, so it won't wake up my aunt.

Jane S (8:34:03 PM): Aud?

Audra S (8:34:06 PM): Thanks.

Jane S (8:34:06 PM): You're still there?

Audra S (8:34:09 PM): Yeah, sorry.

Audra S (8:34:13 PM): I was just putting your number in my phone.

Jane S (8:34:21 PM): Really?

Audra S (8:34:28 PM): ::sigh:: No, not really. I mean, at first I was. But then I sort of stalled out.

Audra S (8:34:32 PM): I just wasn't sure what to say.

Jane S (8:34:35 PM): It's okay. You don't have to say anything. I just wanted to make the offer.

Audra S (8:34:39 PM): It's really sweet of you.

Audra S (8:34:44 PM): I can't promise I will call.

Jane S (8:34:46 PM): No, I wouldn't ask for a promise.

Jane S (8:34:48 PM): Too much stress.

Audra S (8:34:40 PM): Yeah.

Audra S (8:34:51 PM): But I am glad you offered.

Jane S (8:34:53 PM): Really?

Audra S (8:34:58 PM): Yeah. I guess. As much as I'm glad of anything right now.

Audra S (8:35:01 PM): I'm just so tired, you know?

Audra S (8:35:04 PM): Everything's really stressful, and I'm so tired of it.
Audra S (8:35:08 PM): I wish I could go back to when I could just hide in LtT and fanfic and forget about all of this shit.

Jane S (8:35:10 PM): Yeah, I hear you.

Audra S (8:35:16 PM): I know you do.

Audra S (8:35:18 PM): That's why I'm still talking to you.

Jane S (8:35:21 PM): Really?

Audra S (8:35:24 PM): Yeah, really.

Audra S (8:35:36 PM): The whole thing with Rachel being imaginary or whatever was pretty fucked up.

Audra S (8:35:43 PM): But then there are these moments when you explain part of why you did it or what your life's like and it's like you're saying everything I can't find words for.

Audra S (8:35:49 PM): I think we could be real friends. And I need real friends right now.

Audra S (8:36:12 PM): Jane? You still there?

322

Jane S (8:36:18 PM): Yeah, I'm sorry

Jane S (8:36:21 PM): I'm sorry, I've been really overemotional lately

Audra S (8:36:24 PM): I'm sorry, hon.

Audra S (8:36:25 PM): ::hugs::

Jane S (8:36:27 PM): :) ::hugs back::

Jane S (8:36:40 PM): ::laughs:: I'm sorry. I'm all pulled together again now, promise.

Audra S (8:36:44 PM): Yeah right! LOL

Jane S (8:36:48 PM): LOL Okay, okay. Not entirely. But for the moment.

Jane S (8:36:57 PM): So, uh, precisely how many months do you think it will be before the aftermath of this Rachel thing dies down and you and I can have a conversation that isn't either about how one of us is crying or about how my middle name is Christine?

Audra S (8:36:59 PM): LOL!

Jane S (8:37:04 PM): Because, you know, everything sounds and feels so stilted and... yeah. ::flails helplessly::

Audra S (8:37:08 PM): Flails? Really? ;)

Jane S (8:37:12 PM): Oh, totally. Arms pinwheeling, torso completely spastic. I am flailing in helplessness.

Jane S (8:37:13 PM): ;)

Audra S (8:37:15 PM): Poor you!

Audra S (8:37:20 PM): But in answer to your question... well, I don't know. How long's it take for a normal friendship to form?

Jane S (8:37:28 PM): ...you are so asking the wrong person. LOL

Audra S (8:37:36 PM): How's a month or two sound?

Jane S (8:37:39 PM): Oh, come ON. Please tell me that in a couple of weeks at least we won't be talking about sobbing and/or our middle names constantly.

Audra S (8:37:43 PM): Well, that's probably realistic.

Jane S (8:37:51 PM): I guess what you meant is it'll be a few weeks before the conversations get less stilted, and a few months before you can trust me?

Audra S (8:37:53 PM): Something like that.

Jane S (8:37:56 PM): I can live with that.

Audra S (8:37:53 PM): ...

Jane S (8:40:02 PM): ...

Jane S (8:40:07 PM): So is a month over yet?

Audra S (8:40:09 PM): LOL :)

Jane S (8:40:12 PM): Well. Uh. So!

Audra S (8:40:14 PM): :)

Jane S (8:40:22 PM): Well, to jump back to a more familiar topic -- I mean, not to bring up stuff about which I've historically been a pain in the ass :-S, but I'm just curious -- are you going to enter the Lookies after all this year?

Jane S (8:40:26 PM): I'm asking because I don't know if I am, so I was wondering.

Audra S (8:40:29 PM): Oh. For a minute I thought you were going to ask me to contribute to the auction again. Heh.

Jane S (8:40:31 PM): Oh, dear God, no. LOL

Jane S (8:40:34 PM): No, that's pretty much done.

Jane S (8:40:37 PM): I mean, if people want to donate or whatever on their own hook, that's fine, but yeah, I've pretty much given up on it personally.

Audra S (8:40:39 PM): I think maybe that's for the best... :)

Jane S (8:40:41 PM): I'm really sorry about all of that. I was... well, you know what I was, I'm sure. ::eyeroll::

Audra S (8:40:43 PM): Hanging onto a fantasy?

Jane S (8:40:45 PM): No, being a pain in the ass. ::sigh::

Audra S (8:40:48 PM): Ah, we can take a little from column A and a little from column B. :)

Jane S (8:40:50 PM): LOL

Audra S (8:40:53 PM): And it's water under the bridge, anyway.

Jane S (8:41:01 PM): Anyway. Forget the auction, I don't know if I'm even entering at this point. I don't know if it's a good idea for me right now, you know?

Audra S (8:41:04 PM): Yeah, I definitely know what you mean.

Jane S (8:41:08 PM): That giant AU episode I was writing went up in flames anyway. I suppose I should just write the whole thing off.

Jane S (8:41:11 PM): Everyone's going to get on my case about it though.

Audra S (8:41:13 PM): Me too! God, I hate that.

Audra S (8:41:16 PM): Everyone thinks that they're, like, entitled to a new fic from me every three days, and I so don't feel like dealing with it right now.

Jane S (8:41:18 PM): I keep getting emails asking why I haven't been posting.

Audra S (8:41:20 PM): ME TOO. Seriously, people.

Jane S (8:41:22 PM): What do you tell them?

Audra S (8:41:23 PM): Nothing. LOL

Audra S (8:41:25 PM): Why, what have you been saying?

Jane S (8:41:30 PM): Well, I've been saying my WIPs got lost in the computer crash, but that's not going to work forever.

Audra S (8:41:33 PM): Yeah, what was up with that computer crash, anyway? I mean, did it actually happen?

Jane S (8:41:35 PM): Oh, it happened. Well, in a way.

Audra S (8:41:37 PM): "In a way?"

Jane S (8:41:40 PM): Someone was harassing me online, but it wasn't some guy from college (well, obviously). It's a long story -- I don't really feel like going into it now.

Audra S (8:41:42 PM): np. Sorry if I was prying.

Jane S (8:41:44 PM): No, you weren't. It's just that the whole thing was ridiculous.

Jane S (8:41:48 PM): Anyway, so yeah. Forget posting a fic a day like I used to, I'm not even sure I'm entering the Lookies. And I can't imagine how much people are going to ride my ass about that.

Jane S (8:41:51 PM): If I won I probably couldn't even go to the damn convention. Being in foster care tends to put a damper on teenage road trips. :P

Audra S (8:41:54 PM): Yeah, I feel that. Constant psychiatric surveillance will have the same effect. ::eyeroll::

Audra S (8:41:56 PM): You know, the thing is -- I don't mean this in a bad way or anything, honest -- but I never liked your big epics as much as your drabbles anyway.

Jane S (8:41:57 PM): Really? o.O

Jane S (8:42:01 PM): I mean, no offense taken, it's just that no one in the fandom ever cares about my drabbles. LOL

Audra S (8:42:03 PM): Well, you know how fandom is. If it's not Jaerin mega-melodrama, no one ever does care.

Jane S (8:42:05 PM): True. :)

Audra S (8:42:08 PM): And I definitely do like your epics. I thought what you showed me of Grip was pretty good.

326

Audra S (8:42:10 PM): But your drabbles always seemed so heartfelt to me. They're pretty special, IMO.

Jane S (8:42:12 PM): Well, thanks. I like yours, too (big surprise ;)).

Audra S (8:42:19 PM): Thanks. Honestly, I think they're much better training for a writer than longer fics anyway. I tend to get really self-indulgent and blathery in longer fics. Drabbles force you to examine your writing much more carefully and get your point across more concisely.

Jane S (8:42:21 PM): True enough.

Jane S (8:42:22 PM): Also they never win the Lookies. ;)

Audra S (8:42:24 PM): Which is about the best reason for submitting one I can think of right now! :)

Jane S (8:42:46 PM): So you're thinking of entering a drabble, then?

Audra S (8:42:48 PM): Maybe. Honestly, if it will get people off my back, I'm all for it. :P

Jane S (8:42:50 PM): It's not a bad idea. Mind if I copy? The idea of submitting a drabble, I mean.

Audra S (8:42:52 PM): Why not? We could submit companion drabbles.

Jane S (8:42:54 PM): Like a collaboration? That could be fun.

Jane S (8:52:56 PM): And if we win the category you can have the Official LtT Guide. I already have one.

Audra S (8:52:57 PM): I was just about to tell you the same thing... :)

Jane S (8:52:59 PM): Ha. Okay, we'll give it to some poor un-Guided soul.

Jane S (8:53:00 PM): Since we're obviously going to win. ;)

Audra S (8:53:02 PM): Oh, obviously!

Audra S (8:53:03 PM): Anyway, I should go. My mom is knocking at the door for my nightly strip search.

Jane S (8:53:05 PM): :P

Jane S (8:53:11 PM): If you want to call me, please feel free.

Audra S (8:53:15 PM): Maybe I will.

Jane S (8:53:17 PM): Aud?

Audra S (8:53:19 PM): Yeah?

Jane S (8:53:21 PM): I'm glad you're still talking to me.

Audra S (8:53:24 PM): Me too.

Jane S (8:53:26 PM): Good luck with your mom.

Audra S (8:53:29 PM): :) Thanks.

Audra S (8:53:32 PM): Night!

Jane S (8:53:33 PM): Night.

RawKdaSkEEbaLL (6:49:25 PM): hey

RawKdaSkEEbaLL (6:49:29 PM): ur back online :)

thejanethe (6:49:40 PM): :) Hey, Gary.

thejanethe (6:49:41 PM): Sorry I haven't been around much.

RawKdaSkEEbaLL (6:49:54 PM): w/e i see u @ scool

thejanethe (6:49:55 PM): LOL You know, I was just trying to write out this whole long thing about why I've been online less and how I'm all conflicted about the Internet and fandom right now and the complications of the aversion/attraction dynamic, and then you're just like "Whatever, I see you at school." And you're SO RIGHT.

thejanethe (6:49:56 PM): Don't ever change, I like having someone normal around.

RawKdaSkEEbaLL (6:49:48 PM): lol if im the most normel person u know ur probly in trouble

thejanethe (6:49:59 PM): LOL! Well, whatever you are, keep being it. XD

RawKdaSkEEbaLL (6:50:01 PM): ok :)

thejanethe (6:50:03 PM): Anyway, it's a lot easier being online since I got the stupid screen on my computer fixed. It was driving me crazy.

RawKdaSkEEbaLL (6:50:04 PM): i still cant beleive u thru ur cpu @ ur therepist

thejanethe (6:49:56 PM): Dude, I didn't throw it AT my THERAPIST. I threw it on the floor.

thejanethe (6:49:57 PM): I just kind of jumped up to yell at her, it was in my lap, whatever.

RawKdaSkEEbaLL (6:50:09 PM): i thot u said u thru it @ the table

thejanethe (6:49:11 PM): ...it sort of hit the table on the way to the floor.

RawKdaSkEEbaLL (6:49:58 PM): hard enuf 2 brake the screen tho :)

thejanethe (6:50:01): Yeah, well, the corner of the table that the computer hit was really sharp.

329

RawKdaSkEEbaLL (6:50:03): haha w/e

RawKdaSkEEbaLL (6:50:04 PM): 1st u stock ms. miesner on zoom and she dumps u, then u throw ur cpu @ ur new therepist

RawKdaSkEEbaLL (6:50:08 PM): i bet ur new 1 is glad ur like 4'8', ur a dangerus pacient

RawKdaSkEEbaLL (6:50:10 PM): :)

thejanethe (6:50:11 PM): HEY!!! I am FIVE-TWO.

RawKdaSkEEbaLL (6:50:14 PM): ooo scarey :)

thejanethe (6:50:17 PM): Watch out, I could still take you.

RawKdaSkEEbaLL (6:50:22 PM): yea ull throw ur cpu @ my head

thejanethe (6:50:25 PM): Don't be silly, the repairs cost a fortune. I'll use yours. :P

thejanethe (6:50:28 PM): How are you online, anyway? I thought your mom took away your computer after our little escapade to NY.

RawKdaSkEEbaLL (6:50:31 PM): she isnt home

RawKdaSkEEbaLL (6:50:35 PM): neway thats only for 2 more dayz

RawKdaSkEEbaLL (6:50:38 PM): & regionals r in 4!!!!!!!!!!!!!!!

RawKdaSkEEbaLL (6:50:40 PM): can u come?

thejanethe (6:50:43 PM): I think so. My dad might be able to get a day pass to drive me.

RawKdaSkEEbaLL (6:50:46 PM): so I mite get 2 meet him

thejanethe (6:50:47 PM): Quite possibly.

RawKdaSkEEbaLL (6:50:49 PM): that shd be interrestihng

thejanethe (6:50:50 PM): I hope not! LOL

RawKdaSkEEbaLL (6:50:52 PM): how long is he in rehab neway

thejanethe (6:50:58 PM): I'm not sure. They originally said a month, but it's not really a straight rehab, it's some sort of psychiatric facility too, and apparently he's a difficult case. :P

RawKdaSkEEbaLL (6:51:01 PM): im sorrey

thejanethe (6:51:04 PM): It's all right.

thejanethe (6:51:19 PM): Can I ask you sort of a personal question?

RawKdaSkEEbaLL (6:51:22 PM): sure

thejanethe (6:51:26 PM): You said your dad used to drink... did he drink, like, for your whole childhood? Or did he have periods where he stopped?

RawKdaSkEEbaLL (6:51:30 PM): he prety much drank sence i cd remember

RawKdaSkEEbaLL (6:51:33 PM): he wasent that nice

RawKdaSkEEbaLL (6:51:38 PM): like he didnt beat usup or nothing but he just....... wasent nice when he drank

RawKdaSkEEbaLL (6:51:42 PM): what about ur dad?

thejanethe (6:51:46 PM): That's the thing. He used to drink before I was born -- even when my mom was pregnant with me, I think.

thejanethe (6:51:50 PM): They weren't married then. I don't think she got pregnant on purpose. (Yeah, yeah, joke about how I'm an accident. :P)

RawKdaSkEEbaLL (6:51:55 PM): haha im pretty sure i am 2

RawKdaSkEEbaLL (6:51:58 PM): prolly most ppl are

thejanethe (6:52:03 PM): Heh, maybe. Anyway, when my mom found out she was pregnant she told him she'd leave him if he didn't quit drinking. I guess she didn't want me to grow up in that kind of environment.

thejanethe (6:52:05 PM): And he stopped.

thejanethe (6:52:09 PM): And then, almost as soon as she died, he started again. He was tanked at the funeral.

thejanethe (6:52:14 PM): And it's just like... he'd quit for her, but not for me? What does that say about me?

RawKdaSkEEbaLL (6:52:17 PM): well he sorta quit for u

RawKdaSkEEbaLL (6:52:23 PM): like if ur mom was gunna raise u alone &he quit so she woudnt

RawKdaSkEEbaLL (6:52:26 PM): he quit so he coud be ur dad

RawKdaSkEEbaLL (6:52:29 PM): rite?

thejanethe (6:52:34 PM): Maybe. I always assumed he just didn't want to lose her.

RawKdaSkEEbaLL (6:52:38 PM): u dont know wether thats y tho

RawKdaSkEEbaLL (6:52:42 PM): esp. cuz she probly asked him to stop b4 & he didnt

thejanethe (6:52:44 PM): I don't know if she did. I never asked.

thejanethe (6:52:47 PM): I wish I had.

RawKdaSkEEbaLL (6:52:52 PM): did ur mom tell u this stuff

thejanethe (6:52:55 PM): Some of it. Some of it Dad told me.

RawKdaSkEEbaLL (6:52:59 PM): when did ur mom die again, sry i forgot

thejanethe (6:53:04 PM): I don't know if I ever told you. About a year ago, in a car accident.

RawKdaSkEEbaLL (6:53:07 PM): u never talk about her much

thejanethe (6:53:09 PM): There's not much to say. She's dead.

RawKdaSkEEbaLL (6:53:15 PM): yea but ur talking about her now?

thejanethe (6:53:19 PM): I don't know. My therapist thinks I should talk more about her. "Deal with my grief" or whatever.

RawKdaSkEEbaLL (6:53:26 PM): did she say that b4 or after u thru ur cpu @ her ;) ;)

thejanethe (6:53:29 PM): UEDWEIUGUIFWGKJAK I THREW IT AT THE FLOOR OKAY NOT AT HER

RawKdaSkEEbaLL (6:53:33 PM): yea ofeuifwkndfg @ u 2

thejanethe (6:53:35 PM): And BEFORE, btw. That's part of why I threw the damn thing.

RawKdaSkEEbaLL (6:53:37 PM): huh?????????????

RawKdaSkEEbaLL (6:53:42 PM): shes like u shoud talk about ur mom more & ur like CPU HULKSMASH!!!!!!!!!!!!!!!

thejanethe (6:53:45 PM): LOL! More or less.

RawKdaSkEEbaLL (6:53:50 PM): makes perfect sence?????????

thejanethe (6:53:52 PM): Of course it does. :P

RawKdaSkEEbaLL (6:53:55 PM): newayz ur dad didnt drink 4 a long time

RawKdaSkEEbaLL (6:53:59 PM): & he went to rehab 2 stop 4 ur sake

RawKdaSkEEbaLL (6:54:06 PM): thats better then my dad ever did

thejanethe (6:54:09 PM): I guess.

RawKdaSkEEbaLL (6:54:12 PM): oh hay I forgot 2 ask

RawKdaSkEEbaLL (6:54:15 PM): wtf hapened w/jason?

thejanethe (6:54:16 PM): What do you mean?

RawKdaSkEEbaLL (6:54:19 PM): hes going around scool braging he did sumthing else 2 u

RawKdaSkEEbaLL (6:54:22 PM): sumthin abt ur locker?

thejanethe (6:54:24 PM): Oh. Whatever, it's not worth getting into.

RawKdaSkEEbaLL (6:54:29 PM): huh

RawKdaSkEEbaLL (6:54:31 PM): how come?

thejanethe (6:54:35 PM): He just put some shit in my locker.

thejanethe (6:54:37 PM): It doesn't matter.

RawKdaSkEEbaLL (6:54:39 PM): wait like actul shit

thejanethe (6:54:41 PM): No! Ew.

RawKdaSkEEbaLL (6:54:44 PM): so wut was it then

thejanethe (6:54:49 PM): Just some pictures.

RawKdaSkEEbaLL (6:54:51 PM): picturs

RawKdaSkEEbaLL (6:54:53 PM): like wut?

thejanethe (6:54:55 PM): Man, you really don't give up, do you?

RawKdaSkEEbaLL (6:54:58 PM): just cureous

RawKdaSkEEbaLL (6:55:02 PM): u dont have 2 tell me if u dont want 2

thejanethe (6:55:04 PM): ugh

thejanethe (6:55:07 PM): A bunch of pictures out of a porn magazine, okay?

thejanethe (6:55:11 PM): He put my head on the girls and Brad Memphis' head on the guys.

RawKdaSkEEbaLL (6:55:12 PM): wtf!!!!!!!!

RawKdaSkEEbaLL (6:55:15 PM): y dident u tell me???

thejanethe (6:55:19 PM): I don't know. What would you have done about it?

RawKdaSkEEbaLL (6:55:21 PM): idk

RawKdaSkEEbaLL (6:55:24 PM): but thats so fucked up

thejanethe (6:55:26 PM): It's not a big deal. Seriously.

thejanethe (6:55:29 PM): He put them in my locker, I threw them out.

thejanethe (6:55:31 PM): It's not worth getting upset about.

RawKdaSkEEbaLL (6:55:34 PM): dude thats ttly gross

RawKdaSkEEbaLL (6:55:38 PM): & like sexul harrasmant

RawKdaSkEEbaLL (6:55:42 PM): y dident u tell the scool or sumthin

RawKdaSkEEbaLL (6:55:45 PM): or make him go somewere else in a hat w/flours on it ;)

thejanethe (6:55:48 PM): No! Don't you get it? That's the point!

RawKdaSkEEbaLL (6:55:50 PM): huh?

thejanethe (6:55:53 PM): I didn't tell anybody because I earned it and then some.

RawKdaSkEEbaLL (6:55:56 PM): wiat, no u dident at all

thejanethe (6:55:57 PM): Talk about sexual harassment -- do you have any idea how he's getting treated at school because of me?

RawKdaSkEEbaLL (6:56:01 PM): yea i know hes taking shit from sum of teh guys

thejanethe (6:56:04 PM): More than taking shit!

thejanethe (6:56:07 PM): Every other second in English class one of the guys is throwing something at his head or making some disgusting gesture or something.

thejanethe (6:56:11 PM): Half the time when I see him in the halls someone's following him around gay-bashing him.

thejanethe (6:56:13 PM): I can't believe I told people his first kiss was with a guy

RawKdaSkEEbaLL (6:56:17 PM): dude evry1 thot he was gay way b4 tat

thejanethe (6:56:20 PM): Oh, bullshit. It was never this bad before.

thejanethe (6:56:22 PM): Why would they think he was gay, anyway?

RawKdaSkEEbaLL (6:56:25 PM): idk

RawKdaSkEEbaLL (6:56:27 PM): hes wierd

RawKdaSkEEbaLL (6:56:30 PM): hes always tryin 2 impres all teh guys

thejanethe (6:56:33 PM): WTF? That's because he's unpopular, not because he's gay!

RawKdaSkEEbaLL (6:56:38 PM): yea i know

RawKdaSkEEbaLL (6:56:42 PM): its just ppl r assholes

thejanethe (6:56:45 PM): Yeah, well, none of them are bigger assholes than me, apparently.

RawKdaSkEEbaLL (6:56:49 PM): no ur ttly not

RawKdaSkEEbaLL (6:56:53 PM): their doing it all on perpose

RawKdaSkEEbaLL (6:56:58 PM): u dident mean 4 any of this 2 hapen

thejanethe (6:57:04 PM): Yeah, well, it would have been nice if I'd thought for two fucking seconds about what I was doing before I started that rumor.

thejanethe (6:57:07 PM): And then the goddamn thing with Victoria's Secret

RawKdaSkEEbaLL (6:57:11 PM): thats not ur fault, u dident even plan that 1

thejanethe (6:57:15 PM): Yeah, well, if I hadn't set him up with the hat thing none of it would have happened at all, and this is exactly why I didn't want to tell you about it, okay?

thejanethe (6:57:22 PM): Are you seriously going to sit there and tell me none of this is my fault? Because I swear to God I'm signing off right now if you are.

RawKdaSkEEbaLL (6:57:25 PM): ok ok

RawKdaSkEEbaLL (6:57:27 PM): sum of its ur fault

thejanethe (6:57:28 PM): Thank you.

RawKdaSkEEbaLL (6:57:32 PM): but ur blameing urself 2 much

RawKdaSkEEbaLL (6:57:35 PM): & he started it

thejanethe (6:57:38 PM): What are we, in third grade?

thejanethe (6:57:42 PM): Do you never watch the news or something? People commit suicide over shit like this, Gary!

RawKdaSkEEbaLL (6:57:46 PM): ok jasons not gunna comit suicide

thejanethe (6:57:49 PM): How the hell would you know?!

RawKdaSkEEbaLL (6:57:53 PM): its not that bad

RawKdaSkEEbaLL (6:57:58 PM): ppl r alredy starting 2 forget abt it

RawKdaSkEEbaLL (6:58:02 PM): its gunna go away after awile

RawKdaSkEEbaLL (6:58:05 PM): neway i herd he mite be transfering scools

thejanethe (6:58:07 PM): Really?

RawKdaSkEEbaLL (6:58:11 PM): yea his parrents think he shoudent be at spectrum nemore or sumthin

thejanethe (6:58:14 PM): Oh my God, I can't believe I actually made him CHANGE SCHOOLS

RawKdaSkEEbaLL (6:58:17 PM): no its not that, they just dont like spectrum

thejanethe (6:58:21 PM): Where did you even hear this?

RawKdaSkEEbaLL (6:58:26 PM): shana lin was talking abt it, he was telling sum1 in the guidance office abt it & she overherd

RawKdaSkEEbaLL (6:58:30 PM): but if he transfers noone will know abt it @ the new scool

RawKdaSkEEbaLL (6:58:34 PM): its probly beter

thejanethe (6:58:36 PM): I guess

thejanethe (6:58:37 PM): I just...

thejanethe (6:58:40 PM): I just keep thinking about how disappointed in me my mom would be.

RawKdaSkEEbaLL (6:58:42 PM): im sorry

thejanethe (6:58:48 PM): I mean, the bullying thing, the homophobia thing, just... everything

thejanethe (6:58:53 PM): I don't know how I can have just completely not thought about any of that stuff.

thejanethe (6:59:00 PM): She was taking me to pride marches and stuff when I was, like, three. It was really important to her.

RawKdaSkEEbaLL (6:59:03 PM): rly?

thejanethe (6:59:05 PM): Yeah. She was really into stuff like that.

thejanethe (6:59:07 PM): Civil rights, gay rights, religious freedom, whatever.

thejanethe (6:59:10 PM): She was one of those people who had like a half a dozen bumper stickers on her car, HATE IS NOT A FAMILY VALUE and IMAGINE with a picture of John Lennon and COEXIST with all the different religious symbols and whatever.

thejanethe (6:59:13 PM): I used to make fun of her for all the bumper stickers. :P

RawKdaSkEEbaLL (6:59:16 PM): my dad had 1 that said beer, its not just 4 brekfast anymore

thejanethe (6:59:17 PM): LOL! I guess my mom's weren't so bad!

RawKdaSkEEbaLL (6:59:18 PM): yep :)

thejanethe (6:59:20 PM): But the point is, she was really politically active.

thejanethe (6:59:25 PM): She was even in a goddamn anti-bullying organization, for Christ's sake. She helped start it after that girl killed herself in Pinefield last year.

thejanethe (6:59:28 PM): And then this thing with Jason, I just -- when I actually think about it I can't believe myself. How could I do that?

thejanethe (6:59:34 PM): Like, she's been dead for a year and suddenly I'm forgetting everything...

thejanethe (6:59:36 PM): I don't know

thejanethe (6:59:39 PM): Everything about the way she was, or the way she wanted me to be, or something

thejanethe (6:59:45 PM): sorry

thejanethe (6:59:48 PM): brb

RawKdaSkEEbaLL (7:02:18 PM): u ok?

thejanethe (7:02:31 PM): Sorry. Back now.

RawKdaSkEEbaLL (7:02:34 PM): thats ok

RawKdaSkEEbaLL (7:02:38 PM): r u alrite?

thejanethe (7:02:41 PM): Yeah.

thejanethe (7:02:43 PM): Well, sort of.

thejanethe (7:02:46 PM): I just... what if I'm losing her? Even more than when she died.

thejanethe (7:02:50 PM): What if I'm losing the person I was with her?

RawKdaSkEEbaLL (7:02:54 PM): wut like u nevr did anething she dident like when she was alive

thejanethe (7:02:56 PM): LOL! Um, no, not exactly.

RawKdaSkEEbaLL (7:02:59 PM): prolly shed yell @ u, ud appologize & not do it nemore

thejanethe (7:03:02 PM): Yeah, well, you got that last part right. :P

thejanethe (7:03:06 PM): I just keep thinking I need to make it up to Jason, or something.

thejanethe (7:03:11 PM): Can you think of any way I could maybe get them to leave him alone about the gay thing, anyway?

thejanethe (7:03:14 PM): They can still pick on him about the hat and suspenders if they want. :P

RawKdaSkEEbaLL (7:03:16 PM): uh not rly

RawKdaSkEEbaLL (7:03:19 PM): unless u want 2 start dateing him urself ;)

thejanethe (7:03:21 PM): AAAAAAAACK

RawKdaSkEEbaLL (7:03:23 PM): lol

thejanethe (7:03:24 PM): WHERE'S MY BRAIN BLEACH

RawKdaSkEEbaLL (7:03:26 PM): :)

thejanethe (7:03:30 PM): I don't know, maybe I'll think of something.

thejanethe (7:03:36 PM): Look, I should go, my aunt's calling me for dinner.

thejanethe (7:03:41 PM): Before I go, though, do you have the geography assignment for tonight? I forgot to write it down.

RawKdaSkEEbaLL (7:03:45 PM): yea hold on

RawKdaSkEEbaLL (7:03:58 PM): its read ch. 7 & anser discusion questoins 1-5 @ teh end

RawKdaSkEEbaLL (7:04:03 PM): its so wierd 4 u to be doing hw ;) ;)

RawKdaSkEEbaLL (7:04:06 PM): can i copy urs in hr

thejanethe (7:04:10 PM): NO. If I have to do the work so do you. LOL

RawKdaSkEEbaLL (7:04:14 PM): ok ok

RawKdaSkEEbaLL (7:04:18 PM): u r so not helpfull

thejanethe (7:04:22 PM): Thanks. :P Later!

RawKdaSkEEbaLL (7:04:25 PM): l8r shortie ;)

thejanethe (7:04:29 PM): Yeah, yeah. :P

thejanethe has signed off.

From: margaretbaker@spectrum.org
To: janeshilling@spectrum.org
Subject: Makeup Homework Assignments
Date: 5/08/2013
Attachment: MissedAssignments.doc

Dear Jane,

I am in receipt of your email requesting an opportunity to make up your missed homework assignments for this term. On the advice of the administration, I have spoken to your guidance counselor and we have come to a joint agreement that, given the circumstances, it is appropriate to make allowances and permit you to turn these assignments in late. I want to stress that this opportunity will not be available in the future, and that as of next term I expect all assignments to be handed in complete and on time. I would also note that this arrangement is more lenient than what I would have chosen without the input of Ms. Meisner.

I have attached a list of the assignments from your textbook that you should complete. I have not included them in this email in PDF format as they total 27 assignments and I do not wish to crash your computer. I will expect all of these to be turned in by the Friday after next. I also expect you to turn in your regular homework assignments for this week and the next by that Friday. I would suggest that you turn in at least two assignments each day, working forward from the beginning, in order to grasp the concepts and build your knowledge.

You may make up the test you missed during your absence on 4/12 if you can provide a valid note of excuse from a parent or guardian. You may not make up the tests of 3/29 and 4/26, as school records make it clear that you cut my class on those days. If you make up your homework assignments as scheduled above and study diligently for all future tests, it will be possible -- if not easy -- for you to pass for the term.

Sincerely,
Mrs. Baker

http://www.diarynow.com/users/thejanethe/104560.html
Date: 5/08/2013
Security level: Private

1. I am pretty sure Mrs. Baker is the worst person in the universe.
2. I have 27 makeup assignments to do in the next two weeks.
3. I think I might actually be *glad* about that because it might distract me enough that I might be able to stop crying for like two seconds.
4. But probably not.
5. I don't know if everything will ever stop hurting but I'm so, so scared it won't.
6. 27 math assignments.
7. I guess I'd better start.

NoraActon48267382 (3:36:02 PM): Would you rather talk about it via computer?

thejanethe (3:26:05 PM): Huh? What's "it"? I told you, I'm just checking my email.

NoraActon48267382 (3:36:07 PM): That's fine, but there's something you've been starting to bring up, then backing off from for the last five minutes. I thought it might be easier to talk via IM.

thejanethe (3:36:09 PM): I told you it was nothing. I just forgot what I was going to say.

NoraActon48267382 (3:36:11 PM): But did you expect me to believe you? ;)

thejanethe (3:36:13 PM): Whatever! Why do you think it makes any difference whether we talk in IM or out loud?

NoraActon48267382 (3:36:16 PM): I think the vibe is very different. If it weren't, you'd find it as easy to make friends offline as you do online, correct?

thejanethe (3:36:19 PM): ::sigh:: I don't know.

NoraActon48267382 (3:36:25 PM): One of the most interesting things about these IM conversations is that I can see you starting to type out your thoughts, and then deleting them all.

NoraActon48267382 (3:36:27 PM): What's up?

thejanethe (3:36:32 PM): Nothing. I just...

thejanethe (3:36:37 PM): Do I have to do family sessions with Dad?

NoraActon48267382 (3:36:43 PM): I won't force you to. As I've said, I believe they could be helpful to the two of you. But you don't have to do anything you don't want to. And if you object strongly, I believe I can convince your case worker not to insist as well.

thejanethe (3:36:48 PM): I don't know if I want you to meet him.

NoraActon48267382 (3:36:49 PM): Why not?

thejanethe (3:36:52 PM): He's embarrassing.

thejanethe (3:36:55 PM): He cries all the time.

NoraActon48267382 (3:37:01 PM): I'm sorry you feel embarrassed. I promise you there's no need. I have an idea of what to expect from him; I know he tends to carry around a lot of pain, and it's raw. Those aren't things that I find embarrassing, if that helps.

thejanethe (3:37:06 PM): It's not just that.

thejanethe (3:37:11 PM): I don't want him in here talking about me.

NoraActon48267382 (3:37:13 PM): Why is that?

thejanethe (3:37:18 PM): I don't want you to hear about me from other people.

thejanethe (3:37:21 PM): I don't like how I come off.

NoraActon48267382 (3:37:23 PM): What is it you don't like?

thejanethe (3:37:30 PM): I just... my dad's going to tell you how I act at home, and...

thejanethe (3:37:33 PM): it sounds really stupid

NoraActon48267382 (3:37:35 PM): What does?

NoraActon48267382 (3:37:42 PM): You're typing and deleting again.

NoraActon48267382 (3:37:45 PM): What is it you're afraid to tell me this time?

thejanethe (3:37:47 PM): I'm afraid my dad will tell you what a pain in the ass I am and you won't like me, okay?

thejanethe (3:37:51 PM): That's why it's stupid. you get paid to act like you like me, and it doesn't fucking matter, it's REALLY STUPID for me to give a shit, it's not like this is real or something. It's therapy, whatever. I'm an idiot.

NoraActon48267382 (3:37:53 PM): My God, Jane, you're so hard on yourself.

344

NoraActon48267382 (3:37:57 PM): I want you to really hear this -- I won't bring this conversation into spoken words, I know we're talking online for a reason, but I want you to look me in the eye after you read this so you'll see how serious I am: this may be therapy, but it is completely real to me.

NoraActon48267382 (3:38:00 PM): I'm not being "paid to like you". I'm being paid to help you. But I'm not being paid to put on a show, or to pretend anything at all.

thejanethe (3:39:22 PM): It's therapy. You get paid to listen to me talk.

NoraActon48267382 (3:39:25 PM): You know there's more to it than that. And that's why you said what you said.

thejanethe (3:39:27 PM): That's why I said it was stupid!

NoraActon48267382 (3:39:29 PM): But it isn't stupid.

NoraActon48267382 (3:39:34 PM): I do my best to help all of my patients. I don't like all of my patients. I do like you.

thejanethe (3:39:40 PM): ...I don't get that

NoraActon48267382 (3:39:43 PM): What don't you get?

thejanethe (3:39:50 PM): Oh, I don't know! I mean, obviously no one could *ever* fail to understand why you'd like me -- you know, because I've been so wonderfully kind and sweet and joyous and *likable* through this whole time I've known you! Why wouldn't you like me? I can't imagine why anyone wouldn't get that.

NoraActon48267382 (3:39:56 PM): Oh, Lord, Jane, I can't imagine how boring the world would be, let alone my practice, if everyone were kind and sweet and joyous all the time! :)

NoraActon48267382 (3:40:01 PM): But in all seriousness, all that anger and sarcasm and prickliness that you wear like a shield doesn't hide you nearly as well as you think it does.

NoraActon48267382 (3:40:05 PM): As a therapist I enjoy working with you because your intelligence and quick wit make things interesting, but that's not all. You're a lot stronger than you think you are, and you care about the people in your life even when you don't want to, even when it's hard for you to show it.

thejanethe (3:40:08 PM): What the hell? I'm *mean*.

NoraActon48267382 (3:40:11 PM): No, I don't think you are.

NoraActon48267382 (3:40:14 PM): You're sharp-edged when you feel threatened, certainly. You can be awfully sarcastic when you want to be. But I've never seen you act deliberately cruel.

thejanethe (3:40:16 PM): Yeah, well, tell that to Jason Malone.

NoraActon48267382 (3:40:17 PM): Who's that?

thejanethe (3:40:22 PM): Just a guy at my school... sorry, I shouldn't have brought it up, I really don't want to get into it.

thejanethe (3:40:32): He was harassing me and I played an idiotic prank that got way out of hand, and now he's getting bullied because of me and I just... it's really awful.

NoraActon48267382 (3:40:35 PM): Well, whatever happened, I can tell that it's caused a lot of upset all around, so I'm very sorry about that.

NoraActon48267382 (3:40:38 PM): Still, your reaction to all of that dovetails pretty well with what I was saying. Would you have done what you did if you knew he would wind up being bullied?

thejanethe (3:40:40 PM): No, of course not. I wanted to embarrass him, not destroy him.

NoraActon48267382 (3:40:47 PM): But that's what I'm trying to tell you. You're not deliberately cruel. You don't like hurting people and you're trying to learn better ways of dealing with things than lashing out. And you do care.

NoraActon48267382 (3:40:51 PM): I know I won't convince you of this, there's never any way to give someone else self-esteem. But I want you to understand my point. These are the reasons I like you.

NoraActon48267382 (3:41:02 PM): Jane? Can you come back?

thejanethe (3:41:05 PM): What?

NoraActon48267382 (3:41:07 PM): I noticed that you double-clicked on something -- usually that means you've opened your email, or a Word document. Can you stay here with me for a moment?

thejanethe (3:41:18 PM): I DON'T WANT TO DO THIS

NoraActon48267382 (3:41:20 PM): What?

thejanethe (3:41:21 PM): I dont' want to act like this! I'm sosick of this

NoraActon48267382 (3:41:23 PM): It's all right, Jane. Ease up on yourself.

thejanethe (3:40:24 PM): but I AM THE DUMBEST FUCKING PERSON

thejanethe (3:41:29 PM): christ what am I a 3-year-old?

NoraActon48267382 (3:41:32 PM): Why, because you're letting out your emotions? Emotions aren't "dumb", and they're not childish.

NoraActon48267382 (3:41:37 PM): I know you like things to be logical. Maybe it will help to think of it this way -- emotions make sense. They're our natural responses to things that affect us. And if we sit with them and listen to them, we can figure them out.

thejanethe (3:41:39 PM): but this DOESN'T make sense!!!

NoraActon48267382 (3:41:41 PM): What doesn't?

thejanethe (3:41:42 PM): HELLO, I'M CRYING BECAUSE YOU SAID YOU LIKE ME

NoraActon48267382 (3:41:44 PM): What doesn't make sense about that?

thejanethe (3:41:45 PM): NOTHING about it amkes sense, why do I CARE

NoraActon48267382 (3:41:47 PM): I think maybe you haven't felt very likable lately.

NoraActon48267382 (3:41:50 PM): And I think that's been causing you a lot of pain.

thejanethe (3:41:55 PM): whatever

thejanethe (3:42:03 PM): I'm checking my RC

NoraActon48267382 (3:42:05 PM): All right.

thejanethe (3:45:13 PM): Look, it's just stupid, okay? Mom liked me, she was the one who always liked me, and now she's dead.

NoraActon48267382 (3:45:15 PM): What about your father?

thejanethe (3:45:17 PM): He loves me. I don't have a clue if he likes me or not.

thejanethe (3:45:52 PM): I've been so awful since Mom died

NoraActon48267382 (3:45:55 PM): You've been hurting.

thejanethe (3:45:59 PM): And I take it out on everyone else, I go around being selfish and bitchy and awful, okay? At least people liked Rachel.

NoraActon48267382 (3:46:01 PM): Including yourself?

thejanethe (3:46:03 PM): ...duh?

NoraActon48267382 (3:46:07 PM): But that's what I've been saying. It doesn't sound like you've liked yourself very much for a long time.

NoraActon48267382 (3:46:11 PM): Rachel was the alter version of yourself, the one you liked. The person you wanted to be.

NoraActon48267382 (3:46:13 PM): And you lost her.

NoraActon48267382 (3:46:16 PM): In light of all of that, I think it makes perfect sense that it affects you pretty deeply right now when someone tells you you are likable, you, Jane.

NoraActon48267382 (3:46:19 PM): Especially since you've said that the last person who made you feel that way was your mom.

thejanethe (3:46:25 PM): yeah, well, you're not my mom

NoraActon48267382 (3:46:27 PM): No, I'm not.

NoraActon48267382 (3:46:28 PM): I'm sorry.

thejanethe (3:46:33 PM): that you're not my mom?

NoraActon48267382 (3:46:35 PM): That she's not here to make you feel as safe and valued as you used to.

thejanethe (3:46:39 PM): i'm just crying all the time lately

NoraActon48267382 (3:46:42 PM): You've had a lot to cry about.

thejanethe (3:46:46 PM): it makes me feel really stupid, is all

NoraActon48267382 (3:46:48 PM): So you tell me.

NoraActon48267382 (3:46:50 PM): It's tough to be in such a vulnerable place.

thejanethe (3:46:52 PM): no shit, sherlock

NoraActon48267382 (3:46:53 PM): Indeed.

thejanethe (3:48:06 PM): I'm really tired of everything hurting.

NoraActon48267382 (3:48:08 PM): I know.

thejanethe (3:48:13 PM): Is it ever going to get better?

NoraActon48267382 (3:48:16 PM): Yes, Jane. It will.

thejanethe (3:48:23 PM): There you go with the first name thing again

thejanethe (3:48:25 PM): Is it really going to get better? Do you promise?

NoraActon48267382 (3:48:28 PM): If you keep working this hard at it? Absolutely.

thejanethe (3:48:33 PM): "Working hard"? All I'm doing is crying and whining.

NoraActon48267382 (3:48:35 PM): And has that been easy?

thejanethe (3:48:39 PM): ...no.

NoraActon48267382 (3:48:44 PM): Exactly. Don't undersell yourself. This has been incredibly hard on you, and you've been facing it head-on.

thejanethe (3:48:47 PM): I didn't exactly have a lot of options.

NoraActon48267382 (3:48:53 PM): Of course you did. You could have stopped coming in here. You could have stopped going to school. You could have spent all your time online, never told your friend Audra or anyone about your personalities, spent all your time watching Look to Tomorrow and hiding.

NoraActon48267382 (3:48:56 PM): You know better than anyone how to disengage from the world. You've chosen not to.

NoraActon48267382 (3:48:58 PM): You should be proud of yourself.

thejanethe (3:49:03 PM): Maybe.

NoraActon48267382 (3:49:04 PM): Definitely.

thejanethe (3:49:09 PM): I'll try.

Date: 5/12/2013
Mood: indescribable
Security level: Private

I just got back from Gary's Skee-Ball match.
...Oh my God.
I...
...oh my God!
I, it. Well. STARTING AT THE BEGINNING, HERE
Okay. So Dad did manage to get a day pass from the rehab, and chose, touchingly or whatever, to use it to go to Gary's Skee-Ball match with me. I mean, this was the only window they'd allow him, they have eighteen thousand rules and regulations and most of them make no sense to me, but the point is that when I hesitated to say we could meet up today because of Gary's Skee-Ball match Dad really wanted to come. I suppose I could take this as evidence that he genuinely wanted to spend time with me. A championship Skee-Ball match does not really represent hot weekend action.

So we went. The car ride was... weird. I mean, on the one hand, Dad did seem better than he has in awhile. I can't remember when the last time was that I saw him sober *and* dressed in street clothes. Sobriety looks good on him, I guess; he looked about thirty years younger than when he went into rehab, though part of that, I'm sure, is because before he went in he was crying and panicking all the time. As for that, whatever meds they've put him on seem to be helping, too. Of course he spent about a half hour of the hour-and-a-half drive going on about how he was done drinking and how, no, really, he was done drinking and he was *really really* done drinking this time! And, I mean, I know he's proud of himself and all, but... no. I didn't know how to tell him that things are beyond the point where I care what he says anymore. Until he gets his act together and keeps it together for a very long time, I'm not interested in what he says, and he really just needs to not talk about that sort of thing altogether. And the more he talked the more I got pissed, the more I could feel all kinds of angry words bubbling in my chest. But I didn't say them. Because if I

351

said them he might cry and then drop me at the Skee-Ball match and go to a bar instead. And then rehab would kick him out. And then... well, we know what then.

So I kept quiet. As always.

But it was okay. He is a lot better in a lot of ways. I'd almost forgotten, in the last year, how great Dad can be when he's not a complete mess. He's not always the easiest to talk to because we don't share too many interests -- not like Mom and I did, anyway. But he's funny, and sort of goofy, and for the last half-hour of the ride he provided sarcastic commentary on the rustic "attractions" we passed along the way ("look, Jane, an authentic historic horseshoe nail factory!") It was nice to laugh with him. It was nice to feel a little bit like a family again -- or even two-thirds of one.

We got to the Skee-Ball match about fifteen minutes before it was scheduled to start. It was being held at some arcade out in the boonies -- they'd rented the whole place for the day and were restricting it to people associated with the competition, which must have been a serious blow to the social life of everyone living within a hundred miles. (On the plus side, maybe the horseshoe nail factory got an upswing in business.) Dad and I had had to buy our tickets from Gary beforehand. Somehow I hadn't anticipated that they would actually, you know, collect them. Or that they would stamp our hands so no one could sneak in. Who tries to gain illegal entrance to a *Skee-Ball convention*?

But the place was hopping. I swear to God. It was bursting with people, and almost everyone had this taut, electric excitement about them, like Olympic coaches waiting for their gymnasts to be called. Sure, there were a few people like me and Dad, random spectators wandering around and looking dazed, but most of the people "associated" with the competition were *associated* with the competition. I saw a couple of guys erupting in a serious fight over the brand of powdered chalk one of them had brought for the players to dust over their hands before competing, and another girl removing nine flawless Skee-Balls from individual double-knitted Skee-Ball cozies, which in turn were nestled inside a cotton-padded box. Apparently all the teams bring their own balls -- which are painted with the team name and logo, might I add -- and said balls must be weighed immediately prior to the competition. They're not taking any chances that the Skee-Balls provided by the arcades might deviate from the regulation size and weight! OH MY GOD EITHER THESE PEOPLE ARE COMPLETELY DERANGED OR THIS ACTUALLY IS A REAL SPORT

Gary was stoked when we got there. I mean, I suspect he was pretty jazzed even before I showed up, but when he saw me he really went over the moon. I had never seen him as excited as he was before that competition. His face was all lit up and he was hopping from foot to foot like he couldn't contain his excitement and he kept randomly punching and kicking at the air, yelling stuff like "POW!" and "SQUIRRELS KILL!" When he saw me he ran over and hugged me, then shook Dad's hand so exuberantly I caught Dad rubbing his shoulder a few seconds later. I have no idea what Dad made of him. "He's a very... happy young man, isn't he?" he asked diplomatically, after Gary had bounded away again. I blinked, attempting to find a way to explain Gary. Then Dad's eyes caught on something across the room, and I followed his gaze, and everything changed.

They were serving alcohol. In the Skee-ball alley. I don't even know how they could have been doing that -- is that legal at an event with kids? -- but it was a concession stand of some kind, and they were serving beers. Dad's eyes got all big and panicked and he started looking back and forth between me and the bar, like he was pleading with me not to get upset but he couldn't stop looking at the fucking thing. Whatever he was doing, I missed half of it because I'd closed my eyes and was willing it all to go away. First weekend pass out of rehab? Let's go to a bar! What the fuck! Better get your hopes smashed like cheap china on concrete sooner rather than later, huh?

"Jane," Dad said tentatively, "I don't --"

"Whatever." I was still pretending I wasn't there. It would have been easier if he'd've kept quiet.

"Jane," he said, louder. "Look, it's not... I'm..."

"Whatever." Maybe there was going to be a sentence in there, sometime, a few years down the line. I was guessing he'd be at least six beers in by the time he figured out what it was, though. "You want to leave, let's leave." I'd make it up to Gary on Monday or something. More important to a.) convince Dad that he did in fact want to leave, and b.) get the hell out of there before I wound up in DSS custody for good.

"I don't want to make you... I mean, your friend..."

"His fault for not telling me there'd be a bar. Just -- come *on*." I had Dad's arm now, was pulling him towards the door. My back was very deliberately turned to Gary.

"Jane -- no." His voice managed to stop me in my tracks -- I don't know when the last time I heard him sound so stern was, but I know it was before Mom died and I know he was just backing her up on something, whatever it was. "You asked me to bring you here. This is the first time I've done anything for you since your mother died." I had literally never heard him say those words -- *your mother died* -- except when he was on a five-beer crying jag. It was kind of horrible. "We're not leaving."

I was shaking, I was so -- I don't even know. Mad? Sad? Scared? It came out as mad, though. It always does. "Thanks so much for your willingness to risk your sobriety for a Skee-ball match, Dad -- I mean, I know it's been *two weeks* and all, so I can see where you'd figure hanging out at bars is totally A-OK now -- but maybe..." I stopped there, because I honestly didn't know what came after the maybe. Plus I was being an absolute bitch, and for once I had the sense to know it -- or to be terrified of what the consequences might be, anyway. Plus I was about to cry. *Dammit.*

I don't know what I expected him to do. Turn around and head back to the parking lot? Start sobbing? Make a beeline for the bar and drink until he passed out across a couple of Skee-ball lanes? That was about all I could figure, which is why I was about to head for the parking lot myself and hide in the woods until he was finished having whatever kind of breakdown he was going to have.

I didn't get a chance to go, though. His face creased up like he was about to cry for one half-second, and I was one more half-second closer to running, when all of a sudden his face flipped into straight lines and he said one of the weirdest things I've ever heard him say:

"Go over to the bar, Jane, and ask how many bartenders there are." For a second I literally thought he was asking me to go get him a drink, and I nearly threw up on his shoes, but then he kept going. "I think there are three. Can you see?"

I couldn't, really, with the crowd milling around. But I also couldn't say much of anything, so he continued.

"Go over to the bar and ask to talk to whoever's serving drinks. I'll be over there --" he pointed to a chair a ways outside of the crowd, but a ways from the bar, too. "Point me out to them and tell them they are not under any circumstances to serve me any alcohol. Lie to them if you want -- tell them I'm on some medication that'll send me into a coma if I drink, but I'm too stupid to know what's good for me. But they'll be legally liable if they serve to me and I get sick. Or tell them the truth --" his voice broke a little here -- "that I'm an alcoholic asshole on a weekend pass from rehab, and you're my daughter, and you can't afford for me to fu--screw your life up any more than I already have." He coughed, swallowed, went on. "Your choice. I don't care. Say whatever won't embarrass you."

How did he think that was possible? Seriously, what was he thinking? I was going to ask him, but somehow that wasn't what came out.

"I don't want to be your babysitter anymore, Dad." That was what ended up falling out of my mouth. I hadn't even known I was thinking it.

He nodded, once. "I know. But you won't believe me if I do it."

He was right.

So I went over to the bar and I pointed Dad out to them. I gave them the cockamamie story about medication because Dad was right, the truth was way too embarrassing. Meanwhile Dad was sitting there alone in his yellow plastic chair like a statue, pretending to watch the players warm up on the alleys. His eyes were all shiny. I went to the bathroom and stayed there a very long time. I am seriously done with watching him cry. I just... I'm not doing it anymore.

Like I said before, I am not getting my hopes up over this. I'm just *not*.

That was what was in my head when I came back out of the bathroom -- *not getting my hopes up, not getting my hopes up, notgettingmyhopesupnotgettingmyhopesup* -- and while that train of thought certainly has its common-sense recommendations, it didn't do much to ease the atmosphere between me and Dad. We were both trying so hard, and all we could manage was awkward pauses broken by awkward jokes that we both laughed too hard at before falling back into awkward silence again. I was starting to realize with horror that this was what the rest of the day was going to be, maybe what the rest of my *life* was going to be: Dad and I both pasting on smiles and insisting that everything's normal when nothing is normal at all, both of us pretending not to be looking at the other one out of the corner of our eyes, waiting for each other to break down or fall apart. I couldn't see how Dad was going to make it through five minutes of that without drinking. Hell, I was starting to think I might need to go sneak a beer myself if we kept on this way.

But I hadn't been counting on Gary.

He'd been keeping an eye on us the whole time we were there, I think -- from the guilty expression on his face when he glanced our way, it was pretty clear he hadn't known beforehand that there was going to be alcohol, and he was wondering if he'd wrecked everything for me by inviting us. I didn't blame him, exactly, but I also didn't feel like having him pull me aside and try to have some deep conversation about it when I was barely holding it together as it was, so I avoided looking at him whenever I could. He must have seen how awkward Dad and I looked, though, because a little ways in, he started bouncing over our way whenever there was any break in the action at all. I knew he was sacrificing his concentration to do it, too, which for Gary is an awfully big deal. But there he was, bounding around like an overexcited Saint Bernard puppy, going "did you see that shot?" and "oh man, Joey just worked out this new cross-hand skip-shot that's *so cool*, you gotta watch him" and "did you see Jack, on my team? He's seventy-three years old, no lie, and he just threw his shoulder out *two weeks* ago, and he's back in the lanes again!" (Side note: the Squirrels are WAY more intergenerational than I ever expected. Gary's like one of two people under twenty on the team. Apparently it is not a sport for kids.) The whole time he's going on and on, he's hopping from one foot to the other, grinning that goofy grin of his, and that ridiculous lime-green plastic Chuck E. Cheese toy I won for him the first time we hung out was dangling from his watch chain and clacking against his leg.

And his mood was infectious, just like he'd meant it to be. At first he just gave Dad and I a respite from staring at each other, but soon enough we were really getting into it, and we started finding things to chat about even when Gary wasn't around. Ricochet shots, cross-wise double-handers, short-step and spin shots... I knew them all from hanging out with Gary, and pretty soon I realized I could do a running commentary on the match for Dad, who of course had no idea what was going on. I got pretty into it, actually. I think I might have a future as a very specific kind of sports announcer.

And then, just as we were getting into the swing of things, the mood got tense. The mood in the room, I mean, not the mood between me and Dad. They'd narrowed it down to a runoff between two teams, the Squirrels and the Paintballs (the *Paintballs*? One dork-supreme sport wasn't enough without their naming their team after another one?); the Paintballs were up by a couple thousand points and Jack-the-73-year-old-Squirrel had just thrown his shoulder out again and forfeited his final shot. Gary had the final position in the Squirrels' roster, but it was going to be damn near impossible, mathematically speaking, for them to pull themselves out of the hole they were in. To be honest, I didn't think he was going to make it. I was already trying to figure out what I was going to say to console him.

Then he got to his last shot, and he turned around, back to the alley.

A ripple of whispers went through the crowd, like you'd hear at a golf match as Tiger Woods made a crucial putt. "What's he doing?" Dad whispered, but I didn't answer. For one thing, I was concentrating on the match. For another, what Gary was doing was stupid.

He was going to throw the ball over his shoulder. Seriously. He was going to throw a Skee-ball *over his shoulder* and try to get it to roll down the ramp and into one of the holes. He'd explained this shot to me before, always with a tone of near-reverence in his voice: only the *very best* players in the *whole country* could make this shot consistently, he'd tell me. I thought, but never said, that that was probably because the whole thing was basically contrary to all the elementary laws of physics. You can't throw a Skee-ball overhand, *backwards*, and expect it to do anything you want it to do. Gary's been practicing the shot all year and he barely ever makes it. I tried it once and I cracked the Plexiglas shield over the game.

So there he was, standing facing the audience, who were all staring with mouths agape. He reached down to finger that stupid Chuck E. Cheese toy I won for him, and I *really* groaned internally. Some lucky charm that was going to be. A lucky charm from a lucky girl, right? It'd be a miracle if he didn't take someone's head off with this shot.

He raised his arm. He threw.

The ball smacked the ramp and went wild. The crowd groaned -- an expression of pure agony flitted across Gary's face as he pivoted to watch --

-- and the ball smacked off the underside of the Plexiglas, knocked hard against the side wall, and ricocheted back across the board.

Into the 100-point hole.

The room went nuts. I mean, stampede-style nuts. Everyone jumped to their feet in unison and Gary's whole team swarmed him; I saw Jack try to throw his arms around Gary, his face shining, then flinch back and shout something very impolite as he remembered his dislocated shoulder. I was hollering in an entirely embarrassing manner, trying to shoulder my way through the crowd to get to Gary. Finally I made it. "Gary!" I cried, running over to hug him. "You're amazing! When I saw you going for that over-the-shoulder I --"

"WOOOOOOOOOOOOOOOOOOOOO," he yelled, or words to that effect, and then he kissed me.

I had no idea what was happening at first. Suddenly just -- his arms were around me and his lips were on mine and it lasted for about two or three seconds and I'm not sure if I kissed him back, because he was kind of putting enough force into it for both of us? But his teeth banged off my upper lip at first and I arranged my mouth into a more comfortable position, so maybe that's kissing back. And eventually my hand wound up on his shoulderblade. For about a second. So that's sort of like an embrace. And... oh, boy.

I broke it off when I realized the people around us were staring. Both Gary and I were blushing red as beets, and I wouldn't let him kiss me again for the rest of the day, but we held hands the whole time. Except when he went up with his team to get their medals. He kept glancing from me to the medal back to me and back to the medal, and I have never seen a happier human being in my life. "WOOOOOOOOOOOOO" he kept shouting.

After the tournament Dad drove us both home -- Gary first begged his mother to let me ride with them, but Dad looked so crestfallen at the prospect that he switched immediately to asking to be allowed to ride with us. We drove home with one celebratory stop along the way for ice cream, and Gary did not stop talking the whole way. I don't think Dad had a clue what to make of him, but he seemed very entertained; and the more

Gary talked the less room Dad had to get a word in edgewise and really embarrass me to death, so that was good. We learned all about the history of Skee-Ball and how it was invented in 1909 and the ramps were originally 36 feet long, can you believe that, 36 feet? and the first tournament was in 1932 but they died out for a long time but there's been a recent revival and now they're way different, and the 100-point shots are a new addition to the game and there was a lot of debate about whether to use them in tournaments because not all teams had access to practice on them but that was dumb because they're standard at all CECs and teams just didn't want the hassle of not being able to practice in a private Skee-Ball alley in someone's basement anymore, and... He went on and on, and Dad and I were both laughing constantly, and Dad was just sitting there with this too-innocent expression trying to pretend he had no idea what was going on between me and Gary. And Gary ordered a five-scoop banana split with a million toppings. And got a smudge of marshmallow on his nose.

I think I sort of adore that boy.

He tried to kiss me again when we dropped him off, but I moved my head so he kind of banged off my cheek. "*Not now*," I muttered, angling my chin sharply towards my dad. So I hope he got the point that making out in front of parents -- his, mine, anyone's -- is very highly uncool.

But Dad seemed so happy. On the way to Aunt Amy's, before he headed back to rehab, he kept glancing at me and opening his mouth and then shutting it again, but just *grinning*. I know he wanted to tell me what a nice boy Gary is, and how great he was in the match, and how nice it was to see us so happy together, and, oh, God, I don't even know what all. And I know he only just *barely* managed to keep quiet about it, because he and I have never talked about dating and stuff like that, and if he'd started today he would have humiliated me past all possibility of recovery. So he didn't say anything. But, boy, was he grinning. It struck me at one point that Dad seemed nearly as happy as Gary. After a year of basically making everyone around me miserable, both of them were on cloud nine. Because of... me? What? I can't even process it myself. But I can't stop grinning either.

And Gary and I are going to see a movie after school Monday. So... I guess we are dating. Or something.

...!!!!!!!!!

Hi y'all... sorry I haven't been online lately. Things have been really chaotic with that hacker thing, as you know, and I just needed to take some time away. Another thing -- I should probably just put it right out there, I guess: the Boy and I broke up a month back or so, and for a long time I was just having a really rough time of it. I mean, not to worry: it was a mutual decision, if by "mutual decision" you mean "he went to a party and hooked up with some redheaded chick." :P Whatever, dude. I think we were coming to a parting of the ways anyway, to be honest, but that's a long, complicated story that I think I'll save for another time.

It's all right, though; I really don't want to make a big melodramatic thing out of it, especially since things really are pretty good lately. I mean, school's out in a few weeks, the next season of LtT looks like it'll be better than ever -- how much can a girl complain? :) I've even got a little rebound thing going on. Maybe. We'll see where it goes. He's nothing like The Boy at all, but right now that sounds pretty damn good to me. I think I'll keep that sort of close to the vest too for now, but in the meantime, have a cryptic little quiz, written by yours truly:

Which Unconventional Sport Are You?

You are SKEE-BALL!

You're fun-loving, high-energy, and quirky. People may not pay you the attention you're due just yet, but someday they will - and until then, you're doing your thing, and you're doing just fine.

Take this quiz!

You guys ever hear of competitive Skee-Ball?

ACKNOWLEDGMENTS

Thanks first and foremost to the Associates of the Boston Public Library for the support they gave me through their Children's Writer-in-Residence program. The residency gave me time, space, and money to finish this book (and another one as well), and I'm forever indebted to them for that.

More personal thanks go to all the friends I have made and cherished through the Internet; every one of you helped to make this book what it is. Special thanks go to Carol Leister for her unwavering support and encouragement, Karen Tompkins, Emma Holland, John Pachja, Anne Fisher, Melissa Hourihan, and Nicole Catarius for their astute critiques, Eve Dutton for her early help in developing the characters and setting them on the right path, and Lian Parsons, who gave wonderful editorial advice and also let me know when my Internet slang was ten years outdated. Lian, you pwn my soul, and all my gratitude are belong to you.

On the professional side of town, Steve Malk, of Writers House, gave outstanding editorial direction that helped me immeasurably, and Ken Wright and Kristy King gave me industry-savvy guidance and a lot of greatly appreciated encouragement.

Thanks go out to MA Vespry and Maureen Daly for their generous support of the Kickstarter that made this book possible. A huge amount of gratitude is due my family as well, particularly to my mother and father -- for the financial support they gave the Kickstarter, for the emotional support they gave me, and for not being dead or an alcoholic, respectively. You guys win at parenting.

Finally, thanks beyond measure to my wife Kerianne, who was not only my biggest cheerleader and supporter throughout the writing of this book, but is also the reason you are actually holding this book in your hands. Self-publishing is a daunting task and Kerianne basically did all of the work. People don't get any luckier than I did the day that I met Kerianne.

ATTENTION ALL WRITERS AND ARTISTS!

Do you like writing fanfic? Making fanart? Are you interested in giving it a try, even if you've never done it before? Read on -- you could win a cash prize of $100, $250, $500, or $1,000!

4 TO 16 CHARACTERS FANWORKS CONTEST

Kelly Hourihan and Lemon Sherbet Press are hosting the Official *4 to 16 Characters* Fanworks Contest, a chance for you to showcase your literary and artistic talent and compete with other fans for real cash prizes! Write a story or create visual art about the book and submit it to the contest through the entry form on www.kellyhourihan.com/fanworkscontest. Prizes will be awarded in the following categories:

Grand Prize (any style, any length)
Drabble (maximum 250 words)
One-shot fic (maximum 3,000 words)
Chapter fic (minimum 3,000 words)
Fan art (any visual medium)
All entries, ages 12-15 (any style, any length)
All entries, ages 16-19 (any style, any length)

Be sure to read carefully all the rules on www.kellyhourihan.com/fanworkscontest. Then get writing, get drawing, and get ready to show your best work to the world!

GLOSSARY

The following is list of all Internet slang used in the book. For more definitions, the author recommends consulting www.urbandictionary.com, a user-edited dictionary of current slang terms.

GENERAL ONLINE TERMS

askbox: A feature on some social media sites whose basic intent is to allow site users to privately ask questions of a particular user; the user to whom the questions are directed usually responds publicly.

blog: Short for weblog. An online journal where the journal-keeper, or "blogger," can post entries. Topics are broad-ranging and can involve updates on one's personal life, political or cultural commentary, original fiction and/or poetry, and more. The collection of all blogs and bloggers, and the culture that creates, is referred to as the "blogosphere."

chat: A real-time online discussion among a group of people. Can also be used to refer to a conversation between two people; see "IM" for further information.

Chrome: A web browser, run by Google, which is popular among computer nerds.

comm: Short for "community." A group of people who share an interest and gather on a specific site to discuss it. Most journaling/blogging sites have a function allowing people who keep journals to form and join such communities. Can also refer more generally to a "community" of people who are friends or share interests on the Internet.

emo: Depressed, bleak, gloomy. Short for "emotional."

emoticons: Small images of faces, or series of textual characters that are meant to represent such faces, that people insert into conversations online to convey their emotions. See "Emoticons" section for a partial listing.

Firefox: A web browser that is popular among computer nerds.

furry: A broad category of people who are drawn to animal anthropomorphism, ranging from people who enjoy/create media representing anthropomorphic animals to people who identify with a specific animal or believe their soul is that of an animal. Furries are commonly scoffed at on the Internet, largely due to the (generally inaccurate) perception that they are sexually interested in animals.

IE6: Internet Explorer version 6.0, an outdated web browser. Internet Explorer is a default browser installed on all Windows computers, but is unpopular among computer nerds.

IM: Abbreviation for "instant message." A real-time online chat between two people, which can take place using a variety of chatting programs. The most notable feature of such chatting programs is that they update automatically as soon as either participant sends a message, facilitating conversation in that the user does not have to refresh the page manually (as would be necessary, for example, to update a conversation on a forum). The only people who can read the text of an IM are the two people conversing.

invisible: Changing the setting on a chat or instant-messaging program so that it appears to others that you are offline. While invisible, you can chat with people who are online if you choose to do so, but if someone else initiates a chat they will receive a message saying you are offline.

lolcats: A popular meme on the Internet in which pictures of cats are labeled with humorous captions. These captions are written in "lolcat-speak", which diverges from traditional English grammar and spelling but which has developed into a dialect with its own vocabulary and grammatical rules. The website www.icanhascheezburger.com is the biggest and most popular repository of lolcat macros on the Internet.

macro: Any image labeled with a humorous caption.

meme: Material that is passed on from one Internet user to another to another, propagating widely across the Internet.

forum: A website on which users can post messages back and forth. Users do not have to be online at the same time, and their messages remain on the board so that anyone can later access them and respond to them.

IRC: A service that allows multiple Internet users to chat with each other all at once. Divided into "channels" that allow users to find and chat with other people who share a common interest. Short for "Internet Relay Chat."

mailing list: A group of people who communicate about a shared interest via email.

mod: Short for moderator; someone who manages a particular community, site, message board, email list, or chat room by setting down rules and enforcing them.

newbie: A person who is new to a particular group or fandom.

reblog: On a social media site, to repost a post that another user has made, sharing it with one's own friends or followers. Users who view a reblog can themselves reblog the post as well.

selfie: A photograph that a person takes of him- or herself and then posts to the Internet.

sn: "screen name". An online user name that is used in a chat or an IM.

thread: A particular conversation on a forum or in the comments on a journal or a community. Consists of a particular comment and all the direct responses to that comment. A post or a forum may have many different threads going simultaneously.

torrent: A peer-to-peer service enabling Internet users to swap large files, including movies and episodes of television shows. Also used to refer to files traded this way.

troll: A person who says incendiary and/or abusive things to other people online, or posts incendiary messages to public spaces online, in order to stir up controversy, create drama, and/or bully another person.

unfollow: A feature on some social media sites that allows one to stop seeing posts by a particular user or to stop seeing and/or receiving notifications of new posts in a thread.

#: Indicator of a "hashtag." A hashtag is a word or phrase preceded by the # symbol. Hashtags are generally appended to the end of a post to enable users of a particular site or service to find posts by other users about a common interest. (For example, clicking on the hashtag "#television" would allow one to view all posts by other users about television that have also been tagged "#television".) Though originally designed to allow people to find other people with common interests, the use of hashtags has expanded to include quirky phrases that would be singular to one particular user.

FANDOM TERMS

/ symbol (as in "[name]/[name]"): Indicator of a romantic pairing between two characters. For example, a fanfic described as "Thorin/Jaela" would depict a romantic relationship between Thorin and Jaela.

AU: Alternate universe. Refers to a fanfic that deliberately diverges from material that was shown on the show ("canon"); this can mean that the author accepts what happened on the show up to a certain point and then breaks off into a new story from that point on, or that the author creates an entirely new world and places the characters from the show in it.

beta: To read someone's fanfic before it is posted, editing for grammar and spelling and sometimes giving critical suggestions regarding the content as well. Also called beta-reading. A person who does this is also known as a beta, or as a beta-reader.

drabble: Originally defined as a fanfic that is exactly 100 words long, the term has evolved to refer to any very short fanfic.

fanart: Visual art depicting a particular show, movie, or book series, created by fans of same. Graphical corollary to fanfiction.

fandom: The collection of enthusiastic fans of a particular television show, movie, book series, etc., who discuss their interest in said show/movie/series online with other fans.

fanfiction (also "fanfic" or "fic"): Stories that are written by fans of a particular show, movie, or book series. Such stories build upon the characters and basic framework represented in the original show/movie/series in a variety of ways – by telling what might have happened behind the scenes, telling what the writer wishes had happened, telling what the writer thinks might happen to the characters in the future, etc. Fanfics are generally posted online to be read by other fans.

fangirl/fanboy: A person who is an enthusiastic fan. Can also be used as a verb, to mean that someone is acting like an enthusiastic fan.

fanvid: Video corollary to fanfiction and fanart, often consisting of intercut clips of a television show or movie set to music.

gen: A fanwork (fanfic, fanart, fanvid, etc.) that does not depict any romantic relationships.

guyslash: See "slash" below.

pairing: Two characters who are in a romantic relationship, either on the show or in fanfic.

S1, S2, S3, etc: Season 1/2/3/etc.

ship: A pairing that is supported by at least some fans; derived from "relationship".

shipper: A person who supports a romantic pairing between two particular characters.

slash: Refers to a relationship between two characters of the same sex, or a homoerotic vibe between two characters who are not in a relationship. "Slashfic" is fanfiction depicting same-sex relationships, and is sometimes used specifically to refer to fanfic about gay males, with "guyslash" as a variant. "Femslash" or "girlslash" refers to lesbian fanfic. Not to be confused with the "/" symbol, which may indicate a relationship between characters of any gender.

songfic: A fanfic that is inspired by a song and in which original text is interspersed with song lyrics.

UST: "Unresolved sexual tension" - refers to a dynamic in which two characters seem to be attracted to each other, but never quite make it to a relationship.

WIP: "work in progress". Frequently refers to a fanfiction that is being posted in chapters or segments and which the author begins posting online before the whole fic has been finished.

ACRONYMS AND OTHER SHORTHAND

BFF: "best friends forever"

brb: "be right back"

btw: "by the way"

DIAF: "die in a fire"

ETA: "edited to add"

FFS: "for fuck's sake"

g: "giggle"

GTFO: "get the fuck out"

gtg: "got to go"

idk: "I don't know"

IMO: "in my opinion"

IRL: "in real life"

LOL: "laughing out loud"

nmh: "not much here"

np: "no problem"

oic: "oh, I see"

OMG: "oh my God"

ROFLMAO: "rolling on the floor laughing my ass off"

smh: "shaking my head"

ttyl: "talk to you later"

w/e: "whatever"

WTF: "what the fuck"

EMOTICONS

Note: With the exception of the last few, the emoticons below are sideways representations of faces. Most online chat services, when a user types in these combinations of characters, will replace them with a corresponding cartoon face. This is just a small selection of the total number of emoticons available, and every forum or chat program will have different ones; however, the ones listed below are generally widely understood.

:) - smiling

;) - winking

:(- frowning

:-* - kissing/flirtatious

B-) – "cool" face, wearing sunglasses

:-D – grinning

:-S – confused face

:P::::: - blowing a raspberry

D: - horrified

:-O – shocked

XD: very happy/amused

The following emoticons are in a style which originated in Japan rather than in the English-speaking world and are not read sideways like the previous ones.

^.^ - delighted

o.O – confused or disturbed

\o/ - cheerleader

CPSIA information can be obtained at www.ICGtesting.com
Printed in the USA
BVOW01s0608150414

350597BV00001B/35/P